PRAISE FOR
MELANIE BENJAMIN'S
THE GIRLS IN THE PICTURE

"In the era of #MeToo, *Girls* could not be more timely—or troubling—about the treatment of women in the workplace. . . . Benjamin portrays the affection and friction between Pickford and Marion with compassion and insight. . . . [A] rich exploration of two Hollywood friends who shaped the movies."
—*USA Today*

"A boffo production . . . Inspiration is a rare and unexpected gift in a book filled with the fluff of Hollywood, but Benjamin provides it with *The Girls in the Picture*."
—NPR

"Benjamin fully captures the giddy excitement of the blossoming movie business in the 1910s and 1920s and has chosen intriguingly flawed protagonists with compelling life stories that aren't widely known today. This engrossing and rewarding read provides the same mixture of well-researched plot and fascinating characters who have made Benjamin's previous novels so outstanding."
—*Library Journal* (starred review)

"This vibrant portrait of two Hollywood groundbreakers is rich with insights about friendship, ambition, and power. . . . A fascinating read."

—NANCY HORAN, *New York Times* bestselling author of *Loving Frank* and *Under the Wide and Starry Sky*

"Benjamin immerses readers in the whirlwind excitement of Mary's and Frances' lives while portraying a rarely seen character, an early woman screenwriter, and deftly exploring the complexities of female friendship." —*Booklist*

"As riveting as the latest blockbuster, this is a star-studded story of female friendships, creative sparks about to ignite, and the power of women. . . . Dazzling."

—CAROLINE LEAVITT, *New York Times* bestselling author of *Pictures of You* and *Cruel Beautiful World*

"The heady, infectious energy of the fledgling film industry in Los Angeles is convincingly conveyed—and the loving but competitive friendship between these two women on the rise in a man's world is a powerful source of both tension and relatability." —*Publishers Weekly*

"*The Girls in the Picture* brings readers into Hollywood the same way that *The Paris Wife* and *Z: The Story of Zelda Fitzgerald* did the Lost Generation of literary Paris—it illuminates, entertains, and inspires. Populated with world-famous figures and enmeshed with the sexist and political complexities of the era, *The Girls in the Picture* is as important as it is enchanting."

—PAM JENOFF, *New York Times* bestselling author of *The Orphan's Tale*

"Profoundly resonant . . . Deeply affecting . . . This sublime historical fiction reads like an intimate memoir. Melanie Benjamin has resurrected these women in telling the story of their friendship. This book isn't just timely, it's necessary!"

—BRYCE DALLAS HOWARD

"Full of Old Hollywood glamour and true details about the pair's historic careers, *The Girls in the Picture* is a captivating ode to a legendary bond." —*Real Simple*

"Melanie Benjamin creates an astonishing portrait of the early days of Hollywood, when innovation ruled and women wielded power alongside men. *The Girls in the Picture* is a fascinating, fast-paced, and ultimately heartbreaking story about two kindred spirits and their struggle for professional and personal fulfillment."

—LAUREN BELFER, *New York Times*
bestselling author of *And After the Fire*

"A smart, fond backward glance at two trailblazers from an era when being the only woman in the room was not only the norm, but revolutionary." —*Kirkus Reviews*

"Benjamin has a unique way of diving into the minds of notable individuals. Relying on facts, the author creates a fictional story that celebrates the joy of seeing hard work come to fruition and feels the pain of the personal sacrifices that it took to get there. And at the root of the novel is a passionate story about two girls in the picture." —Associated Press

"A scintillating journey back in time to the gritty and glamorous days of old Hollywood . . . With elegant prose and delicious historical detail, Benjamin delivers a timely tale of female friendship—and the powerful duo who dared to dream beyond the narrow roles into which they'd been cast."

—ALLISON PATAKI, *New York Times* bestselling author of *Where the Light Falls* and *Sisi*

"The author of *The Swans of Fifth Avenue* and *The Aviator's Wife* brings her penchant for diligently researched historical fiction to chronicling the dawn of the American film industry. . . . Fascinating . . . The rise and fall of silent film gives Benjamin a perfect framework to build a blend of genuinely fun and tragic moments as her characters try to keep up with both the rapid pace of change and the forces that have come to feel oppressively constant."

—*The A.V. Club*

"Benjamin has an uncanny knack for finding riveting historical characters and bringing them to life in wonderfully rendered settings. Her many fans should get ready for the pleasure of yet another of these Benjamin miracles in *The Girls in the Picture*."

—ELIZABETH J. CHURCH, author of
The Atomic Weight of Love and *All the Beautiful Girls*

"Benjamin has established herself as a beloved historical novelist who brings to life women who have languished in the shadows of their powerful husbands."

—*The National Book Review*

THE
GIRLS IN
THE
PICTURE

A NOVEL

THE
GIRLS IN
THE
PICTURE

....

MELANIE
BENJAMIN

BANTAM | NEW YORK

2019 Bantam Books Trade Paperback Edition

Copyright © 2018 by Melanie Hauser
Reading group guide copyright © 2019 by Penguin Random House LLC
Excerpt from *Mistress of the Ritz* by Melanie Benjamin
copyright © 2019 by Melanie Hauser

Published in the United States by Bantam Books, an imprint of Random House, a division of Penguin Random House LLC, New York.

BANTAM BOOKS and the HOUSE colophon are registered trademarks of Penguin Random House LLC.

RANDOM HOUSE READER'S CIRCLE & Design is a registered trademark of Penguin Random House LLC.

Originally published in hardcover in the United States by Delacorte Press, an imprint of Random House, a division of Penguin Random House LLC, in 2018.

This book contains an excerpt from the forthcoming book *Mistress of the Ritz* by Melanie Benjamin. This excerpt has been set for this edition only and may not reflect the final content of the forthcoming edition.

LIBRARY OF CONGRESS CATALOGING-IN-PUBLICATION DATA
NAMES: Benjamin, Melanie, author.
TITLE: The girls in the picture : a novel / Melanie Benjamin.
DESCRIPTION: New York : Delacorte Press, [2018]
IDENTIFIERS: LCCN 2016047423 | ISBN 978110188682-3
(trade pbk. : acid-free paper) | ISBN 9781101886816 (ebook)
SUBJECTS: LCSH: Pickford, Mary, 1892-1979—Fiction. | Marion, Frances, 1888-1973—Fiction. | Hollywood (Los Angeles, Calif.)—History—20th century—
Fiction. | Motion picture actors and actresses—United States—Fiction. |
Women screenwriters—United States—Fiction. | Female friendship—Fiction. |
GSAFD: Biographical fiction. | Historical fiction.
CLASSIFICATION: LCC PS3608.A876 G57 2018 | DDC 813/.6–dc23
LC record available at https://lccn.loc.gov/2016047423

Printed in the United States of America on acid-free paper

randomhousebooks.com
randomhousereaderscircle.com

246897531

Book design by Barbara M. Bachman

To Benjamin Dreyer,
who rescued this novel from the slush pile

"Perhaps the simplest formula for a plot is: invent some colorful personalities, involve them in an apparently hopeless complication or predicament, then extricate them in a logical and dramatic way that brings them happiness."

—FRANCES MARION

FRANCES
1969

LATELY, THE LINE BETWEEN REAL LIFE AND MOVIES has begun to blur.

There are times when I'm pounced upon by a memory—the cracked rearview mirror of the first car I ever owned, say, or the ghostly dance of a curtain in front of an open window when I was small and impressionable and plastered in bed with a fever. Or the teasing curve of a man's lips, a man whose kiss I must have known at some time in my life. And the longer I dwell on the memory, the less certain I am of its origin. Is the memory really mine?

Or is it borrowed from a movie I've written? Was the curtain dancing because there was an electric fan off camera, trained at precisely the right angle? Were the man's lips curving as they came near mine, or were they moving closer to the camera lens instead?

More and more, I can't always tell the difference. And I'm not quite sure how I feel about that, to tell the truth. On the one hand, it might be easier to live the rest of my days believing all my memories, particularly the bad, were invented for someone else to experience on-screen.

On the other hand, if I can't claim as my own the memory of Fred's head always ending up on my pillow during the night, as if he simply couldn't stand to be apart from me for even the span of his dreams, how on earth would I ever be able to fall asleep again?

And the number of people who might be able to place the memories firmly into either category—real or cinematic—is dwindling.

No, not "dwindling," Fran. That's a prissy word. Say what you mean. They're *dying*. Your friends, your colleagues, all the Hollywood relics like yourself—dying off. Like old war horses put out to pasture; like plants that have hung around far too long in the florist's window.

Even on those occasions when I knew that I was most certainly standing in front of a real house, one I had visited many times before, and that I was being cooled by an actual breeze and not studio fans, I couldn't help but touch the rough stucco on the wall, just to make sure I couldn't poke my finger through it. And so I did. Touch it. Then I rang the doorbell again.

"I'm sorry to have kept you waiting, Miss Marion." A liveried butler opened the door, catching me as I poked at the stucco once more. He squinted at me cautiously, as if I really were the dotty old lady I must have seemed. "Miss Pickford is not receiving visitors today."

"You told her it was me? Frances? That I asked for her? For *Squeebee*?"

"Yes, Miss Marion. Miss Pickford still says she is not receiving visitors today."

"Is she— Is she ill?"

The butler looked down at his polished shoes and declined to answer.

I glanced at my watch and considered my options. Should I walk away, leave, and let the tragedy play itself out? After all, the last time I'd tried, I'd been insulted and thrown out of the house. That time, I'd vowed I'd never come back. Yet here I was. Trying to revise the tragedy one more time like a fool. A sentimental old fool.

Closing my eyes, I pictured my small apartment, the cool tiled floors, the plush embrace of my sofa, a nice tall glass of iced tea at hand, maybe dozing to the comforting chatter of *The Edge of Night* or another of my soap operas. Because I really was too ancient for this, this arduous, thankless business of *saving*.

And where had Mary been when *I* needed saving, so long ago? Here, as a matter of fact. Hiding behind this very closed door. So why was I knocking on it now?

Shared memories; triumphs and tragedies; the heroine doing right in the end despite temptation—all the plots of all the movies I've written tangled together into one gigantic ball of yarn I couldn't begin to unravel. Finally, I tugged on the loosest, biggest thread.

Because time is running out.

I squared my shoulders, sucked in my stomach, and pushed past the startled butler until I was inside the cool front hall of Pickfair. "Where is Buddy—Mr. Rogers?"

"Mr. Rogers is attending a luncheon. He should be back momentarily."

"Let me go up to her. Do you know how many times I've been in this house? How many times I've held her hand and told her everything would be all right? No, of course you don't, you're too young, you're an embryo and I'm a dinosaur, I know. Well, young man, let me tell you—*plenty* of times!"

The young man, sporting the usual Hollywood tan, paled anyway. Sucking in his breath, he showed his enviable cheekbones to their best advantage, daring to give me a glimpse of a blindingly white, perfect smile. I nearly laughed out loud. Of course! The Pickfair butler was exactly like all the other poor undiscovered souls in Hollywood, biding time until his big break. Oh, how some things never changed.

"I know Sam Goldwyn, young man. He's a personal friend of mine. If you want—"

"Of course, Miss Marion, go right on up!"

I bit the inside of my cheek as I started across the hall. "And if you'd like," the young man called out in a suddenly rich, resonant baritone, "I'll give you my headshot when you leave!"

I had to chuckle. Poor boy. He had no idea that Sam Goldwyn was even older than I was, and mad as a hatter, at that.

Shifting my handbag to my other arm, I set off across the slick, polished floor of the front hall, certain that I would not slip or falter, even though I had seen many people do that in the past. Charlie Chaplin once tied some of Mary's monogrammed dinner napkins to his shoes and skated across this floor, reenacting one of his scenes from *The Rink*.

Mary had looked on with an indulgent smile—the same tight, practiced smile she granted Chaplin in all the photographs and newsreels—but she'd been furious, all the same. I could tell by the way my friend's determined chin seemed more determined than ever, rigid with forced cheer. Doug, of course, had not only egged Charlie on, but then had to top him by tying napkins to *his* shoes, and lifting Chaplin onto his shoulders and twirling him around and around, finally throwing the smaller man into the air and catching him, to the delight of the assembled guests.

The Duke of Alba had been there that night. Along with Gloria Swanson, Rudolph Valentino, Vilma Banky, and Aimee Semple McPherson. Just a typical evening at Pickfair, the royal manor of Hollywood, where Mary Pickford and Douglas Fairbanks reigned supreme, Charlie Chaplin their unofficial court jester.

Of course, I'd always attended when invited—or, rather, *summoned*—but I wasn't fond of those formal evenings, when Mary and Doug sat side by side at an enormous table groaning with finger bowls and several different forks. Try as I might— and risking Doug's wrath—I never could hide my amusement at these actors and actresses elevated to deities simply because of their looks, troupers with whom I'd once shared stale cheese sandwiches and glasses of beer who suddenly wrinkled their elegant noses if a servant happened to spill a drop of champagne. *"The help,"* they'd whisper scornfully, these gods and goddesses who had once been maids or gardeners themselves, and we all knew that it was only because of a fluke, a genetic lottery won or a benevolent mogul slept with, that they now wore tiaras and aped the regal characters they played on the screen. The characters I wrote for them.

They took themselves so seriously back then, these newly christened *movie stars,* still too unsure if the fledgling industry in which they worked—that we all had actually created with pluck and luck—would endure to be able to mock it, and none more than Mary Pickford. Sometimes I would gaze at her, draped in diamonds, her golden curls piled upon her head so that her sapphire earrings could be more easily admired as she nodded regally and conversed with true royalty, and I couldn't believe my eyes. How had this happened? How had a fatherless little Irish girl from Canada come to dine with kings and queens?

And how had a twice-divorced bohemian from San Francisco come to be one of her honored guests? I had to lump myself in with all the rest; my own journey had been no less fantastic. I went toe-to-toe with Louis B. Mayer and William Randolph Hearst. I was the highest-paid screenwriter in the industry. And I, too, had "gone Hollywood."

At least, until Fred died. Then I came crashing down to earth, and the tiaras and mansions seemed flimsier than movie sets and props, the only tangibles the emptiness in my bed at night, the silence that answered my whispered questions when I was alone with only my typewriter for company.

Still, I counted myself among the fortunate ones in this cruel paradise. Every night I thanked my lucky stars for my life, tragedies and all, because they had forced me to take a different path, one not blessed and cursed with a grand winding staircase like the one I was now ascending, the chandeliers blazing like a thousand stars, the velvet draperies exquisitely embroidered but designed to keep real life firmly at bay.

Slowly climbing—Good Lord, had these steps always been so steep?—I glanced into the famous drawing room off the entrance hall. There, over the fireplace, hung the iconic portrait of Mary Pickford, the Girl with the Curls, captured forever in the full flower of her youth and beauty, the face that, at one time, had been worshipped and adored by everyone in America—including me.

That portrait. That idealized little girl. *She* was the reason Mary was currently hiding in a dark room, afraid of the sunshine, afraid of a light unforgiving, unfiltered; that same light that had so loved and flattered her when she was young. Mary once confessed to me that her face felt odd, cold, when not bathed by arc lights and baby spots; the heat of the studio lights had become so familiar, actual daylight seemed dim by comparison.

Now, if the gossip was to be believed, Mary Pickford emerged only at night, sometimes standing in front of her portrait, staring up at it. Sometimes playing with her fabled doll collection, down on her knees, arranging Lilliputian tea parties or tenderly changing infant-sized clothes.

"I ought to pull that damn portrait down with my bare hands," I grumbled, not caring who heard. I talk to myself all the time; I consider it one of the perquisites of old age.

Finally I reached the second floor, my limbs trembling from the exertion, my blouse stuck to my clammy skin. For a moment I couldn't catch my breath; the stagnant air seemed to wrap my chest in a vise. Oh, for the days when I had tagged along effortlessly after Mary as she jumped nimbly about the set, playing pranks, the two of us giggling like little girls as we made our movies together.

Eighty. I was now eighty. Even Chaplin had started to slow down in his seventies. I took one more deep breath, smoothed the front of my blouse, felt my damp forehead, then continued down the carpeted hallway lined with more portraits and photographs of Mary—Mary in *Pollyanna,* in *The Poor Little Rich Girl,* in *Little Annie Rooney,* in *Little Lord Fauntleroy.* Photographs of Douglas Fairbanks in costume, his white teeth gleaming in his tanned face, his eyes crinkled with dashing merriment.

No photographs of Buddy Rogers, however. For the hundredth time, I wondered how Mary's current husband put up with the ever-present image of his predecessor. She sometimes called him Douglas. And Buddy always answered with an eager smile that made me slightly ill.

Finally I reached the end of the hall, where I confronted a closed door. I hesitated for a moment—a moment long enough for me to stoke my anger and resentment and remember. All the times Mary had shoved me aside, forgotten my birthday, neglected to phone, to write, to *remember*. A moment long enough to consider turning back one last time—until, in another one of those memories that might have been a movie, I heard myself saying, *"I've never turned back in my life."*

So I knocked firmly on the door, loud enough to banish the memories and ghosts so that I might have at least a passing chance of saving the living.

"Mary? Mary, it's me. It's Frances. Why haven't you returned my calls?"

"No!" That rusty voice, so unused now it really did sound like a little girl's, high-pitched, uncertain, quavering. "No, go away, Fran, dear. I'll call you tomorrow."

"I'm coming in, Mary. I want to talk to you. Right now."

"No! I'm not—Squeebee's not vewy well today, Fwan!"

Grimacing at the baby talk, I grabbed the door handle. "You're perfectly fine."

Pushing open the door, I had to pause when I crossed the threshold. The room was so dark, my hands shot out instinctively to feel my way, as if I were blind. Only the smallest sliver of light had managed to penetrate the tightly drawn curtains and in here, there was dust; particles drifted and danced through the weak sunrays. There was also a familiar odor: the sharp, sweet smell of whiskey and the juniper scent of gin.

Finally, I made out the enormous bed with its draped headboard. A tiny figure was propped up against the pillows—only a shadow, really. It took a long minute for the detailed image to emerge from the gloom. When it did, my heart twisted first with horror, then with pity. I took a step backward, retreating into the safe embrace of another memory, a memory I hadn't managed to banish, after all.

A memory of a different time, a different door, the same tiny figure emerging from the gloom of a darkened room.

THE
GIRLS IN
THE
PICTURE

"Mary? Hey, Mary, here's that girl artist I was telling you about."

Owen Moore thumped on the door, cocked his head, listening. He held up a finger. "Hold on, she's cutting," he informed me dismissively. "Wait here. She'll yell when she's ready."

"Are you sure this is a good time?" I patted my long skirt, sneezing as reddish-brown California dust came flying out of it, and touched my head to make sure my cartwheel hat was still pinned into place. Oh, if only I could have brought my sketches! But the Santa Anas had been too fierce this morning. They would have blown my sketch folder right out of my hands, and of course I didn't own a car, so I'd had to take the trolley, and I had no idea what number to telephone to postpone the appointment—and I wouldn't have done so anyway, not for the world.

So I'd had to leave my sketches behind, and I felt as if I'd misplaced a baby, so used was I to having something in my hands—a sketchpad, a diary, a book, knitting. *Restless hands,* Mother had always scolded. *Daughter, you have restless hands to match your restless mind.*

"Sure, sure, it's a good time." Owen could barely contain his impatience; I knew he'd regretted setting up the meeting the moment he suggested it. "Mary?" Owen hollered again. "Hurry up!"

Still no sound from behind the closed door, until gradually I became aware of a whirring, clicking, mechanical noise. Owen Moore—Mary Pickford's devilishly handsome husband—patted his smooth, rosy cheek. On his delicate white hand, a ruby ring twinkled from his pinkie. I had to bite my lip to keep from laughing. What a ridiculous dandy!

"My wife thinks she's God's gift to movies." He rolled his eyes nearly to the heavens; a movie actor's exaggerated body language. A *bad* movie actor's, at that. "She's merely a pretty Irish girl with an adequate little talent—hardly cerebral, if you ask me."

"I didn't, actually. Ask." Shifting my feet, I tried to find a stance that showed my disapproval but didn't offend him. I couldn't stand Owen Moore from the moment he'd sidled up to me at the party, flashing that ruby ring, and I loathed him even more now. To talk that way about his own wife! He was just another small man afraid of an intelligent woman—the world was full of such fools. Yet my future was held in this particular fool's overmanicured hands.

"Well, it's the truth."

"I think she's a major talent." I couldn't hold it in any longer. "I've always loved her movies, even before I knew she had a name. Even when she was only The Biograph Girl, Little Goldilocks."

"You would," Owen said with a sneer; he had not liked it when I turned down his advances at the party, but still, he'd managed to get me the invitation I coveted. With one last exaggerated grimace of disgust, he turned. "I'm wanted on set, so you'll excuse me." Then he stalked off toward the "set"— whatever that was.

Left alone, I had to pinch myself; I'd never been in a movie studio before. *Studio*. That was quite a fancy word for what was really a collection of flimsy barns and sheds, so obviously hastily built I was surprised they were still standing in the force of today's winds. When I'd arrived, I'd given my name to a disinterested man, makeup visible behind his ears, who served as a sort of a gatekeeper. After consulting a list, he told me to go inside the largest of the sheds to wait for Owen.

This shed was a maze of rooms partitioned so haphazardly that there seemed to be no real hallway. From one corner of the cavernous building I could hear hammers assaulting nails and saws chewing through wood; from another, violins scratching out "Hearts and Flowers." Bare lightbulbs swung from long, fraying cords. Shouts rang out from every corner; cries to "Watch that flat!" or "Are the damn Indians shooting craps again?" or "Is Sylvia wearing that costume we need for Lita's dream sequence?" Outside, through windows and open doors that let in enough dust to coat every surface a quarter-inch thick, I glimpsed a row of tall cubicles, each with three walls but, oddly, no ceiling save a gauzy sheer fabric draped over some ropes, like a canopy. Each was done up in a different fashion—a living room, a bedroom, a western saloon, a Victorian dining room. In front of some of these cubicles, where the fourth wall should have been, clusters of people huddled around a man diligently cranking one single camera. Next to the camera, men or women clutching megaphones bellowed directions as people with ghostly painted faces—pale, almost white skin tinged with an undercurrent of yellow, but dark,

dark eyes and mouths—moved about stiffly in the odd ceiling-less rooms illuminated only by the reliable California sun. Owen had headed out a door toward one of the cubicles; could that be the "set"?

"Hey, are you an outsider?" A man, barely taller than me, poked me on the shoulder.

"I—yes, I suppose I am!"

"What are you here for?" He narrowed his eyes, and I blushed as if I'd been caught trespassing. Were normal people not allowed in movie studios? Had Owen been toying with me? Was this revenge for rebuffing him?

"To see—to see Miss Pickford?" I detested the question mark in my voice, but this young man, despite his short stature, looked capable of picking me up by the scruff of my neck and tossing me outside to be swept away by the hot wind like the rest of the trash.

"Mary? She don't like outsiders. You sure?"

I took a big breath, remembering who I was, why I'd ever thought I had a right to be here in the first place. "Y-yes. I'm quite sure."

The boy took another step toward me, but I held my ground, although I did grip my reticule in case I needed to clobber him over the head with it. The boy's eyes were blue and hard and not a little bit menacing—until I detected a gleam dancing behind them. The promise of mischief, perhaps? That dancing light won out; his face relaxed. Suddenly, he was no longer a menacing thug but a laughing leprechaun with a sur-prising dimple in his cheek.

"Well, okay, then. I guess you'll do. Mary's in there." He stabbed a finger toward the closed door. Odd; this boy had acted much more protective of Miss Pickford than her own husband had. For when you got right down to it, Owen Moore had no idea who I really was, or what my intentions might be.

"I know, Mr. Moore told me."

"Owen!" The boy grimaced. "So, Miss Outsider. You like it here?" He jerked his thumb in the general direction of the set area.

"Yes, yes, I do!" I surprised myself with this answer. But I *did* like it here, chaotic and strange as it was. I had suspected—hoped—that I would, but even so, hearing it out loud, in my own voice, was stunning. It was as if I'd agreed to dive headfirst into a shallow pond.

Movies.

The first time I'd heard the word, it was used to describe people and not those flickering, mesmerizing images on a screen. *We don't take no movies here,* landlady after landlady told me when I'd first arrived in Los Angeles two years ago.

"What's a movie?" I'd ask, bewildered.

"You know, them people running all over the place with those cameras, makin' those flickers. Those *movies.* You're not one of them, are you?" Always a suspicious, squinty-eyed glare as I attempted to look as un-movie-like as possible, because I desperately wanted the room. Still, the back of my neck twitched and I thought, for a moment, of answering in the affirmative; how appallingly prejudiced these landladies were!

"No, I'm not a movie," I'd confess, practicality winning out over solidarity with the downtrodden.

"Fine, fine, then you can rent the room," and I'd be allowed to inspect such modest abodes, baldly furnished with dusty, moldy Victorian furniture and threadbare oriental rugs, that I had to marvel that the owner could afford to look down on anyone, let alone one of the mysterious *movies.*

I was a native San Franciscan, born and bred, and everyone warned me that I'd take one look at Los Angeles, turn right around, and catch the next train home. "It's a wild and wooly town full of heathens!" "There's not a single museum there!" "I heard they drive cattle down the streets, and you can kill yourself on the cacti!"

Mother, especially, pleaded for me to stay put.

"Why you would want to go to such an untamed place is beyond me," she had said with a sniff. "There's plenty for you to sketch here, Frances, if you're still bent on becoming an artist."

I refrained from reminding Mother that my husband—husband number two, a number that definitely stung and so was best not mentioned—was being sent to Los Angeles to open up a branch of his father's steel company, and it was my wifely obligation to accompany him. It wasn't that I was exactly thrilled about moving; I loved San Francisco. I loved its hills, its stately new buildings springing up from the earthquake just eight years before, its museums, its theater and opera houses, the determined genteel quality, even if most of its residents were only a generation—or less—removed from the gold rush.

But the instant I disembarked from the train in Los Angeles, I was enchanted. Far from being a barren cow town, the place seemed drenched in color, crimson and gold and purple and white flowers spilling out of every window box, embracing every streetlamp. I couldn't stop gazing at the tall pepper trees, with their languid, lacy green leaves dripping with clusters of red berries, providing much-needed shade from a sun that rarely found a cloud behind which to hide—something this native San Franciscan thought she would never find tiresome. Orange groves dominated the mountainous landscape that sloped to the beckoning sea, the air so perfumed that I immediately craved the sweet, tangy fruit that I'd never really cared for before.

Everywhere I walked I encountered quaint little squares lined with the small adobe-style homes I'd seen in pictures of Mexico; colorfully tiled fountains centered the squares and people would lounge about, napping or reading or simply relishing being outdoors in shirtsleeves in the middle of February. At first, this drowsiness seemed to embody the town to me, threatening to lull me into a dreamy slumber as well— sleepwalking through a marriage to a man I didn't know, nor, I now realized with exceptionally bad timing, did I care to. Dutifully I sketched away at my job, doing commercial art for an advertising agency, but it was rote now, not at all challenging or fulfilling—how many different ways can you depict a necktie? After the initial enchantment wore off, it seemed to me that I'd come to Los Angeles to sleep my way through a disappointing life I didn't remember choosing.

Sometimes I'd try to rouse myself with a good old-fashioned scolding. *What happened to your early ambition to create, to make something lasting, something worthy, my dear? Weren't you going to be the next Rembrandt or Chopin? Weren't you going to set the world on fire? Make your mark, cast a big shadow?*

Stupidity, my dear; that's what had happened. Two—not just one, but *two*—impetuous marriages I could chalk up only to youthful idiocy; I was seventeen when I married for the first time, twenty-two the second. Every time I encountered a setback on the road to becoming the next Rembrandt or Chopin,

I blindly said "yes" to the first person who asked. Yet as soon as I'd mumbled "I do," I immediately rebelled. I had no desire to be a conventional society wife to the conventional society husbands I found myself married to.

But for the life of me, I couldn't figure out what I wanted to be *instead*—oh, I couldn't figure out anything, *do* anything other than fall into miserable marriages in order to put off, for a time, doing or figuring out anything—it all went round and round and managed to dull my early ambition until its edges were harmless and easy for a confirmed sleepwalker like me to ignore.

In the evenings, after a silent meal with the stranger I'd married—truly, I'd stare at Robert, his features still so unfamiliar to me that after two years of sharing a bed I would have been hard-pressed to sketch him from memory—I would lean over the windowsill. Dreamily, I'd inhale the perfumed air, feel the warm breeze carrying salt from the ocean, gape at the beauty around me, but even so, none of it *roused* me; none of it reached my soul. That remained dormant, waiting. For someone—or something.

One morning, late for work, I scurried around a street corner only to find my path blocked by an immovable cluster of backs. "Excuse me," I muttered, holding on to my hat with one hand, my portfolio clamped beneath my other arm as I roughly tried to elbow my way through the crowd, which stubbornly refused to part. "Please, let me through!"

"All right, bring on the cops!" I heard someone shout.

Frustrated, I pushed my way to the front of the crowd, only to stop and stumble backward. Right there in the middle of the normally busy street stood a man barking through a megaphone, while another man turned the handle of a camera perched atop a wobbly tripod. I glanced around nervously; it was as if I'd stumbled upon something *unlawful,* perhaps. Like a bank heist.

And maybe I had; most of my fellow onlookers wore grim, disapproving expressions as they glared at the spectacle playing out in front of them.

Suddenly a gaggle of men in rumpled police outfits burst onto the scene, skittering around a corner and toward the camera, jumping about, falling down on their behinds, slapping one another with nightsticks. In the middle of the wide, unpaved street stood a narrow gate. Only the gate, no fence. And to my glee, instead of running around the gate—the obvious visual effect—the policemen fumbled with the latch, then patiently took turns spilling through the now-open gate, one by one.

The smallest of the police, a slight young man with curly black hair, didn't simply tumble through the gate; he leaped into the air, turned a somersault, and landed on one foot, the other leg extended in a stunningly graceful arabesque. I couldn't help it; I clapped wildly.

The little man whirled toward me; I could see his eyes gleaming impishly. He tipped his hat, wiggled his nose, and hitched up his baggy pants—then dashed after the rest.

When he did, I felt an unexpected tingle in my breasts; my limbs trembled with something like desire. I looked around to see if anyone noticed the change in me; I felt I must look wanton, aching. And for what? A camera in the middle of the street? The silly men, the graceful little clown who could do ballet? Or was it the dawning realization that I was watching people joyfully working together to create while the camera turned steadily, recording the result—*movies*? Finally, I had seen them for myself, these people whom the landladies deplored; they did exist, after all. And they were doing *something,* something rare and wonderful, right here on this ordinary street I walked down every day.

Whatever it was, my skin tingled as if someone had slapped my cheeks; I heard myself giggling, a sound so foreign that I almost cried. It had been so long—so unbearably long—since I'd felt anything close to joy. Since I'd felt anything at all.

Of course, I didn't cry; who could watch these funny men continue to tumble about and make silly faces and clobber one another with their nightsticks without laughing out loud? My cheeks actually ached, in a delicious way, from smiling so much; I was having the time of my life and I didn't give a hoot that others in the crowd turned their noses up at me. I actually stuck my tongue out at one glaring gargoyle—until a jalopy careened around the corner, roaring right toward us all.

The cops scattered, as did my fellow onlookers, suddenly not so dignified as they whooped and leapt back, dropping parcels and handbags; they were just as funny as the fumbling cops and I laughed at them, too, as that jalopy tumbled closer and closer. Even as I jumped up on a sidewalk, the man with the camera and the man with the megaphone remained at their posts. As the rusty old Ford Model T hurtled toward them, I could only watch, unable to tear my eyes away from the impending disaster.

With a wild screech, a spray of gravel that baptized us all—a pebble hit my nose and my suit was bathed in dust—the car crashed through the gate and came to a jolting stop only inches from the camera.

"Cut! That's a wrap!" the man bellowed into the megaphone, wiping his brow with a dirty handkerchief, as the cameraman lifted the camera off the tripod and calmly began to fold the legs up. "Cut it a little close there, Clyde."

"Nah. Knew what I was doing." The driver rose from his seat, removed his goggles, and grinned, his face smeared with dust. "And that's an extra five bucks for coming within three feet of the camera, remember, Mack?"

"All right, all right. Next location!" And the entire company scattered like marbles, leaping into waiting jalopies and driving away, stealing all the color of the day, leaving the dusty street suddenly empty, drably normal again—but somehow less real than it had been only a moment before.

Watching them go, I yearned to run after them. I wouldn't have been at all surprised if that graceful little clown had actually turned and beckoned to me—the sensation that I *belonged* was so strong. He did not, and for a very long time I stared after the dust the jalopies kicked up, feeling as if an unspeakably precious trinket had been snatched away from me. Finally, I dragged my feet to work.

But I didn't accomplish much that day—I must have sketched the same bottle of cologne fifty times. Disgusted and still missing—*something,* I packed away my pencils, switched off my light, and tiptoed out early. There was a nickelodeon around the corner, a shabby old storefront with a curtain hanging in the back for a screen and a semiconscious man slumped over the keyboard of a badly tuned piano. Furtively—in case anyone from work might walk by—I paid my nickel, took my seat on a flimsy wooden chair, and laughed until my sides ached at the antics of the very same cops I'd seen that morning. Only now, projected on-screen, their costumes were no longer a faded blue but a light gray, and they were jumping about in a different setting—the beach—occasionally accompanied by crashing chords whenever the pianist roused himself.

I glanced around at the audience, people just like me—lost, lonely people, perhaps, or maybe housewives who'd stopped in after shopping because they didn't want to face their chores or their children. Or husbands putting off going home to nagging wives. All of us, somehow, had found our way to the flicker show. And together we sat staring rapturously at the screen, laughing, poking one another in the side, forgetting about the outside world and our troubles or disappointments—all because of these *movies*.

After that day, my eyes were wide open; no longer was I content to sit dreamily in the window or sleepwalk through meals with Robert. I went out of my way to find these *movies* now and I was almost always rewarded. For, as if sprouting from seed planted months before, they were popping up all over town.

"I'm going for a walk," I'd tell Robert, who never seemed to care what I did as long as it didn't cost money, and then I'd roam, sometimes taking the streetcar, sometimes on foot, until I heard a firetruck's clanging bells—there were always several cameras at any fire, churning away despite being warned by the firemen—or spotted a telltale cluster of onlookers.

Once, I elbowed my way to the front of a group watching a reenactment of a wedding party on a church stoop. The "bride" gazed adoringly, heavily kohled eyelids fluttering as if she had a nervous tic, up at her "bridegroom" (wearing as much lip rouge as she was), while the cameraman earnestly turned his crank and the person with the megaphone—a woman this time—called out, "Now, Bessie, close your eyes and let him kiss you but good—try not to smear your makeup!"

A stuffy, overdressed woman to my right gasped and pulled a handkerchief from her reticule. I couldn't help myself; I had to provoke her.

"Wait until the honeymoon scene," I teased.

"Oh, my!"

Just then, a rector threw open the church door. Very dramatically, I thought, nodding with approval. His timing was perfect.

"Get the hell off my church, you, you *movies*!" He raised his fist, and the stuffed matron beside me nearly fainted.

"Oh, what will these awful people do next," the woman moaned.

"I don't think he's part of the scene." Now I saw the cameraman hastily begin to fold up his tripod; he wasn't cranking anymore. Looking back at the rector, I realized that he wasn't wearing any makeup, as his face was an entirely different, more natural color than the highly contrasted faces—pale, yellowish skin and dark eyes and mouths—of the actors.

"Get! Goddamn it, get off the steps of the House of the Lord!" The man continued to shake his fist to the skies. Really, I marveled, he ought to reconsider his vocation. He was a natural in front of the camera.

The company quickly, but without panic, grabbed their various boxes and crates and mirrors and costumes and jumped into waiting jalopies—the "bride" wrapped her long train around her waist and tied it neatly—and the show was over. To the obvious disappointment of everyone on the sidewalk, as we were all now glaring at the panting, triumphant rector.

"Don't they have to get permission?" I wondered out loud.

"Nah, they film wherever they want," a man behind me spoke up. I turned, hungry to hear more; I'd yet to talk to anyone who had any inside knowledge of these *movies*.

"Most of these outfits are so small they don't have any kind of studio or factory," he explained. "The concerned citizens of Los Angeles want to pass some kind of ordinance prohibiting them from working here, but personally, I think that's bunk."

"*Constipated* citizens sounds more like it."

"That's the spirit!" The man grinned at me. "These movie people are good for local business, is my view. Why, I built myself a little lunch counter across the street from that Inceville place on Sunset, and I'm raking in the dough! Actors have to eat, just like everyone else. I even got to be in a crowd scene one day."

"Good for you!"

He raised his hat and walked away; I stared after him, my mind starting to click feverishly. Oh, if only I, too, could find a way into these movies!

As the months passed, the movies seemed to be taking over more of the city—in many ways, they *became* the city. No longer did I have to go out of my way to find them. In the quiet little parks and squares I liked to haunt during my lunch hour, I was no longer surprised to see a man in a long wig, dressed in white robes like Jesus, sharing a box lunch with two dancehall girls from the Klondike, while on a nearby bench a caveman and Marie Antoinette held hands. And every day another orange grove disappeared beneath the pavement of a new movie studio. Very few companies still had to sneak around and film on the streets, ready to pack up and leave at the drop of a hat. And when they did need a location in which to film, smart homeowners were more than happy to lend their homes or gardens for a tidy sum.

More and more movie theaters—bigger than the old nickelodeons, with permanent seats and a real screen instead of a big sheet—were sprouting up to show the finished product. And new magazines, like *Photoplay,* appeared, devoting their pages to profiling these mysterious new movie "stars." Although some boardinghouses still proudly boasted that they did not allow "actors, Jews, or dogs."

Well, I wasn't an actor, a Jew, or a dog, but I felt an instant kinship with these ragtag movie folk. On the verge of divorce number two—Robert decided he'd had enough of me, which I did not take personally, and went back to San Francisco—at the age of twenty-five, I knew a little about feeling like an outsider. And I was an artist, too, I reminded myself daily. Even if I was merely sketching bottles of catsup and jars of face cream.

Of course after Robert left, Mother pleaded with me to return home; surely I could find some position as a ladies' companion, something that would shield me from the whispers.

But I looked around me; in Los Angeles, no one whispered or held your past against you; everyone seemed to reinvent themselves daily. I couldn't go back; I simply couldn't face my family and the few friends I'd had. No, if I ever went back to San Francisco, it would be after I'd done something good and necessary, something I could be proud of. Something, unlike my marriages, I could call my own.

Sick of commercial art, I found a job at the Morosco Theater Company, a legitimate acting troupe run by the impresario Oliver Morosco. There, I painted and sketched portraits of the actors for billboards and programs. It was more interesting than advertising, and I got a kick out of being around theater people; they didn't judge, they didn't ask questions, and they didn't care how many times a girl had been married.

Still, I couldn't help but notice that within the company there was great disdain for these new flickers—some called them "moving pictures" or even "movies" now—and the actors who performed in them. "You'll never catch me degrading my art in a flicker!" Laurette Taylor proclaimed, and everyone else agreed. Yet the company often went around the corner to see a show after rehearsal, and I always tagged along like the kid sister who wouldn't stay home. I was fascinated by the maturing art of these movies.

They'd grown from silly little one-reelers that had no story, simply images flailing about, to longer two-reelers that did at least try to convey a plot, however absurd. There were far too many stories about damsels in distress for my taste. And most of the actors were awful, gesticulating stiffly, clutching their bosoms or slapping their hands to their foreheads to indicate distress, backs turned to the camera, shoulders heaving, when they were supposed to be crying.

But a few actors stood out, none more than the former Biograph Girl—Little Goldilocks, we took to calling her because of her long, golden curls. Of course, we didn't know her name; we didn't know any of these movie actors' identities, because the title cards mentioned only the studio. But this ingenue's pictures were always a higher quality than the others; she acted more naturally, none of that wild theatrical gesturing. And one day, the title card flashed her name—

Famous Players: Presenting Mary Pickford.

"Well, they're finally letting us know who they are!" someone in the theater called out to general derisive laughter.

"If that is her real name. I'd sure as hell change mine, if I was in any of these flickers!"

"I'd still never be caught dead in one of them even if they said my name was Teddy Roosevelt," Miss Taylor proclaimed in her husky voice.

I would, I realized, my heart beating wildly even as I turned around to give Miss Taylor my very best withering glare. There's something interesting going on—no, it isn't only interesting; it's exciting, delirious; something that comes along only once every century or so. It's the birth of a new art form. How exciting it is to witness it!

But maybe I wasn't content, anymore, merely to be a witness.

When I returned to my grubby little boardinghouse that night, I snatched up one of the notebooks I always kept handy next to my bed and made a list of my talents, to see if any of them would be useful in the movies.

Well, I could draw, of course. Glancing at myself in the mirror, I thought I was pretty enough, but really, I had no desire to be an actress like the enchanting Mary Pickford. There was more than one reason why I never went anywhere without a sketchpad in my hand; it was something to hide behind. I couldn't even imagine painting up my face and exposing myself to the whirring, unblinking eye of a camera. As superstitious as it sounded, there was something to the old Indian belief that the camera stole your soul. I didn't want to be held hostage to it; after two husbands, the only eyes I wanted scrutinizing my every thought and movement were my own.

I'd written a few feature articles back in San Francisco, for the Hearst newspapers. They were little society stories; once I'd been sent to interview the theater actress Marie Dressler, who'd laughed at my youth but then spent hours telling me everything about her troubles with men; they all seemed to steal her money and leave her. She couldn't understand why—I stared at her face, really quite ugly, with coarse features, bulging eyes, and lips like a toad, but as she kept talking about her heartaches, those popping eyes shone wistfully, girlishly, until her face became almost beautiful with the generosity and tenderness of her soul. I wrote about that instead—I thought I brought her completely to life on the page—but the article never ran. That was the extent of my journalism career. Nevertheless I printed, in big bold letters, WRITING on my list, as well.

And that was it. I could draw, and I could write. A little. How on earth would these skills find me a job in the movies? I tossed the notebook aside, continued to ply my "art" at the theater, went to the movies every evening, and brooded.

A party—there was always a party, one of the joys of working for a theatrical company. I'd been around long enough now to know that the only excuse necessary was an extra bottle of gin—or a surprisingly good review, or even a new costume that hadn't been worn a thousand times before—and there was a party in someone's room, everybody bring a nickel to pay for the sandwiches, a bottle if you have extra.

This party was different; I'd invited a new friend, Adela Rogers. Adela was a native San Franciscan, too, and we'd met once or twice in the Hearst offices. Her father was a famous attorney in San Francisco, but she'd recently moved to Los Angeles, still writing for Hearst, assigned to cover this strange new movie business for the *Los Angeles Herald*. To my surprise and delight, she'd looked me up. Understandably, through her work, Adela had gotten to know some of these *movies*.

"Hey, Fran, do you mind if I bring along some movie folks to this shindig? Mabel is a hoot. Mabel Normand—she works for Mack Sennett. She's always taking her clothes off." Adela cracked her gum and smoothed her stockings; even though she was a couple years younger than me, she seemed so much more sophisticated, already slightly weary of life.

At this party—held in Bert Lytell's two-room apartment over a garage, so the whole place smelled like gasoline, but after enough gin, who cared?—movie actors mixed freely with their theatrical counterparts. And I couldn't see one speck of difference between them. As usual, some of the women immediately kicked off their shoes to dance, with or without willing partners; most of the men preened about, trying to score. Couples huddled in corners, urgently whispering; some of these couples were men, queers. I wasn't quite the blushing bride I'd been when I'd first moved to Los Angeles; I knew men who liked men and women who liked women, and while I couldn't really understand the latter—I did miss Robert in bed, oh, yes, I did—I wasn't bothered by any of them. To each his—or her—own.

And Mabel Normand found a reason to remove her clothes. If Mother could see me now, I grinned as I sipped a gin blossom from a teacup and watched Mabel shake her pert little derriere to the accompaniment of a ukulele pounding out "When the Midnight Choo-Choo Leaves for Alabam'."

"This here is our little Rembrandt," a deep voice boomed. I looked up; Charlotte Greenwood, the tall, gangly character actress of the Morosco Company, loomed over me, accompanied by a much shorter man. "Fran's a genius at capturing a person with her pencils. She doesn't talk much, though."

"I do, when I have something interesting to say." I smiled; I liked Charlotte. She was one of the few members of the Morosco company who was eager to "slum it" in movies.

"It's a pleasure to meet you, Miss—?"

Stunned, I realized this was Owen Moore himself, Mary Pickford's husband, according to the latest issue of *Photoplay* (which I may have read on the trolley coming over), who was now bending over my hand. He actually kissed it, and I had to stifle a laugh.

"Miss—" Oh, bunk! Which name should I give? While I'd been born Marion Benson Owens, I'd since married Wesley de Lappe when I wasn't even eighteen, divorced him, married Robert Pike, was separated from him—really, I could hardly go around calling myself Marion Benson Owens de Lappe Pike.

"Miss Marion," I answered. Only yesterday, I'd decided to rechristen myself; I was now going by the name Frances Marion. Much simpler. Frances was an old family name; it meant "free one." I looked at it as sort of a present to myself, now that I was almost single again.

"Delighted." Owen Moore leered, leaning close. Too close; close enough that I could smell the gin on his breath.

"I'm a married woman." I quickly hid my left hand—ringless—behind my back. "Frances Marion is my professional name."

"What is your profession, then?"

"I'm an artist, like Charlotte said. I do publicity sketches of actors. I'm very good." I was astonished to hear myself say this; I never tooted my own horn. But something about this man's slimy demeanor made me want to announce myself as someone of substance and worth.

"Hmm. You don't say. Mary might like it if you sketched her—I'm married, too, you know."

"Yes, I've read. I'd very much like to meet your wife." I tried to sound casual even as my heart began to race; was this a way in? A way to meet the actress who already embodied, to me, everything captivating about the movies? "I quite admire her."

"Well, I think I can make that happen." Owen smiled in a way he must have thought beguiling, showing all his blindingly white teeth. This odious man apparently was used to women simply falling at his feet.

"While naturally I'm flattered by your attention, Mr. Moore, I think you'll find other ladies here more—amenable?"

"You bet your sweet ass I will." Owen's face tightened, his eyes narrowed, and he balled his hands into fists. I held my ground; I would not flinch from this man who now seemed on the edge of violence—and quite capable of hitting a woman. Then I shivered, thinking of that poor young woman with the blond curls who had the misfortune to be this idiot's wife.

"Shall I show up at the—what is it called? Studio? On Monday?"

"Famous Players Studio. Yeah, show up, bring your damn sketches, I'll introduce you." Owen sighed into the flask he produced from his vest pocket, then lurched off, no doubt in search of a more "amenable" lady.

And now I stood outside a closed door, waiting for Mary Pickford. The girl with the curls. How ridiculous that I, so much older, a twice-divorced woman of twenty-five, should be shaking like a leaf, nervous and wishing, for the thousandth time, that I hadn't had to leave my sketches behind. What excuse now did I have for intruding upon the famous Miss Pickford's precious time?

Yet this was my chance; in my heart, I knew it. My chance to join the movies; I was no longer content with being a spectator in a crowd. I never again wanted to be labeled an "outsider."

The whirring sound stopped, and the door opened. "Come in," a soft but surprisingly mature voice beckoned.

For an instant I was confused; I'd never heard Goldilocks's voice before. How strange—the girl sounded like a woman!

But I managed to step into the darkened room. An overhead lightbulb was snapped on, blinding me.

"Hello, I'm Mary." My hand was grasped warmly.

Grasped warmly—by a child, not the romantic young woman I'd seen on-screen. Off-screen, Mary Pickford appeared even smaller; shorter than I was, barely five feet. Slight, every bone and muscle finely etched. But all I was aware of in those first moments were those eyes. Perfectly shaped, hazel in color but the whites dazzlingly pure, unblemished. Those eyes that had looked out of the screen so expressively, shining with tears or blazing with merriment or simply thoughtful, grave, capable of betraying an entire kaleidoscope of emotion.

The golden curls, however, were hidden from view; Miss Pickford's hair was wrapped up in a threadbare pink turban atop a head that seemed too large for her narrow shoulders and delicate frame.

"I'm Frances. Frances Marion." Gently I shook the warm little hand, terrified of crushing it.

Miss Pickford gazed at me for a long while, as if sizing me up. As those now penetrating eyes turned fully upon me, taking me in, deciding, *parsing,* my cheeks began to burn.

"It's not my real name, actually. And I couldn't bring my drawings," I heard myself adding in a breathless rush, while this imposing yet tiny woman-child continued to gaze at me steadily. "The winds—the Santa Anas—were too fierce. But I came anyway—I hope you don't mind. I'm awfully good, actually, and your husband—Mr. Moore—said you might like to be sketched . . ."

"Yes, Owen told me." Another probing look; I realized that Miss Pickford must have thought I was one of Owen's more "amenable ladies."

"Oh, no—I mean, he was a perfect gentleman," I lied. "We only spoke briefly, but I was thrilled when he said I might meet you."

Miss Pickford's expression cleared, relief in her eyes. "Thank you. And Mary Pickford's not my real name, either."

I grinned at her and, to my delight, she grinned back.

"So tell me, Frances Marion—not your real name—do you like to draw? Is that what you want to be? An artist?"

"Well, I'm good at it, but I'm not sure it's what I want to do forever. It's not as easy as it might look, not very fulfilling and I'm—I think—it's not enough . . ." I faltered.

"Enough?" Mary Pickford again shot me a piercing look, then softened it with a smile. "Oh, I know what you mean. When you work hard—and look at me!" She gestured to her head. Beneath the pink turban, her hair was wound on cloth strips. "I'm here at dawn, working with the scenarist and the director to plan the day's shooting, then I'm performing under the hot sun or lights, then when I'm finished with that I have to wash my hair and set it, every other day or else it looks flat on camera. And while it's drying, I'm editing—cutting. That's what I was doing when you knocked." She pointed at an unwieldy-looking machine; dangling from it were brown strips of film. "This is how we cut from scene to scene—we literally cut it, then splice different strips of film together."

"It looks fascinating." I couldn't help myself; I had to look at the strip of film hanging out. It was translucent, full of ghostly images. Square after square of images that, when all played together, told a story. "To mold your performance, to, to *touch* it with your own hands—what a thrill that must be. I can't even imagine."

Miss Pickford looked surprised. "It is—I love it, which is why I don't mind the work! When you find what you're meant to do, it doesn't seem all that hard. It's my life, these pictures. I don't know anything else. It doesn't leave me time for many friends, for one thing." Again, a penetrating look—a challenge, perhaps?

Or an invitation?

"I was told you don't like outsiders." I decided to speak plainly; I sensed this was a moment of truth—or at least a moment that required truth.

"I—well, it's hard to explain." Miss Pickford hesitated, apparently deciding whether or not to do so. Finally, she shrugged. "You see, the work is all I know and want to talk about. But not many people—outsiders—really understand. They may think they do, just because they've seen me on-screen. But they don't."

"I think I see. When you're that—feverish—about something, you only want to be around people who have the same disease. But it's not a disease, it's a privilege. I envy you, actually. I haven't found anything like that yet. It's what I—I think it's what I came here to find today, maybe. I didn't really want to sketch you—oh, I mean, I'd love to! But I was hoping for something more. Someone to tell me what to do, I suppose." Ashamed of my unasked-for confession, I tried to laugh. Even to me, it sounded forced.

"Do you want to be an actress?" A frosty glint in those startling eyes.

"Oh, no! Lord, no—not me. But I would love to be able to find my passion, and I've thought—I've begun to hope—it would be in the flickers—the movies. It's just so exciting, so—raw and new!" Tears sprang to my eyes and my heart was near to flying out of my chest, it was leaping so wildly—*hopefully*. But I took a deep breath and reined in my enthusiasm. She must surely be asked a thousand times a day how to get into movies. I was not going to behave like everybody else; I had too high of an opinion of myself. And of Mary Pickford.

"I won't take any more of your time, Miss Pickford, for I know you're busy." I held out my hand, professional and cool once more. "If you'd like me to sketch you, or if you have any other work you might like me to do, you can reach me at the Morosco Theater Company."

Then Mary Pickford surprised me. With a grin—a sly, worldly grin, very unlike the sunny beam she used in her movies—she said, "That sounds lovely. I have to go back to New York after this picture is finished, but I suspect I'll be back in California soon. Perhaps I'll look you up then?"

"If it's not too much trouble." It wasn't even a promise, only a question; still, it was more than I'd hoped to hear. I shook Miss Pickford's hand with far more enthusiasm than was necessary, and opened the door, allowing all the hustle and bustle to invade this quiet little sanctuary.

"Miss Marion—Frances?"

I turned back.

"Please, call me Mary."

Miss Pickford was blushing and staring at her shoes, and suddenly she looked frighteningly young. Then she gave a defiant little toss of her head, a gesture familiar to me from her movies—as if she'd forgotten that her saucy curls weren't bouncing about her shoulders but were held captive by that ridiculous turban. As competent a woman as Mary Pickford obviously was—I was still rather stunned to see her working that dangerous-looking cutting machine without fear, and wondered how old she really was—there was something about this fragile-looking creature . . . I suddenly longed to wrap my arms about her and protect her from people. Especially from people like Owen Moore.

"You know, I'm married, too." I didn't know why I said it, only that I sensed Mary Pickford's life wasn't as glamorous as I had assumed. "Or I was. I'm almost divorced now."

She was silent.

"It's challenging, isn't it, being married?" I babbled on. "Especially if you were married young, before you knew better."

"Yes, it is." That was all she said, and I was certain I had overstepped the invisible, yet plainly obvious boundaries this petite actress had constructed around herself. I turned to walk away, into the chaos of the studio, but before I could take two steps I heard a quiet "I don't think you're an outsider, Frances Marion."

Stunned, I spun around. Mary grinned, waved; I did the same. Then the door shut again and that whirring sound started up.

I knew that I had a goofy smile on my face but didn't care as

I tried to find my way back to the entrance. All of a sudden, that young man appeared out of nowhere again—almost as if he'd been watching the cutting room the entire time, as if he were Mary Pickford's personal guard dog.

"Say, that's the longest Mary's ever spent with anyone that I know of. Except for her mother, of course. Mary never even spends that much time with her husband, if you may pardon the expression." The boy's darkly handsome Irish face grimaced at the mention of Owen Moore.

"I can quite understand that." I shivered with distaste.

The young man suddenly grinned and thrust out a grimy hand. "Mickey Neilan."

"Marion Bens—I mean, Frances Marion."

"Seems like we know everything we need to know about each other." Mickey Neilan shook my hand briskly. "We both like Mary. And we both hate Owen."

"That about sums it up," I agreed, grinning right back at him.

"Well, I hope you stick around, Frances Marion. I think Tad—that's what I call her, 'cause she's no bigger than a tadpole—needs someone like you. She won't listen to an Irish mug like me. See you later!" With a jaunty salute, Mickey Neilan pivoted on his heel and bounded off.

"Yes! See you later!" I waved as he disappeared around a corner. Then I smiled again, that same goofy smile.

Mary Pickford had liked me! Oh, it was absurd—I was no stage-struck youth—but still I felt a warm glow of being picked out, chosen. Mary Pickford had decreed it: I was no longer an outsider. I was no longer a sleepwalker, waiting for my life to begin.

Somewhere off in the shadows of the studio, a popular song was being scratched by a gramophone and I didn't care who heard me; I began to sing along.

"Aba daba daba daba daba daba dab, Said the chimpie to the monk; Baba daba daba daba daba daba dab, Said the monkey to the chimp."

Pushing the front door open, I marched out into the bright sun, white with heat this time of day. I slipped off my jacket and felt light, unencumbered; now I was glad I'd left that enormous sketch folder behind.

Because without it, I was free to skip and dance and sing. And for the first time since arriving in Los Angeles, my dancing feet knew exactly where to take me.

*M*AMA, *I MADE A FRIEND!*

The first time Gladys had said this, she'd been three, and the friend a dog, a mangy mutt Charlotte banished as soon as she took one look at it.

The second time, Gladys was eight, and the friend a little girl who had come backstage at a matinee, shy and lovely, carrying a fur muff in one hand, her other hand gripped by a starched governess who announced, "Miss Josephine wanted to meet the little girl who played Aurora." And Gladys Smith—the little girl who played Aurora—had smiled her best, biggest smile, the one Mama told her to use with producers and directors, and curtsied, then held out her hand. Miss Josephine touched it, very daintily, and she smiled. "I think you're very pretty," she whispered to Gladys, reaching out to pet one of Gladys's golden curls. "Can I invite you to my birthday party?"

Gladys had forced herself not to squeal and clap her hands, which she knew instinctively would have made Miss Josephine regret having invited her. Somehow, Gladys understood she must act as if she might not come; she had to act as if she would be bestowing a favor if she did; as if she were invited to so many birthday parties daily, she simply couldn't begin to choose.

But, oh! The truth was, Gladys had never been invited to a birthday party before, and when, after Miss Josephine bade her a timid farewell, Charlotte arrived to take her back home, Gladys couldn't contain her enthusiasm.

"Mama, I made a friend! Miss Josephine! She came backstage to meet me after the show. And she's going to invite me to her birthday party! May I go? What shall I wear? I don't have anything nice enough but perhaps I can borrow my costume?"

Charlotte hadn't said a word; she'd only looked down at her daughter with unconcealed pity, which Gladys couldn't understand. Why did Mama look so sad? She'd made a friend, finally! A girl her own age, not her sister, not her brother, not one of the actors in the company, but a real little girl, who was going to invite her to a party! And Gladys wondered what a party was like; she'd been in one onstage, in the last play, and the child actors had all pretended to eat cake, and been told to blow whistles when the lead actress entered the scene, and there had been boxes wrapped in brightly colored paper, which were supposed to be gifts, but once Gladys had unwrapped one of them between the matinee and the evening show, and she'd found the box was tragically empty.

That was the extent of her experience.

Likely, a real party had real gifts and real ice cream, and a cake not made of cardboard. Likely, a real party had real children who didn't laugh only on cue. Likely, a real party had elephants and tinsel and stars hanging from the ceiling, and everyone laughed the entire time and they played games and ate candy and came home with bags full of stardust to remind them of how beautiful it all had been.

Gladys waited and waited for the invitation—for Mama said that's how people were properly asked to parties, by written invitation, but she said it guardedly, as if she knew a secret Gladys did not. Which was odd, because Mama and she had promised never to keep secrets from each other. They had to be the strong ones and protect Jack and Lottie, and take care of them. Every week that she was playing, Gladys was thrilled to hand over her salary to Mama, who put it in a soft cloth pouch that she tied around her neck, and sometimes she'd shake her head so that Gladys could hear the clink of the coins. "That's music to our ears, isn't it, love?" Mama'd ask with a smile meant just for her. A conspiratorial smile, one that Jack and Lottie never saw.

But the invitation never came. Impatiently, Gladys waited after every matinee, two weeks straight, for Miss Josephine to return and invite her in person, to tell her where the party was, what time she should be there. But she never saw Miss Josephine again.

Finally, Charlotte sat her down. Mama's blue eyes—wide and shrewd—hardened, after she first wiped away a surprising tear; surprising, for Gladys hadn't ever seen Mama cry, not even when Papa died and she herself had wept until she made herself sick. What would they do, without Papa? Even though Gladys was only six, she was terrified; she understood that unprotected women and children didn't have a chance in the world. That was when Mama and she decided that Gladys would try her hand at acting, in order to keep the family together.

Mama's mouth set itself in a determined line before she began to talk.

"Gladys, your friend isn't going to invite you to her party.

She's not your friend at all, I'm sorry to say. She is a spoiled brat whose nurse took her to a play, probably without her parents' permission. I know the kind. They'll not want their daughter to have anything to do with us—with you—because we're poor, and you're on the stage. Because you're an *actress*. But don't ever forget that being an actress is a privilege, a rare thing to be. You're providing for your family. You're continuing a noble profession. Still, there are rules about people like us. Real society, they don't want to have anything to do with us, except to let us pour our hearts out onstage, make them laugh and cry and *live,* just for a bit. Until they go home to their marble palaces and, if they think of us at all, they think of us as servants. As dogs, even. Less than that. To hell with them, is what I say—but you're only a child, Gladys. And I'm sorry you had to learn this so young."

"But—but—Miss Josephine wanted me to come! She asked! She was shy around me." Gladys struggled to keep her voice from wobbling; she wouldn't make Mama feel sad for her by crying. Mama had it so hard, really; even though Gladys was the one who earned the money, Mama was the one who had to stretch it out, keep a roof over their heads, food in their mouths. Sometimes Gladys did wish she could stay home and play, like Lottie and Jack did, but she always reminded herself that *she* was the lucky one, because it was her privilege to take care of them all. And one day, she would be a star—the biggest star of all!

Jack and Lottie never would be that. Gladys hugged this knowledge to herself, and it kept her warm on lonely nights when Jack and Lottie huddled in their shared bed and whispered secrets about the other children they played with. Real children, not actors. Children like Miss Josephine.

"But she didn't really want to be your friend," Mama continued, pretending she hadn't heard Gladys's voice wobble. "Miss Josephine only *admired* you because you were onstage. And that's not the same thing, not at all. Even if she did want to be your friend, her parents would never let her."

"I hate her, then!" And Gladys meant it; if Miss Josephine had been there, she would have slapped her silly. And not a stage slap, either.

"No, you don't. Don't forget, people like Miss Josephine make it possible for you to keep acting. As long as they show up, you'll work. Don't ever forget that you need them more than they need you. You remember that, precious, and you'll work for life and we'll always be together and happy."

"But I want—I want—"

But Gladys wasn't entirely sure what she wanted, other than to make Miss Josephine cry and feel sorry for not inviting her. But she also wanted to make her come to Gladys's next play, and the next after that. And also, most important, she wanted Miss Josephine to admire her, to want to *be* her, Gladys, even if Mama didn't think that was the same thing as friendship. But perhaps friendship wasn't that important after all. She did still have Mama and Lottie and Jack.

Gladys couldn't articulate any of this; her dreams of a real party came crashing down around her tiny shoulders right then, and she *did* want to cry, very much. But she saved her tears for later. For when she might need them; perhaps in a role where she was supposed to cry on cue.

MAMA, I MADE A FRIEND!

Gladys was thirteen now; she'd been on the stage for five years, ever since she was eight (even though she always told people she'd started out when she was five; five sounded better than eight). But she *felt* as if she'd started that young; she felt as if she'd never known a life before. A life that didn't mean fire-trap theaters and smelly greasepaint and threadbare costumes she had to try so very hard not to grow out of, or split, or spill anything on, because without her own wardrobe, she'd never be hired by the second- (or third-) rate touring companies with which she had the best chances. A life that didn't mean lining her clothing with newspapers in the winter while on tour, be-cause trains were so drafty; a life that didn't include sleeping upright on those trains, using more newspapers as pillows, waking up covered in newsprint and coal dust. A life that didn't mean traveling without her family, all alone, entrusted to the care of indifferent actresses who sometimes forgot to make sure she ate. But sometimes she did get to travel with them all, be-cause the entire Smith clan was on the stage now, Mama and Lottie and even Jack, the very smallest of them all so sometimes he played a girl, which he hated, but Gladys made it her busi-ness to lecture him about not throwing tantrums, about being happy for a job, any job. Because jobs were scarce, and even though the Smiths worked fairly regularly, they were small-time, Gladys knew it. Try as they might, they'd never been able to break into the first tier; they had to tour, always, all over the United States and Canada, playing in terrible theaters, all bunk-ing together in flea-ridden boardinghouses, Mama, exhausted after a performance, managing to scrape together meals on a hot plate when times were good; feeding her brood crackers for breakfast, lunch, and dinner when times weren't. Learning to make soup out of catsup and water.

The Smiths were spending the summer of 1904 in Manhat-tan, which they had done before; of course, nobody played during the summer, when the theaters were stifling. So Mama took in sewing, and that summer she opened a candy stand at Coney Island. And they tried to pool their resources with other players whenever they could.

"Mama! I made a friend! A little girl like me, her name is Lillian, and she and her mother and her sister, Dorothy, are in the theater, too, and looking for a place to stay this summer. We can all room together and save money," Gladys explained to Mama.

Gladys often explained things to Mama, and to Lottie and to Jack; she was the father of the family, and she had to help Mama out and keep the others in line. And she also knew things they didn't: She knew how to get free tickets for real plays by sidling up to the box office manager, widening her eyes, batting her lashes, handing him her card, and purring, "I'm just sure that I could learn so much from your fine actors!"

The first time she led Jack, Lottie, and Lillian and Dorothy Gish on such a foray, Lillian turned to her and gave her a look, an admiring, appraising look. And Gladys understood that perhaps here was a friend, a real friend, not someone who would show up backstage to invite her to a party and then never come back. It was difficult to make friends while touring; companies were constantly being broken up as some actors got better jobs, or finally decided to give up and go back home, wherever home was.

And while she might not see Lillian and Dorothy again—a fate she accepted pragmatically, because that was life on the road—she enjoyed the summer they spent together. Lillian was very much like Gladys; at thirteen, they were the eldest, with frivolous younger siblings who preferred to cut up and play around rather than work. Lillian was close to her mother, too.

And of course, she understood the theatrical life; she wasn't an outsider, as Gladys had started to think of anyone who wasn't in the theater, anyone who didn't consider the smell of greasepaint just as vital as a cup of coffee to snap you awake. Anyone who didn't understand the nuances of billing or the hierarchy of dressing room allotment, or who didn't know that *In Convict Stripes* was a real stinker, but *East Lynne* always made audiences cry.

Lillian looked like a tiny angel, even more ethereal and helpless than Gladys—Gladys was shrewd enough to accept this and understand that some casting directors might prefer that type to Gladys's own more sturdy, self-reliant appearance. But behind that saintly exterior was a spine of steel to match her own. "I'll be a real actress someday," Lillian vowed, as she and Gladys shared not only a stick of peppermint candy, carefully hidden from the younger children, but also a bed one stifling August night. Usually Charlotte didn't allow Gladys to do this; she felt the family should stick together, even while sharing a tiny two-room flat with the two Gish girls and their mother. But this night, she had.

"A real actress on the stage here in New York. On Broadway!"

"I will, too," Gladys promised. "I have a plan. I'm going to see Mr. Belasco!"

"Belasco!" Lillian gave a skeptical whistle through her rosebud lips; everyone knew Mr. David Belasco was the biggest impresario on Broadway. "How?"

"I don't know yet, but I will. I'm tired of touring. It's not getting me anywhere. And frankly, I'm the one with the talent; Lottie and Jack are young now, and appealing, but they'll soon grow out of it. Mama's hopeless! She gets such terrible stage fright, that's why she's only ever cast in bit parts. But I have the talent to be a Belasco actress, and I'm going to!"

"I know you will, Gladys." Lillian's eyes were solemn and admiring.

"And when I do, I'll send for you," Gladys continued grandly. She patted her friend's tiny white hand. "And we can star together for Mr. Belasco. I'll play the leading ladies and you can be the ingénue."

"Well, as long as they pay us the same, that's fine with me." Lillian yawned, then blew out the candle.

Gladys turned over her pillow, trying to find one small, cool corner, and smiled.

Leading ladies always were paid more than ingénues.

Mama, I made a friend!

Gladys was seventeen, and she wasn't Gladys any longer. She was now Mary Pickford, and David Belasco himself had christened her thus. She had appeared on Broadway! In a legitimate play, an elaborate Belasco production for which she hadn't had to provide her own costumes. Oh, the delight of standing perfectly still for the seamstress, being measured and fitted for her very own costume that no one would ever wear but her, a real antebellum dress with actual lace petticoats, a hoop skirt, satin ribbons! While she wasn't a leading lady with a star on her dressing room door, she had a featured part and received very good notices for her work as young Betty in William de Mille's play *The Warrens of Virginia*. William's younger brother, Cecil, had a part, as well.

But after *The Warrens of Virginia* closed, Mama had urged Mary—they all called her Mary now, and even Mama, Lottie, and Jack had changed their name to Pickford—to do a dreadful thing. An absolutely appalling, horrible thing.

She had urged Mary to take a job in the flickers.

"You were a success, and you will be again, but meanwhile, dearest, we owe the rent. And I hear they're paying quite a lot now, down at that Biograph place!"

It was 1909. Mary had seen one or two flickers, passing time while on the road. She hadn't thought much of them; they were a fad, a fancy. And the storefronts that showed them were horrid—much, much worse than even the tawdriest theater she had played. Although the audiences seemed to love them, these flickering, silent images on the screen.

But no actor worth his salt did; it was humiliating to think that she, a Belasco actress, would work in the flickers! How could she do it?

"They pay five dollars a day," Mama said.

The next morning, Mary showed up at the Biograph studio on 14th Street, dressed in her very best new heels and a pretty straw hat that Mama had just retrimmed. She was doing the Biograph Company a great favor by showing up, of course. It wasn't every day a legitimate actress deigned to visit a flicker studio.

But as she confronted the front door of the brownstone, she felt a flush of humiliation; what she hadn't told Mama—or Lottie or Jack or Lillian or anybody—was that she'd already tried the Biograph studio before, a year earlier, and been sent away, deemed not worthy.

Not worthy! Of the flickers!

Things were different now, yet still the same. Yes, she was a Belasco actress, and that stamp of legitimacy could never be removed. Yet she was a Belasco actress with a family to feed, and it was between seasons. As soon as she dropped her card here at this—*flicker*—place, she'd hurry on up to the theatrical offices; maybe some of the fall tours were beginning to cast.

Mary opened the door and stepped inside; the place was mayhem, exactly as she'd remembered it. The lobby was full of men in shirtsleeves and green visors huddled over adding machines and ledgers. Office boys ran back and forth; so did various people with that awful film makeup, layers and layers of ghastly yellowish pancake troweled on. Mary walked up to a receptionist, handed over her card, and then was instructed to "take a seat over there, girlie."

She shuddered, rose to her full five feet (in heels), and perched on the edge of a bench. Across the room was a clock; she would wait exactly fifteen minutes, then leave. Five dollars or not, she would not subject herself further.

One of the office boys, racing past, stopped and gazed at her, up and down. Mary was accustomed to this kind of gaze; every time she auditioned, she was given it. It was the gaze of someone summing up, taking in, deciding; her fate hung in the balance of gazes like this. The office boy lingered a bit longer than usual, and Mary suddenly felt a compulsion to make a face at him. She scrunched her nose and stuck out her tongue. He took a step back, astonished, then he grinned and sped off.

Two minutes later, a very tall, very thin man with a nose like a beak stood beaming down at her.

"Are you an actress?" he drawled with a southern accent.

"Of course I am!"

"What kind of experience?"

"A decade in the theater, and the last year with David Belasco!"

"Hmmm. Well, you're too little and too fat."

"What—"

"Miss—"

"Pickford. My name is Miss Pickford," Mary sputtered, jumping to her feet, quivering with outrage. "And if you think—"

"I think you'll do. I'll guarantee three days' work each week at five dollars a day."

"Mr.—Mr.—"

"The name's Griffith."

"If you think a Belasco actress will work in flickers for only five dollars a day, you're quite mistaken. I require a guarantee of twenty-five dollars a week. Plus extra if I work more than three days."

Mr. Griffith laughed. He stuck his hands in his pockets, shook his head, and laughed again.

"I'll take it up with the board" was all he said, but Mary saw the unwilling admiration in his eyes, and she raised her chin in triumph. "Now, let's get you into makeup and see what you can do." He grabbed her by the arm and ushered her into the women's dressing room, then left her.

"Hey, D.W.," someone called after him, and Mary pursed her lips at the informality of the flickers. In the theater, no one would dream of calling Mr. Belasco by his first name! In the theater, she wouldn't be fearful—as she was now—that someone might burst into the dressing room, perhaps even Mr. Griffith himself, and try to get her to perform "favors" in exchange for a role. She'd heard of such things happening in the flickers. To be honest, she'd heard of such things happening in the theater, as well. But so far, some kind of virginal aura had protected her.

No one propositioned her, however; what happened instead was that Mr. Griffith himself burst back into the dressing room and began to apply makeup on her quite roughly—terrible makeup, makeup that obliterated all her features, making her face look like the moon, pale and without planes, her eyebrows far too dark, almost black, which didn't go with her light brown curls at all. Wielding powder puffs and brushes, he attacked her face with something like fury. Then he tossed her a dress, enormous, and told her to yank it up if she needed to. Finally, with a small grunt of approval, he left, telling her to come right to the set after she changed.

She'd heard that most flickers were made outdoors, to capture the sunlight, but at Biograph, she found herself directed to a basement room, pitch black, crammed with furniture and painted flats, a wall of lamps made of glass tubes that were suddenly switched on with a menacing hiss, followed by more lights beneath metal hoods, hanging from tall poles. The effect was instant, searing heat and blazing light; she held up a hand to her eyes, blinded.

"All right," called that Dixie-tinged voice again. "Let's do this. Little Miss Belasco Actress, you'll be Pippa. In this scene, Pippa will play a guitar, and stroll from crowd to crowd. You're beautiful, you're graceful, you're animated, you're charming. All right, ready—roll!"

A guitar thrust in her hand, Mary was startled by an unholy sound—a clicking, whirring staccato, which seemed timed to the movements of a man behind a camera, cranking away. As the film went through the camera, tiny little dots, like snow, filled the air.

Somehow, without tripping over the debris on the floor—someone had actually left a boot there—Mary managed to grimace and move, pretending to strum the guitar, from group to group, instinctively keeping her face bathed in the harsh lights, turned toward the camera.

"Who's the new dame?" someone muttered, and Mary whipped her head toward the source of the voice; it was an actor, glaring at her, perhaps handsome, but who could tell with all that ghastly makeup?

"I am no dame. Mr. Griffith? Mr. Griffith?" She let the guitar fall to her side, and held her hand up to shield her eyes as she searched the hazy figures assembled behind the camera for one she recognized. The tall, erect figure stepped out of the shadows.

"Mary Pickford! Do not ever, under any circumstances, *ever* stop a scene until I say cut! I'm the director! I am *God,* do you understand? You're just a silly little actress, Belasco or not. Do you have any idea how much film costs per foot? You've cost us two dollars. Which will be coming out of your salary, young lady!"

Mary felt her face burn; tears stung her eyes and she was torn between dropping to her knees and sobbing and hitting that actor over the head with the guitar. She was so confused; there were a few elements that felt familiar from the theater— all the actors, the playing of a scene—but the rest was entirely, bewilderingly foreign. Those blazing lights—she could feel the makeup melting on her face! That horrific turning of the camera, so noisy, like the clattering of a streetcar. The deitylike presence of the director, having no compunction about humiliating an actress. Mr. Belasco treated actresses like goddesses! Like the artists they were, with great care and respect and decorum. *He* would never yell at her!

"Owen, step out and play up to her. Make love, you two. Have you ever made love, Mary Pickford?" Mr. Griffith studied her with that odd combination of admiration and amusement, and she knew he was testing her, trying to break her.

Which was one thing she would never allow him to do.

"Of course," Mary retorted, despite the fact that her heart was racing and her palms were so clammy they did drop the guitar, which landed with a twangy thud. She was only seventeen! And despite the public's notion that actresses lived sordid lives, Mama had never allowed her to go anywhere unchaperoned, or even entertain the idea of a beau. Not that she'd ever met anyone who—

The young actor who had called her a "dame" stepped up to her. "Owen Moore," he said with a gallant smile, then he grabbed her by the waist, pulled her to him with assurance, and Mary found herself fondling his shirt collar, his buttons, nuzzling his neck, resting her head against his very solid, very masculine chest—

"*Roll!*" Mr. Griffith commanded, and this time, Mary didn't even hear the camera, so intent was she on the beating of Owen Moore's heart beneath her ears, her lips, as somehow—she had no idea how she knew to do this; it was as if a switch inside of her had been flipped on by the sound of this man's heart—she kissed his chest, softly, little fairy kisses, and she heard his sharp intake of breath, and felt a smile she'd never smiled before— teasing, victorious—curl the edges of her lips.

And still she managed to keep her face turned toward the camera.

"*Cut!*"

Owen Moore released her with a startled expression on his face; he looked as if he couldn't trust himself to touch her any longer. He also looked as if he'd been the butt of some joke; his eyes narrowed as he studied her.

"You've never done that before?"

Mary, dizzy, her pulse ringing in her ears and not quite trusting her voice, shook her head.

"Come back tomorrow, Miss Belasco Actress," D. W. Griffith boomed down at her. There was laughter in his eyes that he didn't try to hide. "Or would you rather have dinner with me tonight?" His voice suddenly dropped two octaves and took on a tone that reminded Mary of the dusky velvet of the jewel box in which Mama kept her wedding ring, the way the velvet clasped the simple gold band in its soft, yet unyielding grip.

Then she wondered why on earth she'd thought of that box at that moment.

"No, I think not," Mary replied as primly, as ladylike as possible, avoiding Owen Moore's suddenly darkly threatening eyes. "Thank you all very much."

She fled the studio—but not before she'd grabbed the voucher Mr. Griffith handed her and collected her three dollars (oh, how she cursed herself for ruining that first take!) from the cashier. But she hadn't stopped to scrub off her makeup, and she knew that people were staring at her on the streetcar. When she reached the boardinghouse, she ran straight to her room and shut the door.

Would she return tomorrow?

Yes, she would. If only to see her new "friend"—a friend she knew she could not tell Mama about. Not yet, anyway.

MAMA, I MADE A FRIEND.

When she left the studio this evening, after talking to Frances Marion, Mary went home. Not to Owen, but to Mama. Even after three years of marriage, Mama still meant home.

Three years of marriage, five years of making pictures. Mary Pickford was now the best-loved actress in the movies, she was told; her face was in *Photoplay* nearly every issue, she was making a thousand dollars a week, the highest-paid actress in the world. Her last feature, *Tess of the Storm Country,* was an enormous success, her biggest to date.

And every night, after she closed her eyes, Gladys Smith reminded herself that it could all go away in an instant. Audiences were fickle. Tastes changed monthly, even weekly, in these modern, sped-up times. Her looks could fade. She could get fat like Mama. Then she'd be back where she'd started, playing bit parts in low-rent touring companies, and Jack and Lottie and Mama, always, always Mama, wouldn't have enough to eat or a roof over their heads. And it would all be her fault.

For now, anyway, she was a star. A *married* star, with an actor husband who couldn't stand it that her career was ascending faster than his. A *drunk* actor husband who wasn't very good, she had to admit to herself—that first encounter had been pure animal magnetism. Never again had she witnessed Owen Moore acting a scene so convincingly—and so she couldn't respect him, and he knew it. He took it out on her by belittling her in public, reminding one and all that he'd been in the movies first, he was the bigger star than she was then, and he'd taught her everything he knew though obviously it wasn't enough, but who could account for the public's taste?

There were other ways he took it out on her, too.

So Mary sought refuge in Mama's apartment most evenings, instead of the boardinghouse where Owen resided, and happily let Charlotte fix her warm stews, hearty casseroles—the plain food she still preferred after all those years on the road—and after supper, she'd sit while Mama brushed out her curls, winding them up again for the night, so they'd be shiny and sleek in the morning. She was doing just that, sitting in a rocking chair, eyes closed while Mama's hands brushed and twisted and gently smoothed, when she murmured, "Mama, I made a friend today."

"Did you, love?" Charlotte cooed.

"I did. A young woman, an artist. She said she wanted to work in pictures. Not as an actress," Mary added hastily as Charlotte stopped brushing. Mama had warned her, years ago, that she could never truly be friends with other actresses. "Jealousy, competition—it will always be there," she'd said. "Even with Lillian. You two will inevitably compete for roles, and then how will you be friends? Actresses will pretend to be your friend to get favors. Then they'll stab you in the back the moment you have a flop or you gain an ounce of weight."

"Are you sure?" Mama asked now. "A young woman who doesn't want to be a movie actress? I've never heard of such a thing! She must not be very pretty."

"No, she is pretty, actually. Tall, so tall and slender!" And Mary sighed; as short as she was, she knew there'd come a time when she'd invariably put on weight. "Her name is Frances. Frances Marion. She—it's hard to explain, but somehow, she seemed to understand me. Something she said, about husbands—"

Charlotte put down her hairbrush.

"What's he done now? Did he lay a hand on you? So help me, I'll—"

"Nothing. Nothing new. The usual. Oh, Mama, I made such a mistake!"

"Yes, you did, dearest, and I won't sugarcoat it. You made the worst decision in your life. And there's nothing you can do about it now, all because you didn't listen to me, did you? I told you not to see him anymore but then you had to go and marry him. That was my fault. I should have known better than to tell you not to do a thing, because you're as stubborn an Irish lass as I am."

"It wasn't your fault, Mama. It was mine; I was swept away, too young to know any better. This Frances—she said she was married young, too. Now she's getting divorced."

"And you're Catholic." Mama tugged a little too hard on a curl.

"Well, anyway, we're going back to New York City for the next picture, but Owen is staying out here." And Mary hoped, for the thousandth time, that she could simply *wish* her marriage away; spending as much time apart as they did aided in this fantasy. Yet she also felt a pang of guilt; wouldn't a good wife—a proper wife—be living with her husband instead of her mother? Had she ever given Owen a chance? She'd forced him to keep the marriage a secret at first; she knew it was a mistake, being married by a judge on the sly, such a mistake that she couldn't bring herself to tell Mama and Lottie and Jack, knowing it would break their hearts. So they kept it a secret for months, and when they did break the news—and, oh, what a scene it was! Griffith should have seen her then, as hysterical and simpering as he could have wished for the camera—Mama finally turned to Owen and said, "Mary shares a room with me. Where will *you* sleep?"

And it went downhill from there. Mary knew Owen fooled around with other women; she saw the ingénues lining up outside his dressing room, the pitying looks these girls gave her, even though she was the much bigger star.

The biggest star of them all. The one who couldn't keep her

husband satisfied. But the one whom the camera loved the most. And it turned out, so far, the adoring eye of the camera was enough for her. Even as she knew it wasn't for her husband.

Mary kissed her mother good night and crept into bed. It was still strange, going to sleep so early; she was used to the stage, where you didn't dream of retiring until after midnight, so keyed-up after the evening performance that it took hours to settle down. But the movies were different, more disciplined, and that was one reason why Mary loved them. She had to go to bed by nine, in order to look fresh for the merciless— sensitive, adoring, eager—camera at eight in the morning.

But before she shut her eyes—she still sometimes slept with her arms straight up over her head, from her touring days when the three of them, Lottie, Jack, and her, had to squeeze into one seat on the train—she remembered the sympathetic, understanding gaze of Frances Marion. Frances had looked at Mary as if she knew all about Owen, which, of course, she couldn't.

But she seemed to be able to *imagine* she did, all the same.

As Mary's buzzing thoughts kept her awake—they always would, if she let them—she longed to tell them to someone. She longed to unburden herself to someone her own age. Someone who might make her *feel* her own age, because honestly, she never had. She'd always felt like Mama's contemporary, responsible for everything: food on the table, a roof over their heads, the success of each and every picture, the happiness of these new movie "fans," as they were called. And maybe her sister could have been her friend, like Dorothy and Lillian Gish were friends, but Lottie had turned out to be a bad apple, and Mary blamed herself for that; she'd always taken care of her, indulged her, so of course Lottie had no discipline, no work ethic, no matter how many roles Mary secured for her. She was never, ever grateful!

But Frances Marion—something about her unexpectedly pierced Mary's armor, an armor thickening with every pay raise, every interview, every photo of herself in the newspaper. Every letter from adoring fans not only in the United States, but sometimes now from foreign countries. It was heady, but worrying, this newfound fame, even as she sensed it was only a tremor and that something else, either astonishing or tragic, she had no idea which, would follow.

Some movie promoter had just christened her *America's Sweetheart*. Toronto-born Gladys Smith—Mary Pickford—America's Sweetheart. It was all so dizzying, so confusing. If only they knew, she snorted into her pillow. That America's Sweetheart had no sweetheart, even if she was married. That the marriage bed could be the loneliest place in the world, when the man you'd married was a stranger whose only attribute was that he had been the first boy to put his arms around you on the very worst day of your life.

If only America knew about the decisions you had to make when you found yourself caught up in a profession, an industry, whose very existence you were helping to shape; decisions that other married women didn't have to make. Decisions that numbed your soul, the same soul you were so eager to bare to the camera, the one thing constant, the one thing nourishing, in your life.

But Frances Marion—she might know. Mary very much suspected that she did. And with that comforting thought, Mary finally went to sleep. But not before whispering into her pillow,

Mama, I made a friend.

"I DON'T KNOW WHAT TO DO WITH THE EXTRAS." LOIS dropped her arm that held the megaphone and studied the scene before us, a party scene with lots of gaily—if shabbily—dressed crowd extras. "The audience is getting too sophisticated. We're getting letters now saying they can read lips, and so they know what the extras are saying. And most of it isn't fit for decent company."

"Can't you—can't somebody—tell them what to say? Write some lines for them?"

"I don't have a spare moment." For the first time since I'd known her, Lois Weber looked less than bandbox fresh. Her kohled eyes—she was always made up to look as elegant as any of her actors—drooped in exhaustion.

Then those same eyes were staring at me, widening with an idea.

"You can do it, Frances, can't you? I know you said you didn't want to be on camera, but this is different—you'll be helping me. While I'm setting up, go over there and scribble something down and get made up, then while we're shooting, move among the extras with your back to the camera, telling them what to say. I don't really care what it is—just write some dialogue that works for this scene."

"Me? Write dialogue?" My own eyes widened; what on earth did she mean?

I was on set—me, Frances Marion, actually *on set*. I knew the language now, the language of moviemaking. And despite my protests, I'd been on camera once before, doubling for an actress who couldn't ride a horse, but that didn't really count, as it was a long shot and I'd kept my face turned away from the camera.

I could also claim job experience as a cleaning woman, sweeping sawdust into corners. And as a seamstress, mending torn costumes. And as a painter—putting my highly touted artistic talent to use by slathering cheap paint on flats. I'd learned to cut and splice film and had the scars on my fingers to prove it; I'd written actor biographies (both fake and real, but mainly fake) and press releases. I'd put my hand to work making fifty cucumber sandwiches for a party scene, and when they ran out of fruit, had grabbed my hat and scurried around the corner to a grocer to buy more.

And I loved every single minute of it. I couldn't wait to come to work each morning; no longer did I sleepwalk through my days.

Adela was responsible for giving me my big break; I'd phoned her, after that first meeting with Mary Pickford, begging her to help me find a way, any way, that I might be able to work in this industry. Adela had thought for a minute—I could hear her snapping gum from the other end of the phone—then replied, "Lois Weber's always looking for protégées—her little starlets, she calls them. She's at the Bosworth studio, along with her husband. And you know, she saw you once; we were having lunch at the Alexandria Hotel and you were leaving. 'Who's that beautiful girl?' Lois asked me, and I told her, but that was before you got bitten by the bug. So remind her of that, when you meet her."

I did remind her, and Lois remembered the incident with genuine warmth, although she was stunned when I declared that I didn't want to be an actress.

"Then why are you here?" Like everyone I met, Lois seemed unable to grasp the fact that a pretty young woman with connections didn't aspire to be an actress. Not when the trains deposited hundreds of would-be movie stars every single day; not when the studios had taken to hanging signs on their gates declaring *Go Home to Mother! We Have Enough Actors.*

"I want to create something—something permanent. I want to learn everything there is, and be around the kind of people who want to, as well. I want to have a career, I want to go home at night and feel satisfied with a job well done—I want to be able to tell people I do something. Something important, something real, of my own!"

"Oh, my dear!" And Lois Weber had laughed, even as her eyes were full of sympathy; she was a tall, elegant woman with a full bosom but such a tiny waist that she made me feel like a scarecrow. "You're so young, so eager! You remind me of myself. I love my husband, but I didn't want to stay home keeping house for him, either. But of course, Frances, you can't say that kind of thing. Except for here!" And Lois gestured about her office, but I understood that she meant the studio. Or maybe even Los Angeles, in general, the city that was reinventing itself every time the sun rose.

"Is it fun, working with your husband?" I doubted it could be—Lord, I would have killed Robert if we'd worked side by side—but for some reason, I yearned for Lois to answer in the affirmative. She and her husband, Phillips Smalley—Phillips wrote, Lois directed—were such a dynamic couple; the kind of couple that made a two-time divorcée entertain the thought of marrying again, if to the right man. A man who would respect me, be my equal in every way and not be intimidated by me; a man with whom I could create something lasting.

A man, I realized with a wry snort, who didn't really exist— except in the movies.

"It's stimulating" was all Lois said, with an arched eyebrow, and I laughed. We shook hands, and I signed a contract for twenty dollars a week with my new name, subtracting two years from my real age. "Everyone in this industry does," Lois assured me. "You'll thank me later."

She also wrote, beneath my signature, "refined type." When she saw the question in my eyes, she laughed again. "For when you decide you really do want to be an actress, after all."

So far, except for the horse chase, I'd resisted. But now I found myself in a chair before a smeared and cracked mirror dimly illuminated by old lightbulbs, watching the other actresses as they applied that thick pancake, layer after layer. Finally I picked up a tube of the stuff—I sniffed it, recoiling; it reeked of menthol and sweat—and began to make short streaks all across my face, imitating the others. Then I picked up the least filthy sponge I could find and began to smear the lines together, trying not to think of all the actresses who had used the same makeup and sponge before me. Goodness knows, I was no stranger to a little discreet makeup—another new habit I'd adopted, along with smoking; habits that would have caused any number of San Franciscan matrons to faint, but then I wasn't in San Francisco anymore, was I? I was free—I was

Frances—and on my own in Los Angeles, embarking upon an adventure of my own choosing, and even though I had now thoroughly obliterated my features with this disgusting makeup and was in the process of weighing down my eyelids with gummy kohl, still I giggled. Grotesquely made up or not, wasn't I having the time of my life?

After I chose a stained party dress from the meager costume cupboard—extras were supposed to provide their own clothes, but of course I hadn't known I'd be on camera when I'd dressed this morning—I picked my way among the cables and crates surrounding the set. Lois came gliding over to me; her nose was freshly powdered and she'd applied a little scent, I couldn't help but notice. It was as if, being the only female director in the company, Lois felt she had to emphasize her femininity in order to placate the men she was paid to order about—always with a smile, of course.

"Do you know what you want the extras to say?"

"Yes, I've thought up a few conversations. Just light party talk—'oh, I love your dress,' 'what a pretty hat,' that sort of thing. But it should satisfy the lip readers."

"Wonderful. You look lovely, by the way. I can't wait for you to see the rushes!"

I shook my head. Perhaps I did look lovely—my black hair would photograph very nicely, done up in an elegant twist, and my naturally dark eyebrows would also show up well on film. But I knew I wasn't cut out for acting.

And when, later that day after everyone trooped into the darkened projector room—it was a small company and Lois and Phillips made no distinctions between the lackeys like me and the stars like Claire Windsor—and I saw the day's rushes, I was proven absolutely right.

"Oh, God," I groaned, covering my eyes with my fingers, then peeking out, then covering them again as I forced myself to look at the screen. "Oh, I'm awful!" And I *was*. The way I moved—so stiffly, as if someone was prodding me with invisible wires. My arms looked like sticks compared to all the other actresses, and my blue eyes registered too light. They gave me a wolfish look on-screen.

"I think you look swell," one of the cameramen, George Hill, said softly. I flashed him a grateful smile, which made his handsome face—he had a very dashing mustache and soulful eyes—light up. George followed me around like a puppy dog, but he was a baby, only eighteen or nineteen. And I had no intention of leaping into yet another relationship; my divorce wasn't even final.

"What are you talking about?" Lois laughed, squeezing my shoulder. "You look marvelous!"

"No, no—never again!"

Lois nodded. "Well, I appreciate you making the effort anyway. And how did you like writing dialogue?"

"I liked it enormously!" How fun—how freeing—it had been to put myself in other people's shoes! To imagine their lives, their relationships, what they might say, even if it was merely party chatter. I wasn't acting only one role, I was acting several—all of them—all intoxicatingly different.

Yet at the end of the day, sitting here with all my chums, I was still myself; still Frances. The camera took nothing from me but my words. My soul remained my own.

After that day, I continued to do every odd job—including writing occasional dialogue—asked of me, learning, absorbing, happy to be of use, to spend my days among people just like me; talented misfits with no direction until they'd stumbled upon the movies, or the movies had stumbled upon them. The Bosworth studio was in Laguna Beach, quite a trip from my boardinghouse but worth the long trolley ride for the scenery alone, the stunning cliffs and plunging drops to the ocean and the view of Catalina, sometimes vivid, sometimes only a ghost in the mist. I got a kick out of meeting the various stage actors who showed up, some uninvited, all as if bestowing unheard-of favors, to try their hands in "the movies." No longer did the word define the people but rather, what they—*we*—were creating.

One morning I looked up from the reception desk where I was filling in; who was standing before me but my old friend Laurette Taylor, from the Morosco Company?

"I see you're slumming it, Miss Taylor. Or should I put your name down as 'Teddy Roosevelt'?" I couldn't help myself. Miss Taylor glared at me as she swept past on her way to meet Lois.

For some reason, I wasn't at all brokenhearted when Miss Taylor didn't prove to be very good on-screen.

One day Owen Moore showed up, as handsome and full of himself as ever—his thick, dark hair glistened; his even white teeth glowed even brighter. He was to costar with another one of Lois's finds, a girl named Elsie Janis. I liked Elsie; she was enchanting, always bouncing around and doing handstands and joking with the crew, mimicking everyone in sight. Apparently she was very famous on the stage, especially in England, where she sang and performed little sketches showcasing her mimicry of everyone from Nellie Melba to Lord Kitchener.

"C'mon, Fran," Elsie coaxed one day after she'd been made up and costumed as a cavewoman for her latest, *'Twas Ever Thus*. "We need more cavegirls! Put some mud on your face!

Wrap yourself up in some of these animal skins, and ride out with us to the set!"

"Oh, Elsie, no!" Actually, I had plans to stay in while the company was on location, and work on a scenario with one of my new friends. Bess Meredyth was a laughing young actress who, like me, didn't particularly enjoy performing despite her good looks. Bess had her mind set on writing, too, and had written a few screenplays. Now she was teaching me how to flesh out an idea into a working scenario that a director could shoot. "Everyone has ideas, and ideas sell; you can make a little money that way, you know," Bess told me. "But turning an idea into a shooting script is an entirely different thing." And it was; but it was also exhilarating, trying to put myself inside the camera lens, seeing the actors, framing the shots, describing the motivations, learning how to convey emotion not through words but movement—but not silly movement. Not movement for movement's sake, but realistic, controlled.

Putting myself into each character's mind, too, then crawling back out of the dense psychological forest I had created at the end of the day, shedding the weight of these fictional people's troubles and woes and emerging lighter than air—miraculously lighter, gayer, than I'd ever been. Ready to dance and drink and love and laugh and enjoy life as I'd never known it could be enjoyed before.

"Oh, Fran, you can stay inside any old time," Elsie said, pouting. "But you won't have me around forever! I'm heading back to England after this, to cheer up the troops there—this horrid war, you know! I can't believe it's still going on."

"Neither can I." Europe had exploded into flames this past July; it was November 1914 now and still the conflagration burned. From the unexpectedly serious set to her mouth, I could tell Elsie wasn't happy being away from her adopted home in its time of need. Particularly to make a cavewoman movie—and I couldn't blame her one bit.

"All right," I finally agreed, because Elsie was so much fun, and it was a lovely day. Besides, my face would be covered in mud, so who would know it was me?

My face *was* covered in mud—I told myself it would do my complexion wonders, just like any mud mask I might get at a beauty parlor—and two hours later my hands were scraped and my knees nicked from scrambling about a hill full of jagged rocks and cacti.

"This is one time I'm glad I'm not writing dialogue," I huffed to Elsie after the director called "cut" to set up a new shot. "*Oogga booogga* is about all I can think of to say."

"It ain't Shakespeare, that's for sure." Elsie yawned and stretched out on a flat boulder, looking exactly like a lizard sunning itself as she raised her little face—the only one *not* smeared with mud, since she was the star—to the cloudless sky.

"Watch out for rattlesnakes," I warned her. During the previous take, one of the girls almost stepped on one; the director had pulled out a pistol and shot it.

"I checked." Elsie yawned again. "You know, Fran, sometimes I can't see how these crazy movies are going to last—my name is actually Lithesome, in this. 'Oh, fearless women of the Stone Age who fought and died alongside their men'—that's one of the title cards, if you can believe it!"

"Well, I can write better than that." I stomped my feet, in an attempt to frighten away any rattlers that might be lurking about. Then I looked down at my mangy costume, my mud-splattered legs, my scrapes and cuts; overhead the sun was beating down upon all of us on the rocks while behind the camera sat the director and scenarist, the continuity girl and the rest, mercifully protected by umbrellas. "This is the most insane business. Why does anyone want to be in front of the camera?"

"Frances Marion! I thought you weren't going to be an actress!" A petite figure, framed by a lacy parasol, was cupping her hands and yelling up at me; I shaded my eyes and beheld Mary Pickford's sparkling, mischievous gaze.

"Mary!" I couldn't help it; I clapped my hands, showering myself with mud. "Oh, you're back! I'm so glad!" I didn't care about the next shot; I had to scramble down the rocks, even if the director wasn't yet finished with me. "When did you return?"

"Yesterday. I came out to visit Owen on the set, but I don't see him." Mary frowned. Her golden curls were pinned up on top of her head in a grown-up fashion, and she was wearing an exquisite white linen dress with a blue silk sash. She looked fresh and cool, as if she'd just come from a garden party; I itched to change out of my ridiculous costume and take a long bath. How absurd and embarrassed I felt, covered in mud and fur!

"I don't know where Owen is," I lied. Because I knew perfectly well that Owen was behind the rocks, cuddling with one of the other "fearless women of the Stone Age."

"So you couldn't resist being an actress, after all?" Mary teased as she took in my outfit, but I detected disappointment, perhaps resentment, in her gaze.

"Oh, no—it's only a favor to Elsie, I'm still no actress! Actually, I've been learning a lot here at Bosworth, doing a little bit of everything. I've been thinking I might want to learn how to write. Scenarios." I felt bashful, confessing my ambitions to

Mary; after all, I hadn't seen her in months, and we'd only really just met. But she smiled warmly, and put her gloved hand on my dirty arm, not seeming to care that it would soil.

"I think that's marvelous! I knew you'd find a way into this business."

"I have, but the studio is about to shut down—Bosworth is getting out, he thinks he's too old, that it's a young people's business—and Lois and her husband are going to Universal." I'd only just heard the news, and hadn't had a chance to decide if I wanted to tag along with Lois to Universal or not. There were plenty of new studios popping up. Perhaps at a smaller one, I'd be able to work my way up to writing. As much as I loved Lois, and was grateful to her, I suspected that I'd remain her right-hand girl, only doing odd jobs, if I went with her.

"Work for me!" Mary blurted it out—much to her obvious surprise, for she then clapped her hand over her mouth, her eyebrows raised in astonishment. I held my breath, waiting. But she didn't rescind her offer.

"What?"

"Come work for me, Frances! Really, I mean it! You say you don't want to act, but unfortunately that's the only thing I can hire you for—my contract specifies that I can cast my own films. But mainly, I want you to help shape some of the scenarios I'm set to film. We'll have such fun!"

"Are you serious? You're not—I'm not—that is, I'm still *learning*!"

"We all are! That's the exciting part, isn't it? We're making this up as we go along and there's no one to tell us we're doing it wrong!" And Mary gave me that penetrating gaze again; the one that was so at odds with her demure, virginal appearance.

"I'd—I'd love to! Where do I sign?" My hand was already

tracing the air with my signature; I couldn't wait for something as ordinary as mere paper. She might change her mind!

Mary laughed. "I don't carry contracts with me, you silly; you'll have to come over and meet Mama, and we'll take care of business then."

"Oh, of course, of course. All right, Mary." In lieu of an actual contract, I reached out and grabbed her hand, shaking it firmly. "I'm honored and humbled."

"Don't be humbled. I'm no charity; I hire people who I think have talent. I also hire people I like to spend time with."

"Hey, cavewoman, get your ass back up on your rock!" The director turned his megaphone toward me; I shrugged and scrambled back up the hill. But when I reached the top, I turned and waved at Mary, who waved back.

"Fran, are you coming out tonight with everyone?" Elsie stood up, and resumed her "lithesome" pose. "We're going down to the Ship Café."

Normally, I would love to. I'd fallen in with a ragtag, eclectic group of movie people; actors like Mabel Normand and Sessue Hayakawa and Erich von Stroheim; my fellow lackeys at Bosworth, Sidney Franklin and George Hill. Adela, of course, as well as Bess and another scenarist, Anita Loos, who couldn't have been more than seventeen but somehow had talked her parents into letting her live and work in Los Angeles. It was a fun group, and we usually met at the Ship Café—an actual ship, a replica of a Spanish galleon—on the Venice Pier for beer and sandwiches and gossip and dancing on deck after the sun set. We were all young, we were all hungry for fun as well as fame, and we were all in love with our work—and so, naturally, in love with one another. It was intoxicating, being part of such a gang. We said hello with warm hugs and kisses, laughter was the drug of choice (for most of us, anyway; I wasn't sure about Mabel), and we all helped one another; egos were left outside the door. If Adela was stuck on a story idea, we pitched in and worked on the plot. If Lois wasn't sure about a camera setup, everybody had an idea. And some of the gang— von Stroheim, for instance—were so poor, we all reached into our pockets to pay their way, simply because they were so amusing, so full of self-importance—and ambition. The other thing we all shared.

"Not tonight, Elsie. I have an appointment. With Mary. Mary Pickford." I couldn't believe my own ears.

"Mary? She's back?" Elsie turned her gaze back down to the camera area, where Mary was now talking with Owen; even from this distance, it didn't look as if it were a happy conversation. Mary had folded her arms across her chest, allowing her parasol to droop behind her back; Owen was waving his arms wildly.

"Guess my time with Owen's over, for now." Elsie laughed. "I love Mary, but when the cat's away . . ."

"Elsie! You, too?" I couldn't help it, even though I knew I sounded like a prude. But I was shocked; Elsie was so sweet, so gay. A tomboy, really. But, yes, there was something predatory about her, too—as if the entire world was hers for the taking. And I couldn't help but wonder if that was one of the unsavory by-products of success.

"Me and every other cavewoman around here. Except you, apparently. Oh, Fran, don't look so shocked! That marriage is a sham. They know it, we know it, everybody knows it. Except for the fan magazines, of course. Mary's a real cool cucumber, so serious all the time. And Owen, well—he's not. And c'mon, you're no saint."

My face burned. No, I was not. I enjoyed the company of men, and on some of those nights that began at the Ship Café I ended up in someone else's bed. But never a married man—never. I would never do that.

"But you're Mary's friend, Elsie."

"Not really. Mary doesn't have friends. She has acquaintances."

"Even if that's true, that doesn't make it right."

"Oh, lighten up! I'll leave Owen alone now. I have no wish to really hurt Mary—I wouldn't parade it around in front of her. And I'm going back to England anyway, where there's a war on, if you haven't forgotten. I imagine *that* will sober me up right quick."

"No, I haven't forgotten there's a war on," I retorted, although, quite frankly, I had. No one in the States was really talking much about the conflict in Europe. Other than worrying about how it might affect overseas profits; the movie industry was just waking up to the idea that there was an international market for American films.

The director roared "Places, cavewomen!" through the megaphone. "And . . . roll!" I scampered about, waving at the other women, miming toil or exhaustion as the director called out his whims, doing my best to keep my face turned away from the camera.

Mother didn't yet know about my new career; no one back in San Francisco did. Although there was scant chance of any of them happening into a movie theater to see, still, I didn't want to expose myself. I was the lone cavewoman not mugging for the camera, not silently begging for its favor.

"Don't you know there's a war on?" Elsie cried at one point as she picked up a rock and held it above her head, looking as

fierce and determined as any cavewoman. Her voice quavered, and in that moment, I didn't think she was acting.

But under that relentless, pale sun, surrounded by colorful flowers, a blue sky unclouded by smoke or the haze of a battlefield; in that moment of birds soaring overhead and an ocean of opportunities miraculously in front of me, it was impossible to believe it.

Especially after the director yelled "Cut!"

THERE *WAS* A WAR ON. A WAR, UP ON THE SCREEN.

Mary sat next to me in a crowded theater, her hair pushed up into a voluminous velvet hat so that she couldn't be recognized, which was starting to happen more and more. Thank God I never had to worry about that, and if I proceeded down the path I hoped, I never would. I wanted to be *known,* yes— with every ounce of ambition I possessed—but not *recognized*. I could change my hair, decide to throw on an old dress if I needed to run to the store for butter, or wear an evening gown slashed down to my sternum if I wanted.

All things that Mary was beginning to realize that she could not do without repercussions, and I knew she wasn't quite sure how she felt about that. On the one hand, recognition assured her stardom—and fame meant everything to Mary, for reasons I was only beginning to understand.

On the other hand, these new movie fans were different from any fans I'd ever seen; they weren't always satisfied with simply staring, or politely asking for an autograph. No, movie fans were prone to tears, or sometimes even faint screams, and they sometimes reached out to touch Mary, finger her dress or even her curls, as if they had a right. As if they felt ownership of her, from head to toe, the entire package paid for by their movie tickets and their devotion, their laughter, their tears.

Tonight, Mary had so far escaped notice. The tickets had cost two dollars each, so this was a more jaded crowd. I couldn't wrap my head around it; two dollars for a movie ticket! Only a few years ago, I'd paid a nickel and for most movies it was still only ten or fifteen cents. But for D. W. Griffith's newest—promised to be a spectacle unlike anything the public had ever seen—we willingly paid it and now the entire audience was abuzz, more interested in what we were going to see on-screen than who was in the seats. Word had already leaked out from the first showings that what Griffith had done was astonishing. Unprecedented.

The Clansman—or *The Birth of a Nation,* the movie was titled.

From the moment the orchestra down in front—a real orchestra, not just a pianist—began to play original music, composed specifically for the movie—again, unheard of—I don't believe I took a single breath. For three full hours, I knew nothing but what was unfolding on the screen. The images and the stirring music assaulted my brain, punching it like a heavyweight, so that at times I couldn't quite fathom what I was seeing. I could only let it wash over me and hope to make sense of it later.

Ten reels, the movie was. *Ten!* What would this mean from now on? Ten reels allowed for so much more story—epic storytelling, not the sweet little missives we were all used to making. Studios were certain that an audience could really only be expected to sit through two reels, five at the most.

But Griffith didn't care about what had been expected, and the result was electrifying. My mind reeled, both enjoying the movie and struggling to understand the astounding technical wizardry as one innovation after another unfolded on the screen. Not content with linear storytelling, Griffith employed exciting cuts and inserts—how on earth had he thought to do this? How had he known that the audience could make the connection, keep it all straight? It was brilliant, intense, and utterly thrilling; my every muscle was so rigid that by the time the film was over, my entire body ached.

The battle scenes were miraculously staged and lit, like a Brady daguerreotype come to life. The stunning use of the camera iris to zero in or fade out of a scene—I'd never seen such a thing before, but it gave the audience a chance to catch its breath and steel itself for what might come next. The titles were ornate, like beautiful calling cards instead of the plain sentences, in plain type, that everyone else used.

Of course, the story was epic: the Civil War and Reconstruction, played out as background behind the familiar story of two families, one from the north and one from the south. It was Griffith's genius to concentrate on the intimacy of these families, their personal relationships; the spectacle was breathtaking, but it was the fate of the ordinary people that I cared so deeply about.

All through the film, Mary's hand gripped my arm. She was as feverish as I was, her fingernails digging deeper and deeper until, when at last she let go, I had four distinct red marks in my flesh. But I didn't mind. The two of us were one—one living, breathing, stupefied being, wholly and entirely transfixed. Just like everyone else in the audience caught up in this sweeping, emotional vortex that sucked us all in and wouldn't let go until the very end, when the hero and the heroine were together at last, and the image faded to the ultimate title:

Liberty and union, one and inseparable, now and forever!

The orchestra held the final chord, and there was silence, awed silence, as if in church. I heard the thumping first; I looked around and only slowly realized that it was feet pounding, stomping the floor until the whole building vibrated. Then came the thunderous applause, the cheers and then a roar, a heartfelt, deafening cry.

I was on my feet, clapping and yelling until my throat was raw; I felt something rolling down my cheeks and realized it was tears. Next to me, Mary was standing on her seat, cheering, tears rolling down her face, too. Her hat was hanging halfway down her back, her curls on full display, but nobody was looking at her; everyone was still swept up in what had just transpired on the screen.

"Oh, Fran! Oh, Fran! Did you ever? Aren't you *proud*?"

My throat tightened up, and I thought—*Yes!* This is it, this is what I was looking for, waiting for, all those years. This flowering, this opening of hearts and eyes and minds, great vistas, all through the creation of people like me—people whose imaginations were too big for real life, so we had to build another. Build it out of trial and error and sweat and tears and luck and pluck and heart. I *was* proud of this movie—of this industry. *My* industry.

None of us in the stifling hot theater—one of the new "palaces" springing from the earth like the Great Pyramids, but monuments to movies, not kings—wanted to leave; like stunned cattle we remained staring at the screen, blank now, as if we could still conjure up our favorite moments.

"I want to do that to people." I turned to Mary, seizing her arm; her face was still pink, her eyes still shining with emotion. "I want to make them not want to leave; I want to sweep them away with *my* stories, *my* ideas! I want to make art, not merely entertainment!"

"You will. I will. If Griffith could do it—I mean, Fran, I worked for him at Biograph! I knew he was talented but oh, so arrogant! He never wanted to collaborate. I had so many ideas but he rarely listened. Yet that's what made this brilliant, isn't it? He didn't listen to all those who told him he couldn't make a ten-reel movie. He didn't listen to anyone who told him you can't cut back and forth like he did—oh, Fran, that chase, at the end! No one's ever done that before!" You wouldn't know, to look at Mary, that she wasn't simply a movie fan herself. And I knew that really, she was. She loved movies as devoutly as the most feverish of her fans. Perhaps that was why they adored her: in her, they recognized themselves.

"Do you regret leaving Biograph for Famous Players now?"

"No! God, no! I'm so happy for Lillian—wasn't she stunning? And Mae Marsh—of course, she had an affair with Griffith, which I wouldn't, which is one reason why he was so tough on me." Mary grinned slyly, and I tried not to look as shocked as I felt. For some reason, I never could think of Mary as a sexual person, even though, of course, she was married.

"Griffith? He wanted to—to—" I looked about, in case anyone was eavesdropping, then I bent down and whispered into her ear, "He wanted to make love to you?"

"Yes, of course." Mary laughed as gaily as if I'd just suggested we go get ice cream, and for the first time, I felt the less worldly one of our pair. But then I realized I shouldn't be surprised; Mary, after all, was an actress. And I was already learning that actresses had a different—murkier—path to success than women like Bess and Adela and me. I'd seen the way men in power treated actresses; it wasn't an equal relationship at all, and if you were an ambitious actress, well . . . There were many unsavory choices you would have to make. Actresses who wanted bigger roles were fair game, at least for some directors and producers; it was an open secret.

Although it was strange, wasn't it, that I'd never seen Lois Weber proposition an *actor* whom she was thinking of casting?

Mary continued to laugh at my prissy expression, and I had to admit that I was stunned for another reason. The one thing I brought to this blossoming friendship, so that it wasn't as lopsided as I sometimes feared, was the sophistication of the divorcée from San Francisco. I was better educated than Mary; after all, I'd gone to finishing school, studied Latin and the classics, and I'd been raised in comfort—stifling comfort, but still comfort. Mary had been raised in a trunk and hadn't gone to school at all, and I knew my friend was deeply sensitive about this, desperately trying to make up for it.

And I'd known men, many more men than Mary had—yet now, I realized with a shock that since I wasn't an actress and hadn't grown up in the theater, I was far more sheltered than Mary had ever been. Why had I never even thought to ask her about this kind of abuse; what else had she, and others like her, had to suffer—to accept—as part of the steep price some men exacted for a woman's ambition?

"Oh, Fran, don't look that way! Of course Griffith expects to have affairs with all his little actresses—he's hardly the only one, you know. I learned that on my first day working with him, but I never said yes and for some reason, he didn't make me pay the way he did with others. Although—you know, that might be one reason why I fell so hard for Owen." Mary looked thoughtful. "Being with him protected me from Griffith, and then other directors, too." She gave a short, dry little laugh.

"Well, I wasn't going to be simply another one of Griffith's little dolls, so eventually, I left. Although I respected the work we did, I couldn't put up with his controlling ways. He wants his little actresses to simper and curtsy and ask 'how high?' when he says 'jump.' Still, I'm in awe of what he's done tonight. Now people will stop wondering if this movie craze will last. It will, because of what Griffith has done. He's elevated a fad into an art form."

"He inspires me to want to work harder," I confessed as finally the audience began to move, like a herd, to the doors. Mary adjusted her hat so her curls were fully hidden; she glanced around nervously, and seemed to make herself appear smaller and less attractive. It was a neat trick, one that I'd noticed before. "Ten reels, though! The cost of it all—do you think it will earn it back?"

"I don't know. That's the question—what does the audience really want? Short flickers that cost a nickel but only last a few minutes, or something longer, like a book, to get lost in for an hour or two? Or three, in this case." Mary shook her head, and I could almost see the gears in her mind clicking. Another thing I'd learned about Mary, in the short time we'd become close; her mind never rested. She was always thinking, strategizing, ferociously determined to stay one step ahead of everyone else. No wonder Mary and Griffith had clashed; they were so very similar.

"The thing is," she continued thoughtfully, "are there enough directors who can—"

"Miss Pickford? Mary?" A woman stopped in the aisle and planted herself directly in our path, holding out a pencil and a small album. "Can I have your autograph?"

"Mary? Mary Pickford?" Now others were turning to stare,

and even as I reached toward Mary to protect her somehow—shield her, perhaps?—she shook me off and removed her hat, revealing her golden curls, and soon there was a small crowd closing in. Forgotten was our conversation; she smiled happily and signed each and every piece of paper thrust in front of her, shook every hand, accepted every hug.

"Excuse me, miss?" I looked up; a man with a pathetic little mustache doffed his hat and handed me a card. "You're Miss Pickford's maid? Could you give her this? I represent the Mademoiselle cosmetic company and we'd love to talk to Miss Pickford about representing our face cream."

Before I could reply that I was most certainly not Miss Pickford's maid, the man had disappeared into the crowd, just as Mary signed her last autograph.

"Oh, Fran, I'm so sorry!" She came rushing back to me looking anything but; she had a contented smile on her face as she shoved her hair back into her hat. "Mama taught me never to refuse my fans. And they are dears, aren't they? So devoted!"

I accepted her quick hug, and she hooked her arm through mine as we stepped out of the theater.

I also crumpled up the business card and threw it to the ground.

We strolled down the street to Mary's automobile, a black 1915 Buick touring car. It was lovely, and I couldn't suppress a pang of envy at its rich sleekness. Even if I wasn't a maid, I was still a long way from owning my own automobile. Mary pushed the button, the engine sputtered to life, and we drove off, down wide, hilly streets toward the neighborhood called Hollywoodland, where we both rented bungalows in one of many new courtyard complexes that were being built by savvy real estate investors; there was a perpetual housing shortage now that the trains disgorged hundreds of new citizens every day. Los Angeles was a boom town.

Mary parked the car expertly on the street, and we trooped up toward our twin bungalows. They sat side by side, sharing a little side yard. The light on Mary's porch was on, and a plump figure rose out of the shadows with a groan.

"Mama, it was amazing—you have to go soon!" Mary cried.

"Really? That Griffith? I still don't like the way he treated you at Biograph." Charlotte Pickford pursed her wide mouth, turned up her generous nose, and I grinned.

Mary Pickford's mother was already the stuff of legend in the movie industry. "Love Mary, hate the mother," everyone said. "So pushy. She's a drunk, too. Mary doesn't make a move without her."

But I liked Charlotte; I liked her a lot. Now I knew where Mary got her practical mindset that seemed to stun those who only saw her as the sometimes angelic, sometimes adorably pugnacious creature on the screen; a creature made of light and air and wishes. That wasn't the Mary I knew; in real life, Mary and Charlotte Pickford were the most intensely practical women I'd ever met.

It was Charlotte who kept Mary's books, and she'd taken over the job for me, as well; I had no head for figures. Money was meant to be spent, and now that I was earning so much—fifty dollars a week!—and I was on my own, no husband to report to, well—I bought everything I desired. It would all go away soon, wouldn't it? I couldn't imagine that I'd keep earning this much; someone would find me out, see me for the fraud I was, and then I'd be back drawing and living in a boarding-house. But at least I'd be fabulously dressed.

Charlotte did not think this was a prudent course. She urged me to save every penny, as Mary did. Charlotte mothered me, worried after me, almost as much as she did her daughter, and I enjoyed every bit of it; my own mother had only worried about how I reflected upon her in society.

Of course, Mary earned a far greater income—how much, I never wanted to know, only that it was so vast it might as well have been play money—and Charlotte wisely invested it in land, although not in houses. So the highest-paid actress in the world rented a small bungalow in a modest courtyard next door to her new best friend—me.

And I loved it. As busy as I was now at work, and at play, I'd sometimes been lonely since Robert left. I'd moved from one dreary boardinghouse to another, not even bothering to un-pack my trunks. Now, I was practically keeping house with Mary and Charlotte, and I felt younger, more girlish, than I had in years. It was as if I'd stupidly vaulted into adulthood with those disastrous two marriages, growing up too soon, tak-ing myself and my problems far too seriously.

But in the movies, time did not always travel in a linear manner; it zigged and zagged, leaping forward, falling back, and there was always a chance at redemption. Was that what I was having now? A chance to go back and start over? Had Mary given me that?

Living next door to Mary, it was as if I was transported back to my boarding school days, before I allowed men to turn my head and derail my dreams. The two of us gossiped and giggled like roommates; we tried out new hairdos on each other and speculated about the future. Now, if I was lonely or sad or bored, I only had to go out on my porch and yell across the way for Mary to answer in her sweet, lilting voice. We ran in and out of each other's houses without bothering to knock—the doors were always unlocked—and we cooked up culinary experiments—disasters, really; oh, the time Mary decided to put mushrooms in biscuits! But it didn't matter how near we came to poisoning ourselves because Charlotte, den mother extraordinaire, always swooped in to fix our mistakes.

I didn't see my chums from the Ship Café as much as I used to; Mary didn't like to go out. So confident in the studio, when she was outside of it she often seemed poignantly shy and self-conscious; it was her lack of schooling, I decided; it had a way of dampening the spirit that came so alive when only the camera was watching. Most Saturday nights the three of us stayed in, popping corn and sitting out on the porch, while Charlotte regaled us with old Irish ghost stories about faeries and sprites.

As different as I felt and looked, Mary had changed, too. No longer was she the wary, watchful—so very careful—porcelain figure I'd first met, only months before—impossible! In a short time, we'd become each other's entire lives. It was almost as if Mary, upon deciding she deserved a friend, had shed a too-tight corset she'd been wearing for years; the warmth of the trust she'd placed in me was startling.

I genuinely loved this Mary, this girlish, giddy Mary who laughed more easily, allowing more of her surprising wit to escape. Sometimes she'd stop in the midst of some silly thing we were doing—like the time I taught her to throw spaghetti against the wall to see if it was cooked and soon her entire kitchen was draped in stringy pasta—and I'd be stunned to see tears in her eyes, which had just, a minute before, been blazing with merriment.

"Oh, Fran," she told me once as she swiped away those tears. "You don't know, you just don't know—I never had the chance to have fun like this! To be a child. I was always working."

I hugged her so tightly then; with all my heart I wished there was a way I could give her a childhood, to turn back the hands of time.

When the sun disappeared, so, too, would our silliness; nights were for pinning up our hair, or, if it was washing day, we'd go into Mary's kitchen and let Charlotte spoil us both. Of course, my hair was a much simpler thing; it was just hair. Mary's hair was something else; it was almost as if it were a person, the care it took, the time and responsibility. Poor Mary was held hostage by those long blond curls that had to be rinsed in champagne and lemon juice, wound patiently around Charlotte's fingers, and pinned up in rags every single night.

As our locks dried, we'd sit side by side on the wide porch swing, inhaling the lavender Charlotte planted in the courtyard. In the flickering light of hanging lanterns, I'd read book reviews out loud to Mary; we were always looking for a new property to persuade Adolph Zukor, the head of Famous Players, to buy for her.

And I was beginning to sketch aloud ideas of my own, welcoming Mary's input. Mary Pickford knew more about making movies than anyone I'd met—more than Lois, more than Bosworth, maybe even more than the Great Griffith himself. Whenever I shared a story, Mary would instantly grasp the technical aspect—"Well, that's a fun idea, Fran, to have three cars chasing one another, but how will you shoot it? You'll need one camera on each car the way you've written it, and that's not really possible, financially, for a one-reeler. Now, if you expand it to two or three reels maybe, but I wonder. The plot is awfully thin . . ."

And I'd look at my friend, this tiny, sometimes terrifyingly smart sweetheart of the movies, and shake my head, and make notes. And remember everything.

"Are you girls hungry?" Charlotte asked now, despite the late hour. Anxiously, she gazed at Mary; she had privately told me Mary was too skinny, and she was worried about her. But Mary confided that Charlotte didn't understand how the camera added heft to an image; what was an asset in the theater— the ability to be seen from the farthest row of seats—was a liability in movies; that's why she ate like a bird.

I sniffed the air: chicken and dumplings. There was always something bubbling away on Charlotte's stove, something so hearty and fragrant it could stick to your ribs simply by inhaling.

"Smells delicious!"

There was always a bottle or two hidden away in a cabinet, as well, but I pretended not to notice *that*. Charlotte was a drinker, and Mary would not say a disparaging word about it. "You don't know, Fran," she insisted, shaking her head. "You can't know how hard it was on Mama, when we were small. How poor we were, how we never had a home. Mama took her courage where she could find it."

There was a difference, of course, between a drunk and a drinker—and so I looked the other way on the nights when Charlotte started slurring her speech, indulging herself in nostalgic reminiscences of a glamorous life on the road that had no relationship to the harsher one Mary described. And Charlotte's Irish brogue always was a bit thicker on these nights.

"But I'm not really hungry," I decided, despite my growling stomach; even if I didn't want to be an actress, I didn't mind being mistaken for one. "Thank you, though, Mrs. Pickford."

"Charlotte to you, dear. Don't make me tell you again!"

I smiled. "Charlotte."

Mary's front door opened and slammed, and two figures ran out, hooting with laughter.

"Hey, Mary!"

"Hello, Sis!"

"Where are you two going?" Mary's eyes narrowed at her brother and sister. Jack Pickford was slight, almost feminine despite his mustache; Lottie Pickford was a big, boisterous girl who, at the age of twenty-two, already looked blowsy. She had her sister's eyes, but her hair was dark, her manner as free and careless as Mary's was disciplined and cautious.

"Out on a spree. Come with us," Jack called, and Lottie doubled over with laughter.

Mary frowned. "Don't you both have an early call tomorrow?"

"Sure. We'll make it—we might be wearing the same clothes, but we'll make it," Lottie promised gaily, as the two ran to Mary's car without even asking.

Mary watched them go, then she spun around, hands on hips.

"I got them those jobs! They wouldn't be working if it wasn't for me! But it's up to them to keep them. I don't know what to do about them, Mama! I simply don't—I lecture and lecture, but they don't listen to me at all. What have I done wrong?"

"Nothing, dearie, nothing. They are who they are. Just love them, and be the same good girl you've always been, my pride and joy, my rock," Charlotte soothed, and reluctantly Mary smiled again, although her eyes remained hard and furious. I bit my tongue; I'd already learned the hard way that no one could criticize Mary's family but Mary.

But then it was Charlotte's turn to frown.

"*He* came by earlier."

"Owen? What did he want?" ·

"Money."

"I gave him his allowance two days ago."

"Yes, you did, you generous thing. Don't you worry about him. I'll take care of it."

"No, Mama, no. I'll see him tomorrow." Mary's small shoulders sank.

"I'll go with you," I whispered impulsively in her ear. She smiled gratefully.

"You look pale." Charlotte hovered and clucked like the mother hen that she was. "You need to go to bed now, darling. You, too, Fran. I'll bring you both hot water bottles and warm milk."

Mary's eyes now twinkled as she flashed me an exasperated look, but to her mother she meekly replied, "Oh, thank you so much, Mama. But I'm going to sit out here a few minutes with Fran, if you don't mind. You should go to bed, though. It's late." It was, for us; it was nearly ten o'clock, and we had to be at the studio by seven.

"All right, dears, I'll take myself off to my old widow's bed." But Charlotte winked as she said it.

"Fran, you know what I was thinking? I mean, before all—this." Mary gestured wearily, then settled into one of the cushioned wicker chairs on her porch. I took the other, removing my very fashionable—but rather pinching—new shoes with a groan. I tossed them and stretched my legs out, flexing my stockinged toes.

Then I looked up at the stars. They were so close they looked as if, with one poke of my finger, they might scatter, like brilliant billiard balls.

"What?"

"I was thinking about tonight, how excited I am, how besotted, really, by Griffith's movie. By *all* the movies. I'm in love, actually—that's what it is. And I wonder why I can't feel that way about my own husband. Why I only feel weighed down by him."

I was silent for a time, choosing carefully from the array of responses that had popped into my head. Mary could be bizarrely protective of her husband. Even if she couldn't quite bring herself to live with him.

"Well, I think that Owen is threatened by your talent, to be frank. And, darling, you did marry young, before you knew much about him."

"Oh, I know all that. But that's not what I'm talking about. Fran, I wonder if . . . if I'll *ever* feel about any man the way I feel about my career, the movies. The passion I know—whatever passion I possess, I mean, in my heart—it's all caught up in this, in what I'm doing. What *we're* doing." In the moonlight Mary's delicate face looked plainer, more ordinary, than it did during the day. Hers was a face designed for bright lights and camera close-ups. "Sometimes I wonder if I'm less of a woman because I love my work so much, because it's all I want to talk about, think about. We're not supposed to do that, are we? We women. We're not supposed to love something more than we're capable of loving a man."

"But it's fine for men." I was relieved that the conversation had strayed away from Owen, specifically. Owen was Mary's cross to bear; the penance she seemed to think she was required to pay for her success, perhaps. Catholic guilt—that was something that I couldn't begin to argue away.

"Yes, I suppose it is. No one told Edison he ought to stay

home with his wife more often." Mary laughed ruefully. "But the other thing is—I sometimes do feel as if something's wrong with me. Or missing. I worry about that. It doesn't have anything to do with the fact that I'm a woman. It has something to do with the heart—my heart. *My* ability to love."

"Owen's not your great love," I reminded her. "He's not. I was brought up to believe we all get one great love in our lives."

"But am I *capable* of that great love? Would I recognize it, even? Don't you worry about that?"

"You're asking the wrong person." I sighed, allowing myself to think of the past—something I didn't usually do. "Twice divorced, remember?"

"Because you fall in love too easily? Because *you* have a heart?"

"Because I fall in love too stupidly. Oh, Mary, I couldn't think of anything else to do, so I got married, like some silly little doll with no mind of her own. But now, things are different. Now, I have something to do, finally, something I *love* to do. Like you said—I don't know that I want to be in love again. Love, for a woman, it's—"

"Stifling?"

"Complicated. Isn't it? Men can be in love and it doesn't affect anything else they do; it gives them even more cachet. It adds something to them. But for women, love doesn't add, it subtracts. Why do I feel as if falling in love means I have to give something up?"

"That's how I feel, too, Fran! Exactly how!" Mary leaned forward, grasping her knees. "And I don't want to give anything up! I don't want to give up my career so Owen can feel more like a man—and he asks me to, daily. Every moment we're together he nags me, tries to make me feel like less of a woman just because I'm ambitious."

"Owen's an ass." There, I said it, and I didn't care.

Fortunately, Mary giggled.

"Yes, he is. Still, I don't want to see him fail, but I'm not willing to sacrifice my success for his. But if it were a man whose wife was struggling in her career—there'd be no question of *him* stepping back in any way."

"No." I was now sitting up straight, my hands balled into fists, all fired up with anger; anger at all the unrealistic expectations, assigned roles imposed upon us; roles and expectations we had no part in choosing.

But in that moment of righteous anger, I also thought—Why, I'm happy. Right now. Happy to be here, talking to Mary, who feels exactly the way I do. We're alike, the two of us—who else would understand me right now?

"But is it just us? Do other women feel this way?" Mary fiddled with the lace hem of her dress, fingered the button of her satin boot.

I thought of Mother, my sister, all their friends back in San Francisco; women seemingly content to be merely decorous and allow their husbands to tell them what to think. Even Lois Weber; she'd never worked for a studio that also didn't provide for her—less talented—husband, even if that meant turning down opportunities for herself. "Some women are quite happy being married. Was your mother happy when your father was alive?"

"I honestly don't know." Mary sank back in her chair, and I couldn't see her face in the shadows. "I don't really remember much before he died. I was so young—five. Why didn't Mama marry someone, so I didn't have to be the breadwinner of the family when I was only a child? Mama certainly could have had her pick of suitors then—and there was someone, once, when we were touring. But the three of us—Lottie, Jack, and me—we put up such resistance! That poor man never stood a chance. We needed Mama so much, then. Of course we're older—but maybe she's too old now. And maybe she's regretful. I don't ask. I guess I don't want to know."

"I don't want that—to be full of regret when I'm older. I think that's the thing I'm most afraid of, actually—to look back with regret, to think of all the things I didn't do."

"I didn't think you were afraid of anything, Fran," Mary said, and the admiration in her voice pleased me more than it should have.

"What are *you* afraid of? I told you my greatest fear; turnabout is fair play."

"Oh, maybe I've already faced it." Her voice was very soft; I had to strain to hear her.

"Not fair! You have to tell."

"All right." In the darkness, I heard her sigh. "Losing everything. Going back to how it was before, when we were touring and living like dogs hungry for scraps. Not being able to take care of Mama and Jack and Lottie—yes, that's it. That's the thing I'm most afraid of."

"More than being able to love?"

"Oh, yes. Infinitely more than that."

"I don't want to rule out the possibility of love again, though, and neither should you. But right now— Oh, Mary!" I couldn't remain still; I had to jump up. I began to pace the length of the porch. I looked up at the stars again and now they seemed hung there for me and me alone. They were *mine* to corral. And if I could, I would keep the brightest one for myself and give all the rest to Mary.

"There's so much ahead of me!" I spun around and leaned back against the porch railing, and it seemed as if the very ends of my hair were sparkling like fireflies, so electric was the air and my mood. "There's so much I can do on my own terms. I've only found it out, really—allowed myself to *believe*. And now, tonight, watching that film—it is like love, it is. I get dizzy, my heart has palpitations, I can't sleep at night. I feel the way the romance novelists describe love. But I only feel it when I think of my career! I've never felt this way about a man. Never. And right now, I don't give a damn."

"I know, I know!" Mary jumped up, too; she hooked her arm through mine. Everywhere was quiet, everywhere was ordinary calm—everywhere, but on this porch full of ambitious, restless women. "Tonight, all I want to do is dream of that movie. Is that bad? That I'd rather dream of a movie than of a man? Even my own husband?"

"But I don't think I'd want to be 'normal'—if that's what you want to call it. Do you? Would you really want to give any of this up for mere love? A man? *Children?*"

Mary didn't answer, and although we remained standing side by side, I sensed that she had withdrawn from me. She did this at times, retreating from the world and protecting her energy, saving it—saving the best part of herself—for the camera. Each time it happened, I felt as if she was withholding something from me, like I couldn't be trusted, and that stung. I shared *everything* with her.

With a soft little sigh, Mary unhooked her arm from mine.

She stepped away, retreating again into the shadows. She didn't even say good night; she just slipped away.

I looked back at the stars. There was still so much to learn about Mary, and no matter how close, how alike I might think we were, I might never know everything about her. Even despite the eager, almost needy, way she had instantly, dizzyingly, welcomed me into her life, insisting I call her nicknames—"Squeebee, I'm your little Squeebee from Skunkville, remember? How you said my cabbage soup smelled like a skunk? You see, I never had a nickname growing up. So now I do!" Still, she didn't quite trust me.

Did she—could she ever—trust anybody?

As I heard Mary's front door shut, I began to feel the effects of the long day; a yawn turned into a stretch and I held my arms out straight from my sides and began to spin slowly around on the porch, making my own little breeze, feeling the warm night air gently pulsing against my open palms. I began to hum a little tune, nothing I'd ever heard before but plucked from the very air itself, full of promise and possibility. Despite my weariness, I could have remained there all night gazing at the stars, seeing my future written in every one—but suddenly I stopped and hugged myself.

I was alone. Entirely alone for the first time in a long while and I craved even more solitude. I needed to go somewhere where I could refocus my mind and fully process what I'd witnessed earlier tonight, in that movie theater. For Griffith's *Birth of a Nation* wasn't merely an evolution—something that seemed to take place daily in this crazy business—but a *revolution*.

Mary was right; people would have to take movies seriously, after this.

I skipped across the pavers into my own little house—an entire house, just for me; in both my marriages, I'd only lived in apartments. I loved this little bungalow, decorated to my taste; I had to account for no one else's.

I didn't share Charlotte's Victorian tendency toward doilies and tablecloths and tinted prints in heavy gold frames. What Mary's taste was, I honestly couldn't say—and I only just now realized it. But I'd never gone shopping with Mary as I had done with other female friends; we'd never paged through catalogs or magazines together, except for *Photoplay*. I'd never heard Mary express an opinion about anything domestic, not even food; she seemed content to let her mother make all those decisions.

Or was it that she simply didn't have an opinion outside the studio?

My own house was neat—except for all those notebooks and sketchpads scattered about—and spare, the walls hung with a few chosen pictures, most I'd painted or drawn myself, all in simple wooden frames. There were flowers in vases— why not, when every inch of Los Angeles was a garden just waiting to be picked?—and I'd asked Mickey to make me a writing desk out of a piece of plywood, which I'd nailed beneath a window. On weekends when Mary wasn't shooting, I sat there, breathing in the perfume of the lavender and nodding along to the comforting hum of the bees dancing through the geraniums in the flower box, and I scribbled furiously, story after story. Some I mailed off to magazines for publication, others I kept to stretch and pad into workable movie scenarios.

Now that I'd finally given myself permission to write— funny, how we think it's up to others to say yes or no when really, we're our own gatekeepers—it seemed as if I would never run out of stories to tell. They flowed from my brain to my fingers like water from a fountain, an endless supply. Some were good, some were bad—some were *very* bad—but the important fact was that they were always, always *there*. Instincts—that was all I had, instincts and discipline and the desire to work. And my instincts told me that if I never feared running out of words and stories to tell, I would be a success.

I switched off the light and went to my bedroom, where my dresses, cloaks, and shoes filled the entire closet. Stepping out of my new purple velvet dress, I brushed it with the clothes brush, sneezing as the dust flew up, then I hung it back on its hanger and surveyed my wardrobe with a happy sigh. I did love to shop, my one real extravagance. What did I need with a fancy car or expensive champagne? But clothes, ah—that was another story! I had a good figure for the latest fashions—I was slender, slightly taller than average, practically model size. But it wasn't only the way I looked in them; it was the way I felt.

My wardrobe gave me a certain air, a mood; a legitimacy I knew in my heart I hadn't yet earned. Taking a page from Lois Weber's book, I decided that if I dressed better than everyone else I worked with—including Mary—they'd have to take me, the new kid on the block, seriously. Or at the very least, *notice* me.

As tiny as the bungalow was—a far cry from Mother's vast house in San Francisco—it was *mine*. I paid for it, I decorated it. And while I cherished having Mary and Charlotte only steps away, I enjoyed even more being single, finally, after so many years of stifling marriage. Unlike Mary, I had actually lived with both of my husbands.

Still, my bed could sometimes be a cold and lonely reminder of the one thing I'd enjoyed about marriage. There were nights when I lay awake wondering if I should marry again, just for the regular assurance of the touch of a man's hard, warm body, his coiled muscles, thick hair to grab onto, rough, unshaven cheeks like a brand on my flesh. Since moving next to Mary, I'd been hesitant to bring men home. Mary wouldn't approve, I knew.

But then again, Mary was still married; she didn't have to sleep in an empty bed if she didn't want to.

What if Mary was correct? What if I didn't even have it in me to love fully? Would I, knowing that, someday marry again, in order to have a man's body every night? Knowing that I'd not loved either of my husbands? At the time, truly, neither of my failed marriages had seemed a great tragedy, merely a fixable mistake because I'd married men who had been as emotionally uninvolved as I was. But the next time, I might not be so lucky. After all, look at Owen and Mary.

How odd. Despite my past mistakes, I had always assumed that someday, I *would* love a man like in—well, like in the movie scenarios I wrote. But what if I never did—would it be a tragedy?

And did I want children someday?

Oh, bunk! I pulled my pillow over my head, the better to block out these conventional, disgustingly *female* contemplations. I wanted to go back to that theater; I wanted only to concentrate on *The Birth of a Nation*. I wanted to relive how it had felt to be both part of the audience gasping at something never before seen and part of the industry that had created it; the pride, the astonishment. And the fever to create something like that myself.

As I lay there, the beat of my heart in my ears became the stamping of feet again—*that* was what I kept coming back to, that frenzied drumming. It was as if the excitement was too big to be contained in a stilled body. Never before had I heard anything like it, not at the opera, nor in an art museum, or a concert or a symphony.

Removing the pillow from my face, I saw, again, the stars outside my window. And I picked one. Just one star out of all the stars suddenly available to me; just one thing that I wanted to accomplish now. Before—instead of?—husbands and children and everything else.

Perhaps I'd dreamed too big when I was younger and longed to become a singer, a pianist, a painter; scattering my hopes like buckshot ensured I'd never hit a single target square on.

So tonight, I focused on one. I wanted to sit in a dark movie theater surrounded by people like me, people who needed the movies, needed the glamour and laughter and tears and thrills. I wanted to sit among my fellow travelers and see my name on the screen. Not as an actress, but as a creator; the person with the vision.

The person who could move an audience to a frenzy, and start a revolution of her own.

"DID YOU SEE IT, MICKEY? Did you?" Mary darted into her dressing room as I raced after her, spilling the cup of coffee in my hand. Mickey Neilan was already there waiting, his feet insouciantly on the dressing table—a transgression Mary would allow only him.

"Lower your voice, Tad." Mickey winced. "I had an epic night this morning."

Mary shook her head scoldingly, but couldn't restrain a loving smile, and I understood her indulgence. What was it about

Mickey? I'd been trying to puzzle it out ever since I met him, the day I also first met Mary.

Mickey had moved up from an errand boy in the studio; his face was too darkly handsome to ignore, and now he was playing the leading man in some of Mary's movies, including the one they'd just completed, *A Girl of Yesterday,* which featured yet another epic performance by yours truly. Why I allowed Mary to persuade me to play her rival in it, I had no idea—yet of course, I did have an idea. I was incapable of saying no to Mary.

When we watched the rushes, again I couldn't understand why people kept forcing me in front of the camera. "I'm awful! So stiff! Nothing like you, Mary." I meant it sincerely, and I wasn't envious. Mary had a gift I didn't, a gift I'd never be able to learn because I suspected it was something unteachable.

But then, I had a gift that Mary hadn't. For in spite of Mary's ability to become different people in her movies, she had no imagination in real life.

"It takes time," Mary soothed halfheartedly, but she didn't seem upset when I told her—and everyone within earshot—once and for all, that I was through with acting.

Mickey played Mary's leading man, and when I watched them together on set I detected something more, at least on his part. Even when the camera wasn't turning, he let slip a few adoring looks at her. And whenever Owen showed up to take Mary to dinner—although never did I see him spend the night in the bungalow, and I'd given up trying to define this odd marriage—Mickey started drinking even earlier than usual.

"Mickey, are you hungover?" Mary asked fondly as she nudged his feet gently away from her makeup.

"Tad, the worst. The absolute worst. What? Did I see what?"

"Griffith's *Birth of a Nation*. Did you see it? What did you think? Frances and I went last night."

"Did you, now?" Mickey opened one eye up to squint at me; without a word, I handed him the cup of coffee.

"Mickey, it was remarkable." Mary sat down and began to apply her makeup, expertly; no one did Mary Pickford's makeup but herself. "I never liked Griffith much personally, but professionally, I respected him. I respect him even more now. He's changed the industry—you'll see. People will take us seriously from now on."

"That's the worst news I've ever heard," Mickey groaned, finally removing his feet from the table and sitting up straight.

"Now, why on earth would you say that?" I perched on a stool. "Don't you want to be taken seriously? As an artist?"

"Good Christ, no."

"But, Mickey, you're good—really good! Not only as an actor but as a director, too." I hated it that Mickey didn't respect himself and his talent. He seemed to have a chip on his shoulder about movies even as he couldn't seem to stay away from them. And he had such talent—but he seemed to resent that, too. As if his talent got in the way of his drinking.

"Fran, my dear, once we're taken seriously as an industry—as *art*"—he pursed his lips and held out his pinkie, as if daintily grasping an imaginary teacup—"the money men will move in. They'll fuck it all up—excuse me, ladies." He glanced at Mary, who was frowning.

"Quarter, please." She held out a tin cup; Mickey obliged by dropping a coin in it.

"Sorry, Tad. But they'll move in and it won't be fun anymore. Do you think we'll get away with the shenanigans we pull here? The way we play about, improvise, create on our feet? We look like a gang of street urchins, the way we work. And that's all well and good now. But if you want to be taken seriously, you'll have to pay the price. Both of you. Mark my words."

"Mickey, that's nonsense. I'm making money, lots of money, for the studio, and I have plenty to say about my movies. I hired you, didn't I? And Fran? Papa Zukor trusts me to make movies and I trust him to distribute them."

"For now. But you do know what your sainted Papa called you after your last contract negotiation, don't you?" Mickey grinned, his black eyes flashing. I couldn't prevent a smile, either, for I'd heard the same thing.

"No. What?" Mary put her makeup brush down and glared at us both through the mirror.

"Bank of America's Sweetheart."

Mary's cheeks turned scarlet and her nostrils flared. But then a tiny, triumphant smile began to play at her lips, and we all three burst into laughter.

"You're needed on set, Miss Pickford, Mr. Neilan." A boy popped his head in the doorway. He looked at us all laughing, and shook his head. "Must be fun, at the top."

Which made us all laugh even harder, although I couldn't completely ignore the fact that the boy had not meant *me*. No one at Famous Players thought Frances Marion was at the top, or even in the middle. Or if they did, they suspected it was only because of the generosity of the laughing tomboy who put the finishing touch on her makeup, quickly donned her costume of tattered denim overalls behind a screen, then led us all on set, a tiny Pied Piper.

As soon as Mary stepped before the camera, however, she stopped laughing. Her jaw was granite, her eyes narrow and shrewd as she took in the setup; I watched in awe as she went over to the camera and moved it a fraction of an inch to the left, without asking the cameraman. And he let her.

Then she turned to the rest of the cast and crew. "We only have two more days left, so let's do our best today, gang. I've never been over budget yet and I'm not going to be now. I'm also not going to let that Griffith steal my thunder, so let's make a good movie. No—a great movie." Then the little general marched over to her mark, and as the director, James Kirkwood, called "Action," her businesslike attitude instantly melted away and Mary became her character, Rags, a fiery mountain girl in love with a handsome city slicker played by Mickey.

Like a light switch, I thought. And I couldn't help but grin in admiration.

I settled into a canvas chair beside the noisy camera, consulting my notepad for the scenes scheduled for today. Mary had been the one who discovered the original novel, *Rags,* but together we worked on shaping the scenario with the help of Mickey and Kirkwood. We'd stuck mainly to the novel for this five-reel "prestige picture" but I'd worked in some physical bits to keep it lively and capitalize on what I saw as Mary's growing gift for physical comedy. No one could do a pratfall like Mary Pickford, not even Charlie Chaplin.

But when the camera turned, Mary did not do the fall I'd suggested she do as she took her place on a fake log; instead, she primly sat upon it, and commenced a love scene with Mickey.

After Kirkwood yelled, "Cut," I beckoned to Mary, who stepped nimbly over some cables and was by my side in a flash, a pleasant smile on her face.

"Why didn't you do the gag?" I showed her my notes in the scenario. Notes that she'd approved only yesterday.

"Fran, dear, I just didn't think it worked. Not in this scene."

"But you're so good at that stuff, Mary—it really establishes your character."

"I agree. But just not for this scene, Fran. A little goes a long way."

She was still smiling, but her chin tilted stubbornly and her eyes flashed steel.

So did mine.

"Mary, we agreed, we talked it through. Why don't we ask Kirkwood to do another take with you doing it and then we can choose?"

"No, Fran." Mary's voice rose, and I noticed the extras and stagehands were all staring at us.

"Mary, I don't want to make a scene," I whispered, my ears hot. I gripped my pencil so tightly, it broke in two neat halves.

"There's no scene to make. It's my name above the title, not yours. Remember that, Fran. Dear." Mary's voice was clear as a bell; she turned on her heel and told Kirkwood to move on to the next setup.

"Oh, I'll remember it, all right! You never let me forget it!" I threw the broken pencil at her retreating back; someone gasped but I didn't wait around to find out who; I leaped out of my chair, tears blurring my vision, and stalked over to the coffeepot. If there was one constant on a movie set, I knew by now, it was an electric percolator bubbling away in a corner.

Behind me, I heard the usual hustle and bustle of scenery being moved, hammered, the heavy camera groaning as it was hauled to a new spot. Usually the extras would run to the percolator between takes as if to a well in the desert, but because of my outburst, I was a pariah; no one dared to come near. Until I felt a hand on my arm, and looked up. Mickey was standing there in his city slicker costume, a shiny black jacket, bow tie, crisp derby. The heavy makeup couldn't conceal his concern.

"You were right, Fran. But so was Mary."

"What do you mean?"

"The fall would have been brilliant. But she has to feel comfortable doing it, or else it won't work. For whatever reason, she didn't, and it wasn't your place to argue. Not here, anyway. Not now."

"Because it's her name above the title, not mine. I'm *nobody*."

"Yes."

"Thanks a lot," I muttered, and dumped half the pot of cream in my coffee.

"For now, darling," he promised, giving me a whiskey-soaked peck on the cheek. "Only for now." Then he sauntered away.

Holding the heavy coffee cup to my chest, I turned and took a big breath, trying to restore my dignity. As I made my way back to my post, extras and crew parting before me as if I were Moses, Mary appeared, blocking my path.

"Fran, dear, I'm sorry." She said it loudly; loud enough for everyone to hear.

"Really?" I blinked, not believing.

"Yes. I could have at least done another take and tried it. I don't know why I dug my heels in so—I'm used to going it alone, I suppose. All my life, the only person I've trusted is myself. And Mama. But I asked you to work with me, and I do love it—I love you, I love your ideas, and so I'm sorry."

"You didn't ask me to work with you, Mary." I had to laugh. "You asked me to work *for* you."

"Oh, what's the difference?"

Quite a bit, I thought, but didn't say. I only gazed at her, equal parts adorable and formidable, but yet I remembered the night before, how she confessed she was afraid of losing everything she'd worked so hard to achieve. She was scared. Every day on the set—every day of her life—she was scared.

"I'm sorry, too," I said with a smile. Mary laughed and threw her arms about me, not caring if her makeup got mussed.

"The point is, I should have listened. I should have trusted you."

"And I shouldn't have made a scene about it." I kissed her on the cheek, and felt the world right itself again; she ran back to the set, and I nestled into my chair—after I asked someone for a new pencil.

The next scene began, a long scene with a tight shot of Mickey and Mary making eyes at each other. There wasn't much for me to do, so while the camera clacked away beside me, I quietly pulled another notebook from my satchel. Careful not to let anyone see, I opened it up, and began to read what I'd already written of a scenario I'd been working on in secret, the first complete scenario I'd dared to attempt. By myself.

The scenario was for Mary, of course. It *had* to be for Mary. I honestly couldn't imagine writing for anyone else; every story idea that popped into my head featured a slim, laughing girl with golden curls and expressive dark eyes as the heroine. But the idea was mine alone.

The Foundling, I'd written on the front page in big, bold letters. *The Foundling, presenting Mary Pickford.*

Scenario by Frances Marion.

MARY AND CHARLOTTE—AND OWEN—TOOK THE train east the summer of 1915. The offices of Famous Players were still in Manhattan, and contractually, Mary was obligated to make a certain number of movies at the studio in Fort Lee, New Jersey, just across the river.

Unlike many of her fellow actors, she never complained about having to go back to the raw, damp East Coast. Mary liked New York. She enjoyed going to plays, dropping in to see old friends, like Mr. Belasco himself, who still chided her for working in the movies—even as he proudly displayed a signed photo of Mary in costume from *Tess of the Storm Country* on his desk for all the world to see.

Mary also didn't mind dropping in to the business office to read the latest grosses of her films with her own eyes, comparing them to those of the other actors in the Famous Players stable. The business of movies remained firmly in New York even as production was moving more and more to Los Angeles. And unlike most other actors she knew, Mary had to see, first-hand, how her films were doing, how many theaters were booking them and for how long, what the publicity plans were—she was always urging them to buy more billboards; advertising sold movies! She had to study the ledgers, trace the numbers with her fingers as if that was how she absorbed them, ink passing through her own flesh into her bloodstream. How could the numbers exist, otherwise? How could *she* exist—not to mention the house, the clothes for Lottie and the car for Jack, the jewels for Mama? She had to see, she had to keep a running tally in her head, so that she knew with a certainty it wouldn't all vanish into thin air. So that she knew she wouldn't be back touring in the sticks, her hungry family in tow.

Mary also enjoyed her weekly meetings with Papa Zukor.

Papa Zukor—that was what she called him, the man in charge of Famous Players; the man who had met her eye to eye, seen her future the way she had—starring in her own features, movies built around her and her alone, her name above the title—when Griffith had not. "Papa dear," she called him. "Sweetheart Honey," he cooed back. Mary always got a kick at the shock in people's faces when they observed this sentimental familiarity. For no one else would ever look at Adolph Zukor as a loving father figure.

To others—never her!—he was a cold man. A cold, calculating man, an immigrant who still spoke with a thick Austrian accent. A man who had stumbled into movies like everyone else. But who had implacably grasped the business potential. Mary trusted Papa Zukor to distribute her films; Zukor trusted her, for the most part, to make them. Of course, she had to accept the stories he chose for her—although she had been allowed to buy some on her own. She had to work with the stable of directors under contract. But she could cast her own leading men from the Famous Players contract actors, rarely working with the same one twice. Because she, Mary, was the star; the one and only.

Just like she'd vowed when she was a child.

"Sweetheart Honey," Papa cooed whenever they met. "My little daughter. My favorite actress!"

Even as she dimpled and bestowed a kiss on that leathery cheek, Mary had few illusions; Zukor was out to make money for Famous Players and himself, not for her. So why not sometimes sit in his office, just the two of them, his secretary safely outside, because this was simply friends, dear friends, catching up? And, while twisting her curls round her finger in that way he liked, after asking fondly after his family, why not remind him that a car and driver would be a good investment in her career, as it would save time getting to the set in the morning? Or what about a paid position for Mama, who worked as hard as anyone, repairing costumes and making sure Mary got a proper lunch hour—really, with Mama on the set, Mary would be so much more relaxed and perform better, which, after all, was best for all of them, wasn't it? And perhaps a role for Lottie or Jack in someone else's film?

Why not suggest that he stop block-booking her films? Those poor theater owners, forced to pay for all sorts of bad films just to get hers—how was that fair to them?

Not to mention, to Mary?

"Papa dear," she murmured, after a long sleepless night spent wrestling with the realization that her movies were being used to finance other—lesser—ones. "What do you get from theaters to book my movies?"

"Three thousand dollars," Papa said, after pretending to look it up in a ledger on his desk.

"That's fair, of course. Because I've been to the theaters and seen the lines around the block. The theater owners are making that fee back and so much more."

"Yes." Zukor—a small, thin man with a wizened face and eyes like thumbtacks—watched her. Warily.

"But, of course, then they're forced to book other people's films along with mine, aren't they? They can't only book mine; you make them book several at a time, correct?"

A nod.

"And how much do they have to pay you for those other films? The films they only take because they want mine?"

"Two thousand eight hundred." This time, he didn't even pretend he didn't have the figure at his fingertips.

"I see, I see." Mary nodded thoughtfully, and put her finger on her chin. "But you know, Papa dear, I was at the Strand the other day. Remember how I told you when *Rags* was playing there, the lines stretched clear around the block? For every showing? Well, the other day they were playing dear little Marguerite Clark's newest film. And—oh, my!—the theater was empty. Simply empty—the poor theater owner, what a tragedy for him, not to mention for dear little Marguerite's career. But honestly, Papa, you could have fired a cannon and not hit a soul."

"Is that so?"

"And that got me thinking, Papa dear. It seems to me that the theater will never make back their—what was it you said?—two thousand eight hundred dollars. Not from dear little Marguerite's movie. Which I saw, by the way—I thought *somebody* ought to! So the theaters are really losing money with these other films, which means you are, too. But—of course, you're not losing money with *mine*. And it seems to me that's not quite fair, is it? That the profits of my films are being used to shore up the losses of others? When—don't you think?—it would be more fair if the profits of my films, the films I work so very hard to make and promote, were shared more equally by us? And not used to finance other people's films?"

Zukor paled, and Mary did feel sorry for him.

"Now, of course, my contract is up in a few weeks, and—"

"What is it you want, Mary? I never have to go on a diet; I lose ten pounds every time I have to renegotiate one of your contracts. You're already the highest-paid actress in the business."

"Yes. And the most profitable."

"What do you want?"

"I want you to stop block-booking my films, Papa dear. I want my films sold on their own, not with all those others hanging on for dear life. And I want more of the profits."

"I'll bring it up to the board," he promised grimly, and Mary tried very hard not to smile. These men were always "bringing it up to the board" to save face.

"I'm so certain that you can come up with something, Papa dear. You always do!" And Mary tripped around Zukor's desk to bestow a kiss on his balding head.

He smiled, patted her hand. "Sweetheart Honey, you're family, and you always will be. Will you come out to the house this weekend? The kids are dying to see you again."

"Oh, I'd love to!" And Mary blew a kiss as she closed the door behind her. What a dear, dear man he was!

Another day, another friendly visit.

"Papa dear."

"What is it now, Sweetheart Honey?"

"I was thinking."

Papa groaned, pulled out a bottle of seltzer water, dropped an antacid into a glass, and poured water into it, watching it fizz before he swallowed it.

"What?"

"My films. I do think the quality is slipping a little, don't you?"

"You're still very profitable. The most profitable, as I'm sure you're aware."

"Yes, of course. But the last one—*Madame Butterfly*—well, you know, it wasn't quite what my public expected of me. And it made only half of what the film before it did. Now, I was willing to make it for you; I know you were so very keen on the story. But it wasn't quite for me, and I knew it, and yet—"

"Your contract is almost up again, isn't it?"

"Why, I believe it is!"

"What do you want?"

"I've been thinking. Wouldn't it be appropriate for me to have full artistic control over my movies? After all, it is my name on them, and my face on the magazines and the posters and the advertising, and so it's I who suffer when they do. You don't; you're a big studio with other actors and actresses, and let's be honest, Papa dear, nobody really knows that a film of mine is a Famous Players product. They know it as a 'Mary Pickford.' It would break my heart to ever leave you, but Vitagraph and Universal have been calling, and they seem to understand my dilemma. As an artist, of course."

"I'll take it up with the board."

"Thank you, Papa dear!"

After that, she was the first actor—although there was a rumor Charlie Chaplin might be doing the same thing—to head her own production company, the Pickford Film Corporation. Under this new contract, she received a guarantee of ten thousand dollars a week, half the profits of her own films—which were no longer to be part of any block booking, but distributed instead under a new division created solely for her called Artcraft—and much more say in the product. Papa Zukor was president of the corporation, making him her partner now, not her boss. Mama, of course, was treasurer; a few other Famous Players executives were also board members. If Mary did not like the stories presented to her, she could appeal to the board. She also had a voice in the final cut of any of her pictures. And absolute control over director, casting, and advertising.

"Papa dear, you know how far we've come together! I owe everything to you," she purred, satisfied. For now.

But Papa did not melt into a puddle of pure affection, as he almost always did after a contract negotiation. This time, Zukor looked at her, hard, and bit down viciously on his cigar.

A trickle of apprehension snaked up Mary's spine. And days after Mary signed her new contract, Famous Players merged with the Jesse Lasky Company and took control of Paramount, the company both used for distribution.

"It's the only way we could afford your contract, Sweetheart Honey," Papa Zukor explained in his office over a private lunch, just the two of them; he had brought in his wife's scrumptious German apple cake, knowing how much Mary loved it. "The highest-paid actress in history can only work at the biggest film studio. Which we are now."

Samuel Goldfish—who had recently changed his name to Goldwyn—Jesse Lasky, Cecil B. DeMille: these were the new executives joining Papa Zukor, and Mary didn't trust them. These men had done their best to ensure that actors remained anonymous for as long as possible, simply because they didn't want to pay them commensurate with their popularity. If nobody knew their names, they were all interchangeable and salaries could stay low.

That hadn't lasted for long; Mary herself had been responsible for the change as fans began to write Biograph begging to know who the Girl with the Curls was. And now she was the biggest star in the land. And these men weren't happy about that.

"Mickey was right," Mary told Frances one evening, right before Christmas of 1916. They were having tea at the Algonquin, where Frances was living. Dear Fran! She'd come out to New York a few months after Mary, anticipating that their first true collaboration, *The Foundling,* would open soon at the Strand, and the two of them would share the triumph.

But when Fran got off the train, Mary had to break the news to her that the film had gone up in smoke, literally. A fire had ravaged the original Famous Players studio, and the negative for *The Foundling* had been among the casualties, before they'd had a chance to print any film from it. Mary felt so awful! It was to have been Fran's first movie with her name in the titles as scenarist.

Frances had taken it philosophically—one of the things Mary admired most about her friend—and refused Mary's offer to find a role for her in her next production, in order to give her something to live on while they waited to reshoot *The Foundling.* "No, Mary, I'm a writer now. I can't keep accepting your kindness," she insisted with that stubborn yet elegant tilt of her head; Frances had a way of making obstinacy look like a glamorous virtue. "If I'm going to make it in this business it's going to be as a screenwriter, nothing else."

Mary admired her for that, and quickly wrote a letter of recommendation, explaining about the disaster of *The Foundling*. Fran had looked so uneasy asking for this favor, and Mary didn't know why. Didn't Fran know she'd do anything to help her? She hadn't met anyone with as much of a natural feel for the medium as Fran; she was almost as intuitive as Mary was. Working together on *The Foundling* had been a tremendous experience. To spend her days with someone who cared as much as she, Mary, did! Someone who would work late into the night and then be the first one on set in the morning, as if she couldn't bear to be away, as if she, too, found the bright lights, noise, constant flow of people on their way to and from their own joyous work to be more welcoming than any home. And Fran understood Mary's screen persona better than anyone ever had; she wrote lovely little scenes that came so naturally to Mary, because Fran had studied her, put in gestures that she made in real life, but that always seemed to fit, exactly, the character she was playing.

It was simply *easy,* working with Fran. No having to— politely—explain to a man why a woman wouldn't react that way in real life. No having to—again, politely—swallow a dismissive little remark about "sticking to what you know, girlie, and let me do my job." She had more experience than any of them, but still she wasn't always taken seriously, just patted on the head and told to smile prettily for the camera.

Fran did not pat her on the head.

But thanks to Mary's letter, Fran was working for World Film now, writing for Clara Kimball Young, and making two hundred dollars a week—a figure that made her the highest-paid scenario writer in the business! Mary was thrilled for her, but missed her terribly. Especially now, with the merger.

"Mickey was right about what?" Fran settled elegantly into a velvet chair, and removed her gloves to reach for her cocktail—revealing an ink stain between her right forefinger and thumb, which made Mary love her even more.

"It's a business now. Movies. With this merger, the studio isn't merely a studio; it's a conglomerate. And they want me to fail." Mary miserably sipped her tea; no cocktails for her. "A teacup always, Sweetheart Honey," Papa never failed to remind her. "Even if you have a glass of tea, people will assume it's something else. So always in a teacup."

Nor could Mary dress as stylishly as her friend, who was wearing the most sophisticated blue satin evening dress, cut low and square, with sheer sleeves. Mary's upper arms—again, at the behest of Papa—were always covered. As was her décolletage.

"That's ridiculous, Mary!" Fran beckoned to the waiter for another cocktail. She had such confidence now! Fran had seemed like such a shy, yet oddly glamorous, little thing—like a new foal, Mary decided, spindly arms and legs, tentative steps, and a tendency to tremble a little from nervousness—when they first met. Even though Fran was four years older; even though she'd been married twice, Mary had felt herself the more mature one.

"No, really. It's like these men resent me for my success, for wanting to take control of my own career, for making as much money as I do—more than some of them do, and they hate it. Would they resent me if I were a man? If I were Wallace Reid instead of Mary Pickford?"

"No, they would not." Frances frowned and sipped her cocktail. "Do you know what Mr. Brady at World calls me? *Pete*. As if he can't bring himself to accept that the head of his scenario department is a woman. So he gave me a boy's name."

"Oh, Fran!"

"That's why I dress like this." Frances gestured down at her elegant gown. "He may call me Pete, but I'm never going to let him forget I'm a woman. And we shouldn't have to give up our femininity—it's our minds, our brains, that they want. What on earth does it matter if those brains are covered by a pretty cartwheel hat instead of a derby?"

This is why she needed Fran! Because there was no one else she could speak so frankly to about being a woman in a man's world. Other actresses would pounce on any sign of weakness, because they only wanted one thing—to usurp her. But Fran's ambitions were different, non-competitive. And she experienced the same frustrations that Mary did.

"It shouldn't matter *what* we wear, but it always does, doesn't it? Men need to put us in a box all the time. God forbid we ever step out of that box. I love your dress. I wish I could wear one like it!"

"You don't have to dress like that, Mary—like a perfect little saint. You can have a cocktail, for heaven's sake! You're the head of your own production company now. You don't have to listen to them!"

"No, Papa's right—I do have my public to think about. I can't let them down. I can't *scandalize* them." Because if they stop coming to my movies then I'm back where I was, sleeping sitting up on a train, worrying about whether Mama and Lottie and Jack have enough to eat. What was it Mama had said, so long ago?

Don't ever forget that you need them more than they need you.

"So what if these men want you to fail? Don't. It's that simple." Fran said it so decidedly, Mary was almost convinced. But then she laughed; she knew better.

"Right. All I have to do is figure out how to make these vultures at the studio not rub their hands with glee and say, 'I told you so! I told you the girl couldn't do it on her own. I told you she'd fall flat on her own face, given the chance!'"

"Oh, Mary!" Fran leaned forward, her face red, her eyes gleaming strangely. "First of all, don't worry so. You're the smartest person I know in this business. Second of all, I've had an idea. I've been wanting to find a way to—to sort of give you back your childhood, if only for one movie. Don't laugh"— Fran raised a hand as if to forestall any derision—"I know it sounds silly. But listen, I think I've found something. It's called *The Poor Little Rich Girl,* a darling novel about a dear little girl, very rich but very ignored by her busy parents. I read it and I immediately thought of you, Mary—I kept seeing your face on every page. You'll get to be an actual girl this time, not just a girlish woman—a real child who gets to skip and play, all the things you never got to do when you were young. What do you think? If I get leave from World to write it, I mean— would Zukor go for it?"

"Oh, Fran!" Mary sat up straight now. "I don't know what to say! That you want to give me this—and it sounds exactly right for my first film on my own! It will be such fun—such a challenge, too! An artistic challenge—do you really think I can get away with playing a child? I'm twenty-five, you know. I've played young women—adolescents. But never a child. How old is she?"

"Eleven. And I do think you can do this, Mary. I've seen you when we're being silly—the joy, the abandon, just like a little girl. That's why I thought of you when I was reading the novel."

"Fran, I promise. I promise I'm going to work so hard to get this right. It sounds wonderful—thank you, darling! I'll take it to Papa as soon as you give me your treatment."

Frances frowned, fiddled with the silk trim about her neckline, and suddenly looked to Mary as she used to—for guidance, for reassurance. "Do you think he'll let you hire me?"

Mary smiled. "Of course he will, Fran. You've been working for a year now as a writer. *The Foundling* did good business, once we refilmed it. Don't worry about that. I'll take care of you!"

Odd, the look that Frances gave her; not quite as full of gratitude as Mary was used to. But then Fran smiled and squeezed her hand.

"I'll get it to you in the morning."

"I can work on it now with you, if you want. If you want to discuss some camera setups, perhaps? I was just thinking today that I'd like to try something new, lighting-wise—I was experimenting the other day with a mirror and a light and—"

"Mary, darling, you never can stop working, can you? Neither can I, usually, but—tonight I have an appointment to keep." And the way Fran grinned, only the corners of her mouth curling up a little—as if she'd swallowed a secret—made Mary instantly curious. And envious?

"With whom? Is he tall, dark, and handsome?"

"Tall enough, and that's all I'll say. Have a good night, dear." Frances swooped in to kiss Mary on the cheek, and Mary smelled her perfume—musky, with a hint of orchids and sultry air. "Tell Charlotte I said hello."

"I will." And Mary smarted, just a little, as she watched her best friend sail confidently through the Algonquin lobby, pausing to embrace people who called out her name before she disappeared out the door and into the night. Mary wasn't comfortable at the Algonquin; it was famed for its artists, writers, and such, and Mary always felt their smug superiority whenever she was introduced. "Oh, of course. *Mary Pickford.* The film star with the curls."

But Fran was a writer, and so *she* was accepted. And Mary had to admit that Fran was better educated than she was, of course—anyone would be! Which was why Mary spent so much time, when she wasn't on the set, reading. Still, she felt she could never catch up.

The only thing she knew, the only thing she was sure of, was the movies. *Her* movies.

Mary took a moment to put on her gloves and readjust her hat. Did she envy Fran her life—her sophistication, her intellectual acceptance? Her many and varied "appointments"?

She *was* rather tired at the moment; weary of her own life. Owen was drinking—among other things—even more now that she'd signed her latest contract. She had no hope that he would be home when she got back to the hotel. And while she really didn't want him to be, she also didn't want to think about where he might be, instead.

Suddenly very lonely, Mary rose, pulled her veil down low on her face, wrapped herself up in a nondescript beige wool coat, and crept through the lobby, keeping to the perimeter, until she found herself out on the street. She decided to walk back uptown to her hotel; it would be good for her, to remind herself of the days when she couldn't afford a trolley, let alone a chauffeur.

It would be good to remind herself of all she had to lose.

———

WHEN MARY AND FRAN reported to the screening room a few days after the final scene of *The Poor Little Rich Girl* was shot, they could barely contain their excitement, but—with a mutual squeezing of hands—mutely reminded each other that they must behave like the men they had to impress.

Mary bestowed upon all the men her sunniest smile even as she was dressed in her most somber, businesslike dress. She sat down next to Fran in the middle of the room, the only women present save for Papa Zukor's secretary who always sat at his elbow, taking notes. The lights were dimmed, and the picture began to unspool; the studio didn't believe in paying for musicians simply for screenings.

But as the film progressed, the silence in the room grew more pronounced. When she or Fran giggled at some of the humorous scenes, they were quieted by the swivel of heads turning their way, masculine eyes glaring in disapproval. Finally they stopped tittering, stopped clearing their throats, stopped even breathing, it seemed to Mary. And when the film ended, no one applauded. The stillness in the room was bone-chilling.

Mary was too numb even to reach for Fran's hand; Fran herself was slumped down in her seat, shivering.

"It's a disaster," someone muttered even before the light was back on and the projector had stopped. "An unmitigated disaster."

"It's putrid," Jesse Lasky pronounced with such barely concealed glee, Mary longed to slap him. But she couldn't; her hands were trembling too much.

"I don't know what to do with it," Papa Zukor said at last,

and he turned to Mary with such a sorrowful, disappointed expression, she wanted to cry.

"Who put all that ridiculous slapstick in?" Someone else—Mary couldn't keep them all straight, these new, nameless men who all looked alike with their dark suits, their smug smiles, their hands casually in their pockets even as their eyes shot daggers—asked, aghast. Frances started to raise her hand, until Mary quickly slapped it down.

"Don't," she whispered harshly into Frances's ear. "This is all on me."

"Monsieur, I have to speak up." Maurice Tourneur rose, extremely dignified, extremely French. Mary and Frances glanced at each other; they knew what was coming.

"These two—these ladies—on the set, I have to say. They did not respect me."

"Monsieur Tourneur." Now Mary rose, also with great dignity. "I selected you personally to direct this film, as was my prerogative under my latest contract. How can you say we did not respect you?"

"Because," he persisted in his thick accent. "You did not film the script as it was. You and she—" He pointed at Frances. "You two, you—how do you say?—you made things up. You—you—"

"Improvised," Mary supplied. "We improvised. That is what all true artists do."

"Oui! That is it! The, the—what do you say, slapstick?—that was all them. It was not the script I wanted to film. And I felt I could not say no to Miss Pickford. After all, *she* is ze boss!"

"I see." Papa Zukor shook his head, again, so sorrowfully. "I really think it would be detrimental to your career, Mary, if we released this—this—I honestly don't know what to call it. I don't know what it is—is it a tragedy? A Keystone Cops farce? It's all over the place. I don't know what to do."

"We have to release it because we've already sold it into theaters," someone piped up. "They're all expecting the new Mary Pickford, and we don't have anything else ready."

Papa Zukor rose; he wasn't a very big man, really—his shoulders, in particular, were quite narrow—but at that moment, he seemed to Mary to be six feet tall.

"Mary, Sweetheart Honey," and Mary cringed to hear her nickname in front of all these disapproving, powerful men; all of a sudden she despised herself for ever letting him call her that, and for calling him Papa. What on earth had she been thinking? How infantilizing it all was!

"I don't know what to say," Zukor continued glumly. "I have to think about it overnight. I suggest you do the same."

"I'll—I'll go back to the cutting room and see what I can do." Frances was standing. Like someone who had suddenly lost her sight, she groped toward the entrance, reaching out and touching each chair, as if trying to get her bearings.

"No, Fran, no. Let's go home." Mary gripped Frances's arm, praying her friend could hold it together until they got into the car. They must not let these men see her or Frances dissolve into anything remotely close to "a woman's hysterics."

But once inside the safe, plush touring car, Mary began to tremble all over, and Frances started to cry.

"Oh, Mary! How did we go wrong? It was such *fun* on the set, wasn't it? So inventive—and that Tourneur! He had no idea what he was doing, he was so darn *grim*. If we'd let him have his way, this would have been the dreariest movie ever made!"

Mary couldn't even begin to process the disconnect between

what they'd just experienced and the fun they'd had making the film. Except for Tourneur. But all the action, the inventiveness—a truly inspired mud fight with the children the Poor Little Rich Girl yearns to play with; the brilliant way Fran depicted a little girl's literal interpretation of the things grownups say—it had felt so fresh, so innovative. And watching the film, Mary *saw* it. She was sure she did. But it was as if she and Fran, and all the men, had watched two entirely different films.

"I don't know, Fran, I just don't know. They didn't laugh at all! Not even at the scene where I accidentally drank the brandy and got drunk." Of all the things that shook Mary, it was that—the dour silence that greeted this picture. "It was as if they decided ahead of time not to like it. I thought it was brilliant, really, even in rough cut. I—didn't I do it convincingly, play a little girl? I thought—I mean, I worked so hard at it! I watched children, I practiced in the mirror!"

"I've ruined your career!" Frances hid her face in her hands. "Oh, my God, I've ruined Mary Pickford's career!"

"Stop that," Mary snapped. "I don't want to hear that."

"What will we do?"

"What do you mean, *we*? *You'll* keep writing, because you can, because it's not your face up there, only your name. You can change it, you can be *Franklin* Marion if you want, and nobody would care, and it would probably be better for your career, at that." Mary was astonished by how easily this came out—almost as if she'd rehearsed it, and perhaps she had. Frances shrank away from her, and turned to stare out the window; she seemed stunned by Mary's venom.

"But I can't do that," Mary continued, more quietly; she felt drained, as if her veins had been opened up back there in the projection room, her life's blood spilled on the floor for those vile men to step in and smear all over. "Because it's *my* face, it's my image, my name the public knows. I can't change any of that—and I've worked so hard to achieve it, Fran. So hard—and now what? They're all back there drinking whiskey and laughing at me for daring to take control. For talking to them like a man and not a little girl, for being smart and asking questions and simply wanting what's fair, what's right. What's *mine!*"

"I'm so sorry, Mary," Frances whispered. "I thought—I thought what we were doing was magical. I really did. I thought it was perfect for you—I thought I could give you something, something you missed, something you needed. I don't know how I can trust my instincts from now on, if I was so wrong this time."

"Well, you didn't. You couldn't. I should have known, though; I shouldn't have gotten caught up in your excitement, because I've worked too hard to get here. I have to be smarter than that. And I don't know how I can trust my instincts, either, after this." While Fran began to sob quietly, Mary stared out the window; it was starting to snow. The streets of New York looked gray and dreary, and everyone seemed to be dressed in black.

"I just don't know," she repeated dismally.

AFTER DROPPING FRAN OFF at the Algonquin—they couldn't even say goodbye to each other—Mary went home. To Owen.

Not to Mama, even though every nerve, every twinge in her battered heart told her to, to seek comfort where she'd always found it, to find wisdom, or at the very least loving, soothing arms.

But she dutifully went home to her husband. She was a failure at her job; she couldn't bear to be a failure at her marriage, too.

"Well, well, well." Owen greeted her, drink in one hand, a piece of paper in the other. His shirt was rumpled and stained, his eyes bloodshot, his skin sallow, but still, there was enough resemblance to the cocky young boy who had stolen her heart to make her catch her breath.

"What, Owen?" Mary moved to hang her coat on the coat-tree. She felt infinitely weary; it was as if she was trudging against an ocean current. She unpinned her felt hat.

"Zukor phoned. Or should I say *Papa*?" Owen sneered; he despised the relationship between Mary and Zukor; probably because Zukor could never remember Owen's name, always calling him, instead, "Mr. Pickford."

"Did he?"

"He did indeed. And left a message—rather a long message. I told him I wasn't your secretary, but he insisted." Owen had an odd gleam in his eye, and Mary knew that he hadn't minded taking this particular message down, and her hand was trembling as she held it out.

But Owen snatched his away, dangling the piece of paper above Mary's head as if he expected her to jump for it, like a cat with a toy.

"Oh, no. You're not going to deny me this, my darling wife. You're not going to take this away from me."

"Well, then." And Mary sank into a chair, because she could no longer stand, and squeezed her eyes shut. And listened as Owen read the message in a rich, intense voice, imbuing it with more meaning than he had ever graced a line of dialogue.

"'Tell your *wife*'—that's Zukor's word, not mine—'that

she's to report to my office first thing tomorrow. Tell her that she's to *think about what she's done*. That I paid Tourneur a *fortune* because she wanted me to—and Frances, as well. That Marion girl didn't come cheap. Tell her that I did all she asked but she disappointed me *greatly*. So she needs to be ready to go to Los Angeles on the next train, because I'm having DeMille direct her next film, as he's what I've determined she needs right now. A *strong* arm. Frankly, he's hesitant to work with her now. So Mary's to compose a telegram, to bring with her tomorrow for my approval, telling DeMille how *thrilled* she is to work for him and how she promises to be a good girl and not *interfere,* like she's done in the past.' "

Owen set his drink down on a table with a loud crack. Mary heard footsteps, heard ragged breathing, felt the warmth of his body, and she flinched, holding her arm over her face—*always protect your face,* Mama had told her the first time it happened—bracing for the blow. But it didn't come, and after a moment, quivering with fright, she looked up.

Owen was standing over her with the most grotesque smile on his face, and her blood ran cold. She'd never seen her husband happier. Not on their wedding day. Not after their first time together. Not ever.

It had taken this—her abject failure—to finally make Owen Moore happy. Happy enough not to hit her, not to belittle her. Because he didn't say another word; he didn't rub it in. He merely stood there, grinning, before grabbing her under her arms, hauling her to her feet, shoving his hand up her blouse so that he was squeezing her breast, hard; his other hand reached down her skirt where he cupped her, just once. Then he kissed her; his lips tore at hers, he took what he wanted, what he needed, and then as she reluctantly felt herself stirring, felt herself rising up to meet him, her insides thawing until they started to melt, in a trickle, between her legs—

He pushed her away.

"You're not what I want tonight, Mary." Owen wiped his mouth with the back of his hand. "You're never what I want. You're not a real woman, and we both know why."

Then he left. But not before grabbing the leather album of clippings that Charlotte had so carefully compiled, and heaving it across the room; pieces of paper, photographs, flew through the air like ticker tape. "Find your comfort in these, tonight, dear wife." And—odd, really!—he did not slam the door theatrically, like the bad actor he was. He closed it carefully behind him.

Mary touched her breast, reaching into her chemise and gingerly patting her flesh. It should have ached, after the way Owen grabbed it, but it didn't. She groped about for any mark or welt, but she couldn't feel a thing, not even her own icy fingers against her flesh.

Stumbling about the apartment in a trance, Mary found herself touching objects just to see if anything could penetrate her numbness. But nothing could. Not the little celluloid clock on an end table, not even the clippings she'd so carefully saved, now littering the floor: *Mary Pickford Triumphant in New Film! Our Mary Now the Best-Loved Actress in the World!* She knelt, touched, but couldn't feel, so why not move on to the knives in the kitchen? The daggerlike letter opener on the desk?

But then something caught her eye; it was snowing outside. And now she recalled it had been snowing when she left the office; her driver had made some remark about it, but she hadn't really listened. She'd still been reliving the disaster in her mind, and Fran was clutching her and weeping. How long ago had that been?

Mary walked over to a window and pressed her nose against the pane.

The snow—oh, the snow! Fat, ungainly flakes falling swiftly by, and she remembered how she used to try to catch them on her tongue when she was a little girl. Even running to catch a train to some awful theater, knowing she couldn't be late or someone else would take the job, she would sometimes stop, and quick as a lizard dart her tongue when Mama wasn't looking, and try to taste the snow. But it always disappointed; there was no taste to it, no taste at all.

And here it was, piling up so comfortably outside her window.

She was several stories up—what was it? Seven? Eight?— and still she could see it so clearly, drifting on the sidewalk below. A sidewalk blessedly free of the usual New York activity. There wasn't anyone out there; no footprints yet, no stuffy matron walking a dog, no newsboy lustily hawking his wares, no businessmen, heads bent against the wind, hands clutching their homburg hats to their heads as they shuffled along.

The sidewalk looked so very soft, its undulating cover of snow still undisturbed.

And Mary was so very tired. Weary to her bones, flattened by—everything. Zukor and the men and Owen, even Fran, dear Fran. She was tired of being responsible for everything, *everyone*. Placing her hand on the window sash she pushed it up, and knew that the cold air hit her in the face but she couldn't feel it.

Could she feel anything, would she feel anything, ever

again? Except for the beckoning blanket of snow eight stories down, so absolute.

So tempting.

Who would miss her, if she fell?

Certainly not Owen. Zukor would be glad to be rid of her. Fran would be fine. Her public—they'd mourn, but soon enough they'd find another darling to adore. All Mary had to do was look over her shoulder at the understudies waiting in the wings—Marguerite Clark, Mae Marsh, even Lillian, darling Lillian Gish. Who, then, would really miss her?

No one. No one but—

"Mama!" And Mary was surprised to hear her own voice, her own words finally penetrating the ice encasing her, and before she could change her mind, she turned away from the window and reached for the telephone.

"Mama? Mama?"

"What? What is it, dear?"

"Mama, come. Come quick. I need you."

"What did he do? Never mind, stay right where you are. I'm coming." It was almost as if Charlotte had been expecting a call like this, but how? How could Mama know how desperate she was, when she hadn't had an inkling until this very moment? Because she was Mary Pickford, the most beloved movie star of them all! And Mary Pickford had the world, didn't she? The world at her feet, as her oyster, and what could she possibly need?

Her mother, that's what she needed. She was twenty-five years old and she needed her mother like she was six again, a tiny girl whose feet couldn't reach the floor from the seat of a train. She needed to remember she was loved, that was all. Loved, and respected, and forgiven.

Mama came. Mama cried. Mama drew her a hot bath and bathed her as gently as she had when Mary was a baby. Mama put her to bed and told her not to think of those dreadful men, then she had the hotel kitchen bring up some hot milk, and Mary went to sleep, with Mama sitting, watchful, nearby.

But the next morning, alone, Mary went to Zukor's office as instructed. And in two weeks, she was on the train back to California, where not even Mama could help her face the formidable Cecil B. DeMille, who greeted her the first day on the set carrying a bullwhip.

But Mary wouldn't give him a reason to brandish it; she was the picture of docility. She smiled and nodded and showed up on time and stayed late. She saved everything for the camera, and DeMille could not break her.

As soon as the filming was over, she packed her bags and caught the first train east. To Fran. And the opening day of *The Poor Little Rich Girl*.

Mary had a feeling. Just a feeling.

"GOD, NO, MARY! How can you want to go see it? I can't bear to look at it! It almost ruined our friendship." Fran still looked shaken; she was thinner, paler, almost as uncertain as she'd been the first time they'd met. She hadn't recovered her poise, her élan. For that matter, neither had Mary.

But Mary had to see the picture with Fran; she'd had to make sure they did repair their relationship. She had so few things left to count on now.

"Fran, you have to understand. You have no idea what it's been like with DeMille—those jokes were right about him!

'The angels are worried, because God has been having delusions He's Cecil B. DeMille!' It's true, Fran, all true!"

"Does he really dress in riding breeches and carry a whip?"

"And has someone on staff to carry a chair around for him, and the Great Man never even looks around before he sits. The chair is always there."

"Oh, poor Mary!"

"The film—*Romance of the Redwoods*—will be fine, but, Fran, it's been awful on the set. I have to be a good little girl—oh, I'm so tired of being told that! But Zukor has spies on the set, I'm convinced. If I misbehaved, he'd know. I had to come east, even for a couple days. I had to get away."

"I can think of better ways to spend those days than going to see our film. Mary, I'm heartbroken over it! I feel so responsible—"

"No. Fran, no. I trusted you, you trusted me, and, well—we shoulder the blame. Equally." Mary began pinning up her hair, the way she always did when spying on her movies. "I've made twenty-four films in three years, Fran. I'm tired. I have to make this other DeMille film, then—" Mary didn't know what to say; she couldn't see straight, couldn't think, there was so much going on, so many roads to take, so many possible dead ends waiting for her in her career, her personal life. She couldn't see them yet, but she knew they were there. They were always there. Lottie had just had a baby, a baby that Mary would need to feed and clothe and educate because Lottie couldn't care for a mouse. But Mary didn't want to care for a baby! It was too—too—

And Jack was drinking more than ever and chasing starlets and doing such reckless things; flying in aeroplanes, having expensive affairs with married women. And Mama—

Well, Mama was the same. Her rock. Her constant. The reason Mary didn't jump, after all.

"I need to go see a movie, *my* movie, surrounded by my audience. I need to remember why I do this—oh, please, Fran! Come with me!"

"All right." Frances shook her head. "But I feel a bit like Tom Sawyer going to his own funeral."

Mary finished pinning her hair up, donned her dark glasses, and they went to the Strand. There was a line around the block, but Mary knew better than to put much faith in that; no one had seen the movie yet nor read any of the reviews, had they, the poor souls? There was always a line at the first showings of the newest Mary Pickford.

Frances bought the tickets, selecting seats in the very back of the main floor. The lights dimmed, the orchestra began to play, and the first title appeared—

The
Poor Little
Rich Girl

Normally Mary loved to watch herself on the screen. She was able to forget all the work and lose herself in the magical concoction of music and image and story. How did it happen, how did little Gladys, so short and dumpy in real life, transform into this darling, graceful sprite? It was wondrous, the *movies* were wondrous, in their ability to wrench an audience's heart, pull it right out of them and manipulate it this way and that before returning it to them, better somehow, fuller, the moment the screen faded to black.

She simply loved the movies, the whole experience; the movie palace like a modern cathedral—the Strand was especially ornate, with velvet curtains and frescoes and balconies—the musicians or organist in front, the plush seats, the sensation of being one with your fellow moviegoers, all ready, even eager, to be swept away.

But this day, both Mary and Frances paid far more attention to what was going on around them than what was happening on the screen. It was the faces that Mary would remember the most. The faces that reflected all her hopes, her dreams, her instincts as she'd made the movie—faces that laughed, that cried, that frowned, that smiled. Faces that *reacted;* so very different from those faces made of stone, of male privilege and disapproval, that had surrounded her in that screening room two months ago.

Finally, when the Poor Little Rich Girl awoke from her coma to smile up at the worried faces of her parents—parents who had been too busy to pay attention to her until now—the entire audience sniffled. Audibly. Handkerchiefs were being removed from handbags at alarming rates.

Then, as Gwen—or, rather, Mary—rose from her sickbed to walk hand in hand with her now repentant, grateful parents toward a rosy future full of love and freedom, the cheers began. The audience jumped to its feet, applauding and crying.

And Mary couldn't help herself; she did, too.

"Oh, Fran!" She clapped her hands, and her hat fell from her head, exposing those golden curls.

Frances, tears in her eyes, turned to her.

"Mary! Mary, they were wrong! Zukor and Lasky and Goldwyn and all the rest—they were completely—miserably—wrong!"

"Yes, they were! Oh, those men, I could just—"

"There she is! There's Little Mary!"

Later she couldn't remember who had shouted it, if it was someone seated next to her back in the last row, or someone down in front, but it didn't matter. What mattered was that the audience at the Strand Theater in New York began to turn its attention from the now-blank screen toward the very back row, where hands were suddenly grabbing at Mary, tugging, patting, jabbing.

"It's Mary herself! The Poor Little Rich Girl, right here!"

"Mary! Oh, Mary!"

Mary turned toward Frances, who'd gone pale, her eyes wide, pupils dilated—with fear, Mary realized. Yet strangely, she herself wasn't afraid; all she felt was love, affection pouring out of every outstretched arm, every eager smile, every tear-filled eye. Love for her, love for what she—and Fran—had accomplished on the screen.

"We've got to get out of here." Frances snapped into action, waving for an usher, who pushed his way through the growing circle surrounding Mary.

"Yes, but we need to be careful—I don't want to hurt anyone!" Mary smiled at one and all, blowing kisses, acknowledging the cheers.

But then the air became close, pushed in by the pressing crowd, and she did panic, just a little, until she felt herself lifted—her feet now dangling, someone else's arms about her waist—by a policeman in a dark blue uniform.

"Sorry, Miss Pickford, but it's the only way," he said in an Irish brogue.

"That's all right," she replied with a smile, relief now mixed with triumph. "C'mon, Fran, this way!" And Frances picked up their coats—actually, she had to tear Mary's coat out of someone's hand—and Mary laughed even more gaily.

"Leave it if you must! I can get another!"

"Nope!" Frances brandished the coat triumphantly and jumped to Mary's side, holding on to the policeman for dear life.

Mary looked down from her perch upon the policeman's shoulder; she caught one woman's eye, shouted, "I like your hat!" and the woman fainted. Dead away, and Mary felt awful. And wonderful.

"Take that, Miss Josephine," she cried, and Frances shouted, "Who?" But Mary only shook her head and giggled.

"Mary! Mary! Our Mary!"

The chants rang in her ears, and she closed her eyes for an instant, allowing herself to be carried away not only by the love and frenzy but by the stalwart policeman, and she never, ever wanted this moment to end.

Because it was hers. Because she'd been proven right, after all.

"We'll never trust them again," Mary shouted down at Frances as they finally made it out of the theater, through a back door that led to an alley; a lone rat stared at the hubbub before scurrying away with a banana peel in its mouth. The policeman deposited Mary down on the ground with a grunt and blew his whistle, calling for reinforcements; she half expected the Keystone Cops to appear. Soon their car arrived and they were shoved into it like pies into an oven, and they made their escape by turning onto the street in front of the theater. Mary jumped to her knees on the backseat to gaze at all the masses of people running after them, waving their arms frantically. She even blew kisses.

"Dear God!" Frances slumped back into the plush cushions of Mary's new car. Mary's chauffeur stepped on the gas pedal, and the sedan roared around a corner, right into the middle of the traffic on Broadway. "What on earth *was* that?"

"It was victory, Fran, dear!" Despite the torn pocket on her dress, the lost gloves, the disheveled hair—someone had actually tugged on a curl, as if he could remove it from her head!— Mary felt so serene. Peaceful. *Right*. "Those awful men who told us how wrong we were—who punished us!—for making this movie. How I'd love for them to have seen this! Frances, we were wrong. So wrong."

"What do you mean? Didn't you see what happened? We were right!"

"No, we were *wrong*. First, we were wrong to allow those awful men to screen this film in private, without an audience. From now on, I'm previewing my movies with an audience. I'll get it in my contract. That's why no one laughed—because there wasn't anyone else in the room but those men—and you know they came in there *wanting* us to fail."

"Of course." Frances nodded thoughtfully.

"But we were mostly wrong because we allowed those men to shake us. Oh, Fran!" Mary grabbed her friend's hand, clutching it tightly. "*We* let them make us feel stupid and small— these men! How could we allow it to happen? We're smart, we know what we're doing—we have good instincts. Sound judgment. We don't need any man to tell us that we don't, or to make us question ourselves. Promise me, Fran—promise me you won't let them do this to you again!"

"And promise me you won't, Squeebee!"

Mary hugged her friend—her dearest friend, besides Mama—and she kissed her on her cheek.

"We'll never let any man get between us, Fran, dear. Never!"

"Never," Frances whispered in her ear.

Then Mary sank back into the cushions and replayed what had just happened, picking out special moments to hold on to—when the woman fainted away; when the man held on to her curl so desperately. When the entire audience roared to its feet.

Mama had already cut the first glowing reviews from the newspapers by the time she'd dropped Frances off and returned to her hotel. Mama handed Mary a stack of telegrams, pointing to the one on the top.

RICH GIRL A GLORIOUS SUCCESS.
AM THRILLED FOR BOTH OF US.
CAN'T WAIT TO HEAR WHAT YOU HAVE
PLANNED NEXT. LOVE, PAPA

Mary raised an eyebrow and pursed her lips. Then she reached for the phone, to read it to Frances.

CHAPTER 6

FRANCES

AUTUMN 1917

*T*HESE ARE THE GOLDEN YEARS, I'D REMIND MYSELF
at the oddest times; when I was sitting down for a hasty lunch
between setups, or choosing tomorrow's extras after the day's
shooting, or even alone in my office—my own office!—
sharpening my pencils, a task I didn't allow my secretary.
Sharpening my pencils was the most tangible aspect of my new
status, those sharp points smelling of fresh-ground wood and
lead, and it was a delight I didn't want to share.

These are the golden years, we assured each other, sometimes
solemnly, sometimes with a giddy laugh, before one of us
jumped up with an idea or a bit to add to a scene, and then we
were off and running, Mickey scrambling up a ladder behind
the camera to shout out the new setup to the extras, while
Mary got down on her knees and tickled the children in the
cast to get them to act more naturally around her, and I raced
off to the prop department to retrieve the items required: a
dirt-covered baseball, maybe, or an extra-long jump rope for
Mary to clown around with.

These are the golden years, I would whisper right after my head
hit the pillow every night, too exhausted to muster any other

prayer. Long gone were the lengthy, serious prayers of childhood. Now I only had time to remind myself how lucky I was tumbling into sleep, the best I'd ever had in my life. Sleep well earned, sleep absolutely necessary because tomorrow would be exactly as exciting, fulfilling, and exhausting. It's only when you have no idea what you're going to do tomorrow that sleep is elusive, I realized. Because you haven't given yourself permission to deserve it.

But I did deserve it now. After the phenomenal success of *The Poor Little Rich Girl,* Zukor gave Mary everything she wanted. And what she wanted was Mickey Neilan and me; the three of us together again in Hollywood, our own production unit under Famous Players. And we proceeded to make movies. Movies the way *we* wanted to. Without interference from *the men,* as Mary and I referred to them in ironic whispers.

For some reason Mickey, while definitely a man, didn't fall into that category. We treated Mickey like a playmate, the little boy we allowed inside our clubhouse whenever we needed someone to be the groom in a pretend wedding. Mickey— darkly handsome, still a drinker, yet so quick and inventive as a director, unafraid to tell Mary what to do. And she listened to him. He tagged along as Mary and I improvised scenes on set, and he contributed his own ideas because he saw what we were doing and believed in it.

We were molding Mary into a child—and not just any child. *The* child, America's cherished little girl, the embodiment of innocence and playfulness and vulnerability and spunk; a person the entire audience wanted to wrap up in its arms after each and every film to cherish and protect.

And Mary was finally having the childhood she'd been denied; in front of the camera, she played out her every long-forgotten childish dream. Jumping, skipping, discovering, *frolicking*. The camera had always loved her but now it could barely contain her; when I watched the rushes, I felt as if I were peering over a fence and observing a child unaware she was being watched, Mary was so natural, so pure. So joyful.

We were making films come *alive*. Of course, just by their presence, children had a tendency to do that, and we always had a lot of children on set. Child actors had no technique; they hadn't been taught to give stylized performances. I only had to write "Mary and children play tug-of-war" and they did it naturally, spontaneously. No direction needed, because Mickey was brilliant at camera setups, so the children and Mary simply played.

But it wasn't only the presence of children, and childlike stories such as *Rebecca of Sunnybrook Farm* and *The Little Princess* that made our films so unique and beloved by the public. It was the fun we had on set. Joy that seemed to make its way into the finished product; for the first time, I understood that a mood could be captured on camera.

When I saw the finished movie in a theater—I never got over the thrill of seeing my ideas in a notebook turned into a complete, edited, and scored film; *my* words turned into images, emotions *I* had imagined played out on faces thirty feet tall on a screen—I was as enthralled as anyone in the audience.

The three of us shared an equal collaboration of the sort that I sensed, even then, I might never enjoy again. Mary and I picked the stories, often based on popular books or plays. I chose stories based on my gut but Mary always considered the grosses of her last film, and what made it a success, and how it could be repeated. I did the bulk of the writing, winnowing the story down for the screen, suggesting camera angles, writing the majority of the titles, but Mary always added a few things herself. All three of us cast the supporting parts while I took care of the extras and then, on set, Mickey—even when he didn't show up until after noon due to an epic bender the night before—worked swiftly, seemingly making up shots on the fly, shots that a taskmaster like DeMille would have plotted out for months. Yet when you saw the completed film, you were startled by the artistry, the immediacy.

Overseeing it all, like a tiny general in bloomers, was Mary. Hiring only the best: the best cameramen, the best art directors, spending Zukor's money wisely but freely, knowing that she'd make it up to him, a hundred times over, in box office. Then, like a magician's illusion—try as I might, I could never understand how she did it—she somehow shrugged off all the responsibility of running her own production company and stepped in front of the camera fresh, dewy, at least ten years younger: Mary as the little rich girl, as Rebecca, as Sarah Crewe, the little princess. She was so natural on camera that fans now assumed she was that little girl in real life, yet I never met anyone who worked harder at her "natural" performances. Mary spent hours in front of her dressing room mirror trying to get a child's stance precisely right; every morning while I sipped coffee and ate breakfast, she stretched and exercised to maintain a supple body in order to perform all her childlike stunts—jumping on and off beds, scampering up ladders, skipping and running and cartwheeling, keeping up with the actual children on set.

Our set! It was fast becoming notorious on the Famous Players Lasky lot. Every week we'd get a letter from Zukor informing us that other directors on the lot complained, rather snottily, about the noise we made, the laughter, the songs and games. (Mickey, at the end of the day, always burst into some naughty Irish drinking song that caused the mothers of the child actors to hurry their little darlings away, their hands covering their ears.)

Once, Cecil B. DeMille himself stopped by in his jodhpurs, carrying his whip, and he looked so aghast at our merriment, the uncontrollable laughter, that abruptly, we all froze when we saw him.

But as soon as the Great Man walked away with a single raised eyebrow, everyone burst into laughter.

"Whatever will he tell Zukor?" I wiped my eyes, we were laughing so hard we were crying. "I can't imagine what he thinks of us!" I'd been down on my knees, teaching Mary and four little girls on set how to play jacks; to my astonishment, Mary had never before played. But once taught, she played with abandon and pure joy—another little fact that pierced my heart on behalf of my friend, and made me proud that I was giving her this second chance to be a little girl. I looked down; my stylish dress was wrinkled, my manicured hands grubby.

"Doesn't matter what he tells him. We're making money hand over fist!" Mickey grinned and leaned back in his director's chair. He was defiantly not wearing jodhpurs; he was so slight and muscular he looked like a teenage boy. But he did grab a jump rope and crack it, just like DeMille's famous whip.

"Oh, poo!" Mary jumped to her feet. She put her hands on her hips and stuck her determined little jaw out, and the little girls she'd been playing with did the same.

Mickey and I exchanged a glance; "poo" was quite a strong word, coming from goody-goody Mary.

"I don't care what he says," she declared. "Although I do still owe him a film, which I suppose I'll have to make one of these days. But poo to him—our films are making three times what his are. I just saw his latest grosses."

I was tickled, as always, by the contrast between her childish appearance and her fiercely pragmatic mind. But I also had to admire her, for it was true. She had nothing to fear from De-Mille anymore. Mary Pickford had nothing to fear from anybody, and it showed.

Something else showed as well, and I wondered if Mickey had noticed. I hoped he had—and I hoped he hadn't. Mickey still had a massive crush on his "Tad," and although I knew Mary was aware of it, she never encouraged him.

But I saw the occasional flash of pain in his dark eyes, the way he tried, very hard, not to be quite as affectionate around her as he'd once been. The teasing was still there, but not the easy, physical way they'd once had; it had been a very long time since Mickey had put his arm, even casually, around Mary to discuss a scene. He sometimes balled his hands into fists when she happened to brush against him.

And the irony was, Mary, in general, was more relaxed than she'd ever been, freer with her affection, her praise, even her anger; it wasn't all bottled up any longer. Yet even so, there was something—separate—about her now that we were all back in California. Something I couldn't share. I'd assumed we'd return to those quaint little twin bungalows; I'd looked forward to resuming our easy, in-and-out intimacy. But Mary and Charlotte bought a house instead—Charlotte had looked around at Los Angeles, at the houses sprouting up like mushrooms, and declared that it was now time to buy, not rent, and so Mary bought.

I didn't; I couldn't afford to buy where they did. So I rented a place of my own.

We did still spend cozy evenings lingering at the studio in Mary's bungalow, provided and furnished by a penitent Zukor. We'd have dinner brought in if we were going to work on the next day's shooting script, or I'd resume the old habit of reading out loud to Mary, either the classics she'd missed growing up or new novels that might be potential vehicles. We hashed things out equally, arguing freely without fear of hurt feelings; I remembered our first real argument, on the set of *Rags,* with astonishment. Had I ever been so unsure of myself? Mickey had said I was a nobody then. Not any longer; my name was almost—but not quite—as big as Mary's in the titles.

Away from the set, we still made time for each other, riding horses in Griffith Park, going to movies, and Charlotte frequently invited me over for her hearty stews.

Still. I sensed Mary wasn't quite as dependent on me as she once had been. I also suspected why.

This suspicion was confirmed one Saturday morning, when, unexpectedly, my telephone rang. "Oh, Fran," Mary cried in her gay, conspiratorial way, "let's go for a ride! It's such a lovely day!"

Of course, I dressed in my riding habit and jumped in my car. Even though I'd planned to meet Adela for lunch, I canceled and came running to Mary—I still felt the privilege of her friendship, and I doubted I would ever tire of it.

We met each other at the stables at Griffith Park, parking our cars side by side. I loved the three-thousand-acre park, full of paths and streams and untamed greenery. Studios often shot outdoor scenes there; it was where Griffith (no relation to whoever the park had been named for) had shot the battle scenes for *The Birth of a Nation.* The stables were large and always bustling with Hollywood folk; even in this modern era of the motorcar, people still rode, and Mary and I had had many a heart-to-heart while trotting our horses up and down the bridle paths.

"Fran, dear." Mary smiled over at me once we'd mounted our usual horses and were on our way up a favorite path. She was looking exceptionally pretty in a yellow linen shirtwaist paired with wide-legged riding pants and polished black boots; her skin was glowing and her eyes danced with anticipation. "I'm going to ask a favor of you."

"What, Squeebee, darling?" I inhaled, filling my lungs with the jasmine-and-pine-perfumed air. It felt good to be outside; sometimes I longed for the days when our movies were shot out of doors and not on a stuffy set full of blinding, artificial light. My skin welcomed the gentler sun, and I looked forward to a lazy day of riding. Maybe we'd go shopping later. Or to a movie; there was a new Charlie Chaplin film just out.

I always remembered the first time I'd seen Chaplin; he was that black-haired ballet dancer cop I'd applauded that day I stumbled upon the filming in the street, back when I was still a sleepwalker. Now I was alive, and Chaplin was almost as big a star as Mary, having perfected his character of the Little Tramp. Yet whenever I saw him at parties he was so soft-spoken, almost shy, unless he was with his best friend, a new actor named Douglas Fairbanks, who had recently moved to Hollywood from New York. Together, the two would clown around and perform stunts for hours.

"Well—you'll see in a minute!" Mary let out a little cry of joy and kicked her horse into a canter; I did the same, thinking we were going to race—until I spied, up ahead on the path, two other riders on horseback. And one of them, I was—and was not—surprised to see, was Douglas Fairbanks.

I slowed my horse to a walk. I'd heard the rumors at the studio, but I'd dismissed them, defending Mary to anyone who might whisper about this new romance. Still, I'd wondered. For the last several weeks, Mary had, well—Mary had started to look *sexy*. That was the only way to describe the change in my friend. While she was always startlingly pretty, there was something very prim and Victorian about Mary; she had a tendency to purse her lips up in repose, and sit very rigidly, every muscle tense even when she was supposed to be relaxing. But lately, her skin was burnished to a glow, and her lips plump and rosy and eager to smile.

She walked differently, too—her hips looser, almost as if she were mocking the seductive Theda Bara.

As I approached the pair, whose horses were nuzzling each other in greeting, I tried to sort through the tumble of emotions stinging me like bees. It wasn't that I begrudged Mary a romance; God knows, if anyone deserved a little sexual happiness, it was Mary! But that Mary had found happiness—if this was happiness; it was too soon to tell, but I knew Mary through and through; she'd never risk her public image for something that wasn't so all-encompassing she simply couldn't avoid it—in *Douglas Fairbanks*? Another actor—hadn't she learned from Owen? Fairbanks was newly famous for his drawing room comedies, very amusing, extremely athletic, but he surely lacked the depth Mary displayed on-screen? And he wasn't quite a star yet, at least not of the caliber of Mary Pickford.

He was also, as everyone in Hollywood knew, married. With a young son.

"Hey, Fran!"

Shielding my eyes, I saw that Anita Loos was the figure on horseback beside Doug. I kicked my horse into a trot. I liked

Anita, who was writing scenarios for Fairbanks; she'd followed him out to Los Angeles when he signed with Famous Players.

"Ah, my fellow chaperone. Or should I say *beard*?" Anita's ebony eyes gleamed beneath her glossy black bangs. She looked like she was fifteen, although she was in her early twenties. She was wearing a sailor blouse with a tie along with her riding pants.

"Anita!" Doug glared at her warningly, looked around, but we four were quite alone on the path.

Finally he seemed to register my presence. "Miss Marion."

"Mr. Fairbanks," I replied just as dismissively, earning a swift, appealing glance from Mary. I ignored it.

"Douglas, of course you know Frances, my dearest friend in the world. She was at Elsie's, too, that—that particular day." And Mary blushed, and I wondered what that "particular day" was at Elsie's—and then I remembered. Just an ordinary party, nothing "particular" at all, at least not to me.

But it obviously was to Mary and Doug, because they were now gazing at each other unabashedly with longing, which prompted Anita to turn her horse around and beckon for me to follow her. Which I did—while Doug and Mary, without a word or a wave or even an acknowledgment of what they were asking of Anita and me—steered their horses down a different path that disappeared into some woods.

"His brother has a house nearby," Anita finally said, after we settled our horses down to a languid walk.

I heard, but didn't reply; I was too angry, my chest tight with righteousness. How dare Mary involve me in this way? We'd said hello to so many people down at the stables, people who knew us. And here I'd been defending Mary's innocence to all the gossips!

Then my anger dissolved into hurt. Mary hadn't wanted to spend the day with me, after all. She'd simply needed a decoy. When I thought of all I'd done for Mary in the last year or so, all the ways I'd made her life easier—ghostwriting a weekly advice column under her name because she asked, seeking no credit; leaving World Film, where I'd been head of the scenario department, to join her in Hollywood, where I was back to being one of a trio—oh, sure, a coveted, triumphant trio, but still . . .

When I thought of how I always came running to Mary when summoned, no matter what I was doing, no matter my own ambitions . . . all those cozy evenings we'd spent together talking about our careers, how we'd wondered if we'd ever be able to truly love . . . but that *was* love, what was on Mary's face just now. Love, as simple and true as if I'd written it for her in a script.

Except—I hadn't.

Kicking my horse into a canter, I leaned down so that my face nearly touched his neck, breathing in the pungency of the stable. How could I feel jealous of Mary, of all people? How petty I was being.

Finally the expanding warmth of the new day, the birds chirping, the rush of a stream nearby—along with Anita's lively chatter—slowly worked their magic, and I began to relax, understand, and sympathize. These are the golden years, Fran, I reminded myself. Whatever Doug and Mary were doing today, I'd have Mary back to myself on Monday at the studio. And, of course, I never would have been here—trotting on a horse on a beautiful bridle path, one of dozens and dozens of movie people enjoying their day off like children released for recess; I'd never be looking forward to returning to a studio on Monday—if Mary hadn't taken a chance on me in the first place.

And then there was Owen Moore. I detested him. I couldn't abide the abusive, proprietary way he treated Mary, even now, as his own career continued to spiral into decline as men—*men* like Douglas Fairbanks, not dainty little candy-box boys like Owen—became the popular screen stars. Of course Mary had no future with Owen; Owen didn't deserve her. Whatever was going on with Fairbanks wasn't simply a fling, I knew that already. It never could be, to Catholic Mary. But what it might be was still unknown, and so I couldn't help but assume the worst. Or was it the best?

"How long?" I asked Anita. "How long have they been—?"

"Carrying on? Shacking up? Making love?" Anita's dark eyes flashed suggestively. "A couple months. That I know of. Of course, it might have started back in New York."

"On that 'particular day.'" Which had taken place in the east. "But no, probably not then. Mary isn't impulsive."

"But Doug is. Doug's like a little boy. He wants what he wants when he wants it. I'm not just his scenarist. I'm his baby-sitter."

"*Scenarists.*" I had to laugh. All the industry papers still referred to me as "Mary's scenarist," as if I had no name; as if I didn't deserve one. In the eyes of the public, anyway, the person who wrote the films didn't even exist; Mary's fans assumed that Mary made everything up in front of the camera, she was so spontaneous, so natural. When we were mentioned, if you didn't know the truth—and most outsiders didn't—one would assume that "scenarist" was a fancy word for "secretary."

Anita laughed, too; she had a tinkling little giggle, bright as bells. "Scenarists, maids, beards. It's all the same, isn't it? Tidying up their image, on-screen or off."

I nodded, even as I yearned to contradict her. Because I'd thought—I'd *assumed*—that I was something more to Mary. *We'll never let a man get between us, will we, Fran?* How many times had Mary told me this?

I had to laugh at myself, my naïveté. It was ridiculous to think this could be true, completely. We were women, after all. Women, not schoolgirls. And women, even in this new, modern age, could never be completely independent of men. They would always shape us, I realized as I gave my horse an irritated little kick. For good or for bad. It was up to us to decide which.

Two hours of riding and an aching back—not to mention backside—later, Anita and I met up with Doug and Mary back at the same location. With studied casualness, Mary and Doug wished each other a good day, in case anyone was within earshot. I blew a kiss at Anita, and merely nodded at Doug. He didn't even look my way.

Then Mary and I turned our horses in one direction, while Doug and Anita turned theirs in another.

I vowed I would not say one word the entire way back to the stables, but Mary didn't even notice. She smiled to herself the whole time, a dreamy, satisfied smile, and she sighed at intervals. So that's how it is, I thought. She's not even going to talk to me about him.

However, after we handed our horses over to a pair of stable boys and walked back to our cars, Mary suddenly threw her arms about me, hugging me so tightly, I gave a little cry.

"Thank you, Fran. Thank you! I've been wanting to tell you about this, but I was—I was afraid, you see. Afraid of what you might say. I was afraid of—well, everything. Everyone.

But for some reason, especially, I was afraid of you. Isn't that silly?" Mary looked up at me uncertainly, and of course, I wanted to reassure her—isn't that how I always felt around Mary? As if I was responsible for her happiness.

But strangely—unaccountably—I couldn't. Not this time—and how was that? How was this the very first time I couldn't tell Mary exactly what she wanted to hear? Was I that resentful at having this sprung on me? At being forced into a role I hadn't sought? Or was I jealous—petty, but still, I could admit to myself I was capable of it—to see Mary so completely blissful because of someone other than me?

Because of a man?

I didn't know which it was. All I knew was that before I could stop myself, I blurted out, "But are you sure he isn't using you to further his own career?"

Mary froze, then she balled her fists. Her eyes glittered dangerously, and she took a step away from me, pretending to examine the soles of her riding boots. Finally, with some effort, she looked up.

"You don't know him like I do, Frances. I'll ignore this, because you haven't really had a chance to get to know Douglas."

"No, that's true . . ."

"And besides!" Mary shook her head and almost stomped her foot, like she did in her movies, but seemed to catch herself in time. "You've had yours! Why can't I have mine?"

My face burned and my eyes swam with furious—but not guilty! No, I had nothing to apologize for!—tears. Yes, I "had" mine; yes, I enjoyed sleeping with men. But never a married man. I'd never realized until now that Mary must have been envious of some aspects of my life and frankly, I never thought that was possible.

All I knew was that I'd begun the day as Mary's closest friend, and now we were on the verge of our very first argument—

Because of a man.

Carefully—oh, I chose my words with such deliberation; much more than I'd ever chosen any words before—I tried to end this before either of us said anything we could never take back.

"I only want you to be happy, Mary. Truly, that's all I want for you."

Mary nodded—also carefully, warily; we were studying each other as if we'd only just met—then I stepped into my roadster as Mary opened the door to her car. Adjusting the cracked rearview mirror outside the driver's door—*Oh, I must fix that thing one day!*—I hastily dabbed at my eyes. With another cautious wave, returned as gingerly, I eased the car into gear and started to drive back to my bungalow in Hollywoodland.

Now that I had an entire day ahead of me—a day without Mary—I decided to take the long way home. So I wound my way around canyons, up hills, occasionally marveling at the changes that had occurred to this part of California since I'd arrived five years ago. So many more buildings, neighborhoods laid out in winding grids, orange groves plowed under for studios. More roads, too; now I could easily drive either down to the sea or up to the mountains where before, it might take all day if you didn't take the trolley.

This was my home, my life; my career, that career I'd longed for, worked so very hard to achieve. I had it all now. *These were the golden years.*

Weren't they?

I looked down and saw that my hands were waving, brushing the steering wheel, my fingers tracing the air. *Restless hands to match your restless mind.* Mother might also have added, *and restless heart.* For my mind and my heart, both, were in turmoil; leaping about, seeking more, always more. Yes, my career was fulfilling. Yes, I had worked tremendously hard to achieve this place. Yet my bed remained empty at night. And the movies we were making, while fun and creatively fulfilling, lacked a certain purpose. Mary might not mind the dismissive glance of a Cecil B. DeMille, but I did. Our movies were entertaining and beloved but I still hadn't done what I'd dreamed of after seeing *The Birth of a Nation;* I hadn't shaken things up, enforced my vision on a project. Always—*always*—I picked up my pencil with Mary's image before me, Mary's needs, Mary's vision.

Oh, Fran. Listen to you. I glanced down at my fashionable riding habit, newly purchased. The leather boots, which I took to the cobbler to have cleaned and polished every week. Entertaining films made money, pots of money, and I had to admit I didn't mind the fruits of my labors. The roadster, the spacious house. Maybe someday I would buy a place of my own.

But I couldn't really envision it, buying a house of my own without someone to share it with. And then I realized that I must have been thinking that maybe, someday, Mary and I would buy a house together. How absurd, really. How childish. But truly, I wasn't able to envision any life for myself in Hollywood without Mary the central figure in it. And how pathetic was that?

Drying a few pitying tears, I pushed the starter, and shuddered along with the engine as it started up. Then I put the car in gear and nosed out onto the dusty road, this time heading home. *Marion Benson Owens de Lappe Pike*—I glanced at my reflection in that cracked mirror and had a good hearty laugh at my own expense. *You are the luckiest woman in the world. Instead, you're acting like a pathetic little schoolgirl whose best friend decided to sit with someone else at lunch.*

I pulled to a stop in front of my bungalow—yes, it was very nice, much nicer than the one I'd once rented next to Mary, proof that I had grown up a little, after all. I snapped the cracked mirror off and carried it inside; I would replace it first thing on Monday. Life was too short to spend looking into a disfiguring mirror. I deserved better.

Sorting through the mail inside my front door, I was delighted to spy a letter from Elsie Janis among the bills—too many bills—from the dressmakers. Pouring myself a glass of lemonade, I opened it, my mind not really on the contents. Once more, I was thinking of Mary. Should I telephone to apologize? Or let things blow over, wait until we were back on set on Monday and let our shared work, which had brought us together in the first place, heal the rift? Sighing, I scanned Elsie's letter.

Hey Fran, fearless cavewoman in arms! Don't you know there's a war on? Leave Hollywood and its tinsel behind and get your ass over here to Europe where everything is awful and heartbreaking but so much more REAL than anything you will ever experience in California. What are you waiting for?

Movies, romance, publicity, hurt feelings, petty jealousies—what did any of it matter now that America was headed to war? What was I *doing,* hiding out in Hollywood and missing out on the most important experience of my generation? *This* was exactly what I needed to shake me out of myself. There had to be a way to use my skills and my connections to record the heartbreak, the cataclysm, of war. No—to record the heartbreak of *women* at war. Because there already were enough movies being made about the soldiers. But surely, there were plenty of women "over there." Women like me who needed something important to do. Something bigger to contemplate than our own petty sorrows.

I raced to the telephone. But who should I call? I didn't know anyone in Washington, at the War Department, but surely I knew someone who did—

Of course. Yes, I certainly knew someone who had connections in Washington. Someone I knew who could help me; I had only to ask.

Picking up the phone, I didn't even have to look it up. I knew Mary's number by heart.

MARY, TOO, DROVE HOME FROM THE STABLES with her mind all aflutter—even more than her heart. Unlike her friend, she did not possess the gift of storytelling, at least not with words. She'd always found it difficult to articulate her innermost thoughts; she had learned the lesson, far too well, of saving everything for the camera.

But if she could have talked to Fran, dear Fran, she would have told her that she couldn't help it—and she'd tried! Oh, how she'd tried to forget him! But there was no forgetting the moment that Douglas Fairbanks had, on a miserable November day in 1915, literally swept her off her feet. Although at the time, she'd been more concerned about ruining her very best pair of boots, Russian kid and white as snow.

What had driven her, that "particular day," to grab Douglas's wife by the arm and declare, "Beth, we're not going to let Elsie get away with that, are we? We need to protect our property!" Normally, Mary would never have been so bold. And, frankly, she hadn't wanted to be at the party, anyway; this was back when she was worried about the Famous Players–Jesse Lasky merger, and would have preferred looking at her grosses rather than going to a farewell party for Elsie Janis. But Owen had insisted they had to attend, to wish Elsie well before she left for Europe to entertain the British troops. And Mary refused to give him the satisfaction of saying "My wife couldn't be bothered to join me."

So what had possessed her, on that particular day, to be so rash, so daring?

It was the way Elsie had simply stolen her husband, and Beth Fairbanks's husband, too. Owen Moore and Douglas Fairbanks were marched away from their wives by little Elsie Janis, who linked arms with the two of them and called over her shoulder, "I hope you don't mind me borrowing your husbands, ladies!"

And Beth Fairbanks hadn't appeared to mind at all! A sweet, rather placid cow of a woman, she'd been content to stay inside in front of the warm fire and gossip with the other guests, which included Fran.

But Mary had not.

"C'mon, Beth! We have to go after them!" And so she found herself—in her best white kid boots—tramping after Elsie, Owen, and Douglas in the miserable, rainy weather, desperately trying to keep up. But the grounds of Elsie's rented estate in New Jersey were muddy and rutted; the three, laughing and chatting gaily, were far ahead when Beth simply gave up.

"I'm cold, Mary," she announced. "I'm going back."

"Well, I'm not!" And Mary's Irish was up; she may not have wanted Owen for herself, but she most certainly didn't want anyone else to have him.

The trio had disappeared around a bend when Mary, plunging on, came to a little creek. It wasn't very deep, but it was wide, and there was no way she could get across it without ruining her boots. But there was a log—a narrow, precarious log—that had fallen across the creek. She stepped gingerly on it and felt it sway back and forth.

"Excuse me, do you mind?"

Mary glanced up; Douglas Fairbanks was standing in front of her. He smiled, his teeth blinding white in his dark face; he held out his arms as if expecting her to leap right into them, and she was furious.

Didn't he think she could look after herself? Did he believe she—Mary Pickford!—went around letting strange *actors* scoop her up like a sack of potatoes?

But then she looked down at the wobbling log; she heard her husband's laughter far up ahead, somewhere in the woods. With Elsie.

"All right, Mr. Fairbanks." Reluctantly, she allowed herself to be swept off her feet and carried over the log.

"Thank you, Mr. Fairbanks."

"Doug. Please call me Doug, Miss Pickford."

"Mary, then. Call me Mary. But I shall call you Douglas, if you don't mind. You seem more of a Douglas to me."

Douglas flashed his dazzling grin, set her down gently—he had picked her up as easily as if she were a feather, and she had felt how muscled his arms were—and bowed.

"I hope you don't mind that I waited for you. I very much wanted to talk to you, back there at the party, Mary. I've long been an admirer of your movies."

"Thank you." Mary was startled; it had been a very long time since her own husband had complimented her in any way. She felt herself relaxing and blossoming under the unexpected— sorely needed!—praise. "And your films are doing very well, I see."

Douglas shrugged. "For what they are. I'm under no illusion; I'm no great actor. But I'm told I do have a *personality*." His merry eyes crinkled and he grinned again, and Mary decided that Douglas Fairbanks was quite handsome, almost as handsome in real life as he was on the screen in his nice little drawing room comedies.

Eventually, they turned around and went back up to the house; Elsie and Owen staggered in later, laughing, clothes askew, and Mary, humiliated, insisted she and Owen return home right away.

"I hope I'll see you again, Mary," Douglas said as he—not Owen, who had already left to get the car—helped her into her furs.

"I hope so, too, Douglas. Thank you for a lovely afternoon." Mary smiled, and Douglas Fairbanks bowed deeply.

Gallantly.

THAT HAD BEEN IN 1915. Two years ago. Two years in which Mary tried, but failed, to banish all thoughts of the dashing man who had swept her off her feet; two years in which she attempted to avoid him at parties and industry functions in New York. But she couldn't quite avoid him, at that.

One memorable meeting was at a dance at the Algonquin, where Douglas had earnestly asked her opinion of some movie matters, showered her with compliments once again, then waltzed her divinely about the room until her head began to spin and her heart began to thaw.

For her heart had been encrusted in ice for years; ever since her marriage, six long years ago. No one had touched it, except for Mama and Fran. And her work, of course; her heart was in everything she did for the camera, and all those eager, loving fans she could never stop picturing on the other side of it.

But a man. She hadn't allowed herself to entertain the idea of loving a man again. She knew she didn't love Owen, had never loved Owen, could never love Owen. But she also didn't know how to get rid of him short of praying for his death, which she sometimes did. Guiltily.

Frances could marry and divorce; Frances could sleep with men with no consequences. But not good little Catholic America's Sweetheart. Mary's fans scarcely knew she was married—it wasn't something she talked about much in interviews, although once in a while she and Owen did pose for silly features that portrayed them as happily married, to keep up appearances. If she were to divorce—

Mary shuddered.

She was only twenty-five! She was young, so young, and a woman, despite the fact that she continued to play much younger girls in the movies.

But she couldn't. She couldn't entertain the idea of loving another man; she couldn't jeopardize all that she'd worked for. She allowed their friendship to grow, soberly, properly, under Charlotte's watchful eyes. For two years—seven hundred and thirty agonizing days—Mary had told herself, over and over, that she and Douglas were merely friends. She had tea with his wife, for heaven's sake! They were simply colleagues, close colleagues, who talked shop. Douglas was nakedly ambitious and hungry for advice from Mary, while at the same time, he never failed to flatter her. And respect her.

"You do less apparent acting than anybody I know," he'd told her at that dance at the Algonquin, "and because of that, you express more." Mary had wondered if he was teasing her; her back stiffened against his very sure arm. But then she looked up at his face; those dancing eyes weren't dancing. They were brown, so meltingly brown, and she felt herself wanting to do anything—anything at all!—if only to keep those eyes looking at her.

Those miraculous eyes expressed pain, too, exactly like a little boy's, when his mother died and Mary sent a sympathetic note to his hotel. Her telephone rang soon after. "Please come driving with me," he'd pleaded, his voice flat. "I would like a friend."

Hurriedly she grabbed a cloak, left her curls down even though she'd surely be seen, ignored Charlotte's suspicious glance, and raced down to the lobby; he pulled up in a roadster a minute after, and she jumped in the car, and as the roadster roared away, she had the most astonishing sensation of vaulting into her future.

That night Douglas drove slowly once they reached Central Park, meandering through the narrow roads and talking softly of his mother, how much he owed to her, how much he'd been afraid he'd let her down by becoming an actor, by marrying Beth, whom she hadn't liked. Mary listened, occasionally placing her hand upon his arm, and feeling that nothing more was required of her than her presence; this was a man who didn't need her to be anything other than who she was, and for once in her life, she felt that herself was enough.

"I don't know what I'll do now, without her . . . she was, she was . . ."

"Your rock?" Mary thought of Charlotte, how adrift she would be without her mother's constant love and support, the one thing in this life—this chaotic life she'd never even dreamed of because it hadn't existed back when she was innocent enough to dream—she could count on.

"Exactly! It's odd, I suppose—you must think me strange"—Douglas glanced nervously at Mary, and tugged at the collar of his shirt—"a grown man, acting this way over his mother."

"I think it's touching, and I think you must have been a wonderful son."

"I tried, oh, I did try!" He slammed on the brake—they weren't going very fast, and the road was empty, so it wasn't a jolt—and suddenly laid his head on his arms, across the steering wheel. And he began to sob.

Mary looked about anxiously, as if for someone to advise her, but of course they were all alone. What to do now? She yearned to take him in her arms, hold and comfort this wonderful man, so strong and yet so heartbreakingly soft in the very best way; keep him in her arms forever, stay in this car, the two of them, and forget everything—husbands and wives and movies and reviews and box office and most of all, the public with its judging eyes and suspicious minds. To remain trapped in this spell that had been created out of sorrow but had spun itself into something beautiful, something healing and binding and promising.

"Oh, Douglas!"

"What?" He raised his head, his eyes still wet with tears, and Mary's heart gave a little catch. His hair—normally slicked back in perfect drawing room style, like an advertisement for Brooks Brothers—was rumpled. Adorably.

"The clock." Mary pointed. The dashboard clock had a little crack in it. Time, literally, had stood still. Mary took it as some kind of a sign—perhaps because she was looking for one. "Douglas, the clock stopped, just now. Now, when you were—it was like something, or *someone*—"

"Just like Mother. Like Mother was telling me something." Douglas reached for her hand, holding it as gently as he would hold a baby chick. "Mary, I haven't cried all day. Not a single tear. I even made my brother go to a Broadway show with me earlier today. Then when I got back to the hotel and saw your note—I'm trying to say, this moment, with you, I could cry. I could *feel*. And Mother is letting me know that *this* is good, is right."

Mary couldn't speak; she did what she had done for nearly as long as she could remember. She turned to Douglas as lovingly as she turned to the camera, and she let her eyes say what was in her heart.

Two months later, she and Charlotte moved back to Hollywood to set up the production unit with Fran and Mickey. Not very far at all from La Brea Avenue, where Douglas had moved his wife and his seven-year-old son. Of course, Mary paid a social call on the Fairbankses as soon as she had settled in. Beth Fairbanks was warmly welcoming and obviously a little flustered by so eminent a visitor; she'd always been a little flustered in Mary's presence, to be truthful. Douglas Fairbanks Jr., a round, fair-haired child, was kneeling on the floor, playing with an army of tin soldiers.

"I'll ring for some tea!" Beth exclaimed, bustling off, leaving Mary alone with her husband and child.

"Do you mind if I play, too?" Mary asked the little boy, kneeling beside him in her prettiest white lawn dress, a cart-wheel hat framing her face.

"You can be the Huns and I'll be the Frogs," Douglas's son told her solemnly, and she nodded and lined up her soldiers.

She looked up, and Douglas's face was full of emotion—pride in his boy, pure happiness to see her, sadness still there, too. But it was a sadness they had shared, and so it wasn't tragic; it was bittersweet, and Mary couldn't help but think reverently of that evening in Central Park—*By the clock,* Douglas had signed his last letter to her, letting her know he, too, remembered that night with something more than grief.

Suddenly Doug was kneeling beside her, whispering in her ear, his hot breath making the back of her neck shiver, her breasts tingle.

"I can't wait any longer, Mary. I have to see you. Meet me in Griffith Park tomorrow at three."

Mary, unable to look at him for fear of what she might do right there on the floor next to his solemn little boy, shook her head even as her entire body flooded with happiness, with desire.

"Oh, dear, this horrible war!" Beth chirped as she returned with a silver tray full of tall glasses and a pitcher of tea.

Mary jumped up, her knees knocking in terror.

"All my little boy wants to do these days is play war," Beth continued, unaware of the tension in the room. "Because it's all anyone talks about. I'm so afraid my Douglas will be involved somehow, now that we're in."

The war. Mary nearly gasped out loud. The United States had declared war on Germany only a month before, April 1917, finally swept up in the great European conflict. Hollywood was eager to do its part—not to mention eager to move into Allied markets that could no longer make their own films due to shortages of manpower and material—but so far, life was proceeding as usual; movies continued to be made. It hadn't occurred to Mary that Douglas might have to actually fight until Beth said so.

And whatever last vestige of morals or propriety Mary was still clinging to disappeared as she looked at Douglas Fairbanks and realized that she would miss him even more than she desired him.

"I sincerely hope Douglas will find a way to contribute, without being in harm's way," Mary replied as she nodded, just once, and saw Douglas's face flush with joy. "After all, he has his little boy to think of."

Beth beamed, while Douglas turned to look out a window at the pretty, manicured garden.

The next afternoon, Mary met him in Griffith Park. She dressed herself, arrayed herself—oh, so carefully! She hadn't dressed for a man, other than Papa Zukor, in so many years she didn't even know how to begin, and had an impulse to telephone Fran to see if she could borrow something stylish, something adult. But even as her hand reached for the phone, she snatched it back. She couldn't confide in Fran. Not yet. She couldn't confide in anyone; she was trapped in this glass castle of her own making. If she was going to break free of those walls, she would have to do it alone.

So she chose a demure linen dress that didn't have too many frills—or buttons—on it, and practically raced to her car, so excited was she to do this thing she was about to do, throw caution to the wind, risk everything, but also—be caressed, fondled, adored. *Taken.*

When she saw him, standing beneath a tree on the designated footpath, she ran to him, into waiting, hungry arms, and when they kissed for the first time, it was exactly as if they'd done so a thousand times before.

———

THE DAY AFTER SHE and Fran had their little—spat—at the stables, Douglas came to Mary's house for tea with her and Charlotte.

It was part of the game they were playing; they met in public as friends and colleagues, always with someone else in tow, always loudly discussing work. Charlotte—wise as always, disapproving, too, but as of yet, not saying a word—sat behind the tea set as unreadable as a Sphinx.

"You know, Fran called last night," Mary said as Charlotte poured and she sliced into the cake. "She wants to go to war, can you imagine? She wants to be a correspondent of sorts, and she asked if I had any contacts in Washington. Of course, I'm thrilled to help dear Fran in any way. But it got me thinking about my own contribution. And yours, Douglas."

Douglas didn't reply; she knew he was sensitive about the criticism that he—and other able-bodied actors—ought to be in uniform. But the studios had pulled every string imaginable to keep their leading men safe and in front of a camera.

"We could offer to do a bond tour," Mary continued. "Think of how much money we could raise! I suppose we ought to include Charlie, too. After all, we three are the biggest stars in Hollywood." Mary said it matter-of-factly; it was precisely that, a fact. Based on data she pored over every week, comparing box office and grosses and number of theaters.

Douglas—not quite as used to his prominent position as Mary was, as he had only recently attained it—grinned jubilantly, and did a handstand right there in the middle of the parlor. While Charlotte gasped, Mary smiled indulgently; he was so like a little boy, having to express himself right then, in the most physical way; burning off all that energy and blinding charisma. If he didn't do things like leap over couches and stand on his hands and juggle croquet balls, he would combust.

"Charlie and I can do stunts! We can box! We can juggle and do gymnastics! And you can give speeches—there's no one like you, Tupper, when it comes to moving a crowd!"

Mary grinned and blushed; Tupper was one of his new names for her. She had no idea what it meant, but she'd taken to calling him Hipper or Duber, and she had no idea what *they* meant, either. It was all part of the exhilarating world they found themselves in, a world of secrets and hiding and longing, a world in which she found herself—she, Mary Pickford!— donning ridiculous, hilarious disguises and then hopping into Douglas's new Hudson Phaeton, and laughing as they roared around town, up and down hills, around orange groves, finally finding quiet little dead-end alleys where Douglas would stop the car and pull her over to him with a sure grip, and she'd melt into him, and they'd kiss, and touch, and murmur, and tell each other nonsense.

And then there were the times, like yesterday, when they'd throw caution to the wind—because kissing and touching and murmuring weren't always enough, especially for someone with Douglas's ferocious energy—and they'd go to his brother's, or sometimes she'd sneak into his house if Beth was back in New York. And it was heavenly, it was dangerous, it was always rather rushed; they always had one eye on the door. But still, their sex was better than anything she'd ever experienced with Owen. Even if Douglas sometimes did get carried away and bounce her off the bed or sofa. But that was part of him, part of it all—he swept her up and off her feet every time she saw him.

"A bond tour," Charlotte said now, raising an eyebrow. "So you'd all be together, touring the country, then? Making appearances? Together?"

"Yes, Mama, of course. For the war effort." Mary refused to look at her mother. "Of course we'd all have to be together."

"And you think that's wise?"

"I think it's important," Mary responded, choosing her words carefully. Oh, Mama! She saw right through everything but this time, unlike with Owen, Charlotte was biting her tongue. So hard that sometimes she actually winced. Mama had forbidden her to see Owen back then, and that was something she had always regretted. She wouldn't do the same thing this time. But she had her ways, nonetheless; her ways to make Mary feel as guilty as, well—as guilty as she *should* feel. Because Douglas *was* married, and so was she, and there was a child involved, and she had her career and their welfare to think of—

But right now, for the first time in her life, it didn't matter. Not her career, not her public. Right now, she was only thinking with her heart and other parts of her body that hadn't been considered in such a long time. Her conscience would overtake her sooner or later. It always did.

And so Mary Pickford and Douglas Fairbanks and Charlie Chaplin agreed to embark on a whirlwind bond tour across the nation, to raise money for the war. It was her patriotic duty, and she felt her heart swell with pride as she donned her military uniform, made for her by her costume designer at the studio, and set out to review the troops of the 143rd California Field Artillery, which had made her their honorary colonel.

Before they left on the tour, Mary had one more film to make. One more film with Frances, who was acting so strangely these days, feverishly casting about to find an assignment overseas. What was dear Fran thinking? Why would she want to abandon Hollywood just when she had reached the top of her profession?

But of course, Mary was only too happy to help her friend; a few phone calls and the whole thing was taken care of. Fran began to plan her departure—after she agreed to write *Johanna Enlists* for Mary, a film to help the war effort. A film to keep Mary working alongside Douglas, who was filming, too, until they could both embark on the bond tour, leaving Beth and her son at home.

For the troops, of course. Always for the troops.

"MARY, I'M EXHAUSTED, I'M CRANKY, AND I'M too well paid to hold your handbag," I complained as I followed Mary, who was marching, like the little general she was, into a ward lined on both sides with white enameled hospital beds. "I need to go back to my hotel and work on the script." It had been a long day of location scouting for *Johanna Enlists,* which we were filming in San Diego, at the Army's Camp Kearney. The 143rd Field Artillery Regiment—Mary's own regiment; she was its honorary colonel—was training there, and we used them for all the military scenes.

A long day of walking through woods and fields and now, for some reason, Mary had insisted that I accompany her on her rounds at the military hospital, when all I really wanted to do was sit down, have some dinner, and tackle the script, this last script before I left for Europe.

"Why are we doing this?" I couldn't keep the whine out of my voice.

"Fran, you'll see" was all Mary would say, a twinkle in her eyes and a suspicious smirk on her face.

I shook my head, dragging my feet. Mary Pickford was the one they wanted to see.

Most of the hospital beds were empty, anyway. After all, these men hadn't yet seen battle. No, I was irritated by Mary's assumption that I would follow her around, no questions asked. And there was a nice hotel room with a fireplace waiting for me, as well as a typewriter. I needed to quickly finish this movie so I could get overseas before the war was over.

Sometimes I had the irrational feeling—panic, more like it—that if I didn't do this thing, I was doomed always to be merely Mary's *scenarist*. And while I loved Mary, loved writing movies for her and had, not so long ago, only allowed myself this one dream and should be grateful for it, now I wanted more. More for myself, less I had to share. I was still searching for something even as I had my immediate future mapped out—traveling overseas for the very first time as a working journalist, a war correspondent; doing good, necessary work, then coming home and resuming my career as the highest-paid scenarist in the business. Maybe I'd still write for Mary, maybe not. But it should have been enough—only a couple months ago, it was enough.

Why wasn't it enough anymore?

"Mary, please let me go home!" Why did I need to ask Mary for permission just to go back to my room and soak my weary feet? But Mary shook her head and tilted that stubborn chin, her eyes positively snapping with excitement.

"Darling Fran," she said firmly as she stopped, pivoted, and pushed aside one of those not-very-private privacy screens. I hesitated, curious but suddenly squeamish; what was behind this screen? *Who* was behind it?

Then I followed Mary; didn't I always follow Mary?

"Here you go, Fran, dear!" She was perched on the foot of a very occupied hospital bed, grinning up at me with the most impish expression—eyes sparkling, brows raised, a flush to her cheeks. I couldn't understand; it was as if Mary was *giving* me something, the way she looked both possessive and generous—making some kind of claim. And then offering it to me.

"Frances Marion, I'd like to introduce you to Lieutenant Fred Thomson of the One Hundred Forty-third Field Artillery. Lieutenant, as I am the honorary colonel of your unit, I order you to give Miss Marion your hand in greeting." And in a flash, after one more loving—*bossy*—little smirk, Mary was marching down the aisle, greeting all the other patients.

Leaving me all alone with the equally startled lieutenant, who pushed himself up on his elbows to a sitting position and thrust his hand out toward me.

"Miss Marion, it's an honor," a rich baritone voice said, and my heart did a little somersault. The lieutenant smiled. And my heart went through an entire gymnastic routine.

Blinding blue eyes the color of cornflowers. A strong nose and jaw, cheekbones to match—he could have been carved from stone by the Greeks. Sandy blond hair cut short on the sides but the top flopping boyishly into his eyes. White, even teeth. And a hand that gripped mine, not strong as I would have suspected given his broad shoulders and muscled arms, but warmly, tenderly, as if he was terrified he'd crush it.

"Frances Marion," I heard myself say stupidly, before I could recall that Mary had already introduced me. "I'm a friend of Mary's," I stammered, blushing; I hadn't blushed since I was a teenager.

"Yes, I know." The lieutenant smiled kindly up at me, almost as if I were a benign idiot, and gestured to a chair next to his bed. "You might be more comfortable there."

I had no desire to pull my hand away from his, but somehow I did, and I dropped onto the chair. I clutched my handbag on my lap like a fussy old maid, but I couldn't think of any place to put it. It was as if I'd forgotten how my limbs worked, how to do the most basic things, except breathe—that was the only action I seemed capable of doing. Just keep breathing, I commanded myself. And don't pass out, I added, as my heart began to thud alarmingly against my bodice.

"What's—how—are you ill?" I finally stammered, remembering that despite the unnervingly romantic aura surrounding the two of us, as if we were seated together in the back recesses of a cozy restaurant illuminated by candlelight, we were actually in a sterile military hospital, and the handsome lieutenant was in bed and wearing a hospital gown, not a uniform.

"Broke my leg playing football." Lieutenant Thomson smiled ruefully. "But it will heal before we're shipped out, God willing."

"And the creek don't rise," I added automatically, but when the lieutenant gave me a puzzled look, I realized that he had spoken sincerely—he was actually invoking *God*. "Oh, I'm sorry! I—I—"

"Don't worry." He grinned. "I'm the chaplain of the unit, but that doesn't mean I'm a saint."

"Thank God," I breathed—before my hand flew to my mouth and I could only gape at Lieutenant Thomson—pious, holy Lieutenant Thomson—horrified. I was sure I was confirming the very worst of his suspicions about Hollywood, how we were a godless, pagan bunch of sinners.

To my enormous relief, the lieutenant threw back his head and laughed. And so, blessedly, I could, too.

Finally I relaxed and placed my purse on the floor; I maneuvered around until I was comfortably sitting on the cold metal chair, because I knew I was going to be there awhile. A very long while. But *how* did I know?

"It was love at first sight," I confessed to a touchingly eager Mary—who had pounded on my hotel room door almost the moment I returned—later that night. Much later, hours later; oceans and mountains later, a lifetime already planned and hoped for; a lifetime already forgotten. For I knew that from now on, this was the moment that would forever define my life; there would be a "before Fred," and a happily ever "after."

"I could never have written a scene like it—you know me! I hate the mushy stuff. But, Mary, it was like I was playing my first love scene, and writing it, too, and directing it and lighting it and, well—it was mine. Mine, and Fred's, and I can't explain it except to say that he feels that way, too, I know he does. He's not a frivolous person; he's the most serious man I've ever met, yet he made me laugh—oh, he made me laugh!"

"And he's not too bad to look at, either!" Mary did an entirely out-of-character, suggestive little hip wag.

"No, he isn't! He's athletic—I mean, an actual world-class athlete in track and field. He would have competed in the Olympics, but he's morally against competing on a Sunday."

"He's religious? Oh, Fran!" Mary stopped sashaying and plopped down next to me on the bed. I had to laugh, even as I understood Mary's meaning. Me, with my two divorces, my bohemian lifestyle in sinful Hollywood—and a religious man?

"He's a minister, actually," I continued, unable to meet her eyes, even as I knew they must be round with horror.

Religion wasn't very much a part of either of our lives. Even though Mary wrapped her Catholicism about her like a hair shirt whenever Owen was mentioned, I'd never once seen her go to Mass. Although I was raised an Episcopalian, I hadn't gone near a church since moving to Los Angeles; I didn't much believe in God, I had to admit. He and I didn't see eye to eye on hardly anything.

"Fred is also a widower," I admitted further; I'd found out quite a lot about Lieutenant Thomson in a very short while.

"A *widowed* minister? Oh, Fran! I'm sorry I did this to you—I had no idea! I thought he was the most handsome man I'd ever seen—next to Douglas, of course—and I immediately thought to introduce you to him. He's so tall, and I could picture the two of you together, what a pair you would make—I even framed it with my hands, like I would a camera shot! And I wanted to do this for you, Fran, dear. To give you someone who makes you as happy as Douglas makes me. But now, I'm sorry!"

"No, don't be, Squeebee, dear! I told Fred everything, about my divorces, about my career. And do you know what? He doesn't mind! Not at all, not about either of them. 'I think it's important for partners to be equal,' he said. 'I don't want someone to cling to me. I want someone to stand beside me.'"

"Then I'm glad, Fran. So glad my little plan worked out—and that you forgive me for it!"

"There's nothing to forgive. You know, Mary, I told you I'd scribble this screenplay and go overseas as soon as possible. But I think now—well, don't you think it would be prudent of me to stick around during the filming? Just to make sure everything goes well?" I couldn't repress a sly grin as Mary wagged her finger at me.

"I think that not only would it be prudent, Miss Marion, it's actually a condition of your employment. I would have to order you to do so, if you didn't volunteer."

"Oh, Mary!" I flung my arms about her and we sat entwined for a long moment; long enough for me to feel Mary's generous heart beat against my chest, to accept her joy and approval. Not that it was necessary, no, not that; I would have marched right back to that infirmary had Mary said one word against Lieutenant Fred Thomson.

But that Mary didn't, that she approved and rejoiced in this dizzying happiness, only added to my joy. And now I understood how she'd felt that day at the stables, and how much I must have disappointed her.

"Mary, I'm so sorry for what I said about Doug, that time in Griffith Park—that he was only using you." I released her, and grasped her hand although I couldn't look her in the face, I was so ashamed. "I was hurt, you see. Hurt that you hadn't told me about him, and hurt that you were using me only to see him, that you didn't really want my company that day."

"No, you were right, Fran. I'm sorry I didn't tell you before. But I was afraid to tell *anyone*—I still am. You and Mama are the only ones who really know."

"But still," I continued, "it would devastate me if you weren't happy for me, too. So I know how I must have hurt you. Remember, Squeebee—remember how we said we'd never let a man get between us?"

"I remember." Mary shook her head, her eyes darkening, obviously remembering that entire fiasco with the studio and *The Poor Little Rich Girl*.

"That includes the men who love us. Not only studio heads

and businessmen. But our *lives,* Mary—it has to include the men truly in our lives. Douglas, and Fred." I almost gasped to hear myself say his name like this, so sure of him already. But I could say it; he already had taken possession of my heart, why not my vocabulary?

"Of course, Fran. Of course—we'll always be close, but we'll be *more,* because of them. Remember how we used to talk about not being able to love, because of our work? How we had to give something up in order to be loved? That's the thing with Douglas, and I do hope with your Fred—I don't feel as if I have to give anything up! I feel as if he's only adding to everything, my hopes and dreams, my ambition. He doesn't take anything away from me. How did it happen, Fran? How did we get so lucky?"

"I don't know. I only know that we are, and I'm grateful, and now I have to get some sleep so I can look fresh as a daisy for my dashing lieutenant. He's three years younger than I am—do you think that's a problem? I have to admit, I didn't quite get around to telling him *that.*"

"Oh, Fran!" Mary burst into laughter as she rose from the bed to go to her own room. "You told him about your divorces, but you couldn't tell him your age?"

I shook my head, feeling as foolish as I ever had.

"Frances Marion, you are a model woman, and I mean that as a compliment in every way!"

I laughed, waving goodbye as Mary tripped out the door, then I began to unpin my long black hair, remove my earrings—I began to prepare for bed as I usually did, doing all those feminine things I ritualized. Brushing my glossy locks, patting cold cream on my face, my throat, rubbing lemon juice—a tip from Mary—on my elbows. I performed this ritual every single night, almost by rote, but tonight I savored it, drawing out every detail, lingering, caressing my skin more tenderly than I usually did.

Pete! I hadn't thought of that old nickname at World Film in years, but tonight it popped into my head. They used to call me Pete! As if they couldn't bear to be reminded that I was a woman, and I let them. I let them do that to me.

Not anymore, I decided, as I slipped beneath the covers, ready—impatient—to close my eyes and summon up a tall, strapping lieutenant with sandy hair and a dazzling grin. Not tonight.

Tonight, I'm a woman. And I'm going to dream a woman's dream.

WE HAD SO LITTLE TIME. It was a cliché of monumental proportions, given the fact that the entire world was at war. A cliché I would have written into a script, then ruthlessly edited out. But it was true. So little time to get to know each other, to share our hopes and dreams, to begin to lay the first wobbly foundations of a life together.

So little time to love. But this was different, and I sensed it from the beginning; I would not sleep with Fred Thomson, not before our wedding, and if I could have written myself some kind of time-traveling scenario so that I could become a virgin again, I would have. But then, I thought—no, no, I wouldn't. Because if I were still a virgin, I'd still be in San Francisco; whatever my previous marriages might mean now to this upright minister, they brought me to Los Angeles, to Hollywood, Mary, a career—and to him.

"You truly don't mind?" I asked, for the fiftieth time, as Fred and I—his leg almost healed, so he was using a cane— strolled along the neat, flower-bordered paths of the Famous Players–Lasky studio. We were in the middle of filming the interior scenes for *Johanna*. It was only a month ago that Mary had introduced us.

A month of letters and telephone calls and frequent drives back and forth from San Diego and the military hospital to Hollywood; a month in which time had sped up. We'd met, courted, and agreed to marry—all in one dizzying, head-spinning month. Now Fred had a brief leave before departing with the 143rd for France, and the unknown.

"How can I mind your past, Frances?" Fred, entirely dashing in his putty uniform, asked. I couldn't help but keep comparing him to the actors on set—jealous actors who glowered at the strapping young lieutenant, for they couldn't begin to compete. Fred looked every inch a movie star. Maybe, someday . . .

"Your past made you who you are," Fred said decisively. "Just as my past made *me*. They are two very different pasts, that's true, but the future will be the same. Won't it?"

I nodded, too happy for words.

"You'll wait, for me, my love? Until after the war? I don't want to marry before then. I've lost one wife. I don't want to lose another—nor have her lose me." Fred smiled and took my hand; it looked so fragile in his big paw. "After all, you'll be in danger, too. Miss Brave Female War Correspondent."

"Oh, you read it!" I snatched away my hand in dismay.

"How could I help it? When I gave your name to the receptionist here, she handed me a copy of *Motion Picture World*! With that enormous glamour girl photo of you on the cover in uniform—I must say, it's quite fetching, Lieutenant Marion."

"Oh!" I covered my face with my hands, mortified. "You have to understand, I didn't ask for that kind of publicity. But the studio, well—that's the way they do things around here. A little—a whole lot—over the top. It's for the good of the industry, of course—it's so young, still, and we do everything we can to publicize it, keep movies and the people who make them in the public eye, respectable; and a scenarist—a female scenarist—going over—"

"The highest paid scenarist, according to the article," Fred interrupted, and I caught my breath, searching for any sign that he was in any way threatened by that fact. But all I saw in his handsome face was open admiration.

My assignment to the Committee of Public Information as a war correspondent, ordered to film American women behind the battle lines, had been splashed all over the trade papers by the Famous Players–Lasky publicity department. Mary had been quoted as being near tears at the thought of losing her scenarist and very best friend. Publicly, everyone congratulated me; privately, I knew they were scratching their heads at the idea of sacrificing fifty thousand dollars a year for a miserable Army paycheck. Not to mention going overseas and potentially getting bombed or shot at, wearing a drab, unbecoming uniform, and possibly even—gasp!—having to wash my own underwear and drink water out of a canteen.

But now I was so glad I'd volunteered, before I'd even known that a Fred Thomson existed. It seemed to me that this way I came to him as more of an equal; my sophisticated career may have allowed me to dine out well in Hollywood but it was frivolous, I was certain, to a man like Fred. Fred was a man of such quiet integrity that he almost radiated his own aura, although he would have abhorred that notion. Already, I understood that he was not an athlete because he enjoyed the roar of the crowd or medals, just as he was not a minister who sought public attention. Fred Thomson was an athlete because he sincerely believed God had given him an athlete's body and so he must fulfill that promise. And he was a minister because he felt it was his mission to inspire and console those who were not as fortunate. Because he deeply believed that God spoke through him, but quietly. Not like Billy Sunday, who leapt about and screamed into a megaphone and wouldn't appear for fewer than five hundred people.

That I had already decided there was, at least for now, a greater purpose for me than writing movies gave our fragile new relationship more ballast. While already I knew—and accepted—that Fred's would always remain the more upright, morally sound point of view, I also understood my own strengths. Left on his own, a man like Fred Thomson would never survive a place like Hollywood.

"We make a good pair," I said, and Fred nodded.

"A perfect pair."

"And you really don't mind?"

"I'm crazy about you, Frances Marion—no, make that Marion Benson Owens de Lappe Pike—did I get that right?"

Happy—so happy it didn't seem fair to everyone else—I nodded.

"You see, I love every syllable of that ridiculously long name of yours, I love everything about you, and even though I know there will be obstacles—wait until you meet my mother!—I don't care. Because this—" Fred grabbed my hand again. "This is *right*. It's worth the wait until the war is over, and then we'll be together and figure it out. You'll keep writing because that's who you are, and if the church doesn't want me to preach anymore because of my divorced wife, I'll do something else. Preaching isn't who I am; it's what I do. But there are other ways to inspire. You've found one way; I'll find another."

"Fred!" My heart was racing, as were my hands; I reached for a pencil that wasn't there. "You—that was magnificent! I want to write it down! It's perfect, really, and I'm sure I could use it somewhere—"

"In a movie?" Fred laughed, the corners of his eyes crinkling up in the most disarming way, a way that I hadn't noticed until now. Oh, to think of all the disarming, endearing things I'd yet to discover about him!

"Yes! That was a perfect speech."

"It wasn't a speech, darling, it was my heart. And one thing you will have to learn, because I don't think you've learned it yet, is that real life isn't always as magical as the movies—yet sometimes, it's even more so." And Fred put a strong arm about my waist and pulled me to him; holding my breath, I took in his eyes, his mouth, and then I exhaled, closing my eyes, anticipating the kiss that I more than met halfway. A kiss that made my knees weak, deliciously so, because I knew this man, this man who was as tall and sure as an oak tree and just as strong, would hold me up. For as long as I needed him to.

There were no cameras, no lights burning down on us, no costumer creeping in out of camera range to arrange my dress exactly right, no fan trained on us so that my hair flowed fetchingly behind my back. No director to yell "cut."

But even so, I was the heroine of my own movie and for the first time in my life, I didn't mind being the star. Because only as the star of my own life would I deserve Fred Thomson as my leading man.

He was worth it; he was worth everything. Even then, I knew how much I could lose.

WOULD SHE EVER GET TIRED OF HEARING "OVER There! Over There!" The jubilant chorus, the crashing trumpets of the military bands, the roaring crowds shouting, not singing, as Mary raised her arms to conduct them all, stood on tiptoe so they could see her better, even letting Douglas and Charlie hold her up by her legs so the crowd could get a better look at her. She was so tiny and the crowds so enormous, she had taken to wearing the brightest colors, the biggest hats, so they could see her from afar.

"You don't have to worry about that, Mary," Charlie remarked sourly. "You're the only one here in a dress."

"Well, you don't have to worry about it either because you're the only one with a bowler and cane and big floppy shoes," Mary retorted. Even though Charlie wasn't usually dressed as his Little Tramp character. But he walked like him anyway, and his distinctive waddle was so recognizable people knew him from hundreds of yards away.

The two of them stepped back to let Douglas go next; grabbing a megaphone and raising his arms as he exhorted the crowd to "Kill the Huns! Buy war bonds for Uncle Sam," he resembled nothing more than a college cheerleader, even though he was wearing a custom-made suit. He leaped into the air, over and over; he was a jumping jack come to life.

As they watched Douglas Fairbanks, Mary Pickford and Charlie Chaplin smiled indulgently; he was the child of the trio, the one for whom the other two could find a shared affection. For the truth of the matter was, Mary heartily disliked Charlie, and suspected he felt the same way about her, and it was a matter of them being both very much alike—driven perfectionists—and very different. Charlie cared only for the film and nothing for box office. Mary couldn't understand how he was unable to immediately recall the final numbers for each of his films. She knew Charlie thought she was less of an artist because of her business sense.

And they both wanted more of Douglas's time and attention.

"I greatly admire Mr. Chaplin's artistry," Mary told the hordes of reporters following them on this wildly successful, unprecedented bond tour. It was universally acknowledged that the three of them were single-handedly responsible for funding the war; thousands upon thousands of people came out to each stop to gawk at their favorite movie stars, to hear their voices—such a unique experience!—to shower them with love and affection, and then to buy war bonds almost as fast as they could be printed. The war was incidental; it was the opportunity to see movie stars in the flesh that brought the masses out. Nothing like this had ever been done before, because until recently, movie stars hadn't even existed.

"Miss Pickford is that rarest of creatures, a genuine artist as well as a lovely person," Chaplin repeated, over and over. They posed, together with Douglas, clowning about; Mary and

Chaplin each perched on one of Douglas's strong shoulders; Douglas and Chaplin holding Mary aloft, like a beautifully dressed doll; Douglas and Chaplin pretending to fight, with Mary as the referee. They signed autographs, seated three to a table, until their wrists ached; they shouted at the crowds until their voices were hoarse.

Douglas was done making his speech; Mary and Chaplin placed themselves on either side of him; he held their arms, raising them up in victory; the crowd roared so that Mary's ears ached; her face was split in two by a huge grin as she acknowledged the shouts of "Mary! Our Mary!" "Charlie! Old Charlie!" "Doug! Do a handstand, Doug!" And Doug obliged, as Charlie pretended to conduct the military band playing "Over There!" and Mary beamed and waved an American flag.

Tea with the president followed; Wilson was a dour-looking man who managed, nonetheless, to pinch Mary's behind as he held out her chair, while Douglas glowered and Charlie juggled the teacups. Finally they were able to go to their rooms at the Willard Hotel.

"Dinner, Doug?" Charlie asked as they were ushered up to their private floor, bags already having been taken up and unpacked, even though they were leaving for New York the next day.

"Sorry, old man," Douglas replied. Mary looked straight ahead of her, at her hotel room door; she walked steadily toward it, unwavering, ignoring the other two.

"But I have plans," Douglas explained gently. Mary didn't see Charlie's expression. She only felt a warm tickle at the back of her neck that flowed down her spine as she unlocked the door, and Douglas followed her inside.

———

SHE WAS THE OTHER woman. She was Little Mary. Our Mary. The Avenging War Angel. Mrs. Owen Moore.

So many people laid claims upon her! She had so many different roles, it was hard to keep them straight: head of her production company, little father to her brother and sister, devoted daughter to Mama. But the only one that mattered, right then, was Woman. Woman, to Douglas's Man—she was luxuriating in a physical affair the likes of which she'd never known. Her skin hummed under Douglas's frank, desirous gaze. She couldn't keep her hands off him in private; she had to feel the muscles beneath the starched shirts, the flat, iron abdomen, trace the surprisingly soft mustache. When they were together in public, the desire to touch him was so strong she'd taken to carrying a muff, even though it was April. But that way, no one could see her hands clench; no one could see her wedding ring.

On the train from California to Washington, they'd managed only an occasional intimate meeting; once she'd had to hide in the bathroom of his private compartment when a porter made an unexpected visit to turn down his berth. On another occasion, Mary managed to sneak him into her compartment without Mama seeing. But they were able to sit quietly together without attracting attention in public; after all, they were colleagues, soldiers in arms. The reporters got used to seeing them together, usually with Charlie in tow, so no one took notice of the times it was only the two of them.

"I don't know if you're good for Doug," Charlie told her, on one of the few occasions Douglas was absent, writing a letter to his wife, Mary suspected. "I like Beth."

"So do I." Mary narrowed her eyes, as Charlie did the same. They were almost the same height; Mary had never known a man as slight as Charlie, with hands as delicate and expressive as a woman's, narrow shoulders and hips. Douglas towered over the two of them, and he wasn't very tall.

"You have an interesting way of showing it." Charlie's cockney accent clipped the words, even if his tone remained one of mild curiosity.

"Beth is a lovely person. But she's not right for Douglas."

"And you are?"

"I think so, yes."

"How?"

"I'm his intellectual equal. I'm an artist, like he is."

Charlie laughed. "Doug's no artist! He's a great athlete and has a magnetic personality but he's no artist like we are!"

Even as Mary felt a glow of belonging—because Chaplin had, in his few years in Hollywood, laid sole claim to the word "artist," the one true, recognized genius besides Griffith, and to be acknowledged as his equal was, to her surprise, quite a thrill—she rushed to defend her lover. "Douglas is too an artist! A *great* artist!"

"Look, I love Doug like my own brother—maybe even more. I don't know why, but there's something about the man I can't resist, and I'd do anything for him. But I know he's a lucky son of a bitch, in a way; he didn't work half as hard as we did to get here. He'd be the first to admit it, so no use defending him."

"I can still think I'm good for him," Mary insisted quietly. "I know I am. And he's good for me."

"Better than your husband?"

"Yes." Mary was surprised by how immediately she supplied the answer; perhaps it was the first time she allowed that Douglas might one day supplant Owen. The first time she admitted to herself that she wanted to marry Douglas. Even though, for now, she couldn't imagine how she'd begin to untangle the path that could lead to it.

Charlie, too, was surprised; he arched one black eyebrow. "Oh! I didn't—so this isn't merely a fling?"

"Charlie, you don't know me very well. I've never had a fling in my life, and I don't mean to start now."

Charlie didn't respond at the time. But as he hung back, watching Douglas enter Mary's hotel room at the Willard, he called out, "No flinging allowed!"

And Douglas, turning to look back, was speechless. Until Mary pulled him into the room and shut the door behind him.

THE TRAIN WAS ABOUT to pull into Pennsylvania Station; they only had a few more moments together. Then Douglas and Charlie were going to do an appearance on Wall Street before heading off to tour the Midwest, while Mary would remain in New York for a few days before heading to Chicago. It would be several months before she saw him again, back in Hollywood.

And Beth was waiting for him here, in New York. Beth, and little Douglas Fairbanks Jr.

"I'll miss you," she whispered, tears in her eyes. She'd grown so used to seeing him every day, for more than a week now. Even if they weren't able to sleep together every night, to be able to bask in the spotlight of his dazzling smile, the frank admiration always gleaming in those brown eyes; to be the beneficiary of his solicitousness, as he was always anxious to shield her from harm or nosy reporters or rabid fans—simply to sit across a dining table from him every day, to talk about the weather or the war or the latest grosses from their pictures—it had felt so right, so real. So *earned*. And now, the illusion was shattered; she could no longer pretend that it had been anything other than a fleeting, forced intimacy. When they saw each other again, it would be almost as strangers and she couldn't bear it.

She also couldn't bear thinking of him going back to Beth and their little boy.

"I don't know how I'll be able to stand it," she whispered, resting her head on his white shirt, not caring that it would soon be streaked with her tears.

"I don't, either." His voice was husky with emotion; his arms tightened about her. "You're my reason, Mary. My world."

"What do we do now?" She really didn't know, and for once, she didn't want to be the one to decide. All those years of being in charge, first of Lottie and Jack, then of her career, having to make decisions that no one should have to make—she was made helpless by love. At this moment, she wanted Douglas to do all the thinking for her, because she was so very weary of being practical and pragmatic. She wanted only to function on pure emotion and longing.

"We get through this tour, and then, when we're back together in Hollywood, we'll talk about it."

"I'm tired of talking about it!" The train was beginning to slow; even though the window shades in her private compartment were pulled shut, she knew they must be in the city by now. The press would be clustered together on the platform to greet the triumvirate; she had to pull herself together to face them. And she would.

First, she clung to Douglas, and he to her, and she remembered the night before, the luxury of sleeping all night long beside him—the first time they'd ever done so; how she'd watched him sleep, as restless in slumber as he was in real life, tossing and turning and thrashing about. She hadn't slept much, herself, because she'd wanted only to watch him, memorize him.

What was it about him? His respect, his gallantry—of course. His handsomeness, his athleticism—definitely. But it was that feeling, as she'd described to Fran, of being more with him than she was without him. She'd never felt that way with Owen; always, with her husband, the overwhelming feeling was shame and guilt, and that was nothing to base a marriage on, it never had been. But with Douglas, who loved and respected her despite her flaws—the ones she'd shared with him, anyway—

It was intoxicating, to think of them as a couple! A true couple out in the world, in the industry; what they could do together was so much more than they could do individually, which was quite a lot, of course! But the thought of them together—DougandMary! MaryandDoug!—nearly stopped her heart for its breadth of scope.

At night, behind closed doors, it would be just the two of them, as it was last night; her heart nearly crumbled with tenderness at the thought of coming home, every night, to this man. And so she wept a little, and he said, "Here, here, Tupper, dear," and he patted her hair, and her shoulders, and kissed the top of her head over and over until she stopped crying, and accepted the handkerchief he gave her.

"Promise me—" But she couldn't say what she wanted, more than anything, at that moment. It seemed wicked, wrong—and she didn't want to acknowledge that he had ever done such a thing.

"Promise you what? Anything, Mary! Anything you want!" Doug straightened his tie, and looked over the top of her head into a mirror, and she had to smile; he was a man who enjoyed his own handsomeness, and there was something endearing about that.

"Promise me you won't—you won't sleep with her. Beth. Your wife."

Douglas froze, for only a fraction of a moment. Then he put his arms on her shoulders and leaned down to gaze fully into her eyes. "I promise. Mary, how could you—you don't even have to ask. It's abhorrent to me. I'm a decent man, in spite of it all—you know how it pains me!" And the anguish in his eyes was real. She did know that the tossing and turning of the night before wasn't simply the result of too much energy even for sleep. It was guilt, equal to hers. And that made this whole thing, perversely, even more holy—that they both were suffering agonies; they were both miserable sinners.

"I know it's absurd, to ask that—when we can't—"

"Yes, we can!" Now Douglas bounced up on the tip of his toes, as if he was about to turn a somersault in the air. His eyes took on that feverish look she was beginning to recognize whenever he was seized with an idea—which was approximately a hundred times a day. Mary knew some women might be worn out from living with such a man; Beth certainly was. But *she* wouldn't be, she'd never be. In the past, she had sometimes given in to dark moods and too much self-pity. But with Douglas, how could she ever wallow in such thoughts? With Douglas, there would only be sunlight, never shadow.

"We can what?"

"We can do this! Mary, I can go to Beth right now and say I'm filing for divorce. You can do the same thing with Owen. People do, all the time. Why can't we?"

"Because we are who we are—I'm America's Sweetheart! Darling, I want this so much, but I also want my career. You know that about me—I've never had to hide my ambition from you, like I've had to with Owen. Surely you know how terrifying this is to me!"

"I do know, my dearest. I do. But right now, you're riding high—we both are—with this bond tour. America loves you more than ever. When will there be a better time? Mary, I'm mad without you and I can't live this way anymore!" There was real anguish in his dark eyes.

"Douglas, I—I have to think. Perhaps it will do us good, this time apart. We'll have a chance to catch our breaths. You go home to Beth, and see your son, and . . . and . . ." She tried—oh, she tried!—to be pragmatic, but the thought of him going home to his wife was too much, and she couldn't hold back her tears. To go back to her old life with Owen—unthinkable now! Unbearable. She never wanted to see him again.

But he would be trouble, she knew, if she did what Douglas desired. Owen Moore wouldn't go quietly. And then, what about her public—*hers,* she'd worked hard for them, she'd sacrificed so much! Her childhood, her privacy. Every ounce of cake she did not eat; every night when she would have liked to stay up late to read, but couldn't because of her early call the next day. Every grown-up gown she desired, only to have to don a pinafore before the camera, and stick an enormous ribbon in her hair, and become the girl that Frances wrote for her, the girl the public loved.

The one constant in her life was her career. She had always put her career first. She might be able to live without Douglas—although at the moment even the thought made her want to lock herself in a room and howl until she had no voice. But she'd never be able to live without her career. And Douglas wasn't asking that of her, not like Owen had. But would he ever have been attracted to her in the first place, if she hadn't been Mary Pickford?

Had Fran been right about that, too?

Even if she had, however, it had progressed far beyond usefulness, this thing between her and Douglas. What Mary didn't yet know was if it was too enormous, propelled by too much momentum already. Could it be stopped?

Did she *want* it to be?

"We have to go now," Mary insisted, pulling herself together as she always had—squaring her shoulders, thrusting out her chin, remembering, as Mama had said so long ago, that she needed her audience more than they needed her, and that it could all vanish in an instant. Remembering what was expected of her as the eldest, as the first, as the one and only—as the only girl, the artist, the producer, the true head of the family.

"Go home to Beth," Mary told him, once more. "We can't afford to do anything yet."

"I can," Douglas said solemnly.

"I can't," Mary said, just as solemnly.

She kissed him on his dusky cheek, then turned away as he quickly—furtively—slid out of the compartment. She pulled on her gloves, arranged her curls, looked into a mirror and despaired of swollen eyes, flaming cheeks, bruised lips. Anyone with a grain of sense would look at her and know she was in love, and suffering for it.

But as she stepped off the platform, following Douglas and Charlie, who were up to their usual antics, clowning and doing gymnastics, even as she blew kisses to the throngs who called out, "We love you, Mary! Our Mary," she knew no one really could suspect the truth.

Because when the public looked at Mary Pickford, they saw only what they wanted to see. If they ever perceived who she really was, they'd turn their backs on her forever. Wouldn't they?

She didn't glance at Douglas as he finally pushed his way through the crowd. As he finally made his way back to his wife and son.

Except, as she was to learn very soon, he didn't.

"MISS PICKFORD, WHAT IS your comment on the recent separation between Douglas Fairbanks and his wife? Apparently, he hasn't seen her in weeks, and today she held a press conference. We were told—by Mrs. Fairbanks—that you might have some insight on the situation."

Mary nearly dropped her spoon in her soup; across the table, Charlotte gasped so loudly, other diners—who weren't already staring at the two of them in a quiet corner of the hotel restaurant—gaped.

She had said goodbye to Douglas three days ago; he had gone to his wife, as far as she knew. Then he had taken off for his solo leg of the Liberty Loans tour; he must be somewhere in Michigan right about now.

"Mrs. Fairbanks, er, hinted that you might have something to say about what has transpired," the reporter continued as he sheepishly consulted a notepad. Mary was grateful that there was no photographer accompanying him, but she still made a mental note to speak to the hotel concierge about this gross invasion of her privacy.

"I'm sorry to hear about this," she began, after first sipping some water so that she could perhaps, somehow, manage to speak without a tremor in her voice. "But if Mr. and Mrs. Fairbanks have separated, it's no concern of mine."

"But you and Mr. Fairbanks—"

"Mr. Fairbanks and I are associated in business, and we've been working together on this Liberty Loans drive, because every bond bought is a nail in the Kaiser's coffin!" She pounded the table; the reporter jumped, but grinned appreciatively, then saluted and took his leave.

"Mary—"

"Mama, not now." Mary couldn't look at Charlotte; her heart was pounding too loudly, her head was throbbing. How many of the diners nearby had overheard? So she concentrated on eating the rest of her meal, even though her stomach was clenching so that she thought it might all come back up again, treating the public to even more of a spectacle. But she wouldn't allow that, nor would she get up and rush back to her hotel room to try to understand what had just happened. She would remain eating, placidly, until her meal was through.

Charlotte seemed to have understood, for she didn't say another word, and even ordered dessert although normally Mary never ate it. But tonight, both Mary and Charlotte ate their ice cream sundaes with apparent relish, then rose and went back to their hotel suite amiably, arm in arm, smiling at one and all.

But when the door shut behind them, Mary gritted her teeth and faced her mother's fury.

"What in the name of the Blessed Virgin have you gotten

yourself into?" Charlotte was pacing, wringing her hands, looking everywhere—out the window, then tugging down the blinds as if someone could see inside even though they were on the twelfth floor; frowning at an invisible stain in the rug, and stubbing her toe at it. She looked everywhere, in fact, except at Mary.

"Mama, please—"

"Don't 'Mama, please' me, young lady! This woman has obviously named you to that reporter, who was too polite, or too cowardly, to come right out and say it. And you'll probably be given a pass for a while; no one could ever suspect their innocent little Mary of adultery. And you've been good to the press, you've given them lots of exclusives, and they love you. For now. But that won't last. If you keep being associated with that Fairbanks, the press won't be able to ignore it—where there's smoke, there's fire. Now tell me, what did this bastard do?"

"Mama, I don't know. I said goodbye to him on the train and he was supposed to go home to Beth—"

"Which, it appears, he did not."

"I didn't know that!"

"The entire world knows it now!"

"It wasn't supposed to happen, Mama. Not now. Not yet—or maybe not ever, I don't know—"

"Mary, I've held my tongue for weeks. I've known what you were up to, and you were so happy I couldn't speak my piece. I know he was in your hotel room in Washington—heavens, child, I know everything there is about you! And you're no more of a saint than I am, so who am I to tell you to stop? Except—you *are* a saint, to all those millions of people who love your movies, who pay to see them, who depend on you to brighten their days, who are buying bonds left and right because you tell them to, because you're America's Sweetheart, the Little Patriot. And you can't let those people down."

"Because why, Mama? Because if I do, all this will go away?" And Mary flung her arms out, acknowledging their opulent hotel suite with its oriental carpets and antique furniture and state-of-the-art bathroom with brass taps and a deep tub and plush towels; the beds with the fine linens; the silk gown Charlotte was wearing, the dazzling rubies at her throat that Mary had given her for her birthday; piles of hatboxes full of the latest millinery, some with precious ostrich and peacock feathers; glove boxes stacked like dominoes; outside, a car always waiting for whenever Charlotte wanted it, even if it was to get another bottle of gin. "And if it all goes away, where will you be? Back in Toronto living with Aunt Lizzie, taking in boarders or laundry to pay your way?"

"Mary—"

"Without me, you'd have nothing! Without me, Jack and Lottie would actually have to *work*! And you're terrified of losing it all, so you'll get in the way of my happiness to keep it, just like you've always done! Well, I'm tired of it, Mama! Tired of being your meal ticket, all of you! When do I get to be happy? When do I get to love and be loved?"

Charlotte was across the room in two strides; she raised her hand and Mary felt her cheek sting, saw stars, and was so astonished she sat right down in the middle of the oriental rug, her legs in front of her, and she wondered what on earth had just happened.

"You're no better than Owen, Mama," she whispered. She couldn't look up at her mother; her eyes were streaming tears and the entire world looked unfamiliar and *wrong*.

"I *am* better than Owen. I'm your mother, and I love you,

but I'll never let you talk to me like that, missy. You're not the only one in this family who can hold down a job. You're not the only one in this family with talent. You are, however, the only one in this family with a discipline I've admired ever since you were a tyke, and a sense of right and wrong that would make the pope envious." Charlotte—with a loud groan that made Mary want to laugh, so unpredictable were her emotions at the moment—settled down on the rug next to her. And then her arms—her warm, soft arms—were around Mary, pulling her to her expansive bosom. Mary did giggle, despite her hurt tears; Mama was resembling Marie Dressler more and more every year.

"Now, shhh, you dearie, you child. Shhhh, and close your eyes, and forget everything. You're tired, and you're high-strung, which is why you're an actress in the first place. You're my precious daughter, and you need to rest right now, and we'll figure it all out tomorrow. Or maybe not, maybe it will be the day after, or the day after that, I can't predict the future. But I can promise you that I love you now and forever, and so does your public, and, Lord help me, so does that Fairbanks—Jesus, the way that man looks at you—and we'll come up with a way to make it all work out."

"Oh, Mama, do you promise?"

"I promise," Charlotte cooed as she—again groaning loudly, her joints popping—rose to her feet, gently pulling Mary along with her. And Mary allowed herself to be ushered into her bedroom, Charlotte's arms about her.

"I'm sorry I said those things, Mama. I never want to let you or Jack or Lottie down. I never want you to have to take in laundry."

"I know, dearie, I know."

"I wish Fran was here," Mary said between yawns, realizing with a guilty little start that this was the first time she'd thought of Fran since she'd left on the bond tour. Was that what a man did? Made you forget about the other women in your life? "Fran would know what to do. She always does."

"Fran has her own life to live," Mama said, strangely.

"But she'd know what to do. She'd want to help me."

But Fran wasn't here, she was getting ready to go over there. Over there. *Over there*—and Mary couldn't help herself. She began to sing the song, softly this time, and it was almost like a lullaby.

Strange, that one song could be two entirely different things. And so, perhaps one person—one *actress*—could be, too.

Perhaps.

CHAPTER 10

FRANCES

AUTUMN 1918

I WAS THOROUGHLY SICK AND TIRED OF HEARING "Over There!"

A military band was playing it when I boarded the troop ship, the *Rochambeau,* in New York. At least once a day as I strolled the deck of the ship, shivering and imagining a German submarine, like the one that sunk the *Lusitania,* every time I saw a dark spot on the horizon, someone was humming or singing the tune. Twice, a well-intentioned Red Cross nurse got up a little talent show to raise money for the troops and what song was sung at least three times each show? Why, "Over There!" of course.

If I never heard "Over There!" again, I would be happy.

If I ever saw Fred again after this was all over, I would be delirious. Or would I?

Because, of course, I might not see him again. I might not see anyone I knew, ever again, and that included Mary, and thinking of Mary made me think of Hollywood and everything I'd left behind; everything I'd worked so hard to achieve only to leave it all with no more thought than a bee gives to a flower.

Alone on this ship, alone in the enormous ocean, so far from either shore, my bravado had drained away, leaving me feeling foolish and absurd. *What in the hell are you doing, Frances?*

What in the hell are you doing, leaving behind your snug little home in the Hollywood hills to sleep three to a room on a creaky, leaking transport ship? Leaving behind a spectacular career to show up on a battlefield unwanted, most likely. To be shot at, perhaps. To be shelled at, dropped bombs upon, live in mud, never change my clothes. Already on this voyage we'd had three submarine false alarms that made my heart forget how to beat and my hands shake so that I couldn't even tie my life vest as I tried to remember what boat I'd been assigned to, pushed my way through panicked crowds only to hear the piercing whistle of the "all clear" and want to collapse in relief and get a good strong drink at some lively restaurant with music playing. But on ship, the only booze was shots of whiskey begged from one of the Army doctors.

What I *should* have been doing, instead of brooding and panicking and questioning every decision I'd ever made in my life, was studying my fellow passengers, sketching them, writing down my observations. I was only dimly aware of them, all these young men so full of bravado but terrified underneath. I could see it in their eyes; I could tell by how much time they spent writing letters home—I was always coming across a young soldier huddled over a table, pen in hand. They—and I—were hurtling toward something none of us had ever experienced, could never have imagined. And that unknown was looming, like a great yawning mouth ready to devour us at the end of this journey.

Unknown. That was the only constant in my life now and I

had only myself to blame for that, didn't I? Oh, why was I always making my life harder than it had to be?

And Fred. There was another example. Why on earth did I have to fall in love with a God-fearing minister? Fred was everything I should have run from: Pious. Intractable. From a family predisposed to dislike a woman who worked—let alone a woman who worked in the Gomorrah that was Hollywood. A widower—when would the ghost of his dead wife pop up? How often? Oh—and someone who viewed sex before marriage as a sin.

There were only obstacles ahead with Fred, and if I had a lick of sense I'd disappear into France and never see him again. But then, the thought of never seeing him again made my heart seize up. And if he were killed? The very thought made me wretchedly ill. How on earth had this happened? How had this man I'd known for such a short time so colored my world that the thought of life without him was unimaginable? This beautiful, terrible earth would no longer spin on its axis if there was no Fred Thomson in it.

"Hey, miss!"

I looked up; a soldier was leaning on the railing next to me, his boyish face a little green from the roiling motion of the ship. "Do you worry about them submarines? Them Hun submarines?"

I had to smile; funny, how thinking about Fred had pushed even the ever-present terror from my mind. "Yes, I do. We all do. It's normal."

"Good." The young man let out a breath. "Seems like there's no relief, is there? Submarines in the ocean, bombs or worse—have you heard about that gas they're using now?—on land. If one doesn't get us, the other will. Makes you want to hold on to something, doesn't it? Something good?"

And in that moment, I knew the one thing I wanted to hold on to, more than anything. The one person. But what I didn't know—and this was the thing, wasn't it? The crux of the matter, the turn of the plot—was if I *deserved* him. And I hadn't thought of it that way before; the shock of this enormous truth hit me right in the solar plexus so that I had to grip the cold, wet rail even harder. Ocean spray stung my face as I turned away from the boy.

"Yes, it does," I whispered. But when I turned back, the soldier was gone and I had to wonder if I'd made him up.

BY THE TIME THE SHIP reached France—far off-course, so instead of docking in Bordeaux as scheduled, we landed in Brest—I had made up my mind to give Fred up.

I *didn't* deserve him. Plain and simple. I had made a mess of my personal life with my two marriages: now I had to pay the price. I deserved success in my professional life but not happiness in love—that was what I had come to realize on those endless walks on the freezing, slippery deck while I sped toward the unknown. And in making this decision, I was finally ready to go to war; I was ready to accept my fate with a clean conscience, purged of my past. I might die. I might—I most certainly would—see sights that would haunt me the rest of my life. When I thought of those ridiculous photos I'd posed for in my uniform, back in Hollywood, I cringed, and hoped for forgiveness from someone—not God, because I didn't believe in God, and of course that was one more reason why I was no good for Fred, one more reason that I should nobly set him free. As soon as I reached Paris, where I was to meet up with my unit, I would write him. And end it.

Brest was gray, the clouds ominous, the docks full of ships painted dull colors, camouflage, I guessed, from the stalking U-boats. Ours was the only ship that was vomiting out troops of men, all in uniform, all torn between wonder at being across the ocean and terror of what might await. Relief, too, at having crossed the deadly ocean without harm; it was as if the entire ship had released an enormous sigh when we reached port.

I struggled with my duffel bag—remembering my last trip to New York with Mary, and the trunks upon trunks, hat-boxes, handbags, that we brought with us, all ferried by eager porters. Now everything I would need for the next few months, maybe beyond, was crammed into one Army-issued duffel bag of olive green. And there were no porters in sight; over here, we few women would have to fend for ourselves. No, "Over There!"

The moment I'd set foot on the ship in New York and given my name and company, I had faced hostility. "CPI? To make movies? Stand aside, girlie, and let the real soldiers board first," I'd been informed. The sergeant in charge pointed to a stool. "You can sit over there and knit."

I had not gone over there to knit; I'd stubbornly remained where I stood, duffel bag across my aching shoulder, until he finally checked me off his list and assigned me a berth with a surly "Down with the other dames, near the kitchen where youse belong."

"We didn't ask you to come over, lady," more than one orderly had growled at me whenever I asked the simplest things— where was the mess, what time was dinner, what lifeboat was I assigned to. How many times, since sailing, had a soldier asked me to bake a cake? Mend his uniform? Handed me a mop and expected me to clean up his mess? I didn't argue or make a scene; I handed the mop back and went on my way. These were young men away from home for the very first time and headed to war. I needed to be understanding. Smile and move on and keep my head down.

Now I hoisted my heavy duffel bag over my shoulder and grabbed my satchel full of books—Lord, why had I packed so many?—and began to inch my way, in line with everyone else, slowly around the deck, toward the great gangplank miles, it seemed, away. Continually jostled, pushed and told to "get out of my way, lady," I bit my tongue. All around me were men in uniform, which of course only made me think of Fred. Fred, tall and sure, possessive, unlike anyone I'd ever met before. Where was he now? Somewhere here in France, on a battle-field, most likely; I knew nothing specific from his heavily cen-sored letters but still, I was suddenly filled with such desire for him—not lustful, simply the desire to touch him, to make sure he was still alive, still *mine*—that I stumbled, and fell against the man in front of me.

"Hey, lady, watch your step," he grumbled. "Women! I don't know what you're doing here in a war but you ought to be back home, knitting scarves or canning preserves or some-thing."

Straightening my duffel bag, I glared at him and for the first time since boarding, I snapped.

"When I am back home, I'm hardly knitting scarves, young man!"

"Oh, really? What do you do? Go to tea parties? You look like the type."

"I happen to write for the movies."

"You do? Say, do you know Mary Pickford or maybe Chaplin?"

"Mary Pickford is my best friend." And I grinned, triumphant, as a look of first disbelief, then wonder, then something almost like worship spread across his homely young face.

"*What?*" "*You don't say!*" "*Hey, Joe, come get a load of this!*" Suddenly I was surrounded by a cluster of soldiers who had transformed into eager little boys, eyes shining, delighted smiles on their faces.

"Seriously, lady, you're pals with Mary Pickford?"

"What's she like?"

"Is she as pretty in person?"

"Is her hair really gold?"

"You write for the movies? Really?"

"Name one."

"*Rebecca of Sunnybrook Farm,*" I finally was able to answer.

"Oh!" so many of these manly men exclaimed, I had to laugh.

"Well, I went with the wife, you know," one man admitted gruffly, and the others all nodded. "She loves Mary Pickford. She'd love to meet her."

"Well, maybe she can someday," I said. "Look me up in Hollywood when you get back. Frances Marion. Lieutenant Frances Marion."

"Yes, ma'am! Lieutenant, ma'am!" In a flash, I was gallantly relieved of my duffel bag and escorted by officers down to the head of the line, where my passport was stamped and my military ID scrutinized.

"Goodbye, boys!" I waved at my new admirers, proud of myself and of the movies—and maybe a little triumphant. How many times would I have to trade on Hollywood in order to ease my passage? I'd had no idea it would make such a difference but I was glad I'd found it out.

Then my heart twisted; where would these sweet, starstruck boys be tomorrow?

I heard a boom in the distance and I ducked before I realized it couldn't be a bomb or artillery shell. I was in Brest, for heaven's sake. At least a hundred miles away from battle, although of course, a German plane could drop bombs anywhere. But now that I was here, I needed to find some kind of transportation to Paris, where I was to meet my superior officers at the CPI; I began to fumble through my satchel, searching for the letter with my instructions, when I heard my name.

"Frances! Frances—I knew you'd be here!"

Confused, I looked up, looked about, looked everywhere, for—

Fred.

He was here, he was lifting me off my feet, he was kissing me with an abandon I'd never known before; no longer the somber minister but a tall, wild soldier and I was kissing him back, laughing—crying.

"Fred! Oh, Fred—how did you . . . why did you . . . how on earth?"

"I had a premonition." He set me down and took my hand with that lovely gentle possessiveness that thrilled my heart. "I had a feeling, you see. The Hundred Forty-third is stationed here in Brest and we got notice there was a troop ship docking today. That doesn't happen very often. I thought, I bet Frances is on this ship. And you were. And so I was right!"

"You were!" Dizzy now—shivering with cold or something else and my letter a damp, crumpled mess in my hand—I swayed. "Fred, I'm afraid—is there a place we can sit down?"

With such surety—oh, to be with this man forever, this man who knew how to do everything important, who knew himself, who knew *me*—Fred grabbed my duffel bag with one hand and me with the other, steering us up a narrow path to a sheltered bench. We collapsed, and I blew out a shaky breath, relieved I hadn't fainted away like some ridiculous maiden.

"Fred, I don't know what to say . . . During the crossing, I'd about convinced myself that we are all wrong for each other, that I had to write you and tell you that you were too good for me, that I could never deserve—this. You."

"I would have torn that letter up, Frances Marion. And run you down to the ends of the earth to find you and tell you what a beautiful little fool you are."

"You found me here, in all—this! How, I have no idea—do you know, if I'd written this in a scenario, no one would believe it? But they'd love it anyway. The public does love a romance, an improbable romance. Maybe I will have to use this, you know . . . I can imagine a scenario for Mary, she plays a Red Cross nurse, she's in love with a soldier, but she vows to give him up because of her past, and then he meets her, just like this, and . . ."

"Frances, oh, Frances!" Fred laughed, so exuberantly that soldiers turned to stare. "This is why I love you! You never stop, your mind is always spinning and creating. But, darling, I need to make one thing clear. Please don't use our life together in your work. That's ours, it's sacred. I understand I'll always have to share you with Hollywood, and with Mary. But what's between us, every day—every minute—that's *ours*. Do you promise?"

"Yes, dear." I blushed; I'd never spoken so demurely before and I'd certainly never called him "dear." But I understood; a man as sure of himself as Fred was a man who could afford to make compromises, where other—lesser—men felt they could not. Still, a man like Fred was also naturally private, especially in matters of the heart. I would give him that privacy; I would dignify our love, consecrate it, with my silence. It would always be apart from my work. And it would be more important than work—that, I vowed. Oh, I would never give up my career, not even for Fred, and it was easy to say that because I knew he would never ask me to. But in order to make a marriage succeed—and for the first time I understood something I hadn't been willing to in my previous attempts—you had to put it first.

"Now what?" I was happy. Content to sit beside my—*my*—lieutenant in the gray drizzle of a French day, under the dripping eaves of a tipsy tin shed.

"Now, we both do our part."

And I was back to reality; the thought of having to say goodbye to Fred again, after this unexpected—*holy*—reunion nearly killed me. But I mustn't let him see.

"When do you go?"

"To the front? Who knows? I can get leave to join you in Paris for a day or two, but then I'll have to report back. When do *you*?"

"Who knows?" We laughed, and it was perfect.

"I would have to have fallen in love with a suffragette. A militant suffragette."

"I suspect you secretly admire suffragettes."

Fred guffawed. "Don't tell my mother, but heaven help me, I do. Especially when they have blue eyes and a turned-up nose and a very busy brain."

"Why, Fred?" Now I was struck by the brevity of our time together, the enormity of what lay ahead for both of us. "Why me?" I hungered for answers to questions I'd not allowed myself to ask. "On paper, we're as unlike as two people could be. I'm all wrong for you. You're all wrong for me. So why? Why me?"

"Because of your shoes."

"What?" I was dizzy again, utterly confused. "My *shoes*?"

"Your shoes," Fred continued with a confident—cocky on anyone else but him—grin. "When you met me in the hospital, one of your shoes was unbuttoned. I could tell it bothered you—you kept trying to hide that foot with your other one, and sometimes you almost bent down like you were going to fix it, but each time you would stop yourself. I could tell you were aching to. But you never did, and I thought it was because you felt that wouldn't be ladylike. And I loved you for that— your self-control, your femininity, how that one little thing bothered you so much, but still you never gave in to it."

"I had no idea you noticed! I would have died if I thought you had—I wanted to be perfect in front of you because you were so perfect! Even in a hospital bed, you looked like a Greek god, completely unfazed that you were in a gown, and I was all dolled up."

"Now it's your turn. Why me?"

"Because—" I was suddenly shy and I looked away; all around us was chaos—soldiers were tramping, shouting, dragging bags and trunks, lorries honking, whistles blowing, that damned "Over There!" wheezing from a harmonica. I didn't like to remind Fred of my past; that he knew and didn't care was enough. But he deserved an answer. "Because you're unlike any man I've ever met. Because for the first time, I don't feel as if I have to give up any part of myself to love you. Or to be loved by you."

"That's a beautiful speech, Miss Marion," Fred said seriously, even as his eyes gleamed. "Do you mind if I use it in a movie?"

"Oh!" I hung my head. "I promise, Fred, I won't ever do that. I won't ever use anything you say, or anything real between us. I promise."

"You know I love that you're a career woman, don't you? I love that you have your own identity apart from mine. My first wife—Laura—was, well . . ." Fred swallowed, and I steeled myself; he'd scarcely talked about his late wife, and I wasn't sure I wanted him to, even as I was almost torn apart by curiosity and, shamefully, jealousy.

"Laura was lovely. Fragile. Devoted. The most beautiful person, inside and out, I've ever known. But her entire life was wrapped up in me, in being a preacher's wife, and it was a little stifling. I'm not the kind of person who likes to bring his work home with him; I like home to be a haven, an escape. But with Laura, I was always the minister. And very rarely, simply—me. Fred. But don't get me wrong, I loved her. I mourn her. You have to know that."

"I do." I took his hand. "If you didn't, I would have doubts about you. And I don't. Not a single one."

"Well." Fred pulled me to my feet, putting an end to this particular conversation. I consulted my watch; it was nearly 3:00 P.M. and I had to get to Paris by nightfall. I was also bone tired; I'd not been able to sleep well on the ship with all the fear of being blown to smithereens by a torpedo (we slept in our day clothes, in case we had to abandon ship in the middle of the night). The air had been too close in my tiny, shared cabin; my roommates snored. And then there had been the unceasing roiling in my stomach as I'd sped toward the unknown.

But seeing Fred had eased the roiling, if only for now. And I longed to bathe properly in a real tub, not a washstand, and sleep in an actual bed, not just a thin cot. So I stood and—hand in hand with my beloved—I picked my way among the debris of humanity that had washed ashore in France. American soldiers, all. Ready to go to war.

I was one of them. The only woman swimming upstream in a river of men.

LATER, THE ONLY THING I would allow myself to write, or speak, seriously about was the shoes.

It was odd, I knew; I'd come to war for a lot of reasons, one of which, if I were being honest, was to gain experience; experience to write about. Because that's what writers did; they lived, then they wrote about that living.

But during an entire lifetime of writing—writing movies, writing books about movies, novels, essays, articles—I never really wrote about the war, and my time in France. Not in a significant way.

Oh, sure, I'd tell people about the surprise of seeing American soldiers hungrily watching movies played on huge white sheets in their barracks; of seeing firsthand the popularity of movies, how they could distract, soothe troubled minds and hearts and damaged bodies. To my surprise, Doug and Charlie Chaplin were the soldiers' absolute favorites, not Mary Pickford. But of course, these were men. Doughboys.

I'd laugh and make fun of my own poor French and my

absurd attempts to speak it. I'd reveal my delight in how popular Fred was among these men when we got to Paris. In Hollywood, I was the celebrity—nothing like Mary, but still, I was known and, more important, people *wanted* to know me. But in Paris, hordes of men clamored for a look at or a handshake from Fred Thomson, the great athlete.

I did write to Mary about the obstacles I encountered, time and time again, from the men, officers and soldiers both. The war makers who felt that a woman among them was an aberration of nature. Men who openly questioned my mission, my intelligence, even my femininity. Men who assumed I was there for one purpose only.

"Hey, girlie, be in my room at ten o'clock," one doctor in an Army hospital barked after barely glancing at me in a hallway. "I'll give you what you came over here for."

Men who would grow darkly angry, even physically threatening—an orderly once shoved me against a wall when I tartly explained that my orders did not include him; thank God several officers happened to come around the corner before he could do more.

I was not the only woman treated this way, and I would always praise to the heavens the women I encountered in France—the nurses, in particular. I was eager to relate *their* stories even as I was unable to talk about mine. It was a privilege to witness and share their sacrifices, how the wounded looked at them with a peculiar, devoted light in their eyes, not just as women who could alleviate their suffering but as holy women—Everywoman, in a way. Virgin, Mother, Sweetheart, Lover, Eve.

After I bid Fred a tearful goodbye in Paris, clinging to him until the very last and feeling as if gravity itself had disappeared as he walked away, I dried my eyes, powdered my nose, and reported to duty. I was given a canteen and a utility belt and assigned a cameraman, Harry Thorpe, and a director, Wesley Ruggles, and we went to work recording these remarkable women on film. Women who weren't only nurses; women who rode bicycles bearing telegrams to the front lines. Women who ran the canteens. Women who showed the films for entertainment. As my crew and I traveled back and forth from Paris to the front—never all the way to the trenches; our orders allowed us to go no farther than the field hospitals—we filmed these women soothing, laughing, writing letters. Covering bodies with sheets. Arranging for burials. Packing away personal effects into little boxes to be sent back home, this last act always done so tenderly, no matter how busy the nurse might be, no matter how little sleep or food she might have had in the last thirty-six hours. And always, a handwritten letter went into that box, inventing an intimacy with the dead soldier so the grieving loved ones wouldn't think their son or husband had died alone.

So I filmed the horrors of war, and tried to do so unblinkingly, striving not to allow myself to be caught up personally in the moment—it was as if the camera shielded me from emotional involvement, or at least, that's what I told myself. If something hit me particularly hard, like the soldier who wept for hours before he finally died of his wounds because he didn't have anyone at home who would remember him, I somehow managed to stifle my own sobs, taking refuge in the work, pretending that I was filming a scene with actors, a scene I had written and so could yell "Cut!" when it was over. That helped, quite a lot. To pretend that I was on a set and not an actual battlefield.

But at night, when I was alone in my small hotel room or in whatever tent I was assigned if I remained at the front, I wept, quietly, so as not to disturb anyone.

Always I was looking for images, trying to see my surroundings as someone would in a movie theater, where the only sounds would be piano music. The images were *everything;* the dirt, the scars, so many of the men with bandaged eyes from the gas; men and women mingling, striving, suffering, until gender, at least here in the real battle lines, was of no importance. They were all simply people, caught up in hell. And yet managing, if they were well enough, to flash a smile whenever they saw the camera turned their way. I couldn't get over how the camera affected people, even people who were suffering; it turned them all into aspiring movie stars. The soldiers especially would clown about and imitate Chaplin's Little Tramp, using their forefingers to mimic his mustache, their rifles to imitate his cane, and I'd be struck anew by how universal my world was, how what we did on a soundstage in Hollywood could travel across the ocean to the battlefields of France.

What my crew and I couldn't convey on film, but which were no less paramount and horrific, were the sounds. The sobs, the pleadings, the wails of despair; the grim, accepting silences. The incessant tinkling of bloodied operating instruments into tin basins in the hospitals; even at night, far from the wards, my ears rang from that sound. The never-ending crunch of gravel by heavy boots. The accordion music on every corner, in every café and canteen, in Paris. The desperate, high-pitched laughter there. The lack of it at the front. The constant low hum of voices; someone was always talking, ordering, asking, begging. Never once did I hear a bird chirp, except in Paris.

And the smells—I would never forget them, but how to

write about a smell? How to describe how it made your eyes water or your stomach turn over or your hand fly to your nose? The odor of mud and filth and mildew—mossy at its best, pungently acidic at its worst. The sinus-clearing stench of antiseptics. How to describe what gangrene smells like? I didn't even try, because I didn't ever want to remember it.

Perspiration—no, Fran, not "perspiration"; that's such a prissy word. Sweat. Stink. Bodies foul and ripe on men beyond caring, sometimes even on my own body when baths were scarce. Trench foot—those cases were the worst, for some reason. I once witnessed a reconstructive surgery that involved sawing a man's scalp almost entirely off his head, and I saw brain—not pink, as I'd always imagined, but gray. But that had nothing on the cases and cases of trench foot—flesh falling from bone with a moist, sucking sound, and the odor so foul, so decayed, no perfume could ever erase the memory of it. Battlefields—fresh mounds barely covered in mud, wooden crosses hastily nailed and plunged into the earth like hatpins on a filthy hat—had a peculiarly sweet smell. Someone explained that this was how a body smelled after the initial decaying process was over. I wasn't sure I wanted to know that, but thanked the eager young orderly anyway.

Mostly, my letters home—to Mary, to Charlotte, to Adela and Bess, to friends like Hedda Hopper and Marie Dressler, to a new acquaintance, the writer Mary Roberts Rinehart, herself a war correspondent in France, and to Elsie, the reason I was here, but whom I never once met up with—were cheerful, self-deprecating; to them, I made it sound as if I was having the adventure of my life.

When I did finally tell them of my biggest ordeal, my grandest adventure—the one that made headlines for my being the first Allied female to cross enemy lines—I finally gave myself permission to talk about the shoes.

It was soon after Mary had sent a letter. *"Psst . . . the word in the studios is that there are to be no more 'Kill the Hun!' pictures."* And I had already noticed a difference in the very air; people smiled more, all of a sudden. Allowed themselves to joke. So the war must be winding down. Right about then, I received orders to head to the front to join the Signal Corps and the Red Cross, who were crossing into Germany after the retreating German army, to tend to the American wounded left behind in their prisoner hospitals.

That afternoon, I was late; I'd rushed to where I was to meet my caravan in Paris, only to discover it had already left with Wes and Harry and our cameras in it. The rest of the vehicles were filled with doctors and nurses and their medical equipment.

"What do I do?" I hailed a young corporal who was studying a clipboard and waving cars off to their destinations.

"What's your mission?"

"CPI—filming the Signal Corps and Red Cross."

"Filming?" The corporal shook his head. "We don't have any room. My advice is to turn back. Stay in Paris and have yourself a nice, warm dinner and a bubble bath."

"I'll do no such thing!" The back of my neck twitched and I glared at the boy; oh, how annoying it was to have boys ten years younger order me around all the time! "I have a job to do and I'm going to do it. I've never 'turned back' in my life, Corporal, and I have no intention of doing so now."

He sighed, rubbed his eyes, and shrugged.

"Suit yourself. Grab a seat in that truck there. But you're going to be in for a bumpy ride."

"Fine." I snatched up my duffel bag, filled with a change of underwear, a toothbrush, a brush and some hairpins, and not much more, and climbed into the only empty seat I could find, beside the driver of a transport truck who gave me one look and said, "Goddamn, son of a bitch."

"Hello to you, too, Sergeant."

With an explosive sigh, the driver put the car in gear and we lurched away. I didn't know where I was going and I didn't ask. I only knew that I was going to be closer to Germany than I'd ever been before, and I shivered. So far I hadn't actually seen a Hun. The prospect was equally exciting and terrifying.

In my hand, I clutched a letter I'd just received from Fred, the reason for my tardiness that morning. *"Darling, we're finally going to the front. Hooray! Try not to worry, although I know this is a useless request. I will be fine, I have a real feeling I'll be spared, and my men, too, for what better purpose I don't understand yet. Only know I'm pathetically proud to finally be asked to do my duty, when so many other men have already done theirs. And that I will return to you even more pathetically proud to be yours for the rest of my life."*

So he was going, finally! All this time, as I'd darted back and forth from my home base in Paris, never feeling I was really in harm's way except for one air raid that left some buildings only half a mile away from my hotel in ruins, I'd silently rejoiced that Fred and the 143rd had remained stationed in Brest. He did not rejoice; I answered his increasingly irritated letters with proper sympathy but never revealed how thankful I was that he was safe. That wasn't what you told a soldier who had yet to face battle.

But now he was leaving for the front—wherever that was, somewhere deeper in Germany than I was going, surely. From what I could glean from the tight-lipped sergeant driving the truck, we were headed to Luxembourg as there were huge gaps in the rapidly disintegrating Western Front. Finally the sleeping beast that had always resided at the edges of my consciousness awoke; Fred and I were both headed into danger, his the greater, and it was real now. Not a movie.

As the truck lurched on its way, I gave up trying to get the taciturn sergeant to talk. Instead, I decided to try to get some rest. Using my bag as a pillow, I dozed fitfully, but found it impossible when the ruts in the muddy road became deeper and closer together and I was tossed around the cab of the truck like a salad.

"Verdun," the sergeant spat out. "Look."

Up ahead, there were small bonfires set along the road, on either side.

"What on earth? I thought the battle here had happened long ago."

"To keep the fucking rats away, lady. This place—all these son-of-a-bitch battlefields—are crawling with rats. The damn rats love the dead."

My stomach lurched, and I remembered I hadn't eaten since late yesterday, which was a good thing. For now.

The truck swayed, the axles squealed, ahead of and behind us were dozens more trucks, more machinery moaning and groaning, lurching forward. But on either side of the road, as far as I could see beyond the flickering flames of the bonfires, was a vast emptiness, a heartbreaking silence. Abandoned vehicles, walls of a bombed cathedral silhouetted against the pink, twilit sky. Foundations where homes had once stood. So much rubble, piles and piles of it, wood and metal dangerously mingled, ragged edges poking out like gleaming teeth. A skirt—filthy but miraculously untorn—hanging from a clothesline.

Gardens with unpicked, rotting vegetation. Trees with no leaves, their twisted limbs stretching up to the sky like fingers in supplication. A seesaw, lonely, in a park without trees.

Up ahead were the trenches, and we were almost upon them when I saw the shoe. One red shoe, a child's shoe, poking up out of a pile of bricks and rubble. Impossibly small, this shoe; impossible to imagine the tiny foot that once fit it.

All too real to imagine the fate of the child who once wore this shoe, this shoe that must have run and jumped, danced and kicked; dangled innocently from a high chair. All too easy to sit and wonder what became of the other shoe, ponder at the force of whatever had hit this rubble that could separate it from its mate. Far too easy, and too devastating; I began to shake, taking noisy breaths to prevent tears from streaming down my cheeks, trying to stifle a sob.

This was war. Not a pretty picture staged by D. W. Griffith—I remembered how I'd gasped at the realism of the battlefield scenes in *The Birth of a Nation*. How naïve I had been. They weren't realistic, they were artfully staged vignettes, carefully composed, lit, framed. And even Griffith didn't have the courage to film a child's empty shoe.

This is what I should have been filming, not only the women behind the lines—although of course they were important, their stories were important. But perhaps more important were the women caught up in battle without their consent; women struggling to live their lives, feed their families, care for their children, who found war, uninvited, at their doorstep. Who was filming them?

But where were they to be found now? I didn't even know where to look. I didn't have the strength to start tearing through the rubble with my own two hands, and now we were almost out of the town, entering the abandoned trenches, and that sickeningly sweet smell was everywhere so I sat rigidly upright next to my sergeant, who never once seemed to take in his surroundings, after the bonfires. He was concentrating only on the road ahead.

We bounced on in a sudden rain, until without warning the truck gave an awful jolt and my head slammed against the door.

"Bastard of a bitch, this whoring ball biter of a truck!"

In a way, I was grateful that he didn't take any pains to modify his language; he didn't seem to care if he offended me, so for once, I wasn't reminded of my gender. Still swearing—creatively—he coaxed the groaning vehicle toward the side of the road so the few trucks behind us could go on. Then we were alone on this road, surrounded by ghostly trenches, and it was nightfall. And pouring.

Taking my suddenly foulmouthed sergeant's lead, I got out of the truck and immediately sank to my knees in mud; I shivered as my skirt and stockings plastered my skin in a cold, slimy compress. But there was nothing else to do but slosh around to the other side of the truck, close to the road, where the sergeant was on his hands and knees in the slime, peering beneath it.

"Broken bitch of an axle, goddamn it to hell."

"What does that mean?"

"It means we're not going a goddamn inch farther until some other son of a whore comes along and we can hitch a ride."

"When will that be?" I peered up and down the narrow, muddy, pothole-filled road in the dusk; there was no sign of any vehicles.

"Damned if I know, lady."

"Well." I patted my matted hair, deciding. "I'm going on foot. I don't want to wait, because I might miss my crew."

"The hell you are!"

"How far is it to Luxembourg?" I was already slogging through the mud to the front of the truck.

"Fucking miles. At least two hours, maybe three, by truck."

"Look, I can walk faster than this truck is going, anyway." I retrieved my bag. "And I'm sure I'll catch up with someone sometime."

"Yeah." The sergeant was now beside me, leering; I'd never felt so small and helpless before. This man had limbs as thick as trees, stubble on his face, and while he didn't look menacing he did look strong and big; much bigger than me. "You'll catch up with someone, sweetie. Maybe some bastard not as gentlemanly as this son of a bitch."

"The Germans have retreated, haven't they?" I tried to reason with both the man and myself; why I was filled with this insane urge to march on toward my destination at all costs, I had no idea. Except that I had a duty to do and I would do it. Because I had to. Because—unlike the child whose shoe was left behind—I *could*. I possessed two strong legs, strong lungs, my heart was beating true. I was alive. I was going to go on, because to stay here in this field of death was to tempt death—that was how I felt.

"Do you have anything to eat?" I pulled the collar of my coat up, trying to prevent the freezing rain from trickling down my neck. "A candy bar, an apple, anything?" Suddenly my stomach was gnawing at itself.

"Here." The man reached into a pocket and handed me a wad of jerky—what kind, I didn't ask. One of the more enterprising mess cooks at my last field hospital had sold jerkied rat out of his tent. "You're a crazy dame, you know that? What in Christ's name do you do back in the States?"

"I'm— Oh, it doesn't matter." And for the first time, it didn't. I didn't feel proud of what I did, and it simply didn't matter. It didn't matter what any of us did back home; even thinking of Hollywood right now made my head feel like it was stuffed with lightning bugs. Hollywood was fantastic and far away and as flimsy as the ripped canvas covering the back of the truck. The only thing that mattered, that was real, was this road, this moment, this Dante's inferno of a night.

"Go ahead, then, but you'd better stick to the fucking road. And if any bastard comes by I'll tell 'em to keep an eye out for you or I'll blast his balls. Crazy dame," the sergeant muttered, but stuck out his muddy hand, and I shook it. Firmly.

I bit into the jerky—it was so tough my teeth were nearly yanked out of my jaw—and began to chew it slowly to make it last, savoring the juices that trickled into my empty stomach, hoping it would all stay down, for I needed the fuel. Then I began to walk, sticking to the side of the road where sometimes grass met mud and the slog was marginally easier.

The farther I got from the truck, the more ominously silent it became, and I missed my sergeant's colorful cursing; again, I marveled at the lack of birdsong but then scolded myself. It was night. No birds sang at night.

The rain continued to beat down and I gave in to it, stopped fighting it. I let it wash over me, drenching every fiber of clothing, my hat, my hair, and making my journey that much harder, but soon I actually forgot about it and accepted the bone-chilling, teeth-rattling cold and wet as simply part of a new reality. Just as I accepted the trenches and the rubble and the occasional cross that emerged from the gloom, the churned-up devastation of the earth, as if it had been plowed for some future planting, a planting that would never come.

I walked. My wool stockings were soaked; water was pouring into my boots so that my feet sloshed with each step. My lower back began to throb in time with my footsteps; shivering was so constant I didn't know if I'd ever be able to stop. The jerky was long gone, and I began to wonder how much longer it would be until dawn. Surely, I'd reach Luxembourg by then?

Once, I heard footsteps behind me and my skin pricked; I didn't cry out but I did turn around, very slowly, only to find a dog panting next to me. But I had nothing to give him, even as my heart ached at the sight of this starving, mangy animal. And I did begin to cry then, as I hadn't for the child's shoe, and I cursed myself for eating all the jerky, and before I knew it I'd picked up a rock and was throwing it at the dog. "Go! Shoo! I don't have anything!" The poor thing gave a pitiful cry and slunk away into the fetid darkness.

And I knew this was one more thing I couldn't write about, and I wondered again why I'd come, if I never wanted to record any of the real things that were happening all around me, the gritty, desperate reality, the echoing emptiness, the death.

As I continued to trudge down that infinite muddy trail, I found myself thinking of Mickey and Mary and Charlotte and everyone back home in Hollywood. Oh, if only I could be there with them, I'd never, ever leave! And so, in order to shut out everything I was trudging through—that sweet stench of death seemed to be everywhere, permeating my rain-drenched skin—I began to concoct outlines for comedy scenarios instead. Maybe something for Mary that involved a monkey, a circus-themed film. Mickey could do something with that; he was brilliant at those atmospheric kinds of things, busy scenes in the background, children with cotton candy, elephants, clowns on tiny bicycles . . . Mary could be a pretty little high-wire dancer, maybe twelve or so, who had been kidnapped as a small child by the evil circus owner, brought up in the poor but convivial atmosphere of the circus performers who loved her, and tried to protect her from the evil owner, and so she grew to love them. Then, one day, her real parents, still grieving for their lost little girl, saw her photograph on the circus poster, and . . .

The bleat of a horn made me jump, my breath exploding in ragged gasps; I spun around, nearly falling over in a heap, blinded by the headlights of a car that screeched to a stop as I waved my arms wildly. Shutting my eyes, I steeled myself for the impact—

Which never came. When I opened my eyes, I saw the car had stopped only a few feet away, and I let out a shaky sigh of relief. The car had a star in the windshield—the star of a general in the United States Army.

"What the hell is an American woman doing on this road?" an irritated voice barked from the olive green Cadillac touring car, standard U.S. military issue.

Hastily digging through my bag to retrieve my identification papers and pass, I tried to look inside the car but could see no one but the driver, a lieutenant, who was now walking toward me with a shocked—and furious—look on his face.

"Here," I called, my voice bigger and braver than I felt. "I'm Lieutenant Frances Marion, of the CPI." I handed the other lieutenant my papers; he in turn passed them to the unseen general in the back of the car.

"Lieutenant Marion, where the hell do you think you're going?" Again the irritated bark.

"Luxembourg, sir." I saluted. And smiled.

"Damn fool women, poking their noses into a man's war. Well, damn it, get in, Lieutenant."

My hands flew to my hair in order to arrange it in a becoming way—such a foolish, feminine gesture so completely out of place that I felt as if, with that one movement, I'd let my entire gender down.

Besides, there was no fixing to be done; I was a drowned cat and surely looked like one. Giving up, I opened the car door, and slid inside.

I didn't ask the general his name, and he didn't offer it. Squeezing myself into the farthest corner of the seat, as far away from him as possible, I shut my eyes and must have fallen asleep immediately.

I awoke later—how much time had passed? It was still dark, but the car was stopped, the general gone. The lieutenant remained in the driver's seat.

"What time is it?"

"Twenty-three hundred. We're in Luxembourg."

"Luxembourg!" I scrambled from the car, strangely refreshed, almost exhilarated. My stomach rumbled, and I decided to walk around, looking for a mess tent or canteen. After pushing my way through a tangle of uniforms—I scarcely heard their "Hey, watch it, girlie!" protests—I found a stall where a woman sold pitiful sandwiches, the contents of which I had no desire to inquire about. I bought two and wolfed them down, followed by a watery cup of coffee. Then I went off to find my crew.

As I trudged from group to group, seeking a familiar face, I overheard two soldiers talking about an advance guard about to move across the Rhine, the first Allied forces to do so, while the rest of them hung back for a couple days. Advance guard! Without pausing to think it through, I ran back to the car just as *my* general—I laughed at myself for that, how absurd!—emerged from the hotel with the American flag posted in front, serving as headquarters.

"Sir!" I saluted. General William Mitchell—I could read his insignia—saluted back with a grumpy sigh. "I hear there are troops crossing the Rhine? An advance guard?"

"So?"

"I'd like permission to accompany them."

General Mitchell sighed again.

"Lieutenant Marion, I don't approve of women in war. But since you've come this far on your own I'm not going to be the one to stop you from going farther. Permission granted. My aide, Major Brereton, is going on ahead. You can ride with him." He gestured to a tall soldier standing a foot behind him, who scowled down at me, obviously longing to protest. But equally obviously reluctant to contradict his superior.

"Thank you, sir!" Not hiding my grin, I saluted once more. Then I grabbed my bag from the back of the general's car, and raced after Major Brereton—who was not slowing down for any mere female—as he strode to his own touring car. Without asking, I slid into the passenger seat beside him.

"I don't know why you dames are here," the major grumbled in lieu of a greeting. "Look at you, in that uniform! What do you think you're trying to prove?"

"I'm not trying to prove anything." For the first time since arriving in Europe more than a month ago, I allowed my anger—suppressed after weeks of putting up with insults—to flare. "I'm here because I wanted to do something for my country, the same as you."

"What exactly *are* you doing, Lieutenant Marion, if I might be so bold to ask?" The car was easing out onto another muddy road, heading northeast, and I realized I was about to cross into German territory for the first time. How thrilling! Astonishingly, I knew no fear; hadn't I walked through my own valley of death earlier, on that nightmare road from Verdun, and survived?

"I'm filming women. Telling women's stories. Because their stories are just as important as the soldiers'. The nurses, the doctors, the aides, the telegraph operators. Without them, the Allies wouldn't have had a chance."

"Filming?" The major glanced at me, and I realized my hands were empty. Where was my crew? I had no idea; as soon as I'd heard about the chance to cross the Rhine, I'd forgotten all about poor Harry and Wes. My only thought had been of the opportunity. Nevertheless, I was unrepentant. I'd never felt this strong and fearless before. Only hours earlier I'd been so terrified, so defeated, I'd believed that if I ever made it home again I'd never leave. And now here I was, tumbling toward the German army in a military car! No man had been able to prevent me and I felt as liberated as the Statue of Liberty—I might as well have been carrying a torch for freedom, the Allies; for *women*.

"I couldn't find my crew back in Luxembourg," I lied.

"So why are you going on?"

"Well, because they might already have left." But I knew they hadn't, for our orders were to accompany the nurses and doctors. Not to speed ahead of all the Allied forces to be among the first to cross into the Rhineland.

"I don't understand you women," Major Brereton muttered with a scowl. But he accepted the crumpled cigarette I handed

him from my bag. "You don't have to be here. Why would anyone in his—or her—right mind want to go to war, if they don't
have to? If I never see another battle in my life, I'll be a happy
man."

"You're a major. Which means you weren't drafted. Why
are you in the military? You didn't have to be."

"My father fought at San Juan Hill with Teddy Roosevelt.
My grandfather fought at Gettysburg. It's a tradition."

"So you didn't have a choice?"

Major Brereton grunted. "Not really."

"Some people choose to serve. Some people want to be of
use. Even women, you know. We don't all like the idea of sitting home while our menfolk take care of all the difficult things
in life."

"But we menfolk, as you call us, want to take care of those
things. We want to take care of you."

"But not all women want to be taken care of, you see."

"No, I don't see." And the major shook his head, to emphasize his confusion. "I just don't."

I bit my lip. I wasn't going to argue with this man who,
after all, was doing me a favor. I couldn't spend the rest of this
trip—or even the rest of my life—trying to argue with men
like him. No, the only thing I could do was continue my career,
live my life, and let my work speak for me.

And praise the heavens that I was going to marry a man who
didn't expect me to sit at home and knit.

Closing my eyes again—I really was exhausted, and every
now and then the memory of my earlier chill would cause my
limbs to involuntarily shudder—I slept. But not very long. For
Major Brereton suddenly poked me in the shoulder and said,
tersely, "Germany."

I opened my eyes. We were driving through a small village, as miraculously untouched by battle as Verdun had been decimated by it, the street lit up by blazing torches. But here there was the same menacing quiet. Villagers lined the street, all staring with pure hatred at our car with its little American flag fluttering on the hood. One hungry-looking child took a rock and flung it at us, and soon we were being pelted by rocks, clods of dirt, even a brick.

Major Brereton swore, as I shrank back from the window. At the first sign of a back road, he took it, and we stayed off the main roads, even though we had to inch along through the dark. I did my best to navigate with a map full of strange German names, and we journeyed on.

Finally, near dawn—the sky was pink past the tall trees—Major Brereton actually smiled.

"We should be in Koblenz now. That must be the Rhine, up ahead."

Sitting up, I straightened my hair, still in a damp knot at the back of my head, and wondered again at this telltale female gesture. Why on earth did I care that I look my best now, of all times? In all places? But I did, and I decided not to fight it. I was a woman, after all. And being a woman—even a strong woman, even a suffragette, if that was indeed what I was—meant never apologizing for being feminine.

I began to hear music, very faint, in the distance. Could there be some kind of carnival up ahead? But the notes grew clearer, louder, as we sped up and over a narrow stone bridge, and as I waved at the small, proud military band on the other side, I realized.

They were playing "The Star-Spangled Banner." I'd never been moved by it before, but I was now; my chest expanded and tears were flowing down my cheeks, and even as Major Brereton gaped at me, I wouldn't apologize for crying, either. There was nothing weak in being moved to tears, especially after the night I'd just had.

"Satisfied?" Major Brereton asked sarcastically as the car pulled to a stop outside a small building, obviously just confiscated from the Germans because, gathered on the sidewalk, a cluster of townspeople, with coats thrown over their nightgowns and nightshirts, stood eyeing us with hatred. Fortunately there were a few armed troops watching them, so no rocks were thrown.

"What do you mean?" Drying my tears, I stepped out of the car gingerly. Every joint was cold and stiff, and my head was pounding.

"You're here, Lieutenant. Congratulations. The first American woman to cross the Rhine."

"Yes." I smiled. "I am satisfied. Thank you, Major."

"So now you can leave. Go back to Paris—I'll arrange for a plane. It's not safe—there are rumors of riots all through Germany, and we won't have a large presence here for a few days. The only Americans behind us right now are military police. It's really not safe. And I'm not only saying that because you're a woman." The major rolled his eyes. "It's not safe for any of us."

"Nothing in war is safe. I'm staying. The nurses and doctors will be here in a couple days, won't they?" Major Brereton nodded.

"Then I'll catch up with my crew and we'll start filming. Those are my orders, and I intend to follow them. Now, I'm sure you have things to do, Major. I don't require a babysitter. I can manage on my own."

With a smart salute—after all, the man was my superior—I retrieved my bag from the car. I headed to find a place to stay, a cot to lie down on, a morsel to eat, and, if I was lucky, a place with a hot bath, because I was spattered with filth. And my hair—oh, my hair! I caught a glimpse of myself in a shop window.

My hair was an absolute wreck.

Y EARS LATER, SHE WOULD SPEND COUNTLESS HOURS looking at all the photos from that time, marveling at how young she was, how slim, how unlined her face, how luxurious her hair. She thought, When you're older, looking at your younger self is like looking at a promise you couldn't keep. But still, you look, you marvel. You remember.

But there was something else about those photos that she kept returning to; those photos of her and Charlie and Douglas; her and Charlie and Douglas and Griffith; her and Goldwyn and Griffith; her and all the—

Men.

One after the other, Mary was the only girl in the pictures. Occasionally, Fran would be there, too, but Fran never really did seek that kind of publicity; Mary remembered always having to coax her into the photo, Fran reluctantly obliging and then looking so beautiful that Mary had to tease her.

"Why did I insist you stand next to me, Fran, dear? You're so pretty, no one is even looking at me!"

But even as she said this, she knew it wasn't true. In every photograph that she was in, it was Mary whose image drew the first gaze. Especially in those photos where it was only her and her new partners—males all.

How many photos they posed for, the partners in this embryonic endeavor, all of them simultaneously terrified and arrogant! How many interviews they gave, the four of them!

The lunatics have taken over the asylum.

Some wag said it, although no one ever claimed responsibility. Mary knew it could have been uttered by any of the studio heads and distributors who greeted their new studio with forced jocularity but mainly disdain. No one in the industry could imagine that actors, *artists,* were capable of running their own business; that they could produce and distribute their own films. No one could conceive of the idea that actors could pocket their own profits, too. Or that they'd want to, in the first place.

And that a *woman* could be one of them—unheard of! Yet she was. The very first. Mary Pickford—actress, producer, philanthropist. And now, studio head.

It started in November 1918. Right around the armistice, when Mary had reached the very peak of her fame thus far, single-handedly selling more war bonds than even Douglas and Charlie. Headlines such as *Little Mary Wins the War* were not uncommon; even President Wilson publicly congratulated her for doing more for the war effort than anyone else. Mary proudly packed away her custom-made uniform after a victorious parade in San Francisco. Then she and everyone else in Hollywood returned to the studios and resumed the business of making movies.

But movies were different, now that the war was over. *Hollywood* was different. No longer a new, struggling American industry, Hollywood was suddenly big business, big *interna-*

tional business. It would be years before the European film industries recovered, and since the Allied countries had been introduced to Mary and Charlie and Douglas and the rest during the war, millions hungered for even more of their films. So now there was international distribution to think of; international box office to divide.

Papa Zukor at Famous Players–Lasky pressed Mary to sign a new contract, but she stalled. Chaplin had just gotten a deal from rival First National for over a million dollars, and when that studio reached out to Mary offering her more than that if you included profits, plus full artistic control, she called Papa.

"Let her go," one of the men was reported as saying. "Let that bitch get her ego deflated, destroy First National, and come crawling back on her knees."

When Mary heard this, she seethed. Had anyone said a word about Chaplin when he was offered almost the same deal? Had anyone called him a bastard for seeking control of his own movies?

Papa couldn't—or wouldn't—meet her demands this time, and they finally parted ways, each of them teary on that last phone call; neither with anything left to say but "goodbye."

Then Mary dried her tears, fixed her curls, and put on a new dress to go over to First National. There she signed her new contract, smiling for the cameras—the only girl in the room.

But—she should have known!—First National immediately began to founder, underfinanced like so many new studios. And in January of 1919, during an industry conference held at the Alexandria Hotel in Hollywood, the rumors began. Famous Players–Lasky and First National were going to merge. The studio heads were tired of the actors calling the shots. If they all merged, if there was nowhere else for actors to go, to grab bigger contracts, then the executives would be back in control. The way they used to be, before people even knew actors' names. Before there ever was a Mary Pickford or a Douglas Fairbanks or a Charlie Chaplin.

Alarm bells went off, particularly among Douglas, Charlie, and Mary, the Triumvirate. Mary especially panicked. If all the studios merged, she asked Douglas feverishly, then what would happen to them? There would be no bargaining chip in future negotiations. They'd all be cattle in the same barn.

Mary never could remember who came up with the idea of their own studio. She did recall that B. P. Schulberg, a wildhaired young man with popping eyes who saw the writing on the wall and knew that in any merger he'd be out of a job as publicity director at Famous Players–Lasky, somehow got wind of their talk. He approached the three of them with some financial projections, and the idea took root. Why not bring together the five biggest stars in the business—Mary Pickford, Douglas Fairbanks, Charlie Chaplin, William S. Hart, and the great D. W. Griffith—and have them form their own studio? Immediately, it would leave the other studios peddling lesser product. And what theater in the United States—or the world— would fail to book one of these five luminaries' films for a lengthy engagement, at a premium cost?

On the last day of the convention at the Alexandria, as the studio heads met behind closed doors and the rumors of mergers flew, the Triumvirate, along with Griffith and Hart, descended upon the hotel dining room, where they demurely ate a very public dinner together. All the while, as if on cue, every studio executive—including Lasky and Zukor—popped in to take a look, then ran off in a panic.

When they made the announcement days later, the entire

industry erupted. And when the dust cleared, Mary Pickford, Charlie Chaplin, Douglas Fairbanks, and D. W. Griffith—Hart got cold feet and decided to remain at Famous Players–Lasky—were partners in their own studio, United Artists. Each partner would produce, direct, and/or star in five pictures a year, and they would distribute their films themselves, not working with Paramount or any of the other exhibitors. Each would have full artistic control; no more having to listen to men—*the men!*—who thought only of the bottom line. No more having to suffer directors like DeMille.

No more having to split the profits with people who had no idea what making a film took out of you, the sweat, the physical toil, baring your soul to the camera that never blinked, coming home dressed in character, going to sleep as that character, drinking coffee as your character would, learning lines and blocking for that day's shoot. Never eating, because the camera added so much weight. Never cutting your hair, because your audience would riot.

Never being with the man you loved, because your fans would never forgive you.

For in those heady days when Mary posed with the other "Big Four," signing contracts or clowning around for the cameras, giddy with the freedom awaiting them, Mary was thrown into Douglas Fairbanks's company again and again. Posing together behind a table, watching Charlie sign his contract. Douglas with Mary and Chaplin perched on his shoulders like circus performers, arms outstretched in a "Ta-da!" pose. All four standing on a porch looking casually professional—and in every photo Mary was forced to stand beside Douglas, to be near him, feel the heat of his skin radiating through his clothes, sense the tensely drawn lines of his muscles as he strained to look casual, chummy, nothing more.

After the cameras were gone, however, it was an entirely different Mary and Douglas. A Mary and Douglas who still donned disguises, even though Douglas was divorced, for their rendezvous; rendezvous that now, more often than not, started out in giddy passion but ended in angry tears.

"Be with me, Mary! Be mine! I'm tired of sneaking around. I gave up my wife and my kid for you. Why won't you get a divorce for me?"

"Because, Douglas! Because—what will my fans say? What will the public say?"

"My fans didn't care one bit, Mary."

"Yes, but—but I have farther to fall than you, Douglas. Because I'm a woman—no, I'm a girl, an innocent little girl, to them. It's not the same."

"You don't know that."

"No, I don't." She said it quietly, almost in a whisper. "But I'm scared to find out."

Because snotty little Miss Josephine never did invite Mary to her birthday party, after all. Never would Mary forget that. She loved making movies; she loved *acting*—without it she wouldn't know what to do with herself. She particularly didn't know what she would do with the emotions that bubbled too close to the surface for everyday life—sometimes she imagined that she had an armful of emotions, like an armful of the most colorful, varied blossoms, and she threw out her hands and released them to the camera, day after day after day—without that release, what would she do with them?

Who would she be? Gladys Smith of Toronto, Canada, with

a family to support and no idea how to do it. And she had no illusions. Douglas Fairbanks would fall out of love with Gladys Smith faster than she could say *Rebecca of Sunnybrook Farm*.

Why now? Why had Douglas decided, at this moment, when the two of them were linked together through United Artists, when they both had so much to gain—and so much to lose—why had he decided that now was the moment to make such a fuss? Ever since his divorce three months ago, he'd been after her to do the same, but never with such finality. Because *he* understood—that was what she told herself every day. He understood as Owen never could how it was for Mary, how unique her position was to her fans, to the world in general. America's Sweetheart. Little Mary. *Our* Mary.

And—it was different for Douglas; it was different for *men*. He could divorce his wife, because he was a dashing, worldly man on-screen. Divorce would only make him more dashing, in a way. But Mary was placed upon an altar. Most of her fans probably still believed she was a virgin, despite her marriage. Women—unless they were vamps on-screen—weren't allowed passion off it. There were words for women who indulged too much in the pleasures of the flesh; disgusting, tawdry words. The worst you could call a man who did the same was *playboy* or *rogue*.

Mary didn't know what to do, and she had no one to talk to. Not Mama, because Mary knew what Mama would say and it wasn't what she wanted to hear. Not Lottie, not Jack. But one day she received a telegram; Fran was coming home to Hollywood! And Mary almost cried with relief; Fran would know what to do! Fran would understand. Fran had been divorced, too.

"Let me talk to Fran," Mary urged Douglas after another of

their tense assignations—what a terrible word! What a putrid way to describe the holy union between her and Douglas! Yet try as she might, she couldn't come up with a different one. As usual, they'd started out passionate, unable to keep their hands off each other after a long afternoon of United Artists meetings during which they could only look, and smile, and smolder. But as soon as the passion was spent they returned to the same subject—Douglas wanted to stay the night, Mary reminded him he had to leave, he brought up his divorce, and then the whole thing started all over again.

Douglas's eyes hardened, his mouth pursed into a stubborn pout.

"I don't see what Fran can tell you that I haven't," he said petulantly.

"Fran has been with me almost every step of the way. She's responsible for so much of my career. She understands me."

"Mary, you don't understand *me*. I don't want to share you with anyone—not your mother, not your sister, not Frances Marion. Not another man—never another man! Promise me, Mary. Promise me that we'll marry and you'll never look at another man the way you look at me. Promise me, sweetheart. Or else—"

"Or else what?" Mary's heart began to thump; she reached out to him but he threw her arm off and began to put on his clothes, tugging so tightly at his shoelaces she feared they'd break.

"Or else I'm going away. Mary, I can't go on like this. I know I've said it before, but this time I mean it. I'm in love and I want the world to know. If you don't divorce that idiot Moore and marry me, you'll never see me again. Not like this."

Mary shivered; his voice was so different. Douglas's voice

was always booming, full of delights yet to be discovered. But now it was dead, flat. There was nothing left to say.

"Let me talk to Fran," Mary begged him.

"I'm through with talking. You know where to find me."

Douglas stalked out the door, leaving her alone in the hotel room feeling tawdry; all her clothes were scattered on the floor, her silk stockings, her satin step-ins, her lacy camisole. One of her shoes was missing; it must be under the bed. What would happen if someone saw her like this?

She wasn't cut out for this, being the other woman, having assignations in hotel rooms. She wasn't cut out for this kind of drama; everything she did on-screen was simple, truthful, no suggestive eye rolls or shoulder wiggles for her. That was for the vamps. And Mary Pickford—Gladys Smith—was no vamp.

But *who* was she? A child on-screen; a passionate, troubled woman off it.

She began to get dressed, trying to concentrate on one thought, only one, out of all the agonies that were tumbling through her mind, causing her head to ache: Did Douglas mean it? Would he really leave her? How would that affect United Artists? Would Owen cooperate?

At that moment, she was tired of being the only woman in the room. She needed Fran. Fran would know what to do. Fran—who had created Little Mary, who had written her very best films. Fran would write her a way out of this.

Fran would give her the happy ending she so desperately desired.

"FRAN, DEAR! YOU LOOK—YOU LOOK—" Mary felt ridiculously shy after she knocked on Fran's door at the Hollywood Hotel; she stopped short of flinging herself into Fran's arms when she opened it. Something held her back.

Fran had changed! She looked different—older, yes, but not in a haggard way. Her black hair was still lustrous, she was as slim as ever but not too slim, and she even seemed to have grown an inch or two, although surely that wasn't possible?

But still, there was something about Fran—a sadness, yet also contentment. She'd always been cheerful, she'd always been fully in the moment, eager to enter into whatever scheme Mary proposed. But Mary had never detected any bit of regret or sadness, and now she did; Fran's eyes carried some memory of sorrow now. But she also seemed purely content in a way she never had; she seemed thoroughly at home in her own skin, not uncertain, not a bit shy. And that skin was surprisingly rosy in a way Mary could not recall. In fact, Fran was much more beautiful than Mary remembered her; how was that possible? Had she changed so much? Or had Mary simply not noticed before?

"How do I look?" Fran spun around, showing off a new, fashionable dress—Mary always felt a bit frumpy next to dear Fran. Frumpy, and short. "I bought this in Paris!"

"Ooh la la!"

That broke the ice. Something—some barrier—had been between them but now it melted away.

"Oh, Fran, I've missed you!"

"Squeebee, darling, I've missed you, too!"

And in a moment they had kicked off their shoes, loosened their stays, and called down to the kitchen for some sandwiches to be brought up; as the sun set outside the window—that bewitching, brief Los Angeles sunset, the sun hovering, hovering, and then abruptly swallowed whole by the ocean—the two of them sat side by side on a sofa, the only item of furniture in the room that wasn't covered with hats and gloves and dresses and skirts.

"I was in the middle of unpacking," Fran said with a groan. She turned her head to survey the room. "I have too many clothes."

"Frances Marion, that's the first time I've ever heard you say that!"

"It's true. Why do I buy so many? It's ridiculous, isn't it? In Europe, all I wore was the same uniform over and over, just like everyone else. I never even thought of clothes, until the war was over. And as soon as I stepped foot on American soil, I had to go shopping. It's a sickness!" She groaned again.

"What does Fred think about your pretty clothes? As matchmaker, I have a vested interest in the two of you!"

"He doesn't mind," Fran admitted, blushing. "He thinks I'm quite the fashion plate."

"You are. You always have been." But then Mary smoothed the silk skirt of her new violet suit, waiting for Fran to notice; even though she couldn't begin to compete with Fran, she *was* dressing much more elegantly than she used to, as befitted the head of her own studio.

"That's lovely," Fran said, her eyes widening. "No more sashes and lace?"

"I don't think so." Mary grinned; she'd finally grown up, that's how it felt, now that Papa wasn't around dictating her behavior and her style. Still, she'd never go too far.

"I saw all the headlines on the train out. Heavens, Mary! What you've done! What you've accomplished! United Artists—what a perfect name for a studio!"

"It made sense. Business sense."

"I'm proud of you. You've invested in yourself, because you're worth it. That's not an easy thing for women to do, for some reason. Heaven knows, men don't seem to have a problem doing it!"

Mary smiled, basking in the admiration in Fran's eyes. Naturally, Mama praised her up and down, as did most of the press. But Fran's approval meant the most. Hadn't she been the one who'd shared the worst humiliation of Mary's career?

"Oh, Fran! Isn't it exciting? And you'll come with me, of course. You'll write for me at United Artists. I need you for my first picture there. I can't imagine doing it without you!" Mary still had to do one picture for First National, but then she was free to concentrate on United Artists. It was both thrilling and daunting; her first film had to be an enormous hit, and she couldn't think of anyone but Fran to write it. As much as she was longing to stretch a bit as an artist, move into some more womanly roles now that she *felt* more womanly, she knew it would be smart to launch United Artists with a sure thing; another movie in which she played a child, since that's what the public seemed to want. So she had in mind to do *Pollyanna;* Fran would do a brilliant job adapting it.

"Well," Frances stalled; she suddenly became very interested in a loose thread on the sleeve of her blouse. "I do have a contract still at Famous Players, I assume?"

"Oh, you can get out of that! Papa and I parted on excellent terms. I know Papa will let you go if I ask."

"I wouldn't feel right about that, Mary." Fran didn't meet Mary's gaze. "Actually, they've already contacted me. They want me to write for Mary Miles Minter—*Anne of Green Gables*. Just the one picture, then I'm free."

"Mary Miles Minter?" Mary scowled, picturing that simpering little moon-faced actress with golden curls *exactly* like hers! It was such an *obvious* ploy, Papa trying to replicate Mary, as if she could be replaced by just anyone with *curls*! And that Minter was such a terrible actress—and Fran and she had often talked of making *Anne of Green Gables*! Mary had loved the books when Fran read them to her, back when they were sharing the bungalows. They'd make a perfect vehicle for Mary.

But Mary swallowed her rage; it wasn't Fran's fault. She was a working scenarist, after all. This was all "dear" Papa's doing.

"I can't start my picture for six months anyway, so of course, Fran. That's all right."

"And, well—Hearst telegrammed. He'd like me to write for Marion."

"Marion Davies? His *mistress*!" Mary couldn't conceal the priggishness in her voice; she heard it, and winced. Because, of course—*she* was a mistress, too.

Fran gave her a look, and Mary nodded, conceding the point. "I know, I know. But it's different! Douglas has his divorce, and now—I love him, Fran. I love him and he wants me to divorce Owen. And I want to! But—sometimes, I don't know if I *deserve* him and a career. I don't want to lose either—but I don't know that I deserve both. Or if I'm even allowed both."

"Isn't that strange? I wonder the same about Fred—if I deserve him. I mean, I've been divorced twice. But you, Mary—what on earth have you done that would make you think you didn't deserve Doug or your success?"

"No—it's not that, it's just—I'm afraid, Fran. I'm afraid of being alone, and I'm afraid of disappointing my fans."

"I see. You have to decide which is more important."

"Yes."

They lapsed into silence; Fran looked thoughtful, while Mary found she couldn't control her hands; she kept poking her hat pin in and out of her hat until she tore a tiny hole in the straw.

Then she threw the hat across the room, startling them both.

"Oh, Fran, I don't want to decide! That's the thing—I *can't* decide! I want to believe I deserve Douglas, I really do. But at what price? That's what I need to know—that's what I need *you* to tell me, darling Fran. Will my fans let me do this? Will they still come to see my movies? Will I still be able to play a child, which is what they want, even if I'm not sure I want to anymore? But if I divorce and remarry, can I even get away with it? I can't—I *won't*—give up my career, Fran. I can't! What would happen to Mama? To Jack and Lottie—" Mary couldn't remain seated; she jumped up to retrieve her hat.

"Is Douglas sympathetic? Or is he—"

"Like Owen?" Mary spun around and met Fran's gaze unblinkingly. "Does he hit me? No, never. Does he resent me? No. Does he want too much from me? Maybe. But he would never ask me to give up my career, not like Owen. But in a way, Douglas *is* asking me to, though I know he doesn't see it like that."

"He's asking you to take a chance. A bigger chance than he had to take."

"Yes! And he's always been so lucky—nothing bad has really ever happened to him. He didn't have the childhood I did. He didn't have to work as hard to get to where he is—he didn't have to give up anything."

"Except his wife and child," Fran said, gently, and Mary's face burned with shame. Yes, of course. Why did she always forget that?

Because *Douglas* didn't seem to miss them; he didn't lie awake at night agonizing about them. He slept the sleep of the sound and just. How was it that men could do that—simply walk away from a family, a child, without a second thought? Mary supposed there were women who could do that, too. But she didn't think she knew any—until she remembered.

Yes. Yes, she did.

"Mary, I can't tell you what to do." Fran shook her head. "You've made every decision about your career so far, and they've all been right. I can only tell you what I think, after years of watching your fans practically tear you to pieces, they love you so. I think they love you so much that they only want your happiness. If they knew how happy Doug makes you—if you *tell* them, I mean—then they'll love you even more."

"But we can't know for sure, can we? Yet Douglas—he wants me to say yes, right now, I'll divorce Owen and marry him. Or else—or else he'll leave me! And, Fran, I can't bear that!" She hid her face in her hands, afraid for Fran to see the anguish and torment in her eyes; she saw it herself every day in the mirror, the way she had deep circles beneath her eyes, her cheeks were sunken, she was losing weight. How could she go before the camera as long as she felt this torment? How could she play an innocent little girl when her body ached with un-fulfilled longing?

Frances got up and put her arm around Mary, very gently—as if she was as startled by this new, lovesick Mary as Mary had been startled by the new, war-weary Fran. She steered Mary back to the sofa.

"Dearest, I think—I think you should tell Doug you'll divorce Owen. I think your fans will only want you to be happy."

"Mama doesn't agree. She keeps reminding me I'm America's Sweetheart. But oh, Fran—I don't want to be anyone's sweetheart but *his*!"

And as she said it, she knew it was true. This moment, anyway.

Fran bit her lip, her eyes thoughtful, deciding. She took a soft breath. "Then do it. Be Douglas's sweetheart."

"Owen said he'd give me a divorce—if I paid him. A hundred thousand dollars, Fran." And as the familiar anger stiffened her spine, Mary wondered: Was the only thing that had kept her in this marriage for so long anger? If she didn't hate Owen, would she have tortured him for years with her absences, her niggling little allowances? Oh, she could have given him more money, anytime, but she didn't; she doled it out so he'd always have to come back begging for more. Most of all, she wouldn't have tortured him with her *success*. Which he had no choice but to observe, up close and personal, every single day of their miserable married life.

Now he wanted money in exchange for a divorce. She wasn't surprised; the man had no self-respect. But the truth of the matter was, he should have paid *her* for every black eye, every bruised arm, every blow to her self-esteem he'd tried to inflict for so long.

"He never even hesitated to name the price," Mary snapped. "He had it on the tip of his tongue, as if he'd only been waiting for me to ask him. One hundred thousand dollars! He put a price on me, exactly like everyone else does—Lottie, Jack, those men at the studio. Even Mama, Fran. Sometimes, I think even Mama does."

"No, not everyone else," Frances reminded her.

"No." Mary shook her head; her curls were a little loose, tickling her shoulders, half-up, half-down. "Not everyone else. Douglas doesn't want my money. He only wants me."

"Then go to him, Mary. I've always believed we're allowed one great love in our lives. I've found mine, thanks to you. Now it's your turn. We can't know the future. But we can know our hearts."

Mary laughed, hollowly. "Who could have imagined we'd be where we are today? Two girls who used to brush each other's hair. Remember those days in the bungalows? Sometimes, Fran—sometimes, I long for those days. Before things were so complicated. When we only had one dream, and it was to make as good a film as Griffith. Remember that? The first time we saw *The Birth of a Nation*?"

"I thought of it often, in France. How easy—how entertaining!—it was to see a film about a war, and how terrible it was to see war, firsthand. But I remember those days, too. You and me and Charlotte. Before we had to deal with *men*! They complicate everything, don't they?"

"Sometimes I think it would be simpler if we loved women. Like Nazimova. You know?"

Frances burst into uncontrollable laughter; Mary simply shrugged, knowing why Fran was so amused. She was picturing Little Mary with the golden halo—Little Mary, the Girl with the Curls!—a lesbian like Alla Nazimova!

"Oh, Mary!" Fran shook with laughter, and finally Mary saw the humor in it; she grinned.

"Well! It would certainly solve a few problems! We'd never have to think about marriage, or what it might do to our careers!"

"Or children, either." Frances swiped the tears from her cheeks. "I think about children now. Don't you? I never did before but now that I've met Fred, I can't picture our life complete without them. Yet I know how much time they'll take, and I want to keep working—Fred wants me to, as well. I suppose that's why God invented nannies."

"Yes, well, my films are my children." Mary sprang up and retrieved the damaged hat, plopping back down on the sofa again. "And I don't believe for one minute you'd be happy playing marbles in the nursery. I know you, Frances Marion! You live and breathe the movies just like I do, and that's why I love you." She kissed Fran on the cheek.

"Mary, of course I'll write *Pollyanna* for you. But I am going to keep writing for others, too. The war—it made me feel there are other issues to explore now, and I like stretching myself a bit. You don't mind?"

Well, yes, she did. When she was envisioning what United Artists would be like, her very own studio—she and Douglas were drawing up plans right now for the construction of their joint lot—she had pictured Fran with her, just like always. She had even gone so far as to pick out the wallpaper and carpet for Fran's office, right next to hers. But Fran was different now; she'd seen things Mary couldn't imagine. She had been to war, real war, while Mary had stayed behind waving flags, *pretending*. There was a new gulf between them filled with different experiences, different ideas. She could only hope they'd find a way to bridge it; she was certain that they could.

"Fran, no. I don't mind. I have a lot on my plate right now, too. I'm going to be making fewer movies, now that I'm running a studio, but they'll be bigger ones—all ten-reelers or more. Of course I can't expect you not to work as often, waiting for me. But promise me one thing, though, Fran. Will you?"

Fran hesitated, playing with that thread on her sleeve again, but then she nodded. "Of course, Mary. Anything."

"Promise me you'll let me be maid of honor at your wedding? I'll never forgive you if you don't! After all, I'm the one who introduced the two of you!"

"Oh, Squeebee, I wouldn't think of asking anyone else!"

"Then it's settled. Now, let's get you unpacked, Fran—this place is a rat's nest!"

Fran laughed, and they set about hanging up her various clothes, exclaiming over Fran's new dresses, negligees, hats, and shoes galore. Mary couldn't help but notice, as she hung it up, that Fran's Army uniform—drab, not at all like the bright blue uniform she'd had made up for herself—had stains on it that couldn't be removed, and she realized she'd neglected to ask Fran about one very important thing; her guilt poked at her with red-hot prongs. How could she have forgotten? She was so caught up in her own drama, she'd forgotten about Fran's.

"Tell me about the war, Fran. Tell me some of what you saw."

Fran was silent for a long while; her face looked weary, but her eyes were startlingly clear. "Well, Mary, there was this shoe . . ."

And the two continued to unpack, Mary listening intently while Fran spoke softly, painting the picture with her words.

I SHOULD HAVE KNOWN THE MOMENT DOUG, WITHOUT even looking, handed his dripping umbrella to Fred.

Or the moment that Mary, unconsciously (or so I hoped), elbowed me back so that I had to walk a few steps behind her as we entered the hotel.

I should have known the moment that Fred and I, waiting patiently in our train compartment in Southampton for the Fairbankses' boat to dock, heard the roar, saw the airplanes, felt the trampling of thousands of feet all around us as the ship pulled into the harbor.

Goodness, I should have known the moment I read the headlines:

FAIRBANKS AND PICKFORD MARRY!!

THE WEDDING OF THE CENTURY!!

HEARTS AND CAREERS UNITED!!

MARY AND DOUG: LOVE EVERLASTING!!

THE POOR LITTLE RICH GIRL IS POOR NO MORE—TRUE LOVE
HAS MADE ME RICHER THAN EVER, SAYS MARY

LONG LIVE THE QUEEN AND KING OF HOLLYWOOD!!

I AM THE LUCKIEST MAN IN THE WORLD,
PROCLAIMS DOUG

THE WORLD SWOONS AT THE MOST ROMANTIC
LOVE STORY IN HISTORY

"Remember the headlines when we married?" I asked Fred, ruefully.

"*Scenarist Marries Athlete,*" he replied. But he also laughed; he truly didn't care, and I wished I didn't, either.

"I don't think this is going to be the quiet honeymoon we planned," I said, and all Fred could do was shake his head and hold his ears to drown out the cheering crowd rattling the windows of our compartment.

A joint honeymoon, Mary had suggested, after she'd surprised me—and the world—by marrying Doug in secret. I'd been a little hurt, to tell the truth, but I instantly seized on the idea of the honeymoon and somehow convinced Fred, too. And now here we were. Waiting for Doug and Mary.

Fred and I had arrived first, sailing to England a month before, in May of 1920. How could it possibly be 1920 already? A new decade; a new life. Already the horrors of war were a distant memory—or so I told all who asked.

Fred had come through safely, too, and our reunion in Paris in December of 1918, a month after the Armistice, had been right out of any Hollywood movie. I was so nervous, waiting in the lobby of the Ritz; I caught my breath every time the revolving door spun round.

My uniform was packed away, and I'd bought a Parisian dress for the occasion, agonizing over the design. Should I dress as alluringly as possible? Or clothe myself somberly, like a

Quaker, out of respect to Fred, his background, the rubble of war still all around, the memories of those who had been lost? In Paris that December, every woman was clad in black, heavily veiled or wearing a black mourning armband. It was a city of widows and bereaved mothers, and I couldn't stop looking at the faces, beautiful in their grief. Resolute mouths, eyes clear but lined with sorrow, pale cheeks. Jewelry was minimal, often fashioned out of bullets or ammunition, and of course there was a preponderance of brooches or lockets that held a loved one's strand of hair. Edwardian fashions could still be glimpsed, but a young woman named Coco Chanel had set up shop at 31 rue Cambon, where she sold simple day dresses made of jersey and evening dresses shimmering with beads, all made with unfussy, straight lines that slightly hugged a woman's body but did not contort it out of its natural shape. It was already being whispered that corsets were on the way out, something I more than welcomed. I'd rarely worn one throughout the war and rejoiced in the freedom of movement, of being able to relax against a chair, bend over easily, walk briskly without fear of passing out.

I finally chose a midnight blue suit for my reunion with Fred; its lines weren't quite as simple as a Chanel, but it was modern and still somewhat dignified, with a wide black velvet lapel and black velvet embellishment at the hem. I wore a smart black velvet tricornered hat; hats were getting smaller, no longer the enormous cartwheels from before the war.

"Frances! Hey, Fran!"

I looked up, heart racing. But it wasn't Fred who was calling my name; to my astonishment, it was George Hill who was hurrying toward me, hat in hand, through the crowded lobby.

"George!" It was so good to see a Hollywood face, especially one I'd known forever. Ever since my days at Bosworth, when I was Lois Weber's "do anything" girl, George had followed me around, working his way up to a cameraman, sometimes trying his hand at screenwriting, too. He was several years younger than me, and I'd gotten used to the way he gazed at me, with adoring, puppy dog eyes. I never encouraged him, but I didn't mind being looked at that way, either. What woman does?

"What a treat to see you!" George shook my hand, too enthusiastically; my elbow nearly snapped in two. "I can't believe my luck! How are you, Frances? I'd heard you were over here, like the rest of us unlucky mugs. How was your war?"

This was the question we all asked each other in Paris. *How was your war?* As if it was dinner, or a traditional holiday. And not the conflagration that destroyed an entire generation of men.

"Fine, fine. I was with the CPI. We filmed women, nurses, you know. How are you? You came through fine, I see."

"Yes, lots of us were lucky. I was stationed in Italy, where it wasn't so bad. But it's over now, and here you are! You'll have dinner with me, won't you, Fran?" George's brown eyes were wide and hopeful, and I remembered something Mary had once said. *He's your Mickey. George adores you, Frances. But he would never say so. He's lovesick.*

Mary was right, but George was a boy. Even now that he was in military uniform—a captain, even, which added a few years to even the most callow farm lad—I still thought him that. Just a boy. Whereas Fred was—

"Frances!"

"Fred!" I was wrapped up in powerful arms, lifted off my feet, and twirled around. Out of the corner of my eye I saw

George, only a blur. But still I caught the way his grin faltered, and I didn't care, I didn't want to think about him at all, and when Fred finally set me down, George had vanished.

"Fred, Fred! You're here!" My tongue felt loose and stupid in my mouth; words, usually my reliable allies, would not come. Entire sentences seemed impossible. The only thing I could do was sit down on a chair, my knees suddenly wobbly, and stare up at him. Forever.

"We've come through, Frances. Both of us." The light in Fred's eyes dimmed a little, and I understood; he'd seen things he didn't want to talk about. We both had. Hurriedly I suggested all the things we might do together in Paris, now that we both had leave: see the Louvre, Versailles, Napoleon's Tomb.

And so we did; our scant few weeks in Paris together were a kaleidoscope of memories that I knew, even as we were making them, I would treasure forever. Fred posing with his hand in his jacket, à la Napoleon, at the vast marble tomb. Fred trying his first snail, the tiny fork held so awkwardly in his big paw of a hand, a sincerely puzzled expression on his face that made me giggle until I thought I would choke. Fred coaxed into ordering wine with dinner by an insistent waiter; "teetotaler" was not a word the French understood.

Every evening, saying good night, I was aware of a peculiar feeling in the air; a tense vibration that only my ears could hear. It was like a high-pitched violin, stuck on one note, a pleasant note, but still one waited, breathless, for the next. Which never came.

We lingered in darkened doorways—we were both staying at the Ritz, but on different floors—kissing. Other times, we clung to each other, using touch to become better acquainted; his fingers traced my jawline, I brushed his lapel; he nuzzled my cheek, I placed the flat of my palm against his iron abdomen. Always through clothing, which for the first time didn't seem like a barrier. More like a gate that would be opened, soon.

I longed for him. He longed for me. Our two strong bodies, young, in the best physical condition—how could it be otherwise? Especially when the hearts housed within those bodies reached out, as if each was a magnet for the other. And so was that insistent one note that hummed between the two of us.

We talked about everything. Except for one thing: the war. Fred was as reluctant to talk about his experiences, what he had seen, as I was. So we didn't, but still we seemed to understand, anyway, that we each had gone through a trial only to emerge stronger.

Had I, though? When finally we had to part—he was staying behind to organize and compete in the Inter-Allied Games, an amateur athletic meet—I did not feel strong. I was as weak as a parched flower, overwhelmed by the months we would have to endure before we could meet again; trying to hold on to the thought that when he came home, we would be married.

At the gangplank I clung to him, as if I could absorb him, carry some of his physical presence with me across the ocean. But he finally had to pull away and give me a gentle shove so I wouldn't miss my ship. And when I disembarked in New York, I found myself surrounded by cameras and reporters, all under the direction of the head of the Famous Players–Lasky publicity department—and I instantly fell into the old Hollywood ways, smiling, posing, quipping for the reporters.

Poof! Paris and Fred, both, were far more than an ocean away.

Inside my valise were sixteen reels of film I had to edit, and I threw myself into the work, proud when *American Women at*

War was shown, in serialization, at select theaters. But by then, nobody really wanted to watch anything about the war. The film came and went without notice and I had to wonder why I'd volunteered in the first place; what, really, had I accomplished? Who had I really helped? I told these women's stories, but nobody cared. And when, years later, movies about the war *were* popular—movies like *The Big Parade* and *What Price Glory?*—it was the soldiers' stories people wanted. Not the women's.

I lingered in New York, marveling at how changed the city was. Now that Prohibition had been enacted; now that everyone was back from the war and hemlines were rising and morals were plummeting. Everyone knew "a guy." A guy who could get them gin or wine or whatever they desired. Everyone knew "a place." A place—a speakeasy, they were beginning to be called—where with a password or a secret handshake and a wink, a magic door would be opened and you could step into a rabbit hole, like Alice. Only this Wonderland was filled with the new, frenzied music called "jazz," and smoke from cigarettes, and girls in loose-fitting dresses, hemlines creeping up above the ankles, falling into the laps of men in tuxedos whose ties were always a little askew, eyes always a little bloodshot. Everyone drank too much because who knew what would happen tomorrow? There might be a raid, all the liquor might get confiscated by the Feds—it could all be gone tomorrow. *Everything* could be gone tomorrow; hadn't the war taught us that? So drink up, Alice! Drink it all up, grow small or tall, or anything else you might imagine!

I didn't drink up, not like my chums. I enjoyed going to an occasional speakeasy with Dorothy Parker, my old friend from the Algonquin, or with Anita Loos, who was in New York with her fiancé, John Emerson, no longer writing for Douglas Fairbanks. But I felt like an imposter; a visitor from another planet—a planet named Fred Thomson. Goodness knows, I was no prude but I watched the abandon, the sloppy drunkenness, the affairs begun, consummated, and ended in a single evening, with the clinical dispassion of an archaeologist—or a writer. I stored the images up, because I understood that films would have to reflect this new morality. Oh, when I recalled some of those early films with Bosworth—the cavewoman movie!—I shuddered at the idea of these bright young things hooting in laughter at the archaic titles and costumes and story lines. No—movies must keep up with the times; that was one thing I understood. So I observed, I watched, I took notes. But not once did I tuck a flask in my own garter.

When are you coming home? I need you! Mary telegraphed once, twice, three times. Then she called. Then she sent bouquets of flowers bearing the same message.

Why was I avoiding her? My best friend in the entire world? I had no idea; I only knew that I feared returning to the old status quo. I supposed that was one thing I'd learned from war; I was strong, I was capable. I didn't need Mary to pave the way for me anymore.

But I did miss her, and her distress was obvious; once again, I felt the thrill of having been chosen. Mary *needed* me, and I could never say no to that. So after three weeks in New York City, I boarded the train and headed west to Mary, and her dilemma with Doug.

But as soon as Fred returned home in November of 1919, I took the first train back east, and we were married. A quiet ceremony witnessed by Charlotte and Mary, who had come east, too. Finally, that night, we removed the barriers between us. And I never heard that peculiar, stuck note ever again.

We had no time for a honeymoon. I had to get right to work, writing *Humoresque* for Hearst, dashing back to Hollywood for *Pollyanna* with Mickey and Mary. But it wasn't quite the same. We had fun on the set, of course, but I couldn't help feeling stuck in the past; this was the same kind of movie we'd made before the war, and it seemed a little stale. None of us lingered at the studio at the end of the day. Mary went home to deal with her dilemma, Mickey went out on even more epic benders. And I went home to Fred—who was restless, champing at the bit trying to figure out what he would do, now that ministry was out of the question due to his marrying a divorcée.

When I got a call from Hearst asking me to direct my first film, a quickie called *Just Around the Corner,* to be filmed in a week in Manhattan, I agreed. With one condition.

"Fran, I don't know," Fred answered, when I asked him if he'd play a small role. He was being careful; as careful as I'd been with him these last few months. Even while I was so busy, earning all the money, I'd tried to play it down by saying things like "How silly this is!" and "What a ludicrous thing I'm doing!"

I was appalled at myself for disparaging my talent, my industry, just to preserve Fred's ego, but honestly, I didn't know what else to do. Despite his very vocal support of my career, I knew his pride was hurt at not being the provider. I knew it because every evening when I came home, as if on cue, he very pointedly asked me how my day had been. I came home earlier than I ever had, and it wasn't only because Mary and Mickey left early, too. No, I was afraid *not* to come home to dinner; I couldn't leave Fred alone to do—what, exactly? Fred would never behave like so many men did. But I didn't want him to think my work was more important than he was; I never wanted to give him any reason to regret leaving the ministry for me. He may have said he respected my career, but I could never forget that his first wife had always had dinner waiting for him when he came home.

"Please, Fred, help me out with this. I think you're a natural actor—what preacher isn't? And I'm really in a jam. The actor we hired took another job. Please help."

Of course, Fred Thomson couldn't refuse a lady's plea, and so he showed up on set, suffered through makeup manfully, hit his marks, and played his scene as I—very respectfully—asked him to. When I saw my husband on film for the first time in the editing room, I was overjoyed. He was a natural! A star! But I knew I had to be cautious; I couldn't push too hard. Fred would have to come to this decision on his own, and it would take time. I thought the vacation in Europe with Doug and Mary might help; he'd be the odd man out, the only one not in the business.

So we waited in our train compartment for Hollywood itself, in the form of its newly crowned king and queen, to arrive. Which it did—with the ferocity of a hurricane.

Mary and Doug burst into the train compartment where we'd been waiting, laughing, exclaiming, Mary's arms full of flowers, Doug energetically shaking his hat, dripping with raindrops and rose petals.

"Fran! They dropped buckets of petals on us when we docked! From an aeroplane, Fran!"

"I thought they'd tear the missus to pieces, but boy, what a reception!"

Mary flung herself in my arms, the flowers scratching my cheek but I hugged her tightly anyway, while Doug, still laughing, bounded over to Fred and gave him a hearty handshake.

Even as I was caught in Mary's slightly hysterical embrace, I saw the exchange out of the corner of my eye. Fred, so tall, loomed over compact Doug. And Doug registered this with a fleeting sour expression before pumping Fred's hand up and down, then pretending to arm wrestle with him. Fred, however, simply pulled his giant paw away and patted Doug, fraternally—although I suspected Doug didn't take it that way—on the back.

Uh oh, I thought. Right before Doug handed Fred his dripping umbrella to hold.

"Fran, have you ever seen such a thing?" Mary fell down onto a chair and surveyed her clothes—she had a rip on one sleeve, and her collar was torn. "I never imagined a reception like this! You'd think we were royalty!"

"We are," Doug exclaimed, leaping over to Mary's side. "Haven't you read the newspapers?"

"Fran, I couldn't have been more wrong!" Mary pulled off her hat as the train began to lurch away from the station. We would be in London within an hour. "I was so afraid of what might have happened to my career, but you know what someone said? 'The world loves lovers,' and that's so true. Our fans, our dear, dear fans, couldn't be happier for us! You should have seen the mob when we were in New York! We went to the Follies, and the show absolutely stopped when we were recognized. They must have clapped for ten minutes straight, and then Douglas had to make a speech before the show could go on!"

"I'm so happy," I assured her. "I'm so relieved for you both." I nestled down with Fred on a sofa, and waited for Mary to ask how our trip had been so far.

But Mary didn't; she kept popping up from her seat to fix her hair or brush her clothes, or sit in Doug's lap, or relate another amazing headline or letter—she and Doug had received congratulations from the White House, Buckingham Palace, from the emperor of Japan, even! She babbled and babbled, more keyed up than I'd ever seen her. And Douglas was determined to physically reenact it all, so that by the time the train slid into Waterloo Station, I was exhausted just from watching him.

Fred never said a word; he laughed and nodded in all the right places, the perfect audience. But I knew that he felt the way I did. That Doug was ridiculous—but he had always been somewhat ridiculous to me, a man who made up for a stunning lack of intellect with an excess of physicality, a full-body sleight-of-hand so that you wouldn't notice the shortcoming. But to my dismay, Mary had changed, too. Even after so little time together, I couldn't help but notice that she had morphed into someone—something—I could barely recognize. She'd always been so levelheaded, so earnestly anxious to be worthy of the respect and adoration of her fans—that was one of the things I loved the most about her. That she understood how much she owed others, that her position was one of privilege but never permanence. But this Mary Pickford—*Mrs. Douglas Fairbanks*—seemed to take all that love, adoration, for granted. As if it were her *due*.

I bit my tongue even as I longed to take her down a peg or two—I felt I was the only person in her life besides Charlotte who might have a chance at rescuing her from her new self, but now was not the time. The entire world, it seemed to me, was waiting for us at the station.

The moment we stepped out of our compartment we were swallowed up by the most enormous crowd I'd ever seen. Faces—so many faces! Faces eerily white in the glare of photographers' flash-lamps, which kept bursting with frightening "pops" that punctuated the frenzied screams pounding my eardrums. I knew that I was yelling—but what, I couldn't say, because I couldn't hear my own voice. Pummeled from all sides, I searched for Fred, taller than anyone else, and I was able to cling to him, and scream that he should grab Mary, too, which he did; he steered the two of us through the crowd that pressed in closer, toward the waiting touring car—a car with its top down, which made me freeze with terror.

"Mary! Doug! Our Mary!"

Doug managed to grab the back of my coat; he was sputtering, reaching out to grab Mary, and I was stunned to see the anger, the jealousy in his dark eyes as he finally retrieved his wife in time to push her into the car. Someone stepped on my foot; a hand grabbed the back of my skirt as someone tried to shove me aside to get to Mary, but I wrestled out of the woman's grip so that I could hurtle myself into the car, where I plopped down next to Fred. A glowering Doug was staring at him.

Mary, however, was flinging kisses to one and all; there was an enormous bouquet of roses in her lap, the ribbons torn to shreds, most of the petals gone from the flowers. As the car began to push away, just as Mary flung one more kiss, someone yanked her arm, and she was torn out of her seat as we all screamed in terror.

Fred grabbed her by the waist and kept her inside the car; miraculously, she was released from the crowd. She slumped back in her seat with a stunned expression on her face.

I hadn't been able to move; I was unable to process everything that had just happened. But I managed to catch Doug's expression, and was again shocked by the anger, the *jealousy,* as he glared at Fred.

"Unhand my wife, please, Thomson," he said, and then attempted to grin his anger away. "You have your own, you know, old chap."

"Sorry." Fred shrugged. "I was only trying to help."

"Well, don't." Doug's eyes were deadly serious as he still tried to charm with his million-dollar movie-star smile. "I can do the job myself."

"Of course." Fred nodded, then we sank into silence, which was just as well, as the screams of the crowd when our car began to slowly pull away from the station made any conversation impossible. Lord, people were hanging from windows! Climbing lampposts like monkeys! Perched on the tops of roofs! Running alongside the car, panting, yelling, throwing things inside—flowers for the most part, but teddy bears and boxes of candy, too, until I was afraid we might be buried alive.

Fortunately, we pulled up to a back alley entrance of The Ritz, and bobbies were somehow able to keep the hysterical crowd from following. We got out of the car and stared at each other, panting, unbelieving; Fred and I were appalled, terrified. But Mary and Doug were grinning like they'd won a prize for something.

"Tupper, shall we?" Doug said to Mary, giving him her arm.

"Hipper, my pleasure," Mary replied with a regal bow. They ascended the stairs to the hotel, as Fred and I fell dutifully back, a few steps behind. And I remembered there used to be a time when Mary apologized to me whenever she had to stop and sign autographs; there used to be a time when she understood how to be a friend as well as a movie star.

"Lord and lady-in-waiting to the king and queen," I snapped.

Fred nodded, his jaw set; I'd yet to see him angry, and wondered if this was what it looked like. "I don't know about you, Fran, but I think this could get real old, real quick."

I looked ahead at Mary, arm in arm with King Douglas. The girl I knew and loved, the dedicated workaholic, the dutiful daughter, the loyal friend who sat next to me so many sultry evenings on the porch, confiding and laughing and sharing ambitions and fears and dreams—she *had* to still be in there. Beneath the invisible tiara that I could plainly see, perched regally on those golden curls.

"Perhaps it won't be like this all the time," I whispered back.

All I could do was hope, because we had several weeks ahead of us and already I was thinking that this might have been the most foolish thing I'd ever agreed to in my life. Even more foolish than going to war. Because unlike the war, this time I wasn't so certain that I'd come through it intact.

THE NEXT MORNING, I was startled awake by a pounding on our hotel room door.

"What on earth?" I poked Fred, but he was still snoring. So I wrapped myself up in a robe and ran to the door of our suite.

Mary, clad only in a nightgown—a very sexy nightgown, I couldn't help but notice; nothing like the prim Victorian cotton nightgowns I'd seen her in before; this was satin, with thin straps and a plunging neckline—ran into the room, her hands covering her face but even so, I could tell she was blushing.

A furious Doug, in *his* pajamas, came stomping in behind her.

"Oh, Fran! Fran! I never—I opened the curtains, you see! To take in the morning air, to see what our view was. And—oh, Fran!" Mary's hands slid from her face, which was still scarlet. But her eyes were dancing with delight. "There they were! All of them—all those dear people! Hanging from trees, staring up at me from the pavement below. And they all saw me! In—this!" She gestured toward her nightgown.

Fred, sleepily tying the belt around his robe, stepped out of the bedroom, took one look at Mary in full dishabille—and more significantly, at a hopping-mad Doug—then turned on his heel and headed right back inside, shutting the door loudly.

"They saw my wife!" Doug exploded. He strode around the room, swinging his arms, his hands balled into fists. "They saw her like *this*!"

"Oh, Douglas!" Mary giggled, rosy and twittering, and I couldn't help but feel that I was witnessing a play, written and performed entirely for my benefit.

"We have to move out of here! We have to go somewhere quiet!" Doug thundered.

And so we did. No one asked Fred or me if we wanted to leave; it was simply expected that if Doug and Mary wanted to go somewhere else, then so did we. Reluctantly, we bade farewell to the luxury of The Ritz to stay at a secluded estate, at the invitation of some Lord and Lady Something-or-other.

And the same exact thing happened the next morning.

AT THE TOWER OF LONDON, where we were given an exclusive tour after regular hours, we tramped up and down, watched Doug hang from his hands outside a tiny stone window while Mary feigned terror, applauded as he bounded up narrow, steep stairs two at a time, as if he were filming one of his movies. It occurred to me that Doug was always *on*, always playing to the camera whether or not it was there.

It was a lovely day. I wanted to linger at everything—the crown jewels, the tiny room where the doomed little princes were kept—but Doug raced through it all as if he were leading a charge, pausing only to clown in front of the impassive guards in their tall, furry black hats, or to exclaim to the awestruck tour guide that he'd love to borrow some of the armor for his next movie.

"Look here, Mary," he said when we reached the ghostly quiet of the Tower Green. "This is where Henry the Eighth beheaded all six of his wives!"

"Actually," I said after a moment. "He only beheaded two of them, Anne Boleyn and Catherine Howard. The other four died natural deaths."

The look Doug gave me! I hadn't been on the receiving end of such a scolding look since I was in primary school. He pursed his lips, his eyes went dead, and with a childish huff, he turned and stalked away.

"Thank you, Fran, dear," Mary replied as she watched

Doug storm off. "How very informative! But, well—perhaps it's best, in the future, not to contradict Douglas. You know how men are—they do love to tell us women what's what!"

"But, Mary, you've never let any man tell you what's what in all the years I've known you."

"It's not like that, Fran—it's just—it's just a little different, please try to understand." Mary raised her eyebrows in such a meltingly pleading way, I had no choice but to swallow my anger, smile weakly, and nod.

Still, as Mary hurried after Doug, I hung back, taking deep breaths. How petty of that man! How fragile his ego—how strong his hold on Mary! He was so ignorant—this wasn't the first time I'd been appalled at his lack of knowledge and, now that I thought of it, I'd never once seen him reading anything other than a fan magazine—but ignorance is one thing. Jealousy—for he *was* jealous of me, I realized with a small, victorious thrill—was quite another. The idiot was jealous of *me,* of my friendship with Mary.

Then a black mood settled over my shoulders like a heavy, musty old shawl. If I were to remain close friends with Mary, I was going to have to put up with Doug's jealousies, flatter and soothe his vanity, swallow his insults and ignore his fits of temper.

And I didn't *want* to. Being with Fred had taught me that I shouldn't have to; that there were men in this world who weren't threatened by women. He'd not only taught me, I realized; he'd spoiled me for any other man, forever.

"Come along, Miss Smartypants." I looked up; Fred was smiling down at me with wry humor in his eyes. "Let's go mollify the king. Maybe I'll let him win at arm wrestling. That should make him happy."

"You are the best husband in the world," I declared as we strode, arm in arm, after Doug and Mary. "I adore you."

"The feeling is mutual." Fred leaned down to kiss my cheek.

I had to stifle a laugh, however, as Doug, seeing our intimacy, suddenly grabbed Mary about the waist and pulled her to him in a passionate embrace that made the tour guide—and the guards—practically swoon with admiration.

"Goodness, Douglas! What on earth has gotten into you?" Mary gasped, laughing and blushing.

Fred and I exchanged a look. But kept our mouths shut.

THE MORNING OF THE Chelsea Garden Party. A glorious sunny day, the four of us all decked out in our finest. Mary wore a lovely dark blue organza tea dress with a fluttery wide-brimmed hat; I was in an equally lovely embroidered linen dress with a becoming satin bow. We were both in elbow-length white gloves, and we giggled as we surveyed ourselves in the mirror of my dressing room.

"Who'd have thought it, Fran? That me, little Gladys Smith from Toronto, would be all decked out, as prim and proper and fancy as the queen herself!"

"I couldn't have imagined it, either. What a long way we've come!" And for a moment, as Mary beamed at me, I could almost pretend that it really was the way it used to be, between us.

Then I heard a cough, and I dropped Mary's hand as if it were a hot stone. Turning, I beheld an impressive Doug and Fred in tails and top hats, although I couldn't help but notice Fred was the more handsome, the lines of the tails accentuating his slim height, while Doug, to be honest, looked a little dumpy in his.

"Well, aren't we lucky?" I asked Mary. "To be escorted by the two most handsome men in all of England?"

Fred clicked his heels and bowed, very exaggeratedly, but Doug seemed to take me at my word, for he gave me the first approving smile he'd yet to bestow, and thanked me sincerely.

Outside, we stepped into two separate open cars. "Do you think this is safe?" I asked one of the bobbies who was riding with us.

"Don't worry," Mary and Doug's escort, the actor George Grossmith Jr., replied airily. "This is a civilized party. And we are a civilized people. After you, Mr. Pickford."

Mary, Fred, and I all gasped; Doug froze, but then smiled gamely as Grossmith, recognizing his error, began to sputter an apology.

"It's all right, old man. I'm flattered to be known as the man who escorted Mary Pickford to England." And in that moment I finally found a shard of admiration and affection for Doug. At least he was no Owen Moore; how many times had I witnessed Owen, when similarly addressed, respond with fisticuffs or threats?

I settled down with Fred in our unattended car—"Presumably, our lives aren't worth as much," Fred whispered as I grabbed his hand and giggled—and the two motors began to thread their way through surprisingly quiet streets. I relaxed.

"Mr. Grossmith was right," I said with relief. But then the small motorcade turned a corner, approaching the grounds of the party.

I stiffened; Fred exclaimed. For before us was a throng; a great gaping stampede of people screaming at the tops of their lungs at the first glimpse of Doug and Mary. It was far worse than the scene at Waterloo Station; as the crowd reached in and grabbed Mary, bodily tearing her out of the car, I screamed and heard Grossmith sputter, utterly appalled, "I say, unhand that lady!"

Fortunately Doug grabbed his wife about the waist and held on for dear life; in a flash, Fred had leaped out and was helping Doug stagger out of the car with his arms around Mary. Whose face registered pure terror; she was white as a sheet, her eyes huge, her mouth crookedly shaping cries and gasps.

"Mary!" I darted after Fred, and watched—again with admiration—as Doug, strong despite his small stature, managed to stay on his feet with Mary perched on his shoulders. The four policemen were simply staring at the crowd with their mouths open, so I ran up and hung on to Mary's skirt as Fred, reliving his football days, charged in front, clearing a path as best he could.

I'd never heard such a sound—pitched shrieks and hysterical cries. Tears in people's eyes; blind worship and adoration. At one point I locked eyes with a terrified Mary and I knew what she was thinking—of that moment when we snuck in to see the showing of *The Poor Little Rich Girl,* and we both first recognized the effect Mary had on a crowd. At the time it had been scary, but now it seemed like a wade in the kiddie pool compared to this desperate dive through an ocean of—well, "fans" wasn't quite the word. What was the right word for these people, these weeping and laughing and hysterical people who so desperately *needed* Mary and Doug, needed to project their every hope and dream on these two who beamed upon them from their movie screens even during the darkest days of the war that, after all, had only just ended?

I wondered if these survivors of war needed the sun, after so much darkness; Mary and Doug, together, had enough energy and light to power any number of stars. Even I could see that as impressive as they were individually, together the two of them glowed and shimmered and seemed to expand; two small people that flourished in the spotlight, took root and grew tall and proud and seemed to feed and nourish even the most starved for affection, for fun, for entertainment, for something good in lives that had too recently been wrecked with pain and loss.

But how to survive so close to that fiery sun? That was my own personal dilemma as I clung to the hem of Mary's now-torn gown—had it been only a few minutes ago that we were admiring our finery in front of the mirror? Doug lurched about with her on his shoulders, finally stumbling into a tent full of glass jars of jams and jellies for sale; there was a crash and a crunch and suddenly my hands, my face were sticky with goo.

At last, Fred found an empty tent where a panting, huffing Doug could unceremoniously deposit his tiny, terrified wife. More policemen had arrived and formed a perimeter around the tent; despite the frenzied cries, no one broke through. And we were finally able to take a breath, Doug mopping his streaming forehead, his tails no more—only ragged ends where they once had been. Both men had lost their top hats. George Grossmith Jr. was huddled in a corner, utterly befuddled, saying over and over, "I declare I've never seen such a thing in my life!"

Mary was sticky and grimy, her hair a frizzy golden halo, her dress torn and splattered with jam. Somewhere, I'd lost my gloves, and my new satin shoes were covered in strawberry juice, utterly ruined.

"Anyone have some toast? I believe I've found the jam," Doug quipped as he mournfully surveyed his jacket, and I had to laugh, as Mary and Fred did the same, and soon we were all four in hysterics while Grossmith watched us, his monocle raised to his eye in alarm.

"Now what?" I asked when we'd finally laughed ourselves out, but still were trapped in this tent, our enchanting day completely ruined. My voice was ragged and I realized I was parched; what I wouldn't have given for a tall glass of cool lemonade.

Fred sank down in an empty folding chair, his long legs stretched out in front of him.

Mary and Doug glanced at each other.

"I think," Mary said, hesitantly, looking at Doug for confirmation with every word. "I think we ought to go somewhere else for a while. Germany, maybe? The Netherlands? Where it might be quieter?"

"Whatever you say, Tupper," Doug replied after a moment during which he and Mary stared at each other, as if trying to read each other's minds. "You're the one who was nearly torn in two back there. I'll do whatever you say."

But I thought I detected a flicker of disappointment in his eyes.

HOLLAND WAS LOVELY, but Germany was even better, and finally I was content; *this* was the honeymoon I'd envisioned. Leisurely drives and sunny picnics, just the four of us, no crowds. Germany had forbidden the showing of Allied films during the war, so very few people even knew who Mary and Doug were. With no real audience other than us, Doug was different—quieter, moodier, but at least there were no flashes of anger or impatience—and he and Fred spent a lot of time together talking about the physics of some of Doug's stunts, comparing them to Fred's athletic feats. They discovered they both shared a passion for the Old West and an admiration for the few genuine cowboys who still poked around Los Angeles. Many afternoons we all went riding, and Fred and Doug competed to see whose horse could jump the highest.

I managed to keep biting my tongue until it nearly fell off whenever Doug decided to play tour guide, despite his many inaccuracies. Even when we stopped in Koblenz, which of course I remembered from my earlier—fantastic—visit there at the end of the war, I didn't point out familiar sights. I also didn't talk about my war experience; Fred and I had decided privately not to do so now that we were in Germany. For even that might stoke Doug's jealousy and wound his pride, and neither of us wanted to break this fragile peace. I'd gone out of my way to assure both Doug and Mary, many times, that what they had done on their bond tours had been as important as anything Fred and I had done. Probably more so.

Although I didn't really feel that way, if I were being truthful.

Once we arrived at our small inn in Koblenz, Mary received a message from the commander of the occupying American forces inviting us to a ball in our honor. Naturally, Mary accepted, and we decided to pass the morning relaxing with a picnic.

Sprawling on a blanket gazing at the Rhine, somehow smaller than I remembered it from that harrowing night, I was the happiest I'd been in days. When I looked at Mary I saw my friend again, not the reigning queen of the world; she was relaxed, her face youthful without makeup, unlined and open and fresh, her skin radiant. I recognized that being in Doug's presence did something to Mary; it turned her into a desirable woman, which was most definitely at odds with the image she usually projected.

I leaned back against Fred's knees and closed my eyes, utterly peaceful in the bucolic quiet, blissful in the knowledge that we had many more days of this ahead of us. Years ago, Mary and I had talked of traveling through Europe together and this, finally, was like we'd dreamed; meandering days spent with guidebooks in our hands, picnics with baskets full of strange foods—today, the hotel cook had made Braunschweiger sandwiches, which tasted a little bit like liverwurst, and I didn't really care much for either. But still, I'd tried it. Sighing loudly, it was as if I'd exhaled for all of us; how could the day be any more perfect?

Suddenly Mary made a little noise of disgust and leapt up, knocking over a bottle of lemonade.

"I can't stand this! Douglas, can you?"

"What?" Doug, who was sprawled on his back, his darkly tanned face turned to the sun like an acolyte, opened one eye.

"This! This—quiet! Nobody recognizes us here! And I don't know about you, but I've worked too hard to toil away in anonymity!"

"I agree!" And in a flash, Doug was on his feet beside her. "You're right, Tupper! I can't stand all this quiet, either. Nobody even looks at me twice over here. So let's go somewhere where they do know us!"

"Are you serious?" I pushed myself away from Fred, who raised an eyebrow but otherwise remained neutral. "Mary, are you?"

"As serious as a priest. Let's go to this dance tonight and then after that, Douglas, why don't we go to Italy? They showed our pictures there during the war."

"I'll make the arrangements." And Doug looked as if he was going to bound off to do it right then and there, before seeming to remember that Fred and I were still on the blanket, gaping up at him.

I exchanged a glance with Fred. Clearing my throat, I caught Mary's attention.

"I don't think we'll be joining you, then," I began, not knowing how Mary would react—not sure how I *wanted* her to react. If Mary didn't care whether we left, I'd be devastated. If Mary did care, I'd feel guilty.

"That's fine, Fran," Mary said without hesitation. "I understand. You've been here longer than we have, anyway—we did have to join you late. And, of course, you two aren't used to all this attention, like we are."

As the full weight of Mary's words fell upon me, the sun seemed to dim in the sky.

"No, of course we aren't," Fred agreed in his wry way. And as Doug and Mary began to chatter about their plans, only I could tell, by the way Fred's muscles hardened into rocks against my spine, that he was angry.

"Well, we'll miss you, you old beans," Doug chirped, incredibly—ecstatically—joyful. He clapped Fred on the shoulder. "But we'll see you back in Hollywood! I want you to teach me how you won the high jump."

"And, of course, Fran, we'll be back at work too soon." Mary beamed at me. "I love that idea you told me, about the Italian girl—I think that should be our first film when we get back."

Of course, I was happy that Mary had liked the idea I'd pitched; it was bold for me to do so, and the film would be a big departure for her. Perhaps there would be something in it for

Fred. Mary had suggested that I direct it, too, and I was stunned by the opportunity. Directing a two-reeler for Hearst was one thing; directing Mary Pickford was quite another. "I can't think of anything I'd like better than being directed by a woman, especially one who also happens to be my best friend," Mary had declared, and I'd been thrilled.

But still. I couldn't help it. Right now I was hurt. Even if Fred and I had been the ones to suggest parting ways, Mary and Doug should have protested. Just a little. The old Mary would have; the Mary I thought I knew, and loved.

I opened my book, because I didn't want to see Mary's face right then; I didn't want to be reminded that Squeebee had already forgotten about me. So I concentrated fiercely on turning the pages.

But the words were only a blur.

THAT AFTERNOON, FRED AND I DECIDED to remain at the hotel while Mary and Doug went shopping; we spent the time blissfully in bed, and I thrilled at the now-familiar, but still intoxicating, mounds and planes of Fred's body. His muscles were hard and sinewy, his bones long, his stomach a flat, hardened washboard. He, too, delighted in tracing my softer, more pliant body, over and over, as if trying to memorize it.

And at night, even though we both went to sleep on our own pillows, somehow Fred always ended up with his head sharing mine, as if he couldn't bear to be apart from me even in his dreams.

"Don't try to outshine Doug tonight," I warned as, reluctantly, we began to dress for the dance. "I know you don't mean to, but you're so—so—"

"Tall?" Fred laughed as he splashed water on his face from a basin. He dried himself vigorously with a hand towel, and his hair flopped into his eyes—that boyish look that made my heart flutter.

"Well, yes. But you know what I mean." I began to brush my hair, knowing full well that Fred loved to watch me do it; he could sit for hours at the edge of the bed watching me pull the brush through my long black tresses—seductively looking at him through the reflection of the mirror, of course.

He groaned when I picked up the brush but—with his athletic and religious discipline—he turned away and resolutely began to look through the wardrobe for his dinner jacket and pants.

"Well, I'm glad they're leaving," he said, finally acknowledging the black fog that had hung in the air ever since this morning. "I'm glad we don't have to keep it up any longer. I don't know how you've done it all these years."

"What do you mean?" I stopped brushing and swiveled around to look at him.

"I mean coddling their egos, standing a few feet back, never taking the spotlight. I know Mary's your best friend, but it's not an equal relationship. And it should be—you're more intelligent, you're incredibly gifted, you're respected in your own right. But I'm not sure that Mary sees that, to tell the truth."

"You're wrong about that," I snapped—too quickly, before any of my own long-repressed suspicions could bubble up to the surface, released by his words. "Mary respects me. More than any other scenarist around. I'm her equal. She wants me to direct her next film, Fred. She's never had a woman direct her before."

"Did you read this?" Fred reached into a valise and took out a British newspaper. "I bought this in London before we left. Here." He handed it to me, pointing to the article on the front page, beneath a huge headline trumpeting *DOUG AND MARY ECSTATIC ABOUT WELCOME!*

I scanned the article, written about a week after we arrived in London, the usual purple prose. Then I came across one sentence that seemed to have been printed in blacker, thicker ink than the rest: *"Yes," Miss Pickford said, "we're traveling with my scenarist, so we've brought a little bit of Hollywood with us."*

"She didn't even mention you," I said, handing the newspaper back to Fred. I didn't want to read any more.

"She didn't mention *you,* Frances! Not by name, anyway. *My scenarist.* As if she owns you. As if she alone created you."

"You know she did, in a way." I turned back to the mirror, resolutely brushing, as if I could untangle my feelings as well as my hair. I wondered if I could ever make Fred understand how it was in those first years. He'd only known me once I was already the most successful scenarist in Hollywood. He had no idea how unsure of myself I'd been when I first met Mary, how much I needed someone to tell me what to do. "Without Mary I'd have no career. She gave me my first break—she let me in. She helped me find my way."

"I don't buy it. Frances, you're so intelligent, so talented. You would have done it on your own anyway."

"Maybe. But women like Mary—and Lois Weber, and Adela and Elsie—they made it easier for me. I do owe her everything, Fred. And I know I mean more to her than this article says. I know I'm more than simply her scenarist. You have to understand—she's only recently married. She's now the head of her own studio. She's not yet used to this—this level of fame, if that's what it is. Heavens, nobody is! Nobody's ever experienced anything like this before, you know. Not even Teddy Roosevelt." I continued to brush vigorously, then I dropped my brush and bent my waist until my hair fell over my head, my thick black hair, blocking everything out—including Fred, with his doubtful eyes.

I flung my head back and stared at myself in the mirror; my hair was a wild dark nimbus, my blue eyes wide and sparkling, and I looked as exotic, as alluring, as Theda Bara or Nita Naldi, and I wondered, for the first time, why I'd been so afraid to appear in front of the camera back then. If I had done so, I might be Mary's equal right now. I might have had the kind of deity status Mary enjoyed.

But I'd also be Mary's rival; I saw how Mary held herself back from other actresses, even the Gish sisters, her oldest friends. But *had* I allowed my desire for Mary's friendship and approval to keep me back behind the camera, where Mary was most comfortable seeing me?

My hair settled down, sedately falling about my shoulders. I shook my head.

No, this was the career I wanted; a writer could be employed for as long as she could hold a pencil; for as long as her mind still held out. But an actress—even an actress like Mary—had a fleeting shelf life. Already in Hollywood, I'd seen actresses flash like a comet only to fall to earth with a thud. Gypsy Abbott. Maude Fealy. And perhaps the most tragic, Florence Lawrence, the original Biograph Girl, whose title Mary had usurped. Nobody knew where Florence was now; I heard rumors of her death every year or so, but really, nobody cared. Yet at one time she, not Mary Pickford, had been the most famous movie actress in the world.

I patted some cream on my cheeks, rouged my lips a little,

not much—Fred didn't like too much makeup, but I wasn't about to give up my cosmetics. I liked rouge on both my lips and cheeks, and powder, and a little mascara; it was practically a job requirement in Hollywood.

"What Mary and I have is incredible, Fred. You don't know what we've been through at the studios: the sneers, the put-downs, men praying for us to fail. Especially Mary. *I've* been lucky. Most scenarists are women, and so they need us. But an *actress* who dares to try to tell the men what to do? That's entirely different, and that's what Mary's had to put up with. You know, we've always vowed we wouldn't let men get between us or drive us apart. They tried, once. But they couldn't."

"And now?"

"I suppose it's bound to be different now that we're both married. I just wish—I wish she wasn't married to Doug. Is that awful of me?" I grimaced at Fred, who was wrestling with his tie.

"No. But you know, I like Doug. I really do. Oh, sure, he's got a fragile ego. But I've known a lot of men like that—men who have to be the biggest person in the room. They're all compensating for something, although a man like Doug—he has everything now. Fame, fortune, Mary. Still, I like what he does with his movies. I like how wholesome they are, how there's so much action, fresh air. I've been thinking . . . I've been thinking maybe I could do something like that, too." Fred sat back down at the foot of the bed and looked at me uncertainly—for approval, I realized, unable to prevent a surprised, but triumphant, little smile from tickling his lips.

I nodded, appearing to give his proposal grave consideration even though I'd been wracking my brain trying to find a way to get Fred into the business almost as soon as I'd met him. He was so handsome. Such a natural for the camera—I'd learned to recognize the bone structure that photographed best, and he had it in spades. He'd complained about the little bit he did for me in the Hearst film, but there was a hollowness to it, as if he felt he *should* complain as a man. A former minister. A world-class athlete.

I also had to admit, as my heart surged with another—wholly unexpected—little thrill, that the idea of being a Hollywood couple, like Doug and Mary, was intensely appealing. Especially right now.

"I've been dying to find a way to get you back in front of a camera. This film idea I have, the one Mary talked about—there's a role. Not the leading man, but still a very good role."

"You've been scheming behind my back!" Fred grinned, and I could just picture that handsome, beaming face projected large on a screen, lit just right, and I clapped my hands.

"You have, too!"

"I have. I think I can do something, maybe something with the Old West, like William S. Hart, but more for boys. A way to promote good old-fashioned values. I can't preach anymore—thanks to my dear little twice-divorced wife—but I see now that I could reach so many more youths this way. Your way."

"The Hollywood way."

"I don't like the way that sounds, but yes."

"I can't wait to suggest it to Mary! But I think I'll wait until we're all back home. I'm sure she'll be thrilled." *I hope.*

"But will Doug?"

I turned back to the mirror and gave my nose a final pat with the powder puff. No, Douglas Fairbanks would not be thrilled, not at all. But I knew Mary well enough; private life was one thing. Her career was quite another. *That* she would not bend or reshape to please her man. Any man.

"Let's go dancing, darling." I rose, presented myself with a twirl, and Fred kissed my hand.

"Like a queen," he teased, with a grin.

"There's room for more than one." I took my handsome husband's arm, and we left for the ball. Where I found myself, astonishingly, the belle. For who was the host of this military ball but none other than my old friend Major Brereton!

Just as Mary was introducing me as "And of course, my scenarist—" Major Brereton looked at me and exclaimed, "Lieutenant Marion!"

"Major—I mean, *General*!" I saluted smartly, noting the gleaming star on his uniform. Then we both laughed and shook hands; he seemed genuinely happy to see me.

"What, Fran? Who is this?" Mary's eyes were wide with wonder, while Doug's smile was a little tight, but still professionally magnetic.

"Someone who once told me a woman's place was not in a war." I smiled at the general.

"A statement I still stand by." General Brereton bowed. "However, the lieutenant here was as brave a soldier as I've seen, and while I didn't exactly enjoy escorting her across the Rhine, I have to say it wasn't a hardship, either. She required no special handling. She refused offers of help, if I recall. And we've all seen your film over here, *American Women in the War*. It was very enlightening." He nodded tersely, and I knew that would be all he would praise me for my work. But it was, at least, praise.

All of a sudden I was acutely aware that I was wearing a

shimmering, low-cut ball gown and not a mud-splattered uniform. Still, I did not imagine the respect in General Brereton's eyes—and in the eyes of Fred and, surprisingly, Mary. Mary had really never seen me out of her shadow; she'd not had a chance to witness me on my own. I was touched: Mary could still be genuinely happy for me.

"We're so proud of Fran," Mary burst out, and the evening was simply perfect, after the disappointment of the morning.

"Miss Pickford, might I open the ball with you?" The general remembered his duties and his manners; Mary was the guest of honor, and it was protocol for the two of them to dance the first dance.

Mary rose, a delighted smile upon her lips. Until Doug stood, too, and grabbed her by the arm. I held my breath, poised to leap to my friend's aid, but Doug didn't go any further than that; he didn't yank her back or grip her too tightly.

With another stiff little smile, he said, softly but so that every one of us at the table could hear, "You promised me, Tupper, darling. Remember? You promised that you'd never dance with any other man. Only me."

It took all of my self-control not to remind Doug that this was simply ornamental, a matter of protocol, nothing more. It was what was done. Surely he couldn't expect Mary, with her public profile requiring so many of these formal events, never to dance with anyone but him?

Mary's face fell, but then she looked up at Doug, and her eyes softened with understanding as she spoke to him tenderly, almost as a mother to a petulant son. "Of course, Douglas. Of course I remember. I don't know what I was thinking. I'm sorry, General, but as you can see, I made a promise to my husband."

And with that, Mary took her seat again, and General Brereton was left looking ridiculous.

But only for a moment. With a polite nod to Mary, he turned to me and bowed. Delighted, I walked toward him. And I smiled at my handsome, proud husband as the music started and the general began to twirl me around in a sober, stiff-armed waltz. I smiled at Mary, as well. And nodded sympathetically when she flashed me a little grimace, a little shrug.

But that didn't mean I didn't enjoy the spotlight as it fell on me with blinding, unexpected—but most welcome—brilliance.

AFTER THEIR TRIUMPHANT HONEYMOON, THEY
came home to Pickfair, Douglas's former hunting lodge high
up the mountain in the Beverly Hills that they'd remodeled
into a mock-Tudor castle worthy of the new king and queen:
four stories, twenty-five rooms, stables, tennis courts. They
came home to their own studios, which had been built while
they were away. They came home to reign over Hollywood,
hand in hand.

Every morning Mary awoke in a bed so enormous it could
have held her, Mama, Lottie, and Jack back in the day, along
with all their costumes and hand props. A bed as big as the biggest room they'd ever all crammed into on the road. A bed as
big as the future.

And Douglas was there, right beside her, always clad in the
finest linen pajamas. They rose, and Douglas commenced his
calisthenics, jumping jacks and handsprings and sit-ups and
somersaults, then went off to jog around the house for a while.
When they dressed, they went to separate dressing rooms;
Mary's closets were hung with the finest fashions, sober but

luxurious suits, dainty tea dresses, beaded or chiffon evening gowns—all a bit more sophisticated than what Papa Zukor had always picked out for her. She was Mrs. Douglas Fairbanks now; she would dress accordingly.

If she was going to the studio, she always chose a suit; it was awkward enough having to attend business meetings between takes in costume as a little girl. At least when she first arrived, people would see her as who she was: the head of a major Hollywood studio.

Douglas's closets were filled with fifty pairs of handmade shoes, fine linen and silk shirts, tailored suits, custom tuxedos, as well as dungarees and flannel shirts and pants for his various athletic endeavors—golf and tennis and polo and rowing and riding. But usually he was dressed in a suit when he joined her in the soothing breakfast room with its eggshell-colored walls. For breakfast, even if they had houseguests, it was typically only the two of them. Their guests could sleep until noon, but Douglas and Mary had to be at the studio by seven.

After eating sparingly, both of them—Douglas had a tendency to put on weight even with his vigorous exercise regime, while Mary, of course, had to look as slender as a little girl onscreen—they stepped into the waiting car, a 1920 Hudson touring limousine, driven by a liveried chauffeur. Mary would sit up straight and inhale the perfumed air, surveying her kingdom of gardens and stables and the first in-ground swimming pool in Los Angeles, one of Douglas's many gifts. In that pool was a canoe; they often posed in it with guests for photographers.

Winding their way down the hilly drive, they sometimes remarked on a new house going up, for more and more movie people were building homes in the Hollywood hills. Aeries, where they could perch and survey their kingdom. But none ascended higher than Pickfair; none dared.

If they had a little extra time, Mary would speak into the tube-like apparatus that allowed her to talk to the chauffeur, ensconced behind a window, and ask him to stop at Charlotte's cozy little cottage at the foot of the hill. Of course, Mary had assumed that Mama would live with them at Pickfair, but Douglas had most vehemently said no to that, and built Mama her own house down the hill.

Mary would knock on the door, which was always answered by Mama herself; what her two servants did all day, Mary had no idea. For Charlotte insisted on doing everything herself. Mary would kiss Mama on the cheek and say hello to her niece, little Gwynnie, if she was up—goodness, the little girl looked exactly like her mother, poor thing!—then invite Mama to dinner if Douglas was amenable, or promise her a lunch over the weekend if he was not.

It wasn't that he wasn't *amenable,* she corrected herself. Douglas loved Mama. But sometimes, there simply wasn't room. And Mama wasn't always comfortable around some of their more refined guests, Mary had to admit after Douglas pointed this out.

After the morning ritual, she'd step back into the car— Douglas would have been reading the newest fan magazine while she was inside—and they'd take off toward the studio, passing the Hollywood Hotel, rows of neat little houses, or- ange groves, down Sunset, with its wide bridle path in the cen- ter of the boulevard. They'd drive by studios, some destined for oblivion almost as soon as the last nail had been hammered, the business was becoming so crowded; others established, like Fa- mous Players–Lasky and Mack Sennett's madhouse.

Then they'd turn into the gate of *their* studio. *Pickford Fairbanks Studio,* as the sign said, and Mary never drove beneath those arches without at least a little smile of satisfaction, before she assumed the dignity required of her. Douglas did, too, and the two of them would look at each other with wide eyes, and hold hands in supreme satisfaction.

And then they drove into their kingdom.

Eighteen acres at the corner of Santa Monica and Formosa. The former Hampton studios. When United Artists was formed, it was a studio without a lot; the business offices were established in New York City, where all studio business offices were located. Charlie had built his own studio only a year or two before, when he'd signed with First National (another studio without a real shooting lot). So he had his own lot, and Griffith still worked across the country at his studio on Long Island. Which left Douglas and Mary without a place to shoot their movies, so they'd snapped up the Hampton studio and refurbished it.

Sometimes—many times—Mary lay awake at night, going through the ledgers in her mind. Each partner had to put up their own financing for their own movies (and their own studio lots). United Artists was privately owned; there was no stock, no investors, no bankers—precisely the point, because there were no money men to answer to, to have to please: recut a film when they didn't like it, make what they thought you should make, not what you wanted to. But that left the studio dangerously undercapitalized, floating from picture to picture, and they also, alone of the major studios, did not have their own chain of movie theaters for distributorship. Hiram Abrams in the New York office had decided they would rent theaters, and coaxed the owners to pay their rental fees in advance, promising only the next Mary Pickford or Douglas Fairbanks—which was enough, of course. Still, unlike studios such as Famous Players, United Artists didn't have a year's worth of pictures already in the can to sell, a catalog the salespeople could go out and hawk. Running a business and making movies meant slowing things down; at the most, Mary felt she and Douglas could put out two or three films a year apiece. Chaplin and Griffith were even slower.

Still, it was worth it, the agonizing over every penny, every costume, every prop. For they were free, they were in charge. They were DougandMary.

They would walk to their respective dressing room/office bungalows, blowing kisses at the very last. Then makeup, costume, going over the day's shooting schedule, signing the checks and forms. Then shooting all morning under the hot lights. A break for lunch together in one of their bungalows, usually in costume, usually a photographer there to capture the quaintness of Little Mary in her pinafore dining with Douglas in his dashing pirate's outfit. Sometimes Charlie would join them in his Little Tramp costume, even if he wasn't filming. It was all for publicity. All for the studio.

Then more filming, often late into the evening. Some evenings Mary was too exhausted to change clothes, so she went home in costume, dined in costume, only removing it when she went to bed. Even though the thing would be stiff with perspiration, she never stopped marveling that it was made for her, and her alone; that the years of putting on stained and ripped costumes encrusted with the perspiration of all the other actresses who had come before were over. Long over. Even when she was slumped in her dining room chair, tiredly picking at her dinner dressed as a ragamuffin, she still was able to remember how far she'd come, and breathe a swift prayer of thanksgiving.

Still, those exhausting evenings—sometimes all she could do was run a rough towel over her face before dinner, to remove at least the top layer of the heavy camera makeup that suffocated her pores—were the evenings she preferred. Those were the evenings when it was only she and Douglas dining together, side by side at their enormous dining room table, talking about their days, discussing camera setups (although Douglas relied far more on his director than Mary did), casting, publicity. She'd usually try to get him to think ahead about marketing, for he was prone to putting that off. But good marketing had to start early. Billboards, she was always telling him! Billboards sell movies and you have to secure those weeks ahead of time!

But too many evenings weren't like this. Too many evenings were *Douglas's* favorite evenings—evenings when the house was packed with guests, the dining table at capacity. Everyone visiting Hollywood now wanted to visit Pickfair first; it was like the Buckingham Palace of California, someone said—probably Charlie. And Mary thought that was only appropriate. So, like King George and Queen Mary, she put up with the inconvenience, the loss of privacy, for it was her *duty*.

"How's the duke, Doug?" Charlie once asked during lunch at the studio.

"What duke?" Douglas looked up in surprise.

"Oh, any old duke," Charlie replied airily, and Douglas and Mary both laughed. Because Charlie was right; a week without some duke, any old duke, visiting Pickfair was rare indeed.

Douglas loved it; the more royal, the better. Potentates and politicians, too. Charlie was there; Charlie was always there to make Doug laugh, to egg him on. Mary once asked him if he ever dined at his own house, to which Charlie replied, "But your cook is so much better than mine, Mary!"

Well, he was. Because Mary made sure of it. It was her obligation to make Pickfair the most fabulous symbol of Hollywood, the most refined, sophisticated, and elegant. She could still wince at her lack of education, look back with horror at her hardworking, ragtag childhood. Now that she was queen, she must represent Hollywood to the rest of the world, give it legitimacy, refinement. She owed it *everything*.

So she made sure that not only her cook was the best in Hollywood, she made sure *everything* at Pickfair was the best in Hollywood. The linens, the carpets, the drapes, the china, the silver, the gold plate. Fortunately Douglas was a teetotaler, so she didn't have to worry about the awkwardness of serving fine wine during Prohibition and pretending it was left over from before. And she always had her own sip of gin before dinner, sometimes after, in the privacy of her dressing room.

It didn't hurt anyone, her little occasional nip. She had to hide it from Jack and Lottie, of course, who would have taken it for themselves. And who, the poor dears, definitely did have a problem. Lottie had gone through two husbands, left her little daughter to be raised by Charlotte, with Mary's help. Jack had married that little Olive Thomas, who had died hideously in Paris from an overdose, and so it wasn't only alcohol that gripped him. Those two had the family curse. Mama, too, probably, but then again it didn't matter, for Mama deserved every bit of comfort she could take, and she didn't make a scene or get herself arrested like Mary's siblings. She drank quietly in her own home.

But Mary, of course, didn't have to worry about any of

that, because *she* was fine. So she nipped a little before dinner? Who wouldn't, when faced with the daunting responsibilities she had? Who wouldn't be slightly intimidated by the thought of the duke of York staying the night and reporting back to the queen of England herself how he'd been treated at Pickfair? Toronto was never far away when Mary was dressed, draped in diamonds, and waiting to descend her grand staircase and greet her famous guests. How could she, little Gladys Smith, talk to people like George Bernard Shaw? Only a small glass—teeny-tiny!—of gin would calm her nerves and unstick her tongue from the roof of her mouth. And Douglas need never know, because she was so discreet; she always gargled with Listerine after.

Miraculously, that nip would get her through the evening and at precisely ten o'clock, no matter what they were doing—playing charades in the library, watching a new film starring one of their guests—Mary rang for the butlers to show up with cups of Ovaltine for everyone, the signal that it was time to go to bed.

After all, everyone, except visiting royalty, did have to go to work early on the morrow.

And work was the thing that Mary craved—simple work. Oh, those days when it was her and Frances and Mickey on the set, only worrying about their art, what the camera captured. Not worrying about the money it required. Mary longed for those days, and perhaps that's why she agreed to star in Frances's directorial debut for United Artists, *The Love Light*.

"Mary, let me tell you a story," Frances had said in Europe, one afternoon when Douglas and Fred were off doing manly things. Frances and Fred had been to Italy prior to meeting the Fairbankses in Southampton. "I saw this beautiful girl in a small

Italian village. You know some of the German soldiers were kept safe in Italy, when their ships were wrecked offshore. This girl was a heroine. She had been a lighthouse keeper with her father and when a ship ran aground, she fell in love with the soldier. But months later she found out he was a spy, using the lighthouse lamp to signal German ships. And despite her love, she turned him in, and he was executed. The villagers told me this story, and pointed to the beautiful Italian girl with brown eyes—and the fair-haired baby with blue eyes in her arms. And I thought, this would make a movie. A wonderful movie. Don't you agree?"

"It will be my next one!" Mary was still soaring from the dizzying heights of her marriage, her fame, the likes of which had never been seen. The newspapers bore this out; after their European honeymoon, the press spent oceans of ink trying to puzzle what had happened in normally staid, stoic England. Why respectable people had thrown themselves at Doug and Mary—who before had been merely movie stars—and wept and torn their clothing and seemed so desperate with need for them, to see them, to be in their presence.

And so movie stars weren't merely movie stars anymore. And Mary wasn't merely Mary. She was untouchable. She was also ready to grow up on film; she was nearly twenty-nine now. She'd played little girls long past when she should have. She was married, everyone knew it. So why not play a woman now—a passionate woman? And who better than Frances, who had created her little girl persona, to guide her to on-screen adulthood not only by writing, but directing?

It would be like old times! They could work on the script together at night—Mary'd coax Fran to come over to Pickfair, which, to be honest, Fran didn't seem to admire *quite* as much as

Mary thought she should. Oh, of course dear Fran, along with Fred, was always invited to every single dinner honoring every single guest, and she always obliged (although sometimes, Fred did not, begging off for some athletic thing). But something about the way Fran's nose twitched, her mouth continually clamped shut when she was at the table—did she not enjoy meeting all these important guests? And the way she only gazed at Douglas steadily when he pulled one of his jokes that so endeared him to everyone—substituting a rubber knife for a real one, so that some poor duchess couldn't cut her meat, or setting off firecrackers beneath the table—did Fran not think he was funny?

Mary would laugh along with everyone else and say her exasperated "Oh, Douglas!" But Fran always remained politely silent, her eyes downcast, concentrating on her plate.

But surely Mary could coax her over with the promise of hot cocoa and long nights in front of the fire. Surely they could work together as seamlessly as always, one finishing the other's sentence. Surely, between takes, they could huddle together behind the camera, laughing and making up bits the way they did with *The Poor Little Rich Girl;* they could have laughing lunches together in Mary's bungalow, just like before.

Because Mary, to her own astonishment, *needed* this; she needed to escape from the responsibility of being the queen, of hosting dignitaries and crunching numbers and trying to find ways to amuse Douglas, to put up with Charlie who followed Douglas around like a puppy, plopped himself in the middle of whatever was going on in her house (when he wasn't seducing teenage actresses—oh, that man!). Mary needed to go back to the one place that had always seemed safe and right; she needed simply to be an actress again, the camera the only eye upon her.

And with Fran, she could do that. It would be exactly like old times! Exactly like—before.

Mary couldn't wait to begin the film.

"ARE YOU SURE, DEAREST FRAN, we can't shoot this on the lot?"

"Oh, Squeebee! But don't you think it has to look just a little bit like Italy? I found the most marvelous place up the coast, up around Carmel. It's rocky, a lot like the Italian coast, and the town could definitely double for an Italian village. And look what you'll save on building costs! We'll only need a few interiors to be shot here at the studio."

"Yes, of course." Mary nodded; Frances certainly had a point, authenticity was key. Not since *Madame Butterfly* had Mary attempted to portray someone who was not American. She would need all the help she could get, for she refused Fran's request that she dye her curls or wear a wig. She would be a blond Italian; dear Fran didn't quite understand how important this film was, her second under United Artists. After giving her fans *Pollyanna,* even if she was ecstatic to stretch her muscles and play this passionate Italian girl, she still had to *look* like herself. She couldn't risk alienating her fans, not at the box office, not when United Artists needed every penny it could make.

But dear Fran didn't quite understand the cost of going on location; of arranging for trains to carry all the cast and crew and studio hands, who would still have to do some work to the existing village, for there always was something needed—a wishing well, a church, a barn, fake flowers, something; bringing in the materials, arranging for lodging for an entire company, paying for meals to be brought in (and you could bet that any local cooks would charge triple their usual asking price when it came to movie people), warehousing costumes, paying locals to use their houses . . . location was expensive. But Fran didn't really seem to understand, and why should she? She wasn't head of her own studio.

"Will you use a miniature for the shipwreck scene?" Mary consulted the shooting script.

"I think not, Mary, darling. We want this to be absolutely real. You know that there will be a lot of scrutiny; female directors are a rarity these days, aren't they? Oh, I do miss Lois!"

Mary nodded. True, Lois Weber was washed up; her message films were no longer in the public favor. After the war, people wanted escapist fare, dramatic love stories. Not morality plays.

"Fine, we'll send someone out to look for a ship we can buy up there." Mary made a note in her ledger, and Fran smiled happily. "Now, about the cast—"

"I have an idea."

Mary's heart sank, but she wasn't surprised. She had seen the way Fran looked at her new husband. Not only with love, with desire, but with ambition. Calculation.

"You want Fred."

"Yes! For the German soldier. It's not a large part, Mary, but he has to be physically imposing and handsome. I know he's new to this, but with you to play off—you know how brilliant you are, Squeebee, how expressive and generous! He'll be learning from the very best. From you!"

Mary looked down, squelching a smirk. Fran knew her too well; knew her vanity. Still, if Fran was intent on making her husband an actor, he would have no better launch than playing the love interest in a Mary Pickford movie.

"I think it's brilliant, Fran. And you know I wouldn't say that if I didn't mean it—I'm putting up the money, you know!"

"Yes, you've said," Fran murmured, and now it was her turn to look at the ground.

"Then it's settled," Mary said, and they went on to the next item on their agenda. But it wasn't settled, because she had to tell Douglas.

And she had a very good idea of how he would react to the news.

"I'M NOT LETTING YOU out of my sight while you're making love to that man!" Douglas's dark face turned even darker; he ground his teeth. "I saw the way you looked at him in Europe!"

"Oh, Douglas, don't be absurd! You know I only looked at you in Europe—I only look at you, every day of my life!"

There was nothing Mary could say that would placate him; she'd tried before. But Douglas was terrifically protective of Mary; she was learning she couldn't even look at another man without having to deal with the ramifications once she and Douglas were alone. He wasn't physically abusive, like Owen— thank heavens! But he imagined flirtations where none existed; it was as if, since their own relationship had begun out of wedlock, he thought she was a certain "type." A woman who couldn't be trusted. Yet he seemed to put her on a pedestal at the same time; there were moments when he looked at her as if he couldn't believe his good fortune; as if he couldn't believe that she even could exist in the ordinary world.

If he could, he would have locked her away in a pretty little cell full of the finest objects on earth, to which he had the only key.

But *she* trusted *him*. She'd seen him on set filming love scenes; he was no good at it, awkward and always with a panicked look in his eyes. She'd never seen Douglas come even close to a flirtation, except with her. He was not the kind of man, like Charlie, like John Barrymore, like Wallace Beery—like so many in Hollywood!—who looked at all the eager young starlets as his own brothel. Who promised a girl a part in a movie if only she would . . .

No, Douglas wasn't like that at all. He was rather a snob, she had to admit. A prig, at times. She trusted him. Why couldn't he trust her?

"That Thomson is a looker, I know. Your friend certainly chose well."

Mary refrained from revealing that actually it was *she* who had picked Fred Thomson out of a lineup of strapping young soldiers. And obviously she had chosen well; the two were so in love that sometimes it hurt to see. For theirs was an uncomplicated marriage, unburdened by the public's enormous expectations.

Mary shrugged; she knew it would only make things worse if she continued to protest.

So Douglas—who was in preproduction for *The Mark of Zorro,* which meant he had time off—insisted on accompanying the entire company to location.

Obviously, then, this film set was not going to be like old times with Frances.

After they all descended upon the little village, figured out lodging—Fred and Frances and Mary and Douglas were going to share a house—production began. The first scenes shot were easy ones, and for a while, Fran and she did recapture some of the magic of the old days with Mickey; there were fun shots with dogs and children that had them in tears behind the camera, silly bits where Mary had to play the spitfire early in the scenario, doing some comic fighting with her "brothers," clowning around in the "Italian" streets. While they filmed these scenes, Fred and Douglas went off to do some fishing, and so it was just the two of them on set, and if Mary tried hard enough she could imagine it was like when they filmed *Stella Maris* or *M'Liss* or *Amarilly of Clothes-Line Alley*.

Only this time, Frances sat in the director's chair and said, "Cut." Sometimes even before Mary thought she ought to.

"Fran . . ." Mary took a big breath; the scene had involved a lot of physical activity, and she'd given it her all. She consulted a scratch on her wrist and summoned the makeup woman to tend to it. "Didn't you think I could have done a bit more with the bit in the barrel? I thought it would be cute if we had a glimpse of my legs kicking."

"I don't think so, Squeebee. Remember, you're not a little girl in this, you're a young woman."

"Yes, but my fans—they do like those little bits, you know. They've worked well for us in the past—remember *The Poor Little Rich Girl*?"

But Fran only shook her head and consulted the shooting script, setting up the next shot. And this time—for the first time in all the years they'd worked together—Mary had no choice but to move on.

Still, it was such fun at night, even with Douglas and Fred there, to sit in front of a fire with a glass of milk and talk about the day's shoot, gossip about which extras were in love with each other, discuss the next day's schedule. Fran didn't try to tell Mary how to play her part, at least; she never had done that. And Mary was grateful; what she did to prepare, she couldn't really discuss with anyone. She read the script over and over, daydreamed about the girl she would play, her childhood, her life. She'd read some books about Italy for this one. She spent a lot of time in front of a mirror practicing gestures that seemed authentic. When she went to sleep at night, she imagined herself as this other person; pretending to be anyone but who she was relaxed her and allowed her to sleep untroubled.

As they neared the scenes she'd have to film with Fred, however, she noticed that Fran began spending more time with him, talking him through the script. Naturally, Fran had to; that was her job! But Mary did feel, if not left out, exactly, a little neglected. Of course *she* was a pro, she reminded herself. She was the one with experience. Fred was the newcomer.

As they staged the love scenes, Douglas was always on set, glowering as Fran, with the script in her hand, walked them through their paces. Fran always had an arm on Fred, gently guiding him, while she merely pointed at Mary's marks. "Mary, go through there. Walk here. Look there."

When they started to shoot, the camera clicking noisily, the little orchestra on set—accordions and violins playing Italian music—starting up, Fred was very stiff. Take after take was required to get him to relax—and Fran *knew* that Mary was best on her first takes! She was an instinctive actress, and after three or four takes she simply wilted, all her emotion spent. But no, Fred was too inexperienced; it took him that long to stop looking at the camera in terror.

Also—and she did tell dear Fran this, several times, but Fran didn't seem to hear—there were a few too many takes with her and Fred in profile, equally sharing the screen. Mary was accustomed to at least one full close-up in all of her scenes; after all, hers was the face people paid good money to see! But Fran made sure that Fred had a few close-ups of his own. A few more than Mary's typical leading man. Of course, Fred was handsome, but Mary was the star. Which she also—so sweetly—reminded dear Fran. Several times. And dear Fran, while she certainly heard, didn't appear to consider this as seriously as she ought.

The first time she had to be embraced by Fred while the cameras turned, Mary actually heard Douglas growl. When Fran looked at him in astonishment, he quickly smiled and made as if he was clowning around. But Mary's heart sank. What a fool Douglas was! This wasn't *fun,* this wasn't *amorous.* If he could only see the terrified expression in Fred's eyes as he lowered his head toward Mary's! It took all her self-control not to laugh out loud. She tried to guide him, thinking that her character—Italian, of course!—might be the aggressor, and she caught Fran's subtle nod from behind the camera when she reached out to pull him toward her, for the poor man's arms were so stiff, tense, it was as if he had no idea how to make them work.

As the days went on—and they were going over schedule because of Fred's inexperience, but Mary bit her tongue because she knew it would do no good to say anything, even as she stayed up late at night going over the ledgers, trying to move money from one department to another—Douglas paced and paced behind the camera, needing an outlet for both his jealousy and his boredom. He was not accustomed to being merely an observer on set. At one point, Mary suggested to Fran that she might use him as a stunt double, but Fran felt very strongly that the audience would identify him, which would take them out of the picture. Mary had to admit she was probably correct.

Did dear Fran spend a bit too much time on Fred's close-ups despite the delay, insisting on standing behind the camera herself so that he would appear more natural? Yes. But Mary would never say this out loud. She would never complain. She channeled it all into her own close-ups, welcoming the camera into her heart, opening up her face like a flower.

Determined to wipe the screen with poor Fred.

Still, there was a lot to admire about Fran's direction. She had a good grasp of camera setups, if she wasn't as imaginative as Mickey. Mary was proud to have her friend, a woman, behind the camera; she gave interviews wholeheartedly recommending women directors. "It's nice to have someone who understands relationships, who takes the time to establish them," she said. "Women have a natural feel for emotion, and don't allow technical aspects to get in the way."

To all the press who ventured up, the set was one big happy family, the two couples as close as ever, the shoot simply an extended part of their joint honeymoon. They posed together, making spaghetti in their kitchen, laughing, smiling. "It's wonderful to have your best friend as director," Mary chirped.

Privately, it began to dawn on Mary that she and Fran were rarely speaking off the set. She didn't quite understand when or how that happened; it simply had. They both retreated to their respective suites with their respective husbands after the day's shoot, and no longer did the two couples meet in front of the fire to gossip about the day.

"Good night, Mary."

"Good night, Fran."

And—slam. Doors shut.

The last day on set—thank God! Mary couldn't wait until every last bit player and light hanger was on the train south so that she didn't have to pay their living expenses one minute more—was a terrible, stormy day full of heavy blue-black clouds and a lashing, pelting rain that churned the water into terrifying surf. A fitting end to this uneasy shoot.

It was the day they had to destroy that boat—the boat Fran had insisted on buying instead of using a miniature. The storm successfully smashed the boat against the rocks, but a stuntman doubling for Mary got into trouble; he was struggling against the surf, going under time and again, and suddenly everyone was wild with action. Someone screamed, someone else ran around looking for a boat to launch into the water. But Fred and Douglas didn't wait; they both, with a single look between them, tore down the rocks and jumped into the rough water to rescue him. Mary, soaked to the skin despite her heavy raincoat, couldn't bear to look; she could only pray. Turning to Frances, she prepared to fling herself into her friend's arms as their husbands risked their lives.

But Fran wasn't even looking at her. She stood, tall and steady next to the camera, her mackintosh soaked, her black hair undone and unkempt, wet ringlets streaming down her back. But she did not move an inch; she shouted at her terrified cameraman to keep shooting despite the fact that her husband was being tossed about by the churning water as if he were a doll. And in that moment Mary admired her more than she ever had. She doubted even the great DeMille would have remained so calm, so in control, under the circumstances.

The Love Light opened on January 9, 1921. It did well enough, but it wasn't the spectacular hit that United Artists needed and in retrospect, Mary resented Fran talking her into being a mother on screen. Mary's next film returned her to playing a child herself—*the* child, the child her public demanded she remain, the child Fran had written for her in the first place. Although Fran did not write *Through the Back Door*.

It would be ten years before Frances and Mary worked on a film together again. Ten long years, in which so much would happen, so much they couldn't—or wouldn't—share.

WELL, WE'D GONE HOLLYWOOD.

That's what we told all our friends, gleefully and also somewhat abashed. For all the times we'd gone to Pickfair and put up with the stifling ostentation, then come back to our cozy little apartment to kick off our shoes and laugh about it, we'd done the same as Mary and Doug.

We'd built a palace of our own.

But ours was different—or so we told ourselves. What we built wasn't a mausoleum but a living, working ranch with stables and bunks for cowboys. Yes, the main house had an enormous pipe organ, shipped over from Italy; yes, there were gardens and guest rooms and a screening room and a pool. Yes, we were on top of our own hill, like Doug and Mary. The top of Smokey Mountain, in the Beverly Hills, to be precise. Yes, our neighbors were movie stars with their own pools and stables.

But our house was no stuffy showcase.

The first time we went looking for a place to build, we were stunned. "No, Fred, I'm sorry," one of his old friends from college had said, when we inquired about purchasing acreage on one of his hills. "I was so sorry to hear you'd given up the cloth and become an actor. Because I've made a point of never selling to Jews and actors."

And in a flash, I was right back where I'd been nearly ten years ago, when I first arrived in Los Angeles. How some things never changed! Yet how *everything* had changed since then. Jews and actors had *made* Los Angeles, giving it an industry, a shimmering place on the world's map.

"Without Jews and actors you'd be sitting on acreage that you couldn't give away," Fred retorted, just as I was about to do the same. "Go to hell, Larry. You call yourself a Christian?"

I had never heard Fred swear. Not once. But I was bursting with pride as he took my arm and ushered me out of the real estate office. "I think I've been a bad influence on you," I whispered, beaming up at his face, which was tight with anger.

"And for that, I thank you," he replied.

Almost ten years! Ten years since I'd first arrived in Los Angeles, and some things hadn't changed. But so many things had.

I was the most sought-after screenwriter in the business now, no longer known only as "Mary Pickford's scenarist." I'd turned down many offers for long-term contracts at studios, choosing to pick the projects that appealed to me. I'd written pictures for Hearst, not only for Marion Davies but also big successes like *Humoresque*. At the moment, I was writing for Joe Schenck, movies starring his glamorous, raven-haired wife, Norma Talmadge; sophisticated melodramas, a far cry from the slapstick of my early movies with Mary, like *Amarilly of Clothes-Rim Alley* and *Johanna Enlists*. No longer did I only dream up stories featuring a golden-haired little girl; my imagination was given wings by the ever-expanding industry. And how things had changed from the early days of writing on the fly, scribbling as the cameras turned, sometimes writing two pictures in an afternoon—and filming them, too!

Now, I was provided with an office wherever I happened to be working; an office and a secretary. I preferred to write at home, however, in bed; propped up against a wall of pillows, writing in long hand on a little wooden tray desk, or dictating to a secretary who would type everything up. When I was needed at the studio for casting or rewrites, I was chauffeured there in my own car, with my own driver. Films were lush productions now, filmed on great stages with sophisticated arc lights, several cameramen, entire orchestras for mood music, armies of makeup people and wardrobe minions constantly brushing and plucking and powdering stars between takes. And there were many takes; no more rushing to get everything in one, so that the film could be processed and sped into the newest storefront nickelodeon.

Movie theaters were palaces, even in the smallest towns now. Sid Grauman had recently opened up another palace to rival his grand Egyptian Theater; this one was called his Chinese Theater, and the architecture was wildly oriental. Now major films held "premieres" at these theaters; the very first had been Doug's movie *Robin Hood,* at the Egyptian. For the first time, crowds had been invited to gape at movie stars walking along a red carpet, enormous klieg lights lighting up the sky for miles and competing with the blinding flash pots of photographers. Fred and I had attended in support of Mary and Doug, still the biggest stars of all.

Studios came and went like the wind, usually failing because of a lack of financial backing or distribution. There were more consolidations, too. But a new studio, rumored to be something different, had just opened its doors, and one day I found myself being interviewed by a man named Louis B. Mayer.

"So this is the highest-paid screenwriter in Hollywood?" A short dumpling of a man with a beak of a nose, thinning black hair, and round glasses rose from an enormous desk, set high on a platform, to greet me. He dismissed the other men who had been in the room when I entered with a curt nod, save for one. "You stay, Irving."

The painfully thin, slight young man with enormous, intelligent eyes and a shy smile nodded and held out his hand. "Irving Thalberg, Miss Marion."

"It's a pleasure to meet you both." I smiled and ostentatiously arranged my furs—I always wore my furs to business meetings to remind these men that I had earned them myself, that they weren't gifts—and took a seat.

Louis Mayer resumed his perch on his throne, but smiled benignly at me. Mr. Thalberg took notes.

"The highest-paid and the best screenwriter," Mayer continued. "I know I'm new out here, but this is going to be the biggest studio of them all someday. And I want you to join us."

"Mr. Mayer, I'm quite happy working on an independent basis. I don't like to tie myself to one studio. But I'd be happy to write one picture for you—that is, *if* you can meet my asking price."

"Only one? Well, it's a start." Mayer smiled, a cunning little smile. "I'm determined to make only pictures that my little daughters, Edith and Irene, can see. Hollywood has to change, after all these scandals. I'm all for Will Hays. Are you?"

I knew how I was supposed to answer, but was reluctant to.

I was intimately familiar with the scandals that had plagued the industry. In 1921, Fatty Arbuckle—Roscoe, to those of us who were his friends—had been charged with manslaughter, after a tragic Labor Day party in San Francisco during which one of the guests, a girl named Virginia Rappe, had died. The papers all screamed that she'd died of a ruptured bladder and peritonitis, impaled by either Fatty himself or a soda bottle; it depended on which paper you read.

The truth came out in the courtroom—the girl had a venereal disease, and some said cystitis, which were conditions that could be aggravated by alcohol. No evidence was found of rape. Yet poor Roscoe's career was over, just like that. And when the director William Desmond Taylor was found murdered a year later, and whispers were that either Mary Miles Minter or Mabel Normand had done it, my beloved Hollywood was suddenly a modern Sodom and Gomorrah. A few years before, these scandals wouldn't have been national news. Now they were. Because Wall Street had started to invest in studios, smelling the money being made from across the continent. So Wall Street called in a man named Will Hays to oversee the crumbling morals of Hollywood, to ensure that films were made that would not offend, to repair the reputation of this billion-dollar industry so that people in the heartland would still pay for movie tickets.

With the creation of the Motion Pictures Producers and Distributors of America—of which Hays was the first president—the industry changed. It started with a banquet in 1922 at the Ambassador Hotel, hosted by Mary Pickford and Douglas Fairbanks, attended by fifteen hundred industry luminaries such as Gloria Swanson, Cecil B. DeMille, Harold Lloyd, Charlie Chaplin—and Fred and Frances Thomson. A banquet in which all of Hollywood crowned this man, whom I thought looked like a vicious little bat with sharp teeth, their savior.

After the banquet, everything changed. Now, every studio had an in-house censor, and I had to submit my treatments to the MPPDA itself before being given the green light. I was told to make my scenarios look sugary and syrupy on paper, but often that wasn't what ended up being filmed; on the set, we added the same sophisticated, sexy scenes that moviegoers loved.

Yet under this new system, there couldn't help but be an increase in pablum and I'd stopped reading my reviews. Trying to please everybody meant that nobody was completely satisfied, and we screenwriters were the ones who came under the most criticism.

"So you only want to make wholesome pictures?" I asked, and noticed that Irving Thalberg opened his mouth, then shut it quickly after a swift look from his boss.

"I'm a sucker for humanity," Mayer replied with another charming, cunning smile, and I had to laugh. We agreed on an appropriate figure, and shook hands.

"I love giving surprises, so in addition to your salary—a check will be delivered this afternoon to your home—I'm giving you a bonus."

"Really?" I rose, then allowed myself to be escorted to the door by Mayer. I was taller than he was, but I refused to slouch down to soothe his vanity.

"I respect you, Frances Marion," Mayer said. Then he pinched my fanny; outraged, I couldn't prevent a little yelp from escaping. I couldn't get out of his office fast enough. But I had to laugh when I opened up my "bonus" later that day. It was a photograph of the man himself, inscribed with a flourish.

*To a clever young writer
from her friend,
Louis B. Mayer*

Remembering how his greedy fingers groped my flesh, however, I threw it in the trash where it belonged.

LOUIS B. MAYER WAS FAR from the only man who had pinched my fanny, although as a screenwriter, I was accorded a little more dignity than mere actresses, and counted my blessings. But my friends and I put up with the pinches, the sneers, the slights; it was the price we paid, a new price that hadn't quite been extracted in the same way years ago, when everyone was a newcomer and there was no hierarchy. What hierarchy there was now was entirely paternal; investors were now producers who could hire and fire at will. Overnight, the casting couch was born. I'd had my shoulder dampened by many a young actress's shameful, heartbroken tears when, after having done her "duty," she still wasn't cast as the love interest in the new Ramon Novarro (or Rudolph Valentino or Wallace Reid) picture.

Even if I didn't have to suffer the casting couch, I was not entirely immune from the patriarchy. When *The Love Light* opened, some of the reviews indicated that Mary had played a role not right for her as a favor to her "female scenarist-turned-director." But when one review howled at the "obvious miniature" used for the shipwreck, saying that "only a woman director would use something so fake," I was furious. I dashed off a letter explaining how I'd filmed a real boat in an actual storm, at the grave peril of my crew, not to mention my husband. Of course, there was no correction issued.

After that, I wasn't sure I wanted to direct anymore; I'd never received reviews for my screenplays that were so blatantly sexist. Women were being put in a box now; there were fewer female directors like Lois. Apparently, we were much more palatable as screenwriters and editors, roles that were more collaborative, less authoritative. But Joe Schenck pestered me to direct a film starring Norma, so I agreed. To my immediate regret.

For Schenck had a habit of parading groups of businessmen—investors, theater owners—past me on the set, as if I were a circus sideshow. "Look! There's our woman director. Surprised, aren't you, boys, that she's such a looker?"

"I thought you'd be bigger," one man said to me.

"I thought you'd be wearing trousers," another commented, actually reaching out to touch my silk-clad legs. Slapping his hand away, I caught Joe Schenck's expression, and forced myself to smile demurely, even flirtatiously.

"I prefer satin and diamonds," I purred, mentally counting the money I had in my bank account, reminding myself of my true worth. "After all, I can afford them."

Joe and the men laughed. "What a wit," one said in surprise as they all posed for a photograph. I was so tightly surrounded by men that I couldn't shrug off the "gentleman" who happened to drape his hand across my breast.

"What's your husband think about this, honey? Does he mind his wife wearing the pants in the family?"

"I assure you, when we're at home, my husband wears the pants," I retorted, with that same tight smile.

"Wait till the little woman at home gets a look at this," another said. "I hope she doesn't get any ideas! I'd hate to lose the best little cook in all of Kansas!"

"Only in Hollywood, brother. No women behave like this at home, believe me. They know their place," one man said—the man who had moments before squeezed my breast as if it were only what he deserved, after all.

Thinking of my paycheck, I managed to wave as Schenck herded all the bulls down the chute and off the set, then I slid off my director's chair. Storming over to a water cooler, I took a long drink of water—and several deep breaths—before turning around and ordering the crew back to work without my usual apologetic smile. And since when had I started doing that, anyway? Why did I always do something—a little shrug, a smile, a clearing of the throat—before asking, not telling, my cast and crew to hit their marks, set up a shot, roll the camera?

Lois had behaved this way, too, I remembered; her soft femininity, her appealing little glances and gestures. Never outright *telling,* always suggesting or asking. As if she were presiding over a tea party. Is this how women in power always behaved? I had no idea, because there weren't that many of them I could ask.

As my crew stared at me, mouths open, I apologized for yelling. Then I despised myself for apologizing.

Driving home that night, I furiously replayed the day in my mind, rattling off all the things I'd wanted to say to those disgusting males. Then I heard a siren and looked over my shoulder, and channeled the colorful sergeant who'd driven me through Verdun.

"Goddamn son of a bitch of a ball biter!" For a policeman

on a motorcycle was signaling for me to pull over. Still cursing, I did. Then I rolled my window down.

"Do you have any idea how fast you were going?"

"No, officer, I don't." I decided not to protest or even pretend my innocence; I knew I'd been going fast. Now, I just wanted to go home.

"Of course you don't," the policeman mimicked me. "I am so sick of rattlebrained woman drivers. Now that you have the vote, you broads all think you can drive, too."

I gripped the steering wheel, took a calming breath. "These rattlebrains make me over fifty thousand dollars a year, I'll have you know." Reaching into my pocketbook, I took out a wad of bills to pay the ticket, practically throwing them at the man.

Then I roared off. To the understanding arms of Fred. And our mansion on the hill.

WE CHRISTENED IT The Enchanted Hill, and years later, in my dreams that were more hazy bits of memories than actual reveries, this was the house to which I would return, again and again.

To a two-story white stucco mansion with twenty rooms, wide arches, and a red-tiled roof in the Spanish style, designed by Wallace Neff—the same architect who had designed Pickfair. To the long drive bordered with fruit trees and climbing roses that ended at an enormous tiled fountain in the courtyard. To the bougainvillea-clad walls and palm trees and pots of jasmine. To the coat of arms that Fred and I playfully designed to include a movie camera, a horse head, a horseshoe, and a piece of paper and quill pen.

To the massive drawing room, towering beams, floor-to-ceiling plate-glass windows. The swimming pool, the gardens. An Aeolian pipe organ I, summoning my childhood piano training, attempted to play with more enthusiasm than skill. The master bedroom with the ten-foot-tall shower in the bath designed for my strapping husband. Fireplaces everywhere—I was firmly of the belief that no house could have too many fireplaces—as were antiques, tapestries, maids' rooms.

Down the hill was a stable for Fred's horse, Silver King, a handsome, tall animal he had trained for the movies. Fred was determined to be a role model for young boys and had decided that cowboy movies were the way to go—especially because in cowboy films, there were no love scenes, only a hasty embrace of the heroine at the end while they walked off into the sunset. And after the success of *The Covered Wagon* in 1923, studios were eager to invest in them. By the time our house was finished in 1924, my Fred was the number-two cowboy star in the world behind Tom Mix; he costarred in serials with Silver King, who had his own heated house separate from the rest of the stables and round-the-clock grooms to meet his every need.

"That horse eats better than I do," I teased. But I didn't mind; I had nothing to mind, those days.

Those days when the money was pouring in, earned by us both, as fast as we could spend it and goodness, did we try! *Everyone* in Hollywood, all our old friends who used to pool our nickels to share a bowl of spaghetti and a pint of beer—we were all building grand mansions, stables, pools, most of them in these very Beverly Hills. Harold and Mildred Lloyd were our neighbors. So was John Gilbert. And a young newcomer to Hollywood named Rudolph Valentino.

Everyone had gone Hollywood! Now that we knew the in-

dustry we had invented wasn't going to vanish, we were all putting down roots, spending money we'd never before been able
to even imagine—and some didn't have the schooling to be able
to count it all, but that was what managers and business advi-
sors were for. The sons of chauffeurs now employed chauffeurs. The daughters of maids now had twenty maids of their
own. European vacations were de rigueur.

Parties! Everyone threw parties! So did the Thomsons; we
invited all our friends, new and old, to come to The Enchanted
Hill and kick back, let their hair down; ours were not the stuffy
evenings at Pickfair. No one had to wear a tiara; tuxes were
banned at the door. Sometimes we all packed into cars and went
to the prize fights; boxing was the new fad in Hollywood and
Fred's friend Gene Tunney, whom he'd met planning the Allied
Games, was the world's champion.

Other times, we girls laughingly shooed the boys off to go
to the fights by themselves and settled in for what the press
soon began to call "Cats' Parties." I made everyone bring their
pajamas, and we scrubbed off our makeup and let our hair
down, then trooped down to the basement screening room to
watch not the newest release—the usual Hollywood custom—
but our old movies instead. It was astonishing how difficult
those old movies of the 1910s were to find now! We'd never
imagined that what we were making would have any permanence or worth, so those old one- and two-reelers were hidden
away in forgotten storerooms, piled in boxes, not even protected from the light.

But what fun we had, watching ourselves in our unformed
youth! I couldn't bear to watch myself in those old Lois Weber
films any more now than I could back then, but at least now I
knew myself, knew my place in this industry. Bessie Love and

Alma Rubens and Pola Negri—huge stars now—cackled with glee to see themselves as extras back then, supporting stars who were no longer stars. They hooted and hollered as they glimpsed themselves preening for the camera, trying to catch its favoring eye. And my dear friends Anita Loos and Adela Rogers St. John howled with miserable laughter to watch their early screenplays, wondering what on earth they'd been drinking!

I, too, sometimes winced—especially at those films from World—but mostly I was happy. Happy to be in the company of these women, actresses, writers, directors; happy to be able to turn the lights back on and settle down and talk shop, freely helping, supporting, advising.

"Did you hear about poor Gloria Swanson?" Theda Bara—a panther on-screen but a rather dumpy-looking woman in real life—asked one night after I switched on the lights.

"What about her?" asked Theda's equally dumpy sister, who was always with her, even on set.

"Her husband has accused her of adultery in the divorce—naming thirteen other men including Valentino! Poor Gloria, he's such a louse. But now her studio is insisting that she have one of those morals clauses put in her contract, even though everyone knows she wasn't the one who had affairs. At least not with Valentino!"

"My newest contract has a morals clause, too," piped up the beautiful Pauline Starke.

"We all have one," someone else muttered. "Thanks to Will Hays. If I engage in—or am merely charged with, like Gloria—'adulterous conduct or immoral relations,' they can cancel my contract. Do you think any of the studio heads have morals clauses? No. But *they're* the worst—they're the ones with the casting couches literally inside their offices."

"You *know* C. B. DeMille doesn't have a morals clause," I said, pouring out a new round of cocktails. None of the moguls did, and the hypocrisy made me furious.

"No, he has a *harem,*" Norma Talmadge murmured; she was usually quiet at these parties; it was rare that she spoke up. "Everyone knows he's been having an affair for years with his secretary, his scenarist, anyone who moves!"

"Except Gloria—and isn't that the irony?" Bess Meredyth sighed. I loved Bess; she was the one who had so generously taught me everything she knew about screenwriting, back when we were both at Bosworth. "Everyone assumes DeMille and Gloria are lovers because she's starred in so many of his films. But they aren't—although not because C.B. hasn't tried. Poor Gloria. She does have rotten luck with men."

"Remember what happened between her and Wally Beery?" Anita Loos, in her usual youthful outfit—a little girl's high-necked nightgown—piped up. Bess and I exchanged looks; Anita's own husband, John Emerson, was no prize. He tried to take credit for everything that Anita wrote—except for *Gentlemen Prefer Blondes;* that he merely resented and belittled every chance he got—and he slept around when she was away. Why did smart, successful women have such terrible taste in men? It was as if they looked for ways to sabotage themselves, as if they felt they didn't deserve success personally as well as professionally. And I knew that if I hadn't lucked into Fred, I'd be right there along with them.

"Wally made her get an abortion, you know, because he didn't want her to ruin her career; he thought she'd be his meal ticket," Anita continued blithely. "Gloria told me. She was devastated."

"Do you think the doctors are on the studio payroll now?

Do you think they'll tell them, with all this morals clause stuff going on?" Norma Talmadge looked terrified, as did so many.

I knew, of course, that abortion was the dirty little secret in Hollywood. Glamorous actresses weren't supposed to be mothers; the public would stop going to see their pictures if they thought that the desirable vamp on-screen was changing diapers off it. And few actresses could afford to take the time off for a pregnancy; not with trains disgorging hundreds of would-be starlets every day. Francis X. Bushman could go home to his family of seven and not see his screen image suffer. But not Pola Negri. So we women, as usual, paid a price for our passion in a way that men did not.

"The sins you do two by two, you pay for one by one," sang one of Hollywood's most reliable "female doctors" as he passed out champagne to his patients, as if *that* would make the ordeal any less soul-searing. A very few women who found themselves in trouble chose to go away for a while, returning to Hollywood slimmer than ever, then surprising everyone by adopting a child, "Because I simply fell in love with him, when I was visiting the orphanage for publicity!" Barbara La Marr had recently done this, with the requisite photo spread in *Photoplay* with the new baby "who didn't look a thing like her, but a mother's love knows no bounds," as Louella Parsons loyally wrote in her gossip column. Because she, too, was on the studio payroll.

But I knew only the biggest stars would be able to get away with any of this; only the biggest stars would be able to rely on the studio paying to cover up their sins—if passion, love, rotten luck were truly sins, and I didn't happen to think they were. The rest would find their contracts canceled by these new hypocritical morality clauses.

More than ever, I was grateful I wasn't an actress. Fred and I longed to have a baby together, and if we did, it wouldn't interfere with my work at all. Nobody—not even Louis B. Mayer—really cared what a scenarist looked like, and I could write from a hospital bed if I had to. And because I longed for a child, I wasn't quite sure how I felt about those actresses who had—willingly or unwillingly—chosen to terminate a pregnancy, other than to be extraordinarily grateful that I wasn't in their shoes. I understood the devouring nature of this business—chew them up, spit them out, because there are always more on the way. I also understood that men never had to wrestle with that kind of dilemma, and it wasn't fair. Men could have affairs without worrying about the consequences—well, except for homosexual men. Billy Haines, so charming off-screen and on, was known to be queer; so was Ramon Novarro. And both were terrified about the new morals clause.

I was nearly forty; pragmatically, I knew I'd probably missed my chance at motherhood. And in that way, wasn't I exactly like everyone else? We'd all put our careers first, we brilliant, beautiful women. We all sacrificed something. Marriages. Children. Things a man never had to sacrifice.

"How is Mary? Why doesn't she ever come to these parties?" Adela asked me as we got up to pour ourselves more cocktails before settling down for more gossip. Adela had given up her gum snapping and now wore terribly sophisticated clothes, and had bobbed her hair. As usual, I felt like a country bumpkin next to her, even though one quick glance in the mirror assured me that my black hair was coiled sleekly as usual. Tonight we were both wearing expensive silk pajamas, although Adela had topped hers with a glorious kimono I immediately coveted.

"I invite her, of course. Every time. But she always says she and Doug have plans."

"He's trapped her on that estate." Adela shook her head. "I feel sorry for her. I think she's terribly lonely, after all."

"I don't know," I answered slowly; as loyal as I was to Mary, I wasn't blind to her faults. "I'm not entirely sure who has trapped whom. Doug likes people, he likes to go out and have fun. Once I was with them on the beach—of course, not just the beach, not with Doug and Mary. They'd arranged for enormous tents to be set up, and a catered dinner on the Pickfair china. Remember the days when we used to go out to Santa Monica or Laguna? With only a blanket and a picnic basket, and we'd come home covered in sand? And think we were the luckiest people alive to live where we lived, and do the work that we did?"

"We were. We are."

"Well, anyway, we were on the beach and on the drive back, Doug saw a sign for a dance marathon down on one of the piers and he wanted to go. But Mary said—I still can't quite believe it, but she said in that way she has with him, 'Oh, Douglas! You know we can't be seen in those kinds of places!'"

"Oh, Fran!"

"I know. And so, I wonder. Even when—back when we were—" And I struggled to give voice to what I was really thinking.

Back when Mary and I were friends.

Because I didn't know if we were, anymore. And for a moment my hands trembled and Adela quickly took the cocktail shaker away from me, flashing an understanding smile.

"Back when we were *closer*," I finally decided to say. "Even back then, she didn't like to go out much. I used to invite her to join our gang that hung out at the Ship Café, remember? But she never would go. She's always hung back, apart."

"And now, she's royalty. Or so she thinks. Everyone worships at the altar of Doug and Mary. Don't get me wrong, I love Mary and I like Doug, I always have. But they're turning into waxworks, waiting for the world to come see them up at the castle. The only time they leave is to go to work or go to Europe in order to see how much they are adored by people who don't speak English. We all have to pay obeisance to them. It would do her good to come here sometime and join us girls, let those famous curls get tangled a little."

"Well, maybe if you ask." I smiled ruefully, my heart smarting. "Goodness knows I've tried."

As Adela went to freshen up some drinks, I tried to remember the last time I'd talked to Mary, really talked like we used to.

After *The Love Light,* we seemed to have—drifted apart. Of course we saw each other at industry functions and premieres, and Mary always greeted me warmly with a hug and a kiss, touchingly glad to see me. As I was to see her; I *missed* her, missed how easily we used to be able to finish each other's thoughts and shared the same dreams, missed her sober dedication to her craft. I'd now worked with many actors and not one of them came close to Mary's single-mindedness on the set.

And of course, when summoned to Pickfair for one of those glittering, interminable evenings I always obeyed, even when Fred found an excuse to stay home. But every time I visited, it seemed as if Mary were encased in another layer of finely spun glass. She looked more beautiful than ever now that she was in her thirties; her skin still was like porcelain, lit from within by a special glow, and her sense of style was much more sophisticated than it once had been. Her films still did well, if not quite as well as they once had. Some, like *Little Lord Fauntleroy,* were truly works of art. It was obvious that Mary was seeking to be known as someone—something—more than the little girl with the curls that we'd created together, and I could only applaud her growth and risk-taking as an artist. And stifle a sigh when she reverted back to form, as she had in *Little Annie Rooney,* in order to pay the bills—or ensure her stardom.

She was trapped, that's what she was; Mary was trapped like a fly in amber, unable to stray too far from what her public loved, yet facing the cruel inevitability of time, time that would age her out of these roles, into—what? The public wanted her to remain a child on-screen and a queen off it.

But what did *she* want? I didn't know. And that smarted. Quite a lot.

There was no denying it; we weren't as close as we'd been. For the first time in our lives, I had absolutely no idea what Mary did every day, who she saw, what her habits were.

Maybe it was because *The Love Light,* our first movie together in which she truly played a woman, a woman with a baby, hadn't done well? Of course, I knew that Mary wasn't happy on the set; I saw how she rolled her eyes whenever I spent too much time on Fred. But goodness, the final movie was all Mary—I'd made sure of it. Mary heroic, Mary spunky, Mary good. Once upon a time, working with my best friend had been the very definition of happiness. But no more.

Maybe it was because we were married now and it was inevitable that our husbands took up the bulk of our lives away from work. Maybe Mary suspected that I really didn't like Doug. I knew that Mary didn't think much of Fred, despite her constant crowing that she'd been the one to introduce us.

Maybe it was simply the inevitability of time, of two people growing apart, developing other interests, learning to rely on ourselves rather than on each other.

Whatever the reason, as I gazed at the basement full of women I could call, without hesitation, my friends, I knew there was one person missing. One very important person. And for a moment, my vision was clouded with surprising tears.

"I've got a new record," cried Bessie Love. "Fran, where's the gramophone?"

Blinking the tears away, I laughed and rushed over to put the record on Fred's newest toy, a huge RCA Victor cabinet model. I placed the record on the turntable, vigorously cranked the handle, and a wild, jazzy tune began to play.

"C'mon, everyone! Let me teach you this new dance I'm doing in my next movie. It's called the Charleston!" Bessie tossed her sleek bobbed hair and began to dance, an odd dance that required her to bend her knees and kick, arms swinging, as she rotated on the floor. Everyone screamed, and soon we were all trying, arms flailing, knees knocking. I couldn't get the hang of it; it seemed awkward and disjointed. Give me the good old Turkey Trot anytime.

I paused to catch my breath—Lord, I was perspiring, my hair was coming undone, but goodness, were we all having a good time!—and I couldn't help but think that Mary would never fit in here, even if she did accept my invitation.

If Mary did have a place in my life, it would have to be in quiet, unexpected moments, hidden from the view of tipsy flappers and the screaming of the jazz blaring out of the gramophone. This was a new age, an age of rouged knees and short dresses and rolled stockings and flasks tucked into garters.

Mary, with her Victorian curls, would have been as out of place as a china doll in a speakeasy. And I, with my equally Victorian long hair that I refused to cut because Fred would have killed me, should have been out of place, too. I wondered, as I stepped away from the dancing to watch the youthful, vibrant actresses kick up their heels, if either I or Mary would survive this new, younger age. The truth was, we were already known as the sedate dinosaurs in the industry, those of us who had been around since the early or mid teens. How on earth could we keep up with dancing girls such as Bessie and Colleen Moore, girls who had grown up watching movies, worshipping stars like Mary Pickford? An entire generation was now invading Hollywood; a generation that didn't remember a time before Charlie Chaplin wiggled his nose on-screen.

A generation that had no idea how far we'd come, how hard we'd worked to pave the way.

As I walked over to the gramophone, one of my knees creaked and I had to laugh. Lifting the needle off the record, I placed it at the beginning and cranked the handle again so the girls could keep dancing. I was definitely too old for this!

A few days later, however, I discovered, to my amazement and joy, that I wasn't as old as I'd thought, after all. And when I found out, who was the first person I had to tell (after Fred, of course)?

Mary.

It was always Mary.

MARY HUGGED FRAN AS SHE WALKED HER TO the door; she held on tightly, feeling so noble, so generously expansive; feeling as if she'd just played the performance of her life, and Fran hadn't suspected a thing.

"Take care, Fran, dear! Let me know if you need anything—anything at all! We still have a lot of Gwynnie's baby clothes and things. She's almost ten now, so we don't need them."

"Thank you, Squeebee! I have a feeling this is going to be the most spoiled baby in all of Hollywood!" Fran laughingly patted her still-flat stomach. "Louis B. Mayer and Sam Goldwyn both sent telegrams saying they want to be godfather. Although how they found out, I'm not quite sure."

"Louella. Louella Parsons. She knows everything. You know how these so-called journalists are, Fran. They're highly paid gossips. Louella has every doctor in Hollywood on her payroll."

"I suppose. At least I got to tell you myself, Mary. And Fred—at least *he* heard it from me!"

Laughing—looking lovelier than she ever had, softer, more radiant—Fran walked down the drive in that military way she had; she never strolled, she always marched, her heels punctuating the silence.

Mary shut the door, relieved at first to have gotten through the scene without falling apart—and without disappointing Fran. But then she found herself trying to remember the first time she'd seen dear Fran. When was it? 1914? 1915? So many years ago! The door to the cutting room opened, and there had stood Frances Marion, obviously nervous but elegant, so poised and sophisticated. Mary had felt like a grubby little urchin, her hair in a towel, her hands scratched and dirty from the cutting machine. Owen had introduced them. She'd forgotten that! Well, that was one good thing he'd given her, at least.

Mary's stomach lurched, she tasted bile, and she rushed upstairs, ignoring the startled look of the doorman. Running down the wide hall, past colored framed photographs of her and Douglas in their most famous roles, she pushed open her bedroom door and slid on her knees to the toilet just in time. Holding her curls up, she retched into the bowl, then sat back, her forehead clammy, the room spinning. She sat like that for several minutes. Sympathy sickness, she thought with a drowsy smile. Sympathy, for what Fran was going through.

Sympathy, for what she herself could never go through.

Rising on shaky limbs, Mary walked over to the sink and splashed her face with cool water. Then she gazed at herself in the mirror—even though she'd installed soft, faintly pink lights in the bathroom, the most forgiving light there was, she still looked terrible, her skin blotchy, her eyes a little puffy—and spied the medicine cabinet on the wall behind her.

She looked at the clock; it was only two in the afternoon. She had a rare day off, but Douglas was still at the studio. And he would be, for several more hours.

Quickly she padded back out through her bedroom, shut the door, returned to the bathroom, and opened the medicine cabinet. She took out a large amber bottle, the kind that swabbing alcohol came in, and she crept back into her room. Settling herself among the pillows—so many! Douglas said too many, but in Mary's mind she couldn't have enough, not after years of sleeping on rolled-up newspapers—Mary kicked off her shoes, unbuckled her garters, and rolled her stockings down. She had the figure to wear the most extreme flapper fashions without any of the rubbery undergarments usually required, but Douglas still preferred her in more feminine clothes, with waists. "I like my wife to look like a woman," he declared. And true, he had a taste for old-fashioned clothing; he hadn't made a movie that wasn't a costume picture in years. Although she also suspected that he liked showing off his muscular legs in tights.

Settling down among all the pillows—heaven, it was! Each pillow like a puff of cloud!—Mary unscrewed the bottle and took a nice long sip. The familiar juniper smell tickled her nose, and the gin was icy hot down her throat. She waited a few minutes, took another long pull, then finally felt herself relax, her blood warming up, her head a little bit fuzzy, fuzzy enough to dull the sharpest, most jagged edges of her memories and fears.

She didn't indulge herself in this kind of afternoon very often, so might as well enjoy it, give in to everything that she usually tried to keep at bay with work, both in front of the camera and behind it running United Artists—the public appearances expected of her and Douglas, the never-ending parade of dignitaries that always found their way to the groaning dinner table at Pickfair. She was never off duty—that's how she was coming to think of it. Being on duty meant being Mary

Pickford, no matter how tired she was. Off duty, she could become a Smith again, like Mama and Lottie and Jack. A Smith with a taste for gin.

So what? She'd earned a little reprieve. Now and then. She deserved to wallow a little, shut the curtains, keep all the prying—worshipful, judgmental, fickle—eyes outside; blur the equally judgmental eyes staring at her inside, from her own reflection.

As she stretched her legs and wiggled her toes, she thought once more of Owen. When was the last time she'd seen him in person? Before the divorce. He was still working, but the last time she'd seen his face on-screen, she couldn't prevent a gasp. His features were so coarse, hardened. He looked at least ten years older than he was.

But he had given her her first sip of gin. On the first night they were together—not their wedding night!—to relax her, she'd been so tense, so afraid and yet feeling as if she couldn't live one more minute without knowing what this great mystery was. The gin did its job; she remembered how, after the first drink, Owen's voice turned into the most soothing Irish lullaby, crooning songs of love, of passion, and then songs to soothe her to sleep when her heart was racing with fear and shame and guilt, always guilt. Guilt for hurting Mama, for sinning, for being a bad girl—as bad a girl as most actresses were assumed to be, and she'd tried all her life to live above that, to show that an actress could be good and pure. Pure enough even for Miss Josephine.

How she'd prayed for her monthly time, after that night! And it had happened, thank God. She kept away from Owen after that, until she couldn't any longer and then they were married. That whole sham.

Marriage to Douglas was so different! It was a consecration, in a way. She'd almost felt, standing next to him in his drawing room, with the justice of the peace so starstruck he forgot half of the ceremony, that there should be a rite, something involving Holy Water, for their union was so sacred, so just. Not only for them, but for their careers—for the entire *industry*. It was what the previous ten years or so had been leading up to— from the moment the first nickelodeon flickered on a dirty sheet hung on a storefront wall, all through the teens as an art form was created, Griffith made his epic, the frenzy of the *Poor Little Rich Girl* showing and the first time she'd seen that peculiar expression of disbelief and adoration in the public's eyes, through the formation of United Artists—

The union of Douglas Fairbanks and Mary Pickford was the natural progression, the capstone. The crowning moment.

And so there was no shame in their marriage, only happiness and kindness. "This is a house that has never known an angry word," she'd declared to *Photoplay* magazine the other day, in one of the many sit-downs she was gracious enough to give, for the good of the industry. And for the good of her career.

For that was—slipping?

No. No, of course not. She only needed to regain her footing a little. The public said—she'd even asked them! Asked them to send her story ideas!—that they still wanted her to be Little Mary. But the public was also flocking to films starring Rudolph Valentino and Gloria Swanson and now that little Colleen Moore and saucy Clara Bow, the new rising "flappers."

Douglas could still do costume pictures and not suffer at the box office, but every time Mary hid her curls and made one, she took another blow. *Rosita* had not done well, neither had *Dorothy Vernon of Haddon Hall*. *Little Annie Rooney* and the upcoming *Sparrows* had been welcome returns to form as the feisty girl again, the scrappy little heroine Fran had created so long ago. But there had been snipes in the press that she'd never seen before; too many reviewers made doubtful remarks about her age, questioned the wisdom of continuing to play children or adolescents.

A new script had come across her desk; in it, she'd play a contemporary young woman, not quite a flapper, though. Just a simple shopgirl who has a sweet romance with a young man. She was seriously considering it, although her leading man, a youth named Buddy Rogers, would be twelve years her junior—how embarrassing! To graduate, finally, to a contemporary role only to already be too old for it! But she sensed she needed to do it; she needed to move into this new age, speak to a new generation of fans. Or at least she needed to *try*.

New generation! Oh, Lord, how old she was getting! She'd turned thirty-four, this April of 1926. Fran was even older, but now she was going to be a mother, which somehow made her seem both young *and* old. Young enough to give birth, but a child automatically put you in a different category—maternal. Which was fine for a screenwriter.

Not for an actress, however. Particularly an actress whose image was that of a child herself. She did everything she could to stave off time; she took care of herself, her figure. She slathered so many creams and potions upon her face at night that sometimes, Douglas protested he couldn't even kiss her good night. She wore a chinstrap to bed. She always slept on her back, to avoid wrinkles.

Meanwhile Douglas behaved as he always had, and never

looked a year older; his tan skin gave him such a healthy, youthful appearance. But Mary feared the sun's rays; they treated men's and women's skins so differently, caressing the former, punishing the latter. So always a wide-brimmed hat and a parasol for her whenever she ventured out under the punishing California sun.

Mary took another long sip, patting her chin worriedly; it still felt as firm as ever, but for how long? Outside, despite the heavy windows and curtains, she could hear the gardener rolling the lawn, a motor revving up in the garage. Probably one of the chauffeurs was tinkering with it. She imagined that was what chauffeurs did when they weren't driving, although she wasn't entirely sure. All she knew is that they needed to be paid.

Along with the cooks and maids and doorman and Doug's manservant, her French maid, the gardeners—an army of them! Once she'd gone inside the tool "shed"—larger than any house she'd ever lived in before Pickfair—and been stunned by the rows and rows of gleaming shears and clippers and rakes and hoes, lawn rollers and mowers, bags and bags of seed and fertilizer, wheelbarrows of all sizes, coiled hoses. It was like an armory, the weapons required to keep the rugged California wilderness surrounding Pickfair at bay.

It all cost money. Money she and Douglas had to earn. Money that United Artists was bleeding, as Charlie had stubbornly slowed his output, deciding to do everything himself—write, produce, direct, compose the music, design the costumes; taking years to make one of his films, films that were instantly hailed as genius but didn't quite perform at the box office. *A Woman of Paris* was his first UA film and it had been a disaster! *The Gold Rush* had done better but it had taken him three years to make it.

Griffith was no longer with UA: Griffith was no longer doing much of anything, as far as she could tell. They'd forced him out, after one too many failures, in 1924. He hadn't made a film since, although there were always rumors that he was in preproduction. It was a shame, of course, that she'd had to fire him—the man who had made her! The man who had shown her what she could do in front of a camera. She could remember those early days with him at Biograph with fondness, particularly after the third or fourth glass of gin; those days of pure terror at the strangeness of this new thing called "flickers," the clackety-clack of the camera punching out the sprocket holes while they filmed, the inferno of the lights or the unpredictability of the sun, the feeling that she was slumming, that she had let someone down, some muse or patron of the arts, by agreeing to appear in front of the camera. But then the wonder of it all, the first time she saw herself on the screen—she was absolutely mortified, even as she understood she was witnessing something historic; until films, no actor had ever been able to see his performance as the audience did. But then Griffith peeled her hands from her eyes and forced her to look, really look, at how the camera loved her; at how she seemed lit by a different, more special light than everyone else, even though they'd all been lit the same. She had D. W. Griffith to thank for that; for showing her *herself,* the self that, over the years, came to be more real than the self who never saw the loving lens of a camera.

But a business is a business, and despite the memories—which they recalled over a bottle of gin and some tears; shhh, don't tell Douglas!—she'd had to let Griffith go. Now UA had Gloria Swanson and Sam Goldwyn and Rudolph Valentino in the stable. But still, Douglas and Mary and Charlie were the figureheads. The ones who really paid the bills.

But oh, how sometimes she did long to be able to walk away! To hole herself up in her room like this, or take Mama away somewhere, back to Toronto, maybe. Mama—oh, Mama! She had to get well, she had to—but if she didn't, it would be Mary's fault.

"Mama, I need help," Mary had said one day in 1925. And hadn't Mama come to her rescue as she always did? But Mary didn't really need help; she only said it to give Charlotte something to do, because Mama spent far too much time down at her cottage with her bottles. It was as if, now that she and Mary had achieved success beyond their wildest dreams, Mama lost her way. She sometimes seemed so sad, so lost, now that they didn't have trains to catch and theaters to play and contracts to negotiate. So she drank more than usual, and Mary did sometimes worry about little Gwynnie—someone had to, because Lottie had to be reminded that she had a daughter!—and so she started having the little girl over to Pickfair more and more, until now Gwynnie had her own room and a nurse in a separate wing. Which left Mama alone, so Mary asked her to help with the costumes for *Annie Rooney*.

"I can't get this costume designer to understand what I need, Mama," Mary lied. "I'm a girl on the streets in New York in this one. I need my costumes to look adorable, but rather—raggedy."

Charlotte had brightened up; she'd laid off the bottle for a couple weeks, and sketched designs and searched for fabric, before recalling she still had some bolts from the old days up in an attic. "Just the thing, my dear! The cloth is probably all faded by now, but perfect for your new movie."

While Mama was digging in the trunk, the lid fell down on her, crushing her ample chest; it was when the doctor examined her that a lump was found. And it was all Mary's fault! If she hadn't asked her for help, Mama wouldn't have been crushed by the trunk and the lump would never have formed.

Mama refused surgery; she'd become a Christian Scientist, believing fervently in the power of prayer and mind over body. Mary couldn't persuade her otherwise. And now she was wasting away, inch by inch; no longer was her soft chest a warm memory, a place where Mary had found solace, time and again. Now it was a misshapen bomb ticking slowly but steadily, and one day it would explode. And Mary would be left without the one true thing in her life: a mother's love.

Mary wouldn't think about that; no, she wouldn't. She would think about other things, happier things. She had a new gown to wear to Douglas's premiere; *his* movies were doing well. And he wasn't bothered by the things Mary was; he didn't question, he didn't brood, he only stood with his hands on his hips, feet planted firmly, and laughingly dared the world to change, to come at him. And the world, dazzled as Mary once was by the brilliance of that white gleaming smile, the insouciance in his brown, crinkled-up eyes, did not dare. And so Douglas kept making his films and the public kept flocking to them, and he did not get letters asking how old he was, when was he going to grow up, didn't he think he was too old to be playing the parts he'd always played?

He did not get letters asking when he was going to have a baby, if he did have a baby, or why he couldn't have a baby.

Fran could have a baby. And she was. So Mary took another drink of gin.

She should be happy for dear Fran, but she wasn't and that was another thing to feel guilty about. She should be thrilled that Fran and her husband—her successful cowboy star husband—

were having a child together to cement their union. Fran had never particularly talked about children before, only in the vaguest of ways. So it was something of a surprise, and so Mary could be forgiven if she hadn't quite reacted the way Fran had probably hoped.

"Mary, darling, I have something to tell you!" Fran had telephoned earlier that day, then driven over to Pickfair in a rush. She'd grabbed Mary in the foyer, and Mary had to laugh and calm her down, and take her into the drawing room so the servants couldn't hear whatever it was—obviously something important—she had to say. For the servants did whisper and gossip, it was a problem all her movie-star friends had, the help tattling to the press—

Mary bolted upright, sloshing her gin, her heart thumping. She slid out of bed, tripping over her shoes, giggling a little as she locked her bedroom door after first pressing her ear against it, to make sure no one was standing outside. Then she crawled back into her nest of pillows, these linen pillows, embroidered by nuns in Belgium—how lovely! How perfect! Just for her!

"I'm having a baby!" Fran had barely waited until they were seated on the Louis XIV sofa and the maid had left to bring in tea, before she blurted her news. Then she sat back and stared anxiously at Mary.

But Mary didn't know what to say; she didn't know where to look. It only took one glimpse at Fran's joyful countenance to make her own eyes fill with tears, so she couldn't risk that.

"I'm—I'm so happy for you," she heard herself say, and it must have been enough, because Fran let out an enormous breath and began babbling about what a surprise it was, they'd been trying but the doctor wasn't optimistic, and, yes, she was a bit embarrassed because she would be thirty-nine when the baby was born, that was so old, she knew women who were already grandmothers!

Fran kept talking, to Mary's relief; it seemed she was only required to say yes and no and um-hum, now and then. But there was a moment before they said goodbye that Fran seemed to catch herself; she stopped the babbling and put her hands on Mary's shoulders, gazing at her with those eyes that had always looked up to her for approval, for assurance. Those eyes that had been so touchingly hopeful when she'd first seen them, all those years ago.

"Mary, dearest, I do hope you're pleased. Do you remember how we used to talk about things, back in the bungalows? How we wondered if we'd ever love a man as much as we loved our work? If we could ever fit children in?"

Mary nodded, her eyes misting over; those years seemed so long ago. She should be thankful for how far she'd come—triumphant, even. But right now she was dead inside, impervious to feelings. Had she become so used to pouring them out to the camera that she had nothing left over for her actual life?

"And here we are, we both have found our true loves. And now—a child! I think I can do it, Mary—be a good mother and a career woman. But if I can't, I've already done so much more in my career than I could have dreamed, and maybe now it's time for me to be a mother. Maybe that's the most important thing, after all."

"No, Fran!" Mary hugged her friend to her fiercely; she couldn't let her believe this. Because if she did, what did it say about Mary? "No, I won't hear it! I'm so happy for you, but you're still—I *need* you, Fran! I still need you, the industry needs you. You're the best there is, and don't you forget it!"

Fran gasped, then she pulled away, and there was astonishment in her eyes, a rosy flush mottling her already red cheeks. "Mary! Thank you! I—that you think that! Even after—that you think that means so much to me."

"Now go home and put your feet up. Do you still have that little lap desk you used to write on?"

Fran nodded.

"Then take that with you and start writing. Something. Prove to the world that a mother's mind isn't only good for thinking up lullabies, will you, Fran?"

"Mary, you're my dearest friend, and I owe you everything."

"No, Fran, I owe you."

They hugged, Fran left. But Mary didn't know when she'd see her again as she shut the door. When she would be *able* to see her again, that is. She was not going to be able to be Fran's friend the way she ought to be, the way Fran expected her to be. A friend to accompany her to doctors' appointments, take her shopping for layettes, commiserate over the inevitable changes in her body. She couldn't tell Fran why; Fran would never understand. How could she, when Mary herself didn't?

All she knew was that she had to protect herself; she had to save herself for the camera because she didn't know how much longer it would gaze at her adoringly. And in order to do that, she had to cut ties to the real world, with its mess and chaos, its urgent tempo, blaring jazz, dancing flappers. Mothers with fussy babies, mothers with heavy, milky breasts and hampers of dirty, smelly diapers and heads full of nursery rhymes. Mothers who were more enamored of their fussy babies than they were with her. Because babies always came first, didn't they?

Mary was alone now; Fran had gone, but her news remained and it would linger, this dream baby would become real, like little Gwynnie had. And she would lose Fran forever. And she would be even more alone.

But she did still have her bottle; the gin wasn't gone yet, and there was more where that came from. The gin made her forget how quickly time passed, how fleeting was youth and beauty and innocence and fame and fortune; it made her dream wild dreams—fantastic visions of dragons and men on the moon and silly dancing people; dreams that had nothing to do with real life, and so she preferred them, terrifying as they some-times were, to her dreams that were not gin-soaked.

The gin let her forget that Douglas might come bounding in for dinner with a coterie of people to amuse him, because he seemed to need that more and more; he was no longer content only in her company the way he used to be. And if he didn't come home surrounded by others, he would probably come home late. There had been some nights, recently, when he stayed at the studio until almost midnight. Mary didn't ask him why. Just as he didn't ask her what was in the medicine cabinet.

She set the bottle down and snuggled further into the pil-lows, pulling the covers over her. She might as well sleep now; she would look all the better in the morning. The room spun behind her closed eyes and her mouth was already dry as cot-ton, but still it was preferable to remaining awake, thinking about all the things she didn't want to think about; seeing im-ages of people she would only disappoint, or whom she had already disappointed. Seeing images of gurgling babies; babies she could never have. Babies she didn't deserve.

And she wouldn't have to know what time Douglas came home, if she was asleep.

CHAPTER 16

FRANCES

DECEMBER 1926

THE HOSPITAL WAS SO COLD.

That was what I kept thinking as I waited outside his room, seated rigidly on a small metal chair. The very same kind of chair I'd sat on when I met him—and I almost laughed at that, wanting to rush inside and share this with him as I shared everything.

But the doctors wouldn't let me, and the hospital was so cold, and I was shivering so violently my teeth hurt, my joints, too. The last time I'd been this freezing was on that road from Verdun, in the war. The war that brought Fred and me together. The nurses and the doctors went in and out of his room but they always shut the door firmly, as if it could drown out his moans. But it didn't.

I thought that if I could only hold him, I'd stop shivering and he'd get better. I thought that if I couldn't hold him, I wanted to hold our sons, little Fred and Dickie, and I looked around, their names on my lips until I remembered. It was Christmas Eve, and they were home asleep. Oh, God, Christmas Eve, and they'd be expecting a visit from Santa, presents to open, and how could I do it? Who would do it for me?

"Mary," I whispered, and I knew this was not the first time I'd said her name, but I couldn't remember how many times I had, or when. I couldn't remember what time it was or how long I'd been sitting here.

I could only remember that Fred was sick, desperately sick, and I was shivering outside his hospital door, and that it had all started with a limp. A stupid little limp, as we strolled the grounds of The Enchanted Hill one evening the way we always did; surveying our land, taking stock of our blessings, planning tomorrow before heading inside to say good night to our sons, already tucked into bed by their nanny.

"What's that?" I'd ask, as he winced and favored his right leg. "One of your old injuries?" For my husband had many; that was the occupational hazard of being a cowboy star. Fred had been run over by a wagon, injured himself in a jump from a building onto Silver King, and collected countless scrapes and wounds from rolling around in the sagebrush as he wrestled bad guys.

"Oh, nothing." Fred took another step and couldn't hide a spasm of pain. "I think I pulled a groin muscle yesterday."

"Fred Thomson, is there a muscle on that body you haven't pulled or strained?"

"I'm working on it." Fred grinned, pulled me to his good side, and held me close as we turned around and took one last look—I would always remember it that way. *One last look* at the purple twilight, the way the sun's last beams threaded pink through a smear of gray clouds, a few stars beginning to twinkle on. A horse neighed down in the stables as I inhaled the jasmine. I took one last look to remind myself how lucky I was—how lucky *we* were.

Then we went inside. Only a few hours later, the nightmare began.

———

BEFORE THE NIGHTMARE, there was paradise.

A new contract with MGM, when I was expecting Fred Jr. I finally allowed Mayer and Thalberg to persuade me to settle down and work for one studio—a welcome measure of stability right when I was feeling the urge to nest. The better to rock the cradle, which would never fall. And I made good films, too—*The Scarlet Letter,* with Lillian Gish; *Love* with the strange new Swedish star, Greta Garbo. And my favorite of all my films, *The Wind,* again with Lillian.

Irving and I had poured our hearts into that movie, going over the script together time and again. It was a grim story and it had to be filmed on location—something that Mayer balked at, but he was in awe of Irving then, in awe of that frail young man's obvious genius, happy to take credit for it when his movies became instant masterpieces. So Mayer reluctantly agreed to film on location in the desert, an ordeal, but worth it. Even after Lillian had the skin on her hand seared off when she grabbed the handle of a car that had been in the sun all afternoon, she never complained. She was the most dedicated actress I'd ever worked with save for Mary, and she gave a towering performance as the young bride driven mad—and to murder—by the relentless prairie wind.

The ending *had* to be tragic. The mad bride had to walk out into the wind to her death. She'd killed a man. It was the ending the censors would require—it was the ending the audience deserved—Irving and I agreed on that while we worked on the script.

Still, I had a premonition. "Not a happy ending, Irving. Not that," I told him when I turned the treatment in, and he'd agreed.

But when the film was previewed, the audience wasn't happy, and Mayer forced us to change the ending. No argument was heard; I found myself on the wrong end of one of Mayer's increasingly famous icy stares. His little studio had grown by leaps and bounds and was now the grandest of them all, and even though my contract was bigger than most of the studio's stars, I was still only a writer—a profession that seemed to have shrunk in the last few years. Gone were the days when I cast small roles, worked next to the director suggesting setups or lighting. Gone were the days when I could shape my scripts as I saw them. Mayer—and, to a lesser extent, the MPPDA— was the last word. He was God.

MGM spared no expense in its productions; my films were guaranteed enormous distribution and publicity. The actors were the best, as were the costumes and sets. But it was all rather like a factory; so unlike those days when Mickey, Mary, and I caught magic in a bottle through laughter and improvisation. But as long as I had Irving's ear—which I did, and which I cherished—I was spared the worst of it, and allowed some autonomy. To a point.

And true, I didn't care as much; I'd allowed myself to idle after the birth of the baby and then the adoption of Richard only a year later. It wasn't as if I spent all my time in the nursery; Mary had been right about that. I loved my sons but was more than happy for the nanny to do the dirty work. Still, I didn't pursue projects as passionately as I once had. Fred was doing so well and was enjoying fame far beyond what I'd ever hoped; I found myself stepping back into the shadows so that he could shine even brighter.

"You're sublimating your career to his," Adela pointed out

one day. And I had to admit I was, even as I wasn't very proud of that fact.

"It's his turn in the sun." I shrugged, as if I didn't really care. "I've had mine."

"The world would be brighter with two suns shining, you know," Adela remarked sagely. While I laughed and acknowledged it was true, I still remained in a low gear, my career idling, not racing.

Why was that? I'd worked so hard to get here, to step out of Mary's shadow, and now that I had, why did I want to step into Fred's? Was I simply incapable of being in the spotlight? I'd had more chances to direct, but turned them all down. I was capable of pushing other women's careers—I'd urged MGM to get Garbo out of the cheesecake business and play up to her exotic, brooding strengths; I'd pushed Lillian at the studio, gotten jobs for Adela and Anita. But why did I shy away from pushing myself?

Or did I see Fred's career as one of my projects, my own creation, and, in stepping back, I was giving my creation room to grow and flourish?

"I think I've learned to be happy where I am, instead of wondering where else I could be. Fred's done that to me. He's made me happy," I answered Adela.

"You know my grandmother used to say you can't drive three mules at the same time. Career, husband, children—one of these will get the short end of the stick. I guess you've chosen which."

"And I'm lucky I got to choose." The moment I said it, I realized that was the truth; I was simply astonished at my luck—career *and* family—and not inclined to test it in any way.

"I'm happy, Adela. Happy. Completely fulfilled for the first time in my life. No compromises, no disappointments."

"You and Fred are the lucky ones," Adela agreed, then she grabbed her handbag, pulled out a sheet of paper, and made notes. While she was still a screenwriter, Adela was now known as the "Mother Confessor" of Hollywood; she wrote column after column for *Photoplay* and other newspapers about the comings and goings of the stars. I knew that if I asked Adela not to write about my happy marriage, she would comply; our friendship always came first.

But I didn't mind having the truth of my marriage in print, for I was proud of it. It wasn't easy every day; Fred and I both had a stubborn streak, and we could argue, vehemently, about any topic. But we ended every argument with a handshake of respect and a kiss. And while we both had legions of friends, we preferred each other's company and made time for evenings spent with our sons, dining in front of one of the many fireplaces at The Enchanted Hill, or mornings riding together before we went our separate ways to work; me to MGM and Fred to FBO, the studio recently bought by Boston banker Joseph P. Kennedy. Fred's FBO films were huge in the rural markets but FBO had recently lent him to Paramount, to try to boost his box office in big cities.

Mary and Douglas still were the king and queen of Hollywood, but Fred and I had the marriage most movie people looked up to, maybe envied. More and more, Mary stayed shut up at Pickfair while Douglas was seen out and about town surrounded by a coterie of celebrities, royals, and of course, Charlie Chaplin. He'd built Pickfair for Mary—but it was as if he himself chafed within its confines.

Mary didn't always return my calls these days; she hadn't,

since the babies came. Oh, she'd sent beautiful gifts for each of our boys, but somehow had never found time to come and see them. Mary was drifting, that was it; she was drifting, like a fragile water lily, further and further away and I had no idea why, or how to get her back. Adela, Hedda Hopper, Marie Dressler—these were my closest friends now, the ones who were there when the babies came, who didn't mind scrambling around on the floor of the nursery, who stood up at each christening.

And Adela, Hedda, and Marie were the ones who were here now, taking turns holding my hand, day after day, in the hospital. They fetched coffee, drove back and forth to the house to check on the boys, gave out bulletins to the press, for anxious fans were sending telegrams and flowers by the bushel.

But he was too sick to notice.

That first night, when Fred awoke in terrible pain with a 106-degree temperature, the doctors thought it was kidney stones. After a few days they operated, only to find nothing there, but meanwhile, Fred had lost a lot of blood. He had a transfusion, but that didn't help his condition.

And now, ominously, his fever had spiked again, and his jaws had clenched.

"Tetanus," the doctors finally said, relief in their eyes, and so for a moment, I felt it myself. But then I realized that they were only relieved at having stumbled upon the right diagnosis; their grim words pierced my heart with terror. Very few people recovered from an advanced state of tetanus. "Did he have any kind of accident or injury lately?"

"Oh!" My gut was punched by a memory. "Yes, a couple weeks ago—he stepped on a nail in the barn. But he was fine right after—for days! This only just happened."

The doctors exchanged glances and nodded.

"But there's hope?" I couldn't help asking even as I knew it was wrong, useless. They'd tell me what I wanted to hear because they were doctors, because they were *men* and I was merely the wife. The hysterical wife, but that was what I was; the sight of my Fred—my strong, strapping husband—thrashing feverishly in bed, his eyes, when opened, dull with pain. And now his jaw locked so that he could barely moan—that was the worst. The terror in his eyes when he did try to speak, the rigidity of his jaw, his mouth a misshapen slit.

At one point, I thought I saw him try to say, "Children."

"Do you want to see the boys?" Fear invaded my stomach, filling its emptiness so that I was nauseated, but I gripped the rail of his bed, tight, until the wave passed. Did this mean he thought he was dying? Did I want our sons to see their father like this, their last glimpse of him not the laughing man who tossed them effortlessly in the air and caught them with ease, or tickled them until they squealed like little piglets, or chased them all around the tiled fountain outside, splashing them with water? But a wasted nightmare, a clench-jawed monster out of the worst horror movie?

A tear rolled out of Fred's right eye, and I caught my breath, stemmed my own tears, and squeezed his listless hand.

"All right, darling."

Our sons were brought from home, sleepy; it was late, but the doctors had given up the fiction of normal visiting hours; this was a death vigil, and so there were no rules.

"What do you say to Daddy?" I couldn't control my voice; I couldn't write a happy ending this time and God, where was L. B. Mayer when I needed him? Why couldn't he swoop in and tell me this was wrong, the audience wouldn't like this, Fred must live, and so all I had to do was sit down and cross some lines out and write new ones?

"Happy Christmas!" Two-year-old Fred Jr. waved, innocently mixing up his holidays, and normally Fred would have laughed the loudest. But he couldn't do anything but look, and all the love in the world was in that look; all the love he'd never be able to give, an infinite amount.

Little Dickie was only one year old, and so could only imitate his big brother by waving, too. Fred made a sound—a moan, and, so gingerly, tried to move his head away. Was I sobbing, too? Everyone was, the nurses, the doctors, Hedda, big Marie with her beautifully ugly face that the boys adored—everyone was weeping, and my face was wet and my heart hurt, so I must be, too.

"Go home, Fran," someone whispered. "Get some rest."

"Mary," I said again. Or did I? Nobody seemed to have heard.

Hedda whisked the boys away and the doctors shooed everyone out of the room so they could give Fred a sedative. I sat back down on that metal chair, shivering. There was an empty chair waiting for Mary, right next to me.

Instead, to my surprise—everything was a surprise now, wasn't it? There would never be anything familiar in my life again—a cowboy sat down on the chair.

"Mrs. Thomson?" His battered hat was in his brown, leathery hands.

I looked up; the narrow hall was lined with cowboys, spurs on their muddy boots, dusty hats in their hands. One of the nurses, far down at the end of the hall, began to sputter and point.

"We all wanted to come," the cowboy next to me explained.

"Mr. Thomson, he's one of the good guys. He always treats us well on his films. He respects us, doesn't try to tell us what to do, but lets us show him how it's done. We're mighty sorry, ma'am."

"Oh!" I could do nothing but blink and blink, and I almost laughed. It was official; the line between movies and life had completely blurred, as represented by this hall full of actual cowboys who were standing vigil outside a movie-star cowboy's hospital room, talking to his screenwriter wife. "Thank you," I said, and my heart expanded, filled the looming emptiness with gratitude, bittersweet. If only Fred could know how many lives he touched! But he lay listless in his room now, the fever having taken over, smothering him.

I must have worn a path between this cold metal chair and Fred's bed, anxious to be with him but once inside, helpless to give him any comfort, unable to rouse any kind of response, and so I'd rush out so I wouldn't cry in front of him, sit down in the chair but the tears wouldn't fall, and then I'd get back up and start the whole thing over again. Back and forth, like a distraught hamster. It was funny. It could have been funny. On film, it would have been funny.

At one point, I looked up from my little chair and saw that I was alone. The cowboys had left, Hedda and Marie and Adela were gone—I thought they'd said they were going home to check on the boys—and all the chairs surrounding me were empty.

Then I saw a little figure far down at the end of the hall; a figure with golden hair.

"Mary!" I rose, began to walk, in a trance, down the hall. She'd come! Mary had come, she knew I needed her, she'd left her castle and come despite all the—well, all the things she must be afraid of now, but I didn't know what they were. All I knew was that Mary was finally here, and all I felt was relief, lifting me nearly out of my shoes as I kept walking toward her. Mary couldn't change things; that was beyond even her powers. But that she was here, after all—it was the only thing that could have helped me at that moment, and I was simply glad; I held my arms out, already feeling Mary's warm embrace.

"Mary!" But the ethereal figure walked right past me and as she did, I saw that it wasn't Mary after all but merely a nurse with a veil, a veil that had caught the light just right so that it looked like gold. My hands still outstretched as I blinked after the vanishing nurse, I heard my name.

"Mrs. Thomson! Mrs. Thomson!"

Whirling around, I saw another nurse, the one who'd been by Fred's bed, beckoning to me. "Mrs. Thomson—you must hurry!"

Still reeling from the mirage that I had thought, had *known,* was Mary, I stumbled back to my husband's bedside; I fell upon him, grasped those big shoulders in my arms, cradled that beloved head, the hair plastered against the forehead with sweat, and the eyes—

The eyes closed, by someone else's hand. A hand bigger, more authoritative, than mine.

"I'm so sorry," the nurse whispered, and something tore its way up from my stomach through my throat, my mouth, and it was my grief, my sorrow, the realization of all the years left ahead of me alone, without him, and it was my sobbing that was the only sound audible in that room, bouncing off the sterile white walls. My tears that were the only living things left, they stained the collar of Fred's pajamas, the ones he'd asked me to bring, the last thing he'd ever asked me to do.

"Bless you, my child," someone said, and I looked up and saw a priest, and almost laughed, then remembered that Fred was supposed to have been a minister, and I'd put an end to that, and if I hadn't, would he still be here now?

"Mrs. Thomson," someone said, removing me—gently, as if I might shatter into pieces—from his bedside. A doctor approached with a vial and a needle, he took my arm—again so carefully—and there was a sting, a warm sensation spreading out from the puncture, invading me, filling the void that would need filling for the rest of my life.

"Is Mary here?" I asked, my eyes suddenly heavy, my voice surprisingly thick.

No one answered.

No one ever answered.

And then I was asleep.

THE FUNERAL WAS EVEN bigger than Valentino's had been, people were anxious to assure me. As if that mattered.

But—the thing was—it *did*. It did matter that Fred be remembered as a star, one of the biggest. Because I had forced him into that role—or *suggested,* depending on how I chose to remember it—and I needed to know that he had succeeded. That he had been happy. That he had never had a cause to regret that I'd been the reason he'd left the ministry. Seeing the throngs of fans lined up, openly weeping; the stiff unfamiliarity of cowboys in suits, looking touchingly awkward among the luminaries that included Irving and Mayer and Cecil B. DeMille, Marion Davies, Harold and Mildred Lloyd, Sam and Frances Goldwyn and of course Hedda and Marie and Adela and Bessie and Anita and Lillian, all my women friends—

"We've gone Hollywood, Fred," I whispered, settling into my pew, and I smiled a little, to the consternation of Marie and Hedda who were flanking me, two fierce bulldogs protecting me from the press. I'd left my boys at home with their nanny; they were too young to understand what was going on. I envied them their innocence.

Douglas Fairbanks was one of the pallbearers and he was weeping as he and Tom Mix and Buster Keaton and some of Fred's nephews shouldered the big casket up the aisle. And I liked him, for perhaps the first time ever, for that. He was a snob, he was a conceited fool, but he had come down from the mountain often enough for him and Fred to become friends; they'd loved to ride the range together with all the cowboys Fred used on his pictures. They weren't close friends, but they admired each other.

He had come down the mountain today, and I'd not even asked him to. He'd simply done it, because he knew it was the right thing to do.

I never turned around during the entire ceremony; I couldn't take my eyes off that enormous casket, long enough for tall Fred who was inside it. I had to stare at it for as long as I could stand it, because once it was in the ground I was afraid all my memories of Fred would be laid to rest, too; they'd vanish, smothered in dirt.

But even though I didn't turn, I knew one person was missing. Mary had sent an enormous array of flowers, the largest of all the arrangements at the altar. She'd telegraphed her deepest sympathies. She'd said she would be there.

But she wasn't. I knew it; I didn't have to see it with my own red, swollen eyes.

And I knew there would come a day when I would remember this, go over it time and again, worrying it like one does a sore bruise, pressing down on it over and over to feel the pain anew. But not now; I didn't have room for Mary today. So I tucked the grievance—no, Fran, that was a prissy word. It was a *laceration,* no less; what Mary had done was tear apart something that had once been pristine, perfect.

I stitched over the laceration with some of the many dangling, tangled threads of my grief and regret. Someday, I would unstitch it and wallow in it, and march back up that hill to Pickfair and show it to Mary, and demand an explanation.

But not this day. This day was only about Fred. The one pristine, perfect thing in my life, after all. And when it was over, all I wanted to do was sleep, and sleep, and never wake up. For I knew that waking up would mean losing him all over again. But I would, because I had to. Because this wasn't the movies, and I couldn't dissolve into a frame with the title "Years passed."

The years would have to pass agonizingly slowly, 365 days at a time, before I'd ever experience anything like happiness again.

ARY FELT THE BACK OF HER NECK, GRAINY FROM
the talcum powder the barber had brushed it with. She couldn't
remember the last time she'd felt a cool breeze ripple against
her bare neck. Always, her hair had hung there, a heavy curtain
falling down to her waist.

"I hope—I hope you like it," the poor barber—a stone-
faced older man who was suddenly holding back tears, his lips
quivering—stammered. He swiveled Mary around to face the
mirror.

A photographer's flash pan popped, there was a blinding
light and the smell of burning sulfur, and when Mary could see
again, a woman was staring back at her. A petite woman, with
softly waved hair hugging her cheekbones, making them more
pronounced; a woman with enormous hazel eyes, wide, shimmering with tears. Her eyes had never looked this big before.

"Mary, Mary, what do you think?" One of the reporters—
there were about a dozen of them, all crammed into this small
barbershop in Manhattan—wanted to know.

She touched the back of her neck again, touched her newly
shorn hair, and smiled for the cameras even as she quivered in-

side. *What on earth have I done? How long will it take to grow back? What will Mama say—*

Then she realized that Mama couldn't say anything, anymore.

"I think it looks so modern, don't you?" She posed for the cameras, tilting her head, pursing her lips just like any other flapper.

"But your curls! What will you do without them? What will your fans think?"

"I don't think my entire career has been dependent on my hair," she retorted. Looking in the mirror again, she sought reassurance that a movie star would be reflected back, smiling and glowing, the familiar image from the cover of *Photoplay,* the movie posters, the programs. But she couldn't quite see it, at that.

Her entire career *had* been dependent upon her hair. From the moment Miss Josephine came backstage to see her, bashfully touching her curls and saying, "You're so pretty," Mary's hair had been something more than a coiffure—just as Charlie's hat and cane were something more than merely accessories. Her curls had been sacred. As her fame grew, odes had been composed in their honor. Psychologists had written scholarly analyses about their symbolic value.

There were eighteen of them when she was filming. Twelve of her own, six specially made fake ones, each twelve inches long. Curls once wildly copied, not only by her fans but her rivals like Mary Miles Minter, Madge Bellamy, Olive Thomas, even dear Lillian at one point. Then, wildly derided by the press: *When Will Mary Cut Her Curls? Bobbed Hair Is All the Rage.*

Now that she had, she felt slightly nauseous; her reflection in the mirror wavered for a moment, like the way a road looks on a hot day, little shimmering waves obscuring her face. But the press was here—she had invited them, of course—so, still smiling, she removed the huge drape from her clothing and rose. Then they all looked down. Her curls were lying on the floor, fallen soldiers, twelve in all. The barber approached with a broom but she waved him off; kneeling, she carefully picked up the curls and put them in her purse before she could even say why. She simply couldn't bear to see them swept up like—like anybody else's hair! And she couldn't say goodbye to them yet. She'd said too many goodbyes lately.

Blowing kisses to the reporters, she ran out to her car and was driven back to the hotel, and the entire way there, she shook her head, marveling at how light it felt, how her hair didn't whip across her face and get in her eyes. She kept brushing her hands over the nape of her neck, trying to get used to how exposed it felt.

When she opened the door to the hotel room, Douglas was waiting for her, pacing up and down like a husband outside a maternity ward. He stopped, looked, and made a sound that Mary had never heard before; a wail of despair, of disbelief, seemingly originating from the very depths of his soul. He fell down on his knees, and sobbed like a baby.

"Douglas! What? What's wrong?"

"Your—your hair, Tupper! Your hair, oh, your hair!"

"But you knew I was going to have it cut!"

"I knew, but I didn't quite believe. Until now—oh, Tupper, what have you done? What have you done with my Mary?"

"I don't know!" She ran to the mirror again for assurance; she still looked the same as she had at the barbershop—like a woman, like a sophisticated, very pretty woman. But she didn't look like a girl; she didn't look like Little Mary, beloved the world over. She didn't look like the daughter Mama had known, and then she, too, was crying. Not for her hair—no, she was relieved, happy to be rid of it, from a purely practical standpoint.

No, now her tears were for the memories of Mama tending to those curls, so diligently, when Mary was little; of Mama coaxing her dark blond, rather flat, childish hair to grow and grow with special egg-white shampoos and beer rinses, wrapping up the hair at night, twining it about her loving finger when it was finally long enough. And encouraging Mary to rinse it with champagne to lighten it up so that it was really golden in real life and not only when strategically lit for the camera.

She wept for all the loving, cozy nights, like a warm cocoon, or being back in the womb, when she and Mama had chatted while Mama tended to Mary's hair, brushing it, twirling it, pinning it up so that Mary could sleep. Her hair was almost as much their mutual creation as her career, or perhaps they were the same. Little Mary would never have been Little Mary without the curls—that was the truth, the terrifying truth. So what would Little Mary become now? If only Mama could tell her—

But Mama was gone now. Two months ago, she'd passed away. Mary was still picking up the telephone every day to call her; still planning treats and surprises for her before remembering, then having to cancel them.

Mama had died, peacefully—truly, she had. The cancer had taken her away; no amount of prayers could heal her but Mary believed, finally, that this was the right way to go. No doctors, no surgeries, no interventions. Simply a wasted body at the end of its life.

"Mary, don't cry," Mama had whispered at the end, a strange, beatific smile on her face. A smile of peace, which was so odd, for Mary had never really seen her driven mother at peace in her life. Happy, yes. Proud, always. But never entirely at peace.

"Who will love me when you're gone?" Mary tried not to cry; she tried to be strong, as she'd always been. But oh, it was so hard!

"Your public, darling. Your public will always love you. We made sure of that, didn't we?" And Mama smiled again, closed her eyes—and soon after, drew her last breath.

Someone's hands were on Mary's shoulders, pulling her away from Mama so that the doctors and nurses could do whatever they had to do. But Mary didn't want to leave; she never wanted to leave and so, urged on by a roaring sound, like a freight train, in her ears, and a sudden, white hot light in front of her eyes, she fought whoever it was, twisting, lunging, slapping the person—and then the clouds parted and she saw that she had hit *Douglas*.

And that was it; after she saw his stricken face, she calmed down, took charge, did everything the way Mama had wanted her to. Everyone said that Mama'd had a good life, Mary was such a devoted daughter, and with such a loving relationship as theirs had been, Mary would be comforted and soon, back to normal. Mary nodded and agreed and knew they were all as wrong as wrong could be. She would never be normal again; she was all alone in the world. There was no one left who truly knew her. Mary would always feel gravity weigh down on her more, now that Mama was gone; she would always be utterly alone in the world. And while she knew that wasn't a very loyal thing to think, considering she was married, it was true. No one would ever love her, ever understand her, like Mama did.

Not even Douglas. Not even Fran.

Dear Fran! She came to Mama's funeral and was so broken up; she stared and stared at the coffin while tears ran down her face and Mary came up to put her arm about her. "I loved her," Fran said, simply, and while they didn't take the time to reminisce about the old days, Mary knew she was thinking about them, the days when they were next-door neighbors, and Mama was the den mother who took care of them both. But she couldn't talk, not even to Fran; she was too overwhelmed with grief. And Douglas had an iron grip on her arm in that way he had; he wanted to be her only comfort. She thought she even detected some relief in his eyes that Mama was gone, and he finally had Mary all to himself. But he didn't; he wouldn't. As much as she loved him, knew their love to be the biggest love of all time, he would never have her all to himself. A part of her was buried along with Mama.

But now—watching Douglas still sobbing, unable to look at her, she had the strangest notion. She had killed his Mary. Murdered her, intentionally. And it seemed right, for it was 1928, a year of death.

Deaths of careers, as well as people.

Only a couple months after Mary cut her hair—*Famous Golden Curls Go! Mary Pickford Cuts Her Hair! The Little Girl with the Curls No More!*—Fred Thomson died, so tragically. Poor Fran! With her own grief still so raw, Mary knew how Fran would be feeling, and she did want to go to her; truly, she did. She even put on her best black dress and hat and descended the stairs to the door, before turning back around and running up to her room.

Fran had her children, after all, for comfort. Children *were* a comfort, in times like these; sweet little babies to cuddle and watch over, taking refuge in their innocence. And the more she thought of it, the more she realized—rationalized?—that if Mary went to the funeral there would be so much publicity, it would absolutely take away from poor Fred, and so that day, she stayed home. Even when Douglas surprisingly told her, with a disgusted look—a look that he gave her more and more, and she had to wonder just what else she had destroyed that day at the barber—that she owed it to Fran to be there. But she waved him away, ordered the most expensive floral arrangement possible, and retired to her room for a little "nap."

That was what she called it, and he knew what it really was, but he went along with the fiction, because he understood. He was terrified, too, and he had other ways to cope, ways that didn't involve the bottle but were no less destructive.

Everyone in Hollywood was terrified, that deadly year of 1928.

"Wait a minute! Wait a minute! You ain't heard nothin' yet!"

Al Jolson spoke those words on-screen; the words leaped from his mouth into the air and everybody gasped, cheered, rose to their feet. And everything changed. Eleven words, heard 'round the world. Now all of a sudden movies were supposed to talk. There was even a new word for them—"Talkies."

Ever since *The Jazz Singer* premiered in October of 1927, Hollywood had been trembling like one of its frequent earthquakes—only this one was man-made. *Warner Bros.* made.

"It's a fad, it'll pass." "People still want the artistry of silent films." "Silent films are a universal language. When people have to talk, they can only speak one. It will never happen."

"Speaking movies are impossible," Griffith pronounced.

"It's like putting lipstick on the Venus de Milo." Mary herself issued a press release. "Silent film is a perfect art. It doesn't need embellishment."

But it wasn't a fad. When Warner Bros. released another "talkie" starring Al Jolson, called *The Singing Fool,* it did even better than *The Jazz Singer.* Now every movie theater was frantically wiring itself for sound; every studio was hiring callow young undergraduates from Stanford or UCLA who had completed even one class in sound engineering, making them the heads of newly formed sound departments. Production had ground to a halt; silent movies that could have some kind of sound added—even just noise effects—were being held in order to do so.

And actors, all of a sudden, were expected to speak.

Of course, Mary was a trained stage actress; so was Douglas. Of course they had nothing to fear, or so they told themselves, told the press, told the money men at United Artists.

But privately, they hired a vocal coach from New York who came to Pickfair every evening to train them to speak properly for the screen. "Enunciate, enunciate," she intoned, making them walk around with books on their heads and their hands on their stomachs to feel their diaphragms as they recited poems and snippets of Shakespeare.

Mary and Douglas had spoken into microphones before— many times. At banquets, at premieres; they'd given interviews on something called "radio" that was beginning to make inroads into America. They even had their own radio receiver at

Pickfair, an enormous black cabinet monster that looked as frightening as any piece of medical equipment with all its dials and tubes. But there wasn't much to receive; some sporting events, news programs, and quite a lot of symphony music.

Still, apparently they didn't speak well enough; they were told to broaden their vowels, speak slower, and hit every consonant equally hard. It wasn't unheard of, these days, for dinner parties to end with all the guests sitting around the table hearing each other recite, sharing tips and breathing exercises. Gone were the wild days of drunken charades after dinner; now everyone was sober as a judge, for tomorrow, or the next day, they had to face a sound test at the studio.

"He has a voice! John Barrymore has a voice!" Mary was visiting MGM one day when a young man—earphones still clamped over his ears—stepped out of a small building and proclaimed it to all the land, jumping up and down with triumph.

You either "had a voice" or you didn't. And many of Mary's contemporaries did not. Vilma Banky, who'd done so well with Goldwyn with her delicate blond beauty, playing against suave male stars like Valentino and Ronald Coleman, unfortunately had a guttural Hungarian accent and could barely speak English. She announced her "retirement" shortly after her sound test. Ramon Novarro, who was so boyishly charming onscreen, had a Mexican accent that made him sound like anybody's gardener. His career was over.

So was Aileen Pringle's, John Gilbert's, Alma Rubens's, Pola Negri's. Overnight, houses were on the market, cars were being sold, belongings shipped back to wherever their owners had come from. And an army of new hopefuls was marching east from New York—and Broadway. Talent scouts filled the bulk of the seats at Broadway plays and fought over anyone with two legs, a pretty or handsome face, and a pleasing speaking voice. Acting skill not required.

Mary and Douglas, ensconced at Pickfair, untouchable—at least for a while—put it off for as long as they could, as did a few other stars like Clara Bow and Gloria Swanson and Greta Garbo. Charlie refused even to wire his studio, he was so disgusted by the idea of sound. "But you have to," they pleaded with him. "We can't ignore this. Our films have to turn a profit!"

"The Little Tramp can't speak. It would break the spell," he said, his own voice—a pleasant baritone with traces of a cockney accent—ironically perfect for sound.

But Mary and Douglas couldn't afford to be so self-righteous. Fortunately, they were their own bosses and so didn't have to go through the terror of a sound test, knowing they could be let go any minute. They refurbished Pickford-Fairbanks studios for sound productions at enormous cost, and prepared to make their first talkies. Well, Douglas fudged a bit; his first "talkie" was the silent *The Iron Mask,* but he recorded a prologue in which he recited a poem; his voice was good for sound, although Mary could tell that his heart wasn't really in it. Douglas was all action, all movement—like Charlie in certain ways, although Charlie's movements were controlled, small, and Douglas's were enormous leaps and bounds. Still, they shared a same graceful physicality. And in sound, of course, you couldn't move more than a few inches away from the microphone.

Mary's first talkie would be *Coquette,* a film in which she would play a southern flapper, a flirt, whose lover is murdered by her father. Shorn curls, a grown-up role, and sound—all at once, her career was staked on terrifyingly unfamiliar ground.

And Mama wasn't here to guide her and tell her everything would be fine.

No wonder she "went to bed" very early the night before.

That first day on the set was terrifying! Always, she looked forward to the first day of shooting; her crew remained the same, they were all one big happy family who looked forward to working together. They respected and deferred to Mary but she also felt protected by them on set. Everyone wanted her to succeed, to look and act her best, because their paychecks depended on it.

The moment she walked on the set for *Coquette*—on rubbery legs—she saw the trepidation in every eye, even the lowliest grip. Even those whose jobs had nothing to do with sound, like the costume ladies, looked deathly pale. As if this was no longer a film set, but death row.

Back in 1909, when she first started out, everyone was unsure of themselves, too. But it was different; back then nobody had anything to lose. They could take risks without worrying about the consequences because who cared? They'd all just go back to what they were doing before, touring or on Broadway or vaudeville, living out of a trunk because that's all they knew.

Now, however, Mary—and her director, her cameraman, the lighting director, all the crew, the extras, especially the new sound engineer—had *everything* to lose. Mary most of all.

Everything was so strange on a talkie set! The comforting thing about filming silent movies, oddly, was all the noise. The noise of the camera, whirring and clacking. The director calling out directions and cues as the camera was whizzing away. The orchestra playing mood music. It had taken a special concentration to perform among all that chaos, but there was something safe about it, too. The hum of collaboration, the din of happy professionals who knew their jobs. It was a safety net, all that racket; it was what they all knew, had invented themselves, this method of making movies.

But now the slightest noise could be picked up by the sound engineer. The camera, once so mobile, so friendly—Mary's shadow, following her faithfully as she clowned around—was encased in a giant soundproof closet. It couldn't move, and neither could the actors; all staging had to be static. The microphones did not have a big range, and were large and unwieldy; they were often placed in vases of flowers or hidden in lampshades, and the actors were always positioned right next to them, unable even to turn their heads.

Outside the soundstage—that's what they were called, these enormous, cement-block, soundproof buildings where they now filmed—it was different, as well. No more dashing in and out of sets to watch what was being filmed, laughing along at the jokes or sobbing at the tragedy being portrayed. Concrete paved over everything, even the beautiful flower gardens, to deaden the sound, and huge red lights ominously flashed when filming was going on, to prevent anyone from opening a door and ruining a take.

Mary's biggest tool as an actress, aside from her face, had always been her supple body; now she had to stand or sit perfectly still so as not to rustle her dress; the microphone would pick up even the softest movement of fabric and magnify it ten times over, ruining the take.

But she had a voice. She was stage-trained. And so, while far from confident about the final result, she wasn't afraid of speaking on film; she declaimed loudly, distinctly, clipping every consonant, broadening every vowel as she'd been instructed. When filming was finished, while no one knew for sure what the reception would be, neither did anyone rush out to sell their homes. There was a feeling of a job done as best it could be, under these strange new circumstances.

Coquette did well; reviews were, for the most part, encouraging and of course, as Mary's first talkie, her fans came out in droves so the box office was decent. *Little Mary Grows Up,* the headlines screamed, and she even won an Academy Award—the second one in history—for Best Actress.

Of course, she and Douglas—along with L. B. Mayer, Cecil B. DeMille, Fred Niblo, Conrad Nagel, and others—had been instrumental in founding the Academy in 1927. Some people carped about her win but Mary felt that truly, she had been awarded only for her performance, not all the money she had donated to the Academy of Motion Picture Arts and Sciences. She was very proud when she received her statuette; the standing ovation was heartfelt, for if Mary Pickford could succeed in talkies, then so could the rest of them. Mary should have been relieved; she should have assumed the danger had passed, and all would be rosy again, just like it had been, before. Before Mama died; before the talkies came.

But she was not relieved; she couldn't help but think that the success of *Coquette* was simply curiosity on the part of a public who wanted to hear Mary Pickford's voice. And now that they had, there was no reason to return. Unless she gave them one.

"Let's do a movie together, the two of us—the king and queen. A grand love story to resemble our own," she suggested to Douglas, who was—losing interest? In her? Or in himself? Or in Hollywood?

Douglas did not feel the urge, as Mary did, to reinvent himself for sound. "Maybe this is it, Tupper," he said, when the grosses for *The Iron Mask* were tepid. "Maybe this is it for us. We've had a good run."

But Mary wasn't ready to accept it. Yes, she heard the whispers that now she had proven herself in talkies, it was time to retire, to let a new generation of sophisticated women like Greta Garbo and Norma Shearer, married to Irving Thalberg, and Joan Crawford, married to Douglas Fairbanks Jr.—that adorable little boy of Douglas's had grown up—take her place.

The feeling was that as Hollywood rang in 1930—cautiously, trying to weather both sound and the Crash of October of 1929—the mood of the country, too, was changing. People were out of work, had lost their fortunes; nobody was making money hand over fist in the stock market anymore. Salaries were being cut in Hollywood, to make up for all the changes.

And child-women like Mary, like Lillian, like Janet Gaynor, were through. Washed up. A symbol of a more innocent time. Nobody wanted to worship a little girl with curls anymore. And even though her curls were shorn, that was what Mary knew she was, in the eyes of the public. Her hair could be as short as Peter Pan's, and the public would still see her as that little girl. The ghost of that little girl, at any rate; never again would Mary be that sprite who had made her famous.

But who would she be, now? That was the question that kept her up at night.

"Let's forget Hollywood, and take a trip," Douglas implored instead, and she agreed—if he would make a movie with her first. For years, their fans had begged for the two of them to star together but it never made sense; why split their profits, when they were both making money on their own? But now they weren't. So why not film *The Taming of the Shrew*—

perfect for Mary to show off her stage voice and for Douglas to do his usual physical antics?

Perfect for a couple who weren't quite sure if they were still in love.

"Hipper, dear, can we retake that?" Mary asked one day on the set, when she hadn't felt she'd made her entrance right; her heavy Elizabethan gown had gotten caught in the door-frame. "I think I can do better. Would you mind?"

"As a matter of fact, I would," Douglas snapped at her, for the first time ever. In public.

"But, Douglas, dear, I think—"

"For God's sake, don't you get it? No one cares anymore, Mary. Let's just get this thing over with."

She swallowed her retort; it wouldn't do to argue in front of the crew. Shakily, she waited for the next setup.

Douglas didn't speak a word to her off camera for the rest of the day. And she had no idea why. She was losing him, losing her career, losing everything and what could she hold on to? Who could she turn to now that Mama was gone?

Not Fran, who wouldn't understand. Not Fran, who was moving smoothly into writing talkies at MGM; her *Anna Christie,* starring Greta Garbo, had been a smashing success. *Garbo Talks!* the headlines roared. Yes, she did. Because Fran put the words into her mouth. Just as she had once found the perfect phrases for Mary.

No one would understand, but someone might help her forget, take her mind off her growing irrelevance, the feeling that she—only thirty-nine!—represented what some were already calling the Stone Age of Hollywood. Someone young, someone handsome, someone who adored her.

Buddy Rogers—her costar in *My Best Girl*—was filming nearby. That movie, her last silent and one of her best, had been a big success. Buddy was twelve years her junior and worshipped her; their flirtation on-screen—and off—had been so real, Douglas couldn't bring himself to watch the entire film. Mary had welcomed his adoration; what woman, nearing forty, wouldn't be flattered by such a young, handsome man's attentions? But she'd kept the relationship platonic, of course; it was fine for Buddy to gaze at her as if she were the *Mona Lisa,* but she never so much as held his hand, off camera. She would never do to Douglas what she had done to Owen. Douglas was—well, he was Douglas. Hipper. Duber. Her consort. She could never betray him.

Unless Douglas strayed first. Which he would never do. Would he? They were DougandMary, MaryandDoug.

But she no longer had golden curls, and he no longer could leap quite so high.

The Taming of the Shrew did not make money—she knew it wouldn't from the very first take—and Mary went off with Douglas on a trip around the world, as promised. A trip around the world! Once, it would have represented heaven; together with Douglas in a stateroom for weeks on end, no prying eyes, no worries about Beth or Owen or Mama, only the two of them, touching, nuzzling, cuddling, stroking. Waving to their adoring public in exotic cities; "DougandMary" sounded the same in every language.

Now, it was hell. Separate staterooms seemed prudent, as they brought so much luggage—that's what they assured each other. Douglas simply wouldn't stay still; he had no desire to sit next to her on a deck chair, watching the waves or reading or even holding hands. He had to clown around on deck, intent upon impressing everyone on board; everyone, except his wife.

"Why can't you stand to be with me?" She couldn't help herself; she had to ask, just like any other shrewish wife, which she supposed she was. And that was as devastating as anything else; that they had turned into just another husband and wife who nagged and argued and had nothing to talk about at dinner.

"Why do you have to have the weekly box office telegraphed to us in every port?" Douglas asked in response. "Why do you insist on reading scripts? Why won't you stop thinking of work?"

"You used to like that about me," she whispered, but Douglas pretended not to hear. His face—so tan, too tan; sometimes he received letters asking if he were really a darkie—tightened, he straightened his tie, then stalked out. She would see him later, at the captain's table, where they'd put on an act, pretending to be the happily married, enchanted, favored-by-the-gods couple everyone wanted them to be. They were doing the best acting of their careers on this trip.

Mary missed home; she missed her own cook, her own bed. She couldn't eat exotic food, and was growing weary of dry toast and coffee. She was *tired*. She'd been working since she was five. And being on a cruise with Douglas in his current state of mind—what was it, exactly? What was making him irritable, twitchy, driven by something she couldn't begin to identify and so could only continue to do the things she'd always done, because once, that was enough? Was it simply her *hair* that bothered him so? The talkies? Middle age? Whatever it was, he was unhappy and, like the man-child he was, intent on making everyone close to him unhappy, too.

It was a lot like work, that's what this cruise was. Being with Douglas—the miraculous being who had rescued her from Owen and placed her on top of the world like the cherry on top of a cake—was suddenly a lot like work.

The crowds were still the same; that was the one saving grace of the entire trip. In India, in Budapest, where American silent films still played, they remained the king and queen, their public as feverish, as adoring, as ever, screaming their names, crying whenever Mary deigned to shake a hand or touch a shoulder. But as soon as they returned home, Mary sensed a change in the very air; there weren't as many photographers and reporters waiting for them when the ship docked. It was a week before *Photoplay* asked her for an interview about the trip. And there weren't nearly as many welcome-home floral arrangements in the entryway of Pickfair; she didn't have to pack them all up and send them to local hospitals, as she once would have done.

Douglas must have sensed it, too, for he packed his bags again almost immediately and took off, this time not asking if she wanted to join him. She kept track of him through telegrams and once in a very great while he would show up at Pickfair, unannounced. He wasn't making any films and he didn't appear very interested in sharing the burden of running UA. He couldn't seem to be able to stand being around her even in their beloved home; he bounded away from the house at dawn—their cozy breakfasts together only a memory—and played endless rounds of golf or clowned around with Charlie, then took off again without telling her his plans.

Ignoring the spiteful headlines—*Are Mary and Doug Through? Is Pickfair No Longer a Love Nest?*—she threw herself back into work as she always had, because she had no idea what else to do. Work and Douglas. *Kiki,* a film in which she played a French streetwalker, did miserably. She didn't even go to the premiere, loyally staged at the Chinese Theater by Sid Grauman, who was merely being kind. A Mary Pickford movie was no longer an Event.

And what on earth did she know about playing a French streetwalker? Once upon a time, she'd known her strengths as an actress; now, she wouldn't have been able to name a single thing she could do that any other actress couldn't. Everything about making these new films was so foreign to her. All of a sudden, she had no idea what to do with her hands—her *hands!* The first thing any decent actress learns to deal with. She, who had been heralded as the most natural actress of her time—suddenly, she had *hands.*

One day Adela called. "Mary, have you heard of Lady Ashley? Lady Sylvia Ashley?"

"No, Adela. Who is that?" Mary struggled to make her speech as clear as possible; she'd had a couple drinks with breakfast, because she didn't have anywhere to go. And no one was there to care whether or not she did.

"Douglas has been seen with her in London. Many times. It seems they're an item."

"Douglas does like to go out, Adela. I can hardly keep him home these days! But there's nothing to it. Douglas and I are fine, we're fine!"

She hung up, roamed the house—the vast, empty house, walls echoing with the memories of happier times when everyone wanted to come, everyone wanted to breathe the same refined air as she and Douglas did. People did still come, sometimes; after all, she was Mary Pickford, the woman who ran United Artists, the woman who helped found the Academy of Motion Picture Arts and Sciences, the woman who had founded the Motion Picture Fund, so that industry folks down on their luck would have a place to live. She was still the reigning queen of Hollywood society; she just happened to be without a king at the moment.

She had no desire to reign alone.

It was 1932. She was forty years old. Mary Pickford, the Girl with the Curls, was *forty years old,* and looked it. She'd never had a childhood but she must remain forever a child on screen; that was her own special hell, a hell of her own making. Or was it?

With Douglas, it might be bearable. Without him . . .

Desperate, she felt she had one last chance to win Douglas back. She *had* to succeed! Not only because she loved Douglas still, although loving him now primarily meant missing who he once had been. Who *she* had once been.

No, she had to succeed because if their marriage failed, it would be the same thing as if Hollywood itself—*their* Hollywood, the Hollywood that the two of them had invented and put on the map—broke off the continent and fell into the sea. That was how much Mary fervently believed in the holiness of their union and all it stood for. She must remind him of all that they'd created together—not only Pickfair and United Artists and the Academy of Motion Picture Arts and Sciences; not merely the biggest, the best movies ever made. But also, the greatest love of all time; the love that all their fans looked up to, and desired for themselves.

The love that she nearly sacrificed her career for.

So how would Mary win Douglas back?

The same way she'd won him in the first place; by making a movie, of course. She'd sacrificed her youth to the camera; she'd sacrificed more. The movies *owed* her. She would woo Douglas back to her side, where he belonged, with a movie. He would look at her on-screen and fall in love with her again, just as he had long ago.

And there was only one person she trusted to write this movie for her; one woman. Because it had to be written by a woman. Only a woman would understand. And the best woman she knew, the only woman she thought of, was Fran.

But for the first time, Mary didn't know if Fran would even answer the phone when she called.

"*And the 1930 Academy Award for best writing goes to—Frances Marion for* The Big House*!*"

I was frozen, shocked to hear my name. As much as I'd told myself that awards didn't matter, and that this banquet was merely another work obligation that had to be fulfilled, I realized that I was happy to have won. Even though I knew that happiness wouldn't last the night; these days, happiness clung to me only briefly, like a piece of lint.

George Hill, to his credit, kissed me on the cheek and whispered, "You deserve this, Fran," and I was grateful. His eyes were full of tears, although I wasn't sure if they were of happiness or sadness or both. "Go on, Fran." My husband gave me a gentle shove, and I realized I'd been sitting for too long, and people were applauding, waiting for me to go up to the podium and accept the award.

My husband. Yes, George Hill was my husband, and how could that be? How could I be married again, a mere two years after my world shattered? How could I have fallen into the same old trap I'd fallen into before I'd found Fred?

Terror, it was. The fear of raising our two sons alone. Oh,

just say it, Fran—*stupidity*. George asked, with his devoted, puppy-dog eyes, and I said yes, even though I didn't love him, I knew I never could love anyone but that big strapping cowboy of mine who had gotten on his horse and ridden into the sunset, forever.

It couldn't last, and it didn't; even though George was seated next to me at the MGM table—he'd directed *The Big House*—we were already separated. Our marriage was a casualty of his drinking, and my career (George wasn't nominated for his direction). Another Hollywood marriage gone bust.

George finally reached over and grabbed my arm and hauled me out of my seat, and I dropped my napkin on the table. My friends were now standing as they cheered—Hedda Hopper, tall and elegant, laughing hysterically; Marie Dressler, dear Marie, her face wet with tears. I ran to hug her, then Irving Thalberg gave me a shove so I would make my way across the banquet floor to the podium. I had to stop at every table to shake someone's outstretched hand; there were so many, it felt as if I was at a wedding reception. I accepted all the congratulations, trying to move forward all the while, when suddenly there was a tiny figure with golden bobbed hair, eyes shining, blocking my path, her arms waving as if she were trying to stop a train.

Mary.

"Fran! Fran, darling, congratulations! I'm so glad I'm here to share this with you!"

"Thank you, Mary." I eyed her warily, not sure how—stable—she was tonight. I didn't see Doug anywhere, but surely he'd come with her? He never missed these things.

"Isn't it marvelous, Fran? I'm so proud of you! I won last year and now you win and—"

"Yes, Mary, it is. Now, excuse me." I slipped out of her feverish embrace, but not before I saw the hurt tears in her eyes—bloodshot, confused eyes. But I told myself I didn't care; I was through caring about Mary.

None of it mattered, anyway. These awards—I looked around; Louis B. Mayer was actually standing on a chair and cheering me, even though only yesterday he'd chewed me out in his office and told me he *owned* me. And tomorrow, despite my trophy, he'd do the same. It was all so stupid, so self-congratulatory, yet it meant nothing. Because there was one person missing and how I would have loved to see this evening through his eyes, but I couldn't.

Robert Montgomery—who had starred in my movie—was holding the statue at the podium and waving me up. Without another word, I marched up to the podium, where I accepted my award.

"Thank you very much." That was all I said; that was all I needed to say. I returned to my seat, clutching the gold statue, and left soon after the last award—*The Big House* lost to *All Quiet on the Western Front;* the war movie I could never bring myself to write, after all, and why was that?

Why was my life, the real, sad, dirty, wonderful, terrible, heartbreaking life *I* lived, not the fantasy I wrote for Mary and for all the others—why was it the one thing I could never find the proper words to describe? Was it too much for me; too much for me simply to survive, so I couldn't spare it more mental energy? Did I fear examining it too closely?

Probably, I would never know, and frankly I didn't spend a lot of time worrying about it. I was too busy trying to give a passable impersonation of living, these days.

After I unlocked my front door, I threw my cloak on a chair

in the living room that Fred had never seen; The Enchanted Hill was someone else's now. I'd sold it right after his funeral; the memories would have buried me alive within its walls.

Holding my award, I wondered why I didn't want to share that moment with Mary; why I'd frozen at the sight of her, as if I was *ashamed* of her. It wasn't that—although being Mary Pickford's best friend these days wasn't the coveted role it used to be, that was for certain. No, I was still angry with her—and at myself. Angry because I'd never asked her where she was when my children were born, when Fred was ill, when he died. I deserved to know, but was afraid to ask; ever since Fred died the world had seemed so impermanent, flimsier than movie sets. Mary, despite her flaws, was still someone I couldn't bear to lose. Or rather—because I couldn't lie to myself—I couldn't bear to lose the memory of who Mary *used* to be; what we used to mean to each other.

I curled up in an armchair and fell asleep, not the first time I'd done so but always before Fred had been there to carry me upstairs and put me to bed, then slip in beside me. But when the weak rays of early morning filtered in through the closed drapes, I was still in the chair; my neck was stiff, my back ached, and there was no one to carry me upstairs. My only companion was my statue from the night before; that strange little bald man on a pedestal lay at my feet, looking up at me with a blank expression.

With a groan, I picked it up. Stiffly, I trudged up the stairs to my bedroom, looking for a place to put it—the mantel was too narrow, my bureau too crowded with pictures of the boys, of Fred. My bookshelves were crammed with books and bound scripts. Finally, I gave up and placed the golden statue on the floor; a doorstop was as good a use for it as anything.

That morning I went to work as usual, leaving my sons in the care of others—a nanny for now, boarding school eventually. I was their sole support; I had to work. And if I was being honest with myself, I was also terrified of them. I was a woman who didn't trust men; my sons represented a challenging puzzle I knew I would never solve. So I took refuge in my work, telling myself it was for their own good.

Back to work—that meant MGM now, exclusively. And Louis B. Mayer, who—after taking out enormous ads trumpeting my win for MGM—reverted to his usual antics; haranguing me, treating me like chattel. Even though I had written some of the most spectacular hits of my career for him—*Anna Christie, The Big House, Min and Bill, Dinner at Eight*. Unlike Mary, my first sound movies were enormously successful.

Why was that? Because I didn't automatically think of Mary anymore when I sat down to write? Or was it because I was exhilarated to learn a new craft, for wasn't that what writing for talkies represented? From the beginning, I instinctively grasped that the ornate language of silent movie titles couldn't be an easy substitute for dialogue; sentences such as "The rosy dawn breaks over the majestic hills" could not be spoken, at least with a straight face. Dialogue had to sound like people actually talking; a simple enough idea, yet surprisingly hard for some screenwriters to do. Still, film was a visual medium, and I hesitated to fill my screenplays with too many words. So many of these new "talkies" were simply vignettes of people standing about and *discussing,* nonstop. Silence still had a place in talking pictures; in fact, it could be even more powerful.

But as I grew more confident in my mastery of this new craft, I also witnessed a change at the studio; a change, unlike talkies, I wasn't sure I could weather—or that I even wanted to.

At MGM, Irving had gone on a hiring spree as the studio grew. Most of the new writers—mostly male; novelists and playwrights from Broadway—were only on short-term contracts, never knowing where their check would be coming from in a few months. Gone were the days when one screenwriter would work solo, seeing a picture through from pitch to finished product. Now screenplays were passed around, worked on by committee until it became an issue as to who would get credit. Irving didn't seem to care who did; all he cared about was the finished product.

I cared. My films—along with Bess Meredyth's and Anita Loos's—had so far escaped this writing by committee. But more and more young screenwriters came to me frustrated by the system, wondering how on earth they could build a career this way, and when I brought it up to Irving, I was shocked by his attitude. Irving had always been the creatives' champion, always shielding us from the blunt business mind of Mayer.

"We already have the stagehands unionizing," Irving now said with disgust. "Don't tell me you writers are thinking about it. I swear, Frances, I swear our friendship will mean nothing if you go that way."

"Heavens, Irving, who said anything about a union? I'm talking about what's fair."

"Stick to writing your scripts and let me run the studio, Fran. Don't get involved with these ingrates." And Thalberg turned away—which only made me more determined to help organize a writer's union. But I was most upset about the way he dismissed me; as if I was simply—anyone else. Any one of these new, interchangeable young men he'd hired, and not the woman—the highest paid screenwriter then and now—whom L. B. Mayer had begged to come work for his fledgling studio.

There were very few of us women left at the studio these days.

"The trouble with you girls," Mayer recently scolded me, "is that you don't take any of this seriously. You dash in and out of each other's offices like it's a dormitory at some girls' college, laughing, singing songs. You go home to give your brats dinner instead of staying late and attending meetings. You just don't take it seriously."

I couldn't believe what I was hearing. Didn't the work count? We all—Bess and Anita and Adela, too—had been responsible for very successful pictures; practically *every* successful picture. That we chose to help one another, support one another, enjoy one another's company—not to mention see our children more than once a week—did not mean that we didn't take our work, this business that *we* had been responsible for creating even more than L. B. Mayer, seriously.

But I didn't argue with him. I didn't have the heart. I missed—oh, I missed! I missed the old days; Fred, I missed Mickey, I missed—

I missed Mary. A year and a half after I won my Academy Award, I was still missing her when one day the phone rang.

"I need you, Fran."

Not even a hello, how are you. Only this—*I need you, Fran.* I swallowed, wondering what she'd do if I said the same thing to her. No, not wondering, actually. I knew.

"Fran, are you there? Fran, you're the only one who can write my next movie. It's a wonderful story—I want to remake that Norma Talmadge film, *Secrets.* Remember? You wrote it for Norma back then—back in 'twenty-four, wasn't it? I think it's perfect for me now, don't you? This is very important—my career, you know, it's—it's rocky. And then, Douglas—won't you do this for me?"

I couldn't speak for a long moment; too many thoughts assaulted my mind. Mary was too old for the part. It had been a creaky, old-fashioned story back in 1924, and it was even creakier now. Audiences didn't go for that kind of sappy costume stuff these days—not unless it starred Garbo.

"Please, Fran. For your Squeebee?"

It must have been the nickname; the memories it brought flooding back of good times, happier days. I could get Mayer to loan me out. With Mary producing, I'd have full control of the script again. I could probably even help with casting—something I missed doing, now that the studio system was in full swing and writers wrote for whom they were told to write.

Whatever the reason—loneliness? frustration? weakness?—I heard myself saying, "Yes, Mary, I'll do it."

And so I found myself back on the set again with Mary, and despite all I knew, all I suspected—not to mention all I couldn't say to her—I was as excited as I'd been the first time I walked into a movie studio. Because if there was a way back to Mary—to myself, the intact self I was before Fred died and everything, including Hollywood, changed—it was here.

On a crowded, noisy, dirty, chaotic—wonderful, inspiring, exhilarating, wondrous—movie set. I'd never been so happy to see arc lights and flimsy sets in my entire life, the day I showed up to work with Mary again.

LIGHTS! CAMERA! ACTION!

I had no idea when these words became symbolic of the

glamour of a movie set. Because I'd never heard these words in my entire life.

I knew, because I read the fan magazines just like everyone else, that the public had an idealized notion of what a movie set was like. Hushed tones, everyone cooperating, everything moving smoothly, exactly on schedule. One director in charge, confidently commanding "Lights, Camera, Action!" And then glamour and music and beautiful, unattainable people magically being magical.

But a film set was anything but that. Sound had changed everything about the actual filming; of course, while the camera was rolling, the crew couldn't make noise. But between takes the set was just as wonderfully chaotic as it used to be; people dropping hammers, bumping into flats, tripping over cables, props crashing to the floor, costume girls cursing because an actress tore a skirt, actors cursing because they messed up their lines, directors cursing—because directors always cursed. Shared jokes, easy camaraderie; there was still no place I felt more at home than on a movie set.

"First day, Fran, darling!" Mary appeared on set, trailed by several costume girls holding the hem of her enormous pink hoop skirt, just like ladies-in-waiting. The dress nearly dwarfed her tiny frame, but it was period appropriate. "We're going to make a darn good movie, gang, I just know it!"

I grinned, thinking of how many times she'd said this, how many first days we'd shared. I wasn't as jaded and sophisticated as some people—like Mayer—thought; I nearly jumped up and down, my insides doing excited somersaults. I *loved* making movies—especially with Mary.

"Break a leg, Squeebee dear! You look beautiful!"

She pirouetted and tapped me on the shoulder with her

parasol; I curtsied, and then we collapsed in each other's arms, giggling.

"Oh, Fran, I just know this is it—this is going to be the hit I need! Because of you! We're at our best together, don't you think?"

"I do." And I knew it then, and wondered why we'd waited so long to make another film. "We'll be making movies together until we're in wheelchairs!"

"And maybe even then—*Rebecca of Sunnybrook Farm for Old Folks!*"

"Places, Miss Pickford!" the AD shouted.

Mary stopped laughing; her eyes grew anxious and for the first time I saw that there were shadows beneath them no makeup could completely cover. "Oh, Fran! I just need this to be—" She broke off and looked away, unable to finish her thought.

But I could. I always could.

"It will be. Just wait until Douglas sees you like this! You look exquisite!" She did look radiantly pretty; despite the shadows beneath her eyes, her face was still that pretty cameo, if slightly softer in profile. Her eyes were still perfect ovals of glittering emotion. But in my heart, I knew that she was a beautiful *forty-one-year-old,* not a girl of eighteen, which was what she was supposed to be in this scene. Her costar, the new British actor Leslie Howard, was twenty years her junior. And looked it.

My job, however—as it had always been on set, once the script was done—was to help her, ease her way, come up with lines and little bits in which she could shine. So I kept my thoughts to myself, gave her another careful hug—so as not to crush her costume and hairstyle—and filming got under way.

It was the first time, of course, that we'd made a sound movie, and so things were different right away; she looked up at the boom mikes (a new invention) with visible trepidation as she hit her mark. I thought her voice very good for sound; a nice, modulated register.

But unlike the Mary of old, who walked onto a set as if it were her kingdom, this Mary seemed uncertain of herself. There would be a little hesitation sometimes before she said a line, and her readings were letter perfect; too much so. She sounded as if she were reciting from a chalkboard at times, intent on emphasizing every period, every comma. She didn't seem to trust the cinematographer or the director, Frank Borzage. When he yelled "Cut!" she always looked to me for approval instead of him.

"While you're at it, Frances," Frank told me one day after yet another muffed take by a nervous Mary, "maybe you can direct Her Highness to hold off on the gin until after we're done with the day's shoot?"

I nodded, but didn't know what to do. This was another obstacle I'd never encountered on a set of Mary's: For the first time, she was letting her drinking get in the way of the most important thing in her life, until now—her career.

In the morning, she was just like she'd always been—clear-eyed, witty, making jokes with the crew. But after lunch—which she took alone in her dressing room now, instead of sharing it with me—she was a different person altogether. She never stumbled, she always knew her lines—although she did sometimes slur them a little so that the sound engineer had to call out "Cut!" before a scene was over. But she was testy, prone to lashing out at everyone around her; something she'd never done before. I'd never once heard Mary Pickford raise her voice

to her crew. But now she'd yell at her dresser, or harangue anyone who moved behind the camera during a take. And poor
Leslie Howard—he hardly knew what to do with her; he was
uncomfortable enough playing a rough-hewn westerner. He
could hardly be expected to help his equally terrified and
slightly tipsy leading lady who, after all, was Mary Pickford,
Queen of the Movies—his absolute favorite movie star, he
more than once confided to me, when he was a boy.

My heart suffered for Mary. I knew she drank because she
was terrified, because this was her last chance. I *understood*. But
that didn't mean I approved.

"This has to be a success, Fran," she told me one day, between takes. It was before noon, so she wasn't drunk. But she
was still edgy; she picked at her costume until I had to grab her
hands, lest the costume designer throw a conniption. "It has to
be! I need a hit. I need this. Douglas—he's given up. On his
career. On us. But I can't! And it's a great role, isn't it, Fran?
This woman—all she suffers!"

"Yes, but . . ."

"But what, Fran?"

"But is it *you,* Mary? Is this role you?"

"You should know, Fran," she said with a cold smirk. "You
wrote it for me."

Yes. Yes, I had. Because she'd asked. But this woman wasn't
Mary—Our Mary; this woman suffered throughout the film,
suffered heartache and betrayal and still she stayed by her man,
which was precisely what Mary wanted to say to Douglas, but
couldn't. Because she didn't know how to live away from the
camera, and so she had to use it to pour her heart out to her
husband, to tell him that she loved him anyway despite his infi-
delities, and that she would always be there for him.

But Mary *suffering* for an hour and a half—that wasn't what her audiences wanted. I knew that, because I was one of them—I couldn't stand to see her suffer as piteously as she did in this movie; I had to turn away during the filming of those scenes. I couldn't bear to watch her cut her veins open for the camera; it was too personal. Everyone knew what she was saying, and to whom. Her desperation was so palpable, it should have had its own dressing room on set.

As filming went on—Frank Borzage was sure to film all the scenes in which she had to portray a young woman during the morning—Mary began to lash out at me, too.

One evening we were watching the rushes; I had my notepad, jotting down some thoughts—Mary might need a pick-up scene to establish the illness of her child. The prop baby wasn't registering; could we refilm that scene? Mary held it too casually, as if it were a football; I would have to teach her how to really hold an infant. The makeup for Mona Maris, who played Leslie's mistress, was a little harsh; could it be softened in other scenes?

"Fran! Fran!" Mary turned to me, and I smelled so much mint on her breath, I knew she had gargled to disguise the gin she must have swigged on her way to the screening room.

"What?" I kept my eyes on the screen.

"Fran!" Mary actually grabbed my arm, and I looked at her, annoyed.

But she looked even more annoyed at me; she was glaring, her eyes hard and mean.

"I sssound ridiculous in thisss scene," she slurred, glancing at the screen, then twisting back to me. "The lines you wrote me are terrible! Thisss scene is terrible—Mona isn't any good in it, either, even though you wrote *her* some decent dialogue, anyway. I'm sssurprised you had it in you."

"Mary!" I tried to swallow my anger, but it wouldn't quite go down; it sat square in the middle of my chest, waiting. I glanced around the darkened room; the projector sputtered off, then someone turned a light on. Frank, Leslie, Mona, the others all crept away, leaving the two of us alone.

"All I do in that scene is sit there and—and—*take it*!"

I told myself I knew what this was about; she was talking about the scene in which her husband's mistress confronts Mary with the truth and asks her to set him free so the two of them can marry. It was a scene that hit very close to home and Mary had come to the set to film it unsteady on her feet. Fortunately, I'd written it so that she wasn't required to say much, only react—the one thing that Mary Pickford still did better than anyone else in Hollywood. She'd soldiered through the take. We could use it, with some clever editing.

"Mary, darling, remember the scene coming up? I wrote you a great big beautiful speech that's sure to win you another Academy Award!" And I had; I'd listened, I'd watched, and I'd written a speech that allowed Mary to say everything that she wanted to say as a wronged wife; she was a saint, a martyr, it was the scene she'd desperately wanted—demanded—and so, of course, I'd written it for her.

But it wasn't the Mary I loved; it wasn't the spunky little girl who would kick her wandering husband out the door. That was *my* Mary; that's how I would have written it, written *her*.

"But this scene, Fran—it's terrible!"

I bent down to pick up the portfolio containing the next

day's shooting script, so that I could compose myself. She'd never said this to me before. All our lives together, our work was a product of mutual respect. If we didn't agree—and we didn't always—we would work it out together, not resorting to disparaging words or vicious attacks.

"What's happened to you, Fran? What's happened to your talent?"

I dropped my portfolio and faced her, releasing the monster on my chest.

"*My* talent is still intact, thank you very much!"

"What do you mean by that?"

"I mean, Mary, that perhaps you're not entirely right for this role? If you'd only let me write it like I wanted—what if you kick him out? What if you do that thing you've always done so well on camera—that spunk, that fire? Let me make you triumphant in this, Mary, just like before! Not so, so—"

"Real?" Mary's face was twisted, her heavy pancake makeup now cruelly emphasizing the lines along her mouth, between her eyes. "Fran, the reason I want to portray this woman is because I know her. I *am* her. She's a real woman. I thought you knew how to write a real woman—apparently, I was mistaken. I should have remembered *The Love Light*."

"She's not a real woman, she's a doormat. And *The Love Light* was a beautiful screenplay!"

"No, Fran." Mary looked down at her lap; her hands were clasped penitently, as if she were in church. "*I'm* a real woman. Terrified. Terrified of a life without him, her great love—her only love. You wouldn't understand."

"Oh, Mary." I couldn't look at her; I had to turn away. But it didn't matter because tears blurred my vision so that I couldn't have seen her anyway. How could she say that to me? Me, of all people?

"Mary, I do know," I whispered. "I know what it's like to lose a husband. I know what it's like to be terrified." Because I was terrified, every day; terrified of growing old alone, terrified of what my fatherless boys might become. Terrified of an empty bed at night. But I didn't let it keep me locked in my house when I wasn't working. I didn't let it drive me to drink.

And I never confused real life with cinema; I never used my craft to manipulate or control.

Did I?

As if she could read my mind, Mary grabbed me by the shoulders and whipped me around so that she could give me one of those penetrating stares; she didn't look drunk anymore, only bitterly amused. "Have you ever thought, Fran, that if you hadn't made Fred a movie star, he might still be here? Still be alive? Douglas and I used to wonder that. A lot."

I gasped; she had no right. No right at all to say this to me; she wasn't *there*. She didn't know. She couldn't know—

How did she know? How did she know that I couldn't sleep at night, wondering the very same thing?

"Mary, it's late." I pushed my chair back blindly and stood, blinking my tears away furiously; I yanked on my gloves so viciously I split a seam. "I need to get home to check on the boys before they go to sleep. I'll look at your scene again for tomorrow, but it's a fine speech, I think. For what you want it to be. Try to rest. And please, Mary—for God's sake, try to be sober tomorrow on set, all right?"

Never before had I mentioned her drinking. She flinched, paled, didn't look at me. But she did nod. We said goodbye and went our separate ways. Not once, since this movie started, had either of us suggested that we order dinner to be brought to her bungalow so that we could laugh and work through the night.

I had children to tuck in. She had an empty palace to go home to.

The next day, Mary arrived to film the scene letter-perfect. She was sober, and Frank Borzage shot me a look of gratitude. "Maybe she'll pull it off, after all," he muttered, and for the first time, I realized that everyone else had doubts about this film, too. I looked around; the faces of the crew were wary, and I did feel for poor Mary, having to perform for this audience. Always before, she was surrounded by faces full of wonder, of joy—of pure delight at being allowed into her magical orbit.

Now her crew—her audience, the public in general—were skeptical. Simply waiting for her to fall flat on her face. No longer did the world pull for Mary Pickford. And that broke my heart; I couldn't imagine what it did to hers.

I walked over to her as her costume was being given a final brush by the costume girl. I couldn't hug her, as I longed to, so I took her hands, and looked her right in the eyes.

"Mary, I believe in you. You're going to be wonderful, darling, I know it. You'll win another Academy Award, mark my words!"

"Thank you, Fran." She flashed me a smile of pure gratitude, and took her place in front of the camera. The various assistants barked out their readiness—lights were set, actors were on their marks, sound was rolling—as Borzage called out "Action!"

Mary Pickford turned to the camera, but I knew she was seeing her husband, her missing husband who had not once visited her on set, laughing, clowning for everyone, proud of his little wife, his best little girl. Douglas Fairbanks was somewhere in Italy, and he was not alone.

But his wife—my friend—was pouring her heart out on camera to him, saying my words, the words I'd written, the words that would melt anyone's heart, anyone who had a heart, anyway. She was telling him she still loved him, would always love him, that nothing he could say or do would ever drive her away. But the words didn't sound like her, not to my ears; they fell flat, pitiful, and I couldn't look at the crew's faces.

Borzage yelled "Cut!" Mary took a shaky breath, there was some scattered applause. Then she looked to me for approval.

What could I do, but give it?

"AND THE WINNER of the Academy Award for best original screenplay is—Frances Marion, for The Champ*!"*

The applause was as startling in November of 1932 as it had been in 1930, although some things were different. George wasn't my escort; our divorce was final. And Mayer, instead of standing up on a chair to cheer, sat back in his seat like a potentate and proclaimed, "It's a good night for my studio!"

"No, Louis, it's a good night for *me*." I barely glanced at him as I rose to accept my statue, smiling and accepting the congratulations of my peers. Who, I couldn't help but notice, were a tad less enthusiastic the second time around. That's Hollywood, I thought. Happy for your success—as long as it didn't last too long.

Once again, a tiny figure blocked my path.

"Fran!" Mary shook her finger at me, half scoldingly. "Not again!"

She smiled brilliantly—of course, there was a camera snapping away—but her heart wasn't in her eyes, which were dull, her pupils dilated. She was swaying on her feet, and Buddy Rogers—not Doug—was next to her, his arm about her waist to keep her from swaying too far in any direction.

Filming of *Secrets* had ended months before; it wasn't due to be released until the spring. But she knew, and I knew—everyone in Hollywood knew, for there were no secrets in this town—that it wouldn't win her husband back, after all. And Mary would win no Academy Award for it. I steeled myself for some smart, wounding remark; I didn't really know how else to approach her these days. It was as if I had to have one hand outstretched, ready to ward her off—or pick her up—as soon as I saw her.

But to my astonishment, she lurched toward me again, clutched my arm, and whispered in my ear, "Squeebee's soooo happy for you, Fran, darling."

"Mary!" I hugged her, so tightly; I didn't care that now everyone was shifting in their seats, eager for me to hurry up and get my award so the rest of them could collect theirs. But I was touched by her words, and I gave her a kiss on the cheek before I wound my way up to the podium.

Once there, I closed my eyes for a moment in the blinding spotlight, Mary's approval still ringing in my ears—warming my heart. I would always need that, I knew. No matter how old we grew, Mary's were the congratulations—or sympathies—I would always seek. She had given me my start, and here I was—accepting an award for writing a movie that starred a child! I'd not made the connection before, but it was true; I'd first written for children because of Mary. And now I'd won the Academy Award for writing *The Champ* for nine-year-old Jackie Cooper.

The symmetry pleased me, and I smiled. Turning toward Mary's table, I started to thank her for her friendship, for giving me my start—

But her seat was empty; she had left before I could accept my award.

I looked at all the golden statuettes arrayed before me, waiting to be collected by the restless, striving audience. Clark Gable, at a front table, looked pointedly at his watch. So I smiled, thanked the Academy, picked up my trophy, and went home. I found a good place for it; there was a creaky door in my bathroom that wouldn't stay open.

Thanks to the Academy, thanks to L. B. Mayer, thanks to Jackie Cooper, thanks to *Mary*—

Now it would.

SHE CAME DOWN TO LUNCH WITH A HEADACHE, AND she thought it was because of the tiara; she hadn't worn it in so long but of course, she must. Mary Pickford must look her best for luncheon at Pickfair because surely there would be a queen or a duke or someone else accustomed to a crown. So she asked her maid to bring her a tiara, and she draped herself in jewels— several necklaces hung around her neck, nearly dragging her down, and she clasped five bracelets on one arm and six on another, and as she descended the stairs—carefully, for her feet were a *trifle* unsteady—she giggled at the commotion she made as silver and gold and diamonds and pearls all clanged together. She was a jingle bell! She giggled again.

When she got to the dining room, she paused to catch her breath and rearrange her tiara, which had slipped a little over one eye. Then she flung open the door to greet her guests grandly.

The long table was only a quarter full, but of course, this was a luncheon. She wondered who Douglas had brought home this time? He always brought home such wonderful characters!

"Hello," she said, her voice deep and dignified. Douglas rushed to help her to her seat; she fumbled around for her chair, and sat down carefully.

Her guests were all women, and she recognized some of them. There was Adela, so wrinkled now! Her face looked like a raisin, the poor dear. And Gloria, darling Gloria, so thin and ferocious looking. Anita was there, too—hunched over now with a widow's hump.

And there was Fran, too. Fran—*Fran!*

"You!" Mary pushed herself out of her chair, knocking over a water goblet. "You!" she shrieked. "Get out! Get out of my house! You wrote *Anne of Green Gables* for Mary Miles Minter! You betrayed me—get out!"

There was a shocked silence; Adela had risen to her feet and Anita was looking at her plate. Fran had gone scarlet; her eyes blazed, and she grabbed her butter knife as if it were a weapon. Then her face softened; she looked at Mary with something new, something strange—something Mary had never seen before in Fran's eyes.

Was it *pity*? How dare she?

"Mary, darling, you're not yourself—"

Why did everyone say that? What did that mean, anyway? When had Mary Pickford *ever* been herself? The last time she'd answered to "Gladys Smith," that's when. And that was so long ago there was no one left who remembered.

"Get out, you bitch. How dare you? You knew I wanted to star in that—it was perfect for me! You knew you were *my* scenarist! You only got your start because of me—where would you be if I hadn't hired you? And then you had to put your husband in my movie—*mine*! The cowboy was dreadful, you know." Mary turned to Adela. "Simply awful. I carried him through that picture."

There was a crash; Fran had dropped the knife on her plate, her cheeks red, her nostrils flaring. "You're drunk, Mary." Her voice was high, tight with fury. "Drunk as a skunk! No wonder Douglas—"

But Fran stopped, and wouldn't say anything more about Douglas, even though Douglas was right here, his face red now, too.

"You've always been jealous of Douglas and me. The way you pouted on our honeymoon! Remember, Douglas? Oh, what a triumph it was!" Mary turned to her husband, but her husband—so strange, for Douglas!—wouldn't say a word.

"That's it—I'm leaving, don't you worry, Mary." Fran began to gather up her purse and gloves. "I'm leaving and I'm not coming back. All my life I've come running back. Never again. I'm sorry, Buddy—" Strange, that Fran was talking to Douglas but calling him Buddy! "I'm sorry for you, but this is the last straw."

"Fine! Take your two Academy Awards and go home! I won mine first, you know." She addressed the rest of the table fondly, waving her arm expansively, and was about to tell the story of how she won hers, what was it for—that movie, some movie . . . she could go get it and show it to everyone . . . but suddenly, everyone else got up and walked out after Fran.

How odd! But Mary didn't mind; she wasn't hungry, anyway, and her tiara was so heavy, she could barely hold her head up. She allowed Douglas to help her up the stairs and back to her room.

"Thank you, Hipper, dear," she murmured, and his handsome face crumpled. "Thank you, Douglas."

Then she shut her bedroom door. And never opened it again.

THAT HAD BEEN TWO YEARS AGO, or so her husband said, although Mary didn't keep count. What was the point? She had everything she needed right here; a big, luxurious bed and a television, newly installed, and a maid to dress her and bathe her and make sure she ate something, although no one could ever make Mama's stew, which she craved. Sometimes, just for kicks, she made soup out of catsup and hot water, and remembered the old days with fierce love, almost protectiveness. Was that when she'd been her best? When she was plain little Gladys Smith, taking such good care of her entire family?

And of course, here in her room she had access to her liquor; no longer did she hide it because no one cared. Lottie and Jack and Mama were all gone now, all her fans had forgotten her, so she didn't have to set a good example for anyone.

She stayed in bed and watched television. Sometimes, she caught one of her old movies. Late at night, after the news was off the air, and everybody else was fast asleep. Everybody who *could* sleep; everybody who could close their eyes and let go of the memories, and fall asleep looking forward to tomorrow.

Mary wasn't one of those people. She didn't have anywhere to go, anyone she wanted to see. Well, there was one person she wanted to see. But Fran didn't come around anymore, and most days, Mary couldn't remember why. But surely Fran wouldn't stay away forever! Fran always came back.

Except this time, she didn't, which was awful, simply awful! How could Fran do that to her—leave and never come back? Didn't she remember all they'd been through together?

Nobody understood her anymore. Not even Douglas, who kept asking her to get dressed and come downstairs, who often knocked on her door, so politely, telling her she had visitors. Poor Douglas didn't understand—no, no, not Douglas—poor Buddy. *Buddy* was her husband now.

Wasn't he? How on earth had that happened?

It was all so confusing! Husband meant *Douglas*. But Douglas had left her, and Buddy had stepped in seamlessly to take his place and Mary didn't seem to recall having much say in any of it, but perhaps she had. It was so long ago now. Thirty years or more.

Sometimes Mary tittered behind her closed door when Douglas—no, *Buddy!*—knocked on it. She could hear the impatient shifting of feet as whoever was out there—friends or foes, she had no idea—waited for Mary to throw open her doors and emerge, eyes wide, arms waving, like Norma Desmond in that movie *Sunset Boulevard,* whom that director, Mr. Wilder, had wanted her to play but she said no. It made her sick to her stomach, that script with all its tawdry innuendo, the character of Norma entirely pathetic, and so the role had gone instead to Gloria Swanson, dear Gloria, who had been very good in it. Mary was big enough to admit that, and she'd sent dear Gloria a note saying so.

But perhaps dear Gloria had been *too* good, because now every silent screen star was supposed to be living in the past and crazy as a loon, and that's what Mary knew those people outside her door—who were they, anyway? Who had invited them? Whoever they were, and whoever had invited them, Mary knew what they wanted to see. They wanted to see the Girl with the Curls staggering out the door, crying out for her close-up, grotesque and *old.*

Well, she wasn't about to give them the satisfaction. So she stayed right where she was, safely tucked into bed, and giggled as Buddy—always pleasant and pleasing Buddy—pretended that Mary was talking to him through the closed door.

"What's that you say, Mary? You say you're sorry that you can't greet your guests today? You say that you're touched they wanted to see you, but you're a little under the weather? You say you hope they had a pleasant day at Pickfair?"

Meanwhile Mary tittered and fell back among her pillows and waited until they finally walked away. Then she might get up and open the door and peer out, rejoicing in the empty hallway, tickled that she'd managed such a trick.

And her husband would come back in the evening and scold her, very gently, and Mary would listen and nod and say, "But Douglas—" and his face would fall and she wouldn't understand why, and then he'd leave her alone, which was what she wanted, after all.

She preferred it this way, living in shadows and dreams, not entirely sure what year it was or whom she was talking to. Because those moments when she did remember were far worse.

Those moments when she remembered that Douglas had left her, had betrayed her, had told her he didn't want her anymore. Those moments when she remembered how, after she did file for divorce and he remarried, he moved back to Los Angeles with his new British wife, sneaking away to spend long, silent evenings with her at Pickfair out by the pool, the two of them lying in separate deck chairs, remembering. Different things, she knew; she thought of the crowds cheering and the clock stopping in the car and the possessiveness that once had rankled but now seemed like the very notion of love and attention. She had no idea what he was picturing, only that it must be something sweet, something perfect. Something lost.

It was so sad, that's what it was. Tragic. Their love had been too big for a little life. And that was the kind of life she was living now; it was the kind of life she told herself that she *wanted* to live. As much as she loved Douglas, and always would, DougandMary had become too exhausting to keep up forever; it was best to lay it to rest, along with the last remnants of the silent era, like the shorn curls she still kept in a shoe box, high atop a closet shelf.

Buddy Rogers proposed several times, and finally in 1937, once the divorce was final, she married him. Did she love him? No. And she never pretended otherwise.

But he was young, handsome, with black hair, big brown eyes and boyish good looks, and perfectly nice. Rather like a loyal Irish setter. And to have such a handsome young man in love with her, at her age—she didn't mind *that*. Especially after Douglas had so publicly betrayed her with a younger woman.

Douglas died, didn't he? She remembered where she was, in Chicago, in 1939, when the phone rang; Buddy's band was playing and in those days, at least, she still put in public appearances in support of him, or United Artists, or the industry as a whole. But she was the grande dame, trotted out as a remembrance of the old days, then pushed back into her cupboard until the next occasion.

She was only forty-seven at the time.

That night the phone rang in the hotel room, and she answered it before Buddy did. It was her niece Gwynne, dear Gwynne all grown up now, who was sobbing. And she knew.

"He's gone, Mary." And Gwynne didn't have to say who; there was only one "he" in Mary's life, and it wasn't her current husband. The words were like a whip across her face; she flinched from the impact of all the emotions that rushed in behind them: grief, loss, anger, sadness. Then came the memories, cruel and taunting, and she had to get up and go into another room, so that Buddy wouldn't hear her cry.

Once, when she and Douglas were still courting—he always used that old-fashioned word, for he was an old-fashioned man—he'd taken her to an amusement park far down the coast, as far away from Los Angeles and its prying eyes as they could get, almost to Mexico. He convinced her to ride a rickety Ferris wheel, the wind off the ocean pummeling her hair and assaulting her ears; she shut her eyes and gripped the bar in front, terrified that the whole thing would break apart because it looked as flimsy as a set piece.

"Open your eyes, Mary," Douglas shouted above the wind. "Open your eyes, and see!" She did open them; they were high above the rest of the people, little tiny figures below, looking up at them. And that was how she always viewed their union— two people high above the rest of the world, sharing a view only the two of them could see; a privileged, lucky, hard-earned view. The very best view there was.

She had lost the one person who knew how it felt to be on top of the world; she had lost the one person who had shared that view, for so long.

When she put a call through to Charlie the next day, the two of them burst into tears at the sound of each other's voices and this time, she didn't try to stop them.

"Oh, Charlie, what will we do without him?"

"I have no idea," Charlie replied, his voice thick with loss.

In that moment of shared grief, Mary forgot all the annoying things about Charlie—how he was so possessive of Douglas, always trying to sneak off with him behind her back. How he could never be counted on to come to stockholder meetings for UA, how he never read a ledger, how he seemed to think his films were above hers in every way, precious jewels that had to be polished for years before being unveiled in front of an undeserving audience.

No, in that moment all Mary remembered was that Charlie was a bridge to those glorious, heady days of the bond tour and Pickfair and DougandMary; they both had loved Douglas very much, and so now, during this phone call anyway, Mary loved Charlie.

"I always showed him my movies first, Mary, remember? He was the best judge, my best audience. No one laughed like Doug."

"He loved you," Mary was generous enough to say, and Charlie said the same thing. Even though Charlie was still making movies, the Little Tramp was almost as much of a symbol of a bygone era as the Girl with the Curls. And in that moment, Mary couldn't help but envy Douglas; he didn't have to live the rest of his life a relic of the past, like she and Charlie did.

A past that faded more and more into memory, into history, even legend, as the years rushed by. Now Mary Pickford movies were no longer shown in theaters unless they were part of a "silent film retrospective." People came to Pickfair, but only to genuflect at the mausoleum of early Hollywood. Hollywood was no good at preserving its past; all the old studios had been plowed under, there was no museum full of costumes, even the films themselves hadn't been properly saved. Pickfair was the most tangible remaining symbol of the silent era, and to Pickfair the worshipful came. Young actors, hoping to get some kind of blessing from the woman who had invented the term "movie star." Journalists hoping for a good story along the lines of *Sunset Boulevard*. Documentary makers who wanted to air, generally on public television, tributes to a bygone era.

Mary met with some of them; she went to a few of the retrospectives, until she couldn't bear looking at her face any longer; couldn't stand to gaze into the youthful beauty of Little Mary, shaking her fist at the camera in the very embodiment of "spunk," saving her tears for the camera, too; all the tears she didn't allow herself to cry in real life. And when she couldn't bear it any longer; when she couldn't stand to be introduced as "the very first star of the silver screen, the queen of the silent movies, that beloved little girl, the legendary Mary Pickford" one more time—

She shut her bedroom door so she didn't have to see the disappointment, the disbelief, in the public's eyes when they realized she was no longer that beloved little girl.

They deserved each other, finally, Pickfair and she. When night fell and Douglas—*Buddy?*—and all the servants were asleep, she and the house told each other their secrets. Only then would she open her door. And as she shuffled down the halls, touching the chair rail to keep her balance, the house whispered names of long-ago guests: *Albert Einstein, the Duke of York, George Bernard Shaw, Mrs. Calvin Coolidge*. They'd all come to see *her*, the biggest star of them all. The star she'd set out to be when she was such a little girl, responsible for Mama and also Lottie and Jack, who got to have a real childhood, not like her.

They were all gone now. Long gone. And she had all the time in the world.

So while the house kept lookout for prying eyes and gossiping tongues, Mary would play with her doll collection as she'd done in *The Poor Little Rich Girl,* slide down the polished halls like she'd done in *Rags,* raid the kitchen as she'd done in *Pollyanna.* And the house never once betrayed her; the walls and the windows and the curtains and the rugs all seemed to smile in understanding as she took refuge in childhood memories. Memories that were created by Fran for her to play in front of the camera as an adult.

Which were the only childhood memories that she had.

The house was enough, it was *hers,* and she knew that nobody really understood why. The only one who might have understood was Fran.

Sometimes she'd catch an old movie of theirs on television—like she did last night. *Secrets.* Mary thought it really wasn't a bad film, although it had done so poorly at the box office. Leslie Howard played her love interest—poor Leslie, shot down in the war. Which war? She couldn't remember. He was younger than her, of course, something that Fran had worried about in casting, but Mary had overruled her.

Secrets was a flop. It was her last film, too. She was afraid of the camera after that—impossible, but true. The camera who had always been her friend, her lover. She simply had nothing left to give. And the camera had only loved her as a little girl. Just like everyone else, including Douglas.

Douglas had died. Hadn't he? And so had Mama. Everyone was dying; there was no one left who cared, not even her public. They were gone, now. Everything was gone. Never again would she know the desperate throngs who'd greeted her on her honeymoon with Douglas; never again would she receive thousands of fan letters a day.

Never again would she recognize herself in a mirror. In order to remember who she was, she had to creep downstairs at night to gaze at her portrait and weep at its loveliness, and all that little girl had achieved, and lost. Then she would creep back upstairs and shut her door.

Until one day, the door opened. And Fran came barging in.

I STEPPED BACK IN HORROR AFTER I OPENED THE DOOR; it was no little girl with golden curls who emerged from the gloom, after all.

A tiny, puckered figure sprawled on an enormous bed, wispy gray hair standing up all over her head, little downy puffs, like a baby chick. Pink patches of scalp peeking through. On a table next to the figure stood a detached head and I almost screamed—until I realized it was a wig. A wig, styled in blond curls, perched on a wig stand. The figure was propped up on pillows, so many pillows she was almost swallowed by them. She was emaciated; a pink-and-white flowered nightgown enveloped her so that only the tiniest bits of scrawny neck and her clawlike hands were visible.

Except for the face—the face was too visible. The face that had no eyebrows, only watery hazel eyes, still almond-shaped. The chin was still recognizable; that stubborn Irish chin, the outline softer now, a bit jowly but still evident.

And the lips; the rosebud lips. Which were moving, trying to form words.

"*Mary.*" My heart lurched, and I was sorry. Sorry I'd barged in; sorry I'd invaded my friend's privacy.

Sorry that I had to see Mary like this—that Mary was *reduced* to this, a ghostly creature drowning in gin and memories. For I was assaulted by them, too, all the time; but my dreams were fragments of movies I'd written, vacations I'd taken, arguments I'd had with my sons, people I'd lost. And Fred. Always Fred. Sobriety was the only defense against the avalanche of regret and loss that comes with old age. An alcoholic had no defense; an alcoholic was the most vulnerable, raw, walking wound of a person in the whole wide world. Especially an alcoholic who had once been the most beautiful, the most admired. The most.

"Mary, Squeebee, darling."

"Oh, Fwan, I told you not to come up!" Mary brushed one skeletal forefinger with the other in a scolding gesture, one she'd used on film many times. "Didn't you get my message?"

"I did. And I came up anyway."

"Well, go away. It's too late!" Mary flouncingly turned her back to me, crossing her arms, and I had to wonder if this was really happening; if I was truly witnessing this tottering creature acting like a ten-year-old child, the child she'd been in the movies, so long ago.

"I'm not going away, Mary, not this time. I did once, and I'm sorry."

Mary was quiet, she fell back against the pillows and closed her eyes, her blue-veined lids fluttering. Amazingly, her eyelashes were still as long—almost grazing her cheekbones—as they always had been. Then she pushed herself back up on her elbows and suddenly her eyes were blazing, she was raising that skeletal hand toward me, pointing. Accusing.

"You! You wrote *Anne of Green Gables* for Mary Miles Minter!"

"Oh, Mary, stop it!" I hated myself for snapping at her—she was so old and fragile and obviously not herself. Or perhaps, too much herself? "This is ridiculous, darling. That was fifty years ago and we're both too old to care. In case you haven't noticed, we don't have a lifetime ahead of us anymore."

She rubbed her eyes in confusion; then she began to cry.

"Oh, Mary, I'm sorry—I didn't mean it!" I rushed to her side, intending to comfort her, but something held me back. Was it the shock that this creature bore no resemblance to the woman I had known and loved? Was it because I felt somehow responsible for this wreck of a person? I had stayed away for so long because it was easier that way; hearing about Mary's decline through the grapevine allowed me to protect myself. But now, I had to ask—from what? What was so important about my own survival, anyway? I was just another Hollywood relic, too.

"We relics need to stick together," I said now, my voice too loud, too bright—I was speaking to her as one did to a child. A fretful, willful child, and I despised myself for it.

Mary looked at me suspiciously, then she fumbled for a bottle on her nightstand.

"That's a good idea," I heard myself say, still sounding like an aged Florence Nightingale. "Pour me one, too, will you?" I didn't think that she would—I didn't see any glasses around—but I roamed about the room, giving her the time she needed to shore herself up.

The room was clean, but there was a musty smell like a museum—because it *was* a museum. The enormous cabinet television was the only concession to modern times. Everything else hadn't changed since Mary redecorated in the thirties; the same photographs were on the dressing table in shiny Art Deco frames; the same gleaming, once-modern end tables, the same patterned silvery wallpaper, like something out of an old Astaire–Rogers musical.

So many photos were of Mary—and Douglas, always Douglas. You didn't have to look farther than your nose to see who Mary's great love was. I understood; there were photographs of Fred all over my small apartment, photographs of him in uniform, when we'd first met; photographs of him in costume on Silver King.

But there were other photographs here, too, and I picked one up, smiling in remembrance. I had the same photo at home. It was of the two of us at United Artists, Mary and I, along with Cecil B. DeMille and Sam Goldwyn. I glanced at another photo on her dressing table; again, we two, this time with Charlie and Doug. And another of us with Zukor and Lasky.

"Mary." I held up the one with DeMille and Goldwyn. "Remember this? How close we were? Why can't it be like that again? Now that it's only the two of us left. Now that everyone else is gone—why can't we go back to how we were? We need each other, Mary."

"Oh, really?" She set the bottle down on her nightstand with a hard bang, gin sloshing all over the place. "I need you? For what, Fran? You can't write me a movie now."

"Was that all I was to you?"

"Yes."

"I don't believe it!" Now I did go to her, because I had to; I had to shake her into some kind of sense, because she did not mean that. She couldn't mean it. If she did—then everything I knew was wrong. *Everything*.

"Mary, I don't believe it! Look at this photo—look at us!"

"That was then, Fran. I'm not that person anymore."

"But don't you see, Squeebee, darling? You can be! That's why I'm here—to rescue you, to get you to live again—so you can go outside, darling, and see the sun, and get out of this musty place!"

"Oh, Fran!" Mary laughed now, a real, genuine, throaty laugh. "You always did have a high opinion of yourself!"

"What do you mean?"

"Oh, don't pretend—you always thought you were better than me, smarter than me. Now you think you can *save* me?"

I perched on the foot of her bed, more than a little uncomfortable. Did I think that? No matter how much I respected Mary, I supposed I had always felt a tad—smug—about my education. "Is that how you really feel, Mary?"

"You were that way with everyone. Poor Fred didn't stand a chance with you, did he? And on the seventh day Fran created—*a movie star*!" She clapped her hands and giggled again.

"That's not fair." I didn't like this Mary, this startlingly sober, vicious Mary. Where was the pathetic drunk who needed to be rescued? That was the Mary I'd come to see; the Mary, in fact, I'd counted on seeing.

Not this suddenly clear-eyed oracle who could see inside my soul.

"But it is, Fran. I don't know how you sleep at night—do you, Fran? Do you sleep at night?"

"No," I whispered, looking away.

Because of course, she was right. I *had* pushed Fred into an acting career. Despite the fun he had making movies, I'd always known his heart wasn't in it; he'd never been comfortable in

Hollywood. Oh, he made many friends—many genuine friends—but he'd always had much more fun camping out with our sons and the real cowboys he worked with than he ever had at a movie premiere. But I was in the movies, and I wanted my husband to be, too—just like DougandMary.

"I'm sorry, then, Fran. Sorry you can't sleep. Neither can I, so we're even." Mary poked me with her foot, and I looked up; she had tears in her eyes, too.

"Thank you, Mary." I started to scooch up the bed, to be near her, but then she smiled at me again.

"But you did the same thing to me, you know," she continued, plucking at her covers with her gnarled hands—the nails beautifully sculpted and painted a pretty pink, to match her nightgown.

"What?"

"You came here to rescue me, did you, Fran? You think I hide away because I'm too afraid, too used to being the queen, and so I hide away here in my castle—that's what you think, isn't it? And so here you come—Saint Frances!—to rescue me. Isn't that right?"

I had no answer.

"But what you don't understand, Fran—you never did!—is that it's all your fault I'm here. Fred died, Douglas died—but I didn't. I grew old—too old for my public. I had to remain a little girl to them, you know—I couldn't be a woman, not like you. I couldn't have children, a real family. I had to remain a child—*their* child. And whose fault was that?"

"What on earth do you mean, Mary?" Now I wasn't merely uncomfortable; I was terrified. It was as if I'd stumbled into a madhouse and would never be able to leave. I'd be trapped here forever with Mary. I'd become a ghoul, just like her—a ghoul spouting outrageous accusations, held hostage by false memories.

"It was *your* fault, Fran! Yours! You made me a child, didn't you? You thought you were so clever! *The Poor Little Rich Girl*—that was my first film playing a little girl."

"And it was a hit—the biggest hit of your career up until then. Remember, darling, that day we went to see it at the Strand?"

She shook her head impatiently. "No—yes, of course—but that's not the important thing. *You* made me a child—what did you say? Once, you said that you were . . . you were . . ."

"I was giving you your childhood." I was struck by the memory; I hadn't thought of it in so long. But yes, that's exactly what I'd said. But it was a good thing! I wanted my friend to have what was so cruelly denied her; I wanted to give her that.

But did *she* want that childhood? That idyllic, made-up childhood? It wasn't her idea, it was mine, that was true. But we'd had so much fun making those movies! How many times on set had Mary told me that she was doing something for the first time; skipping rope, playing jacks, making mud pies? I gave her the chance to do all those things she'd never done, and the public loved it, *she* loved it—you could see it on the screen, how much fun she was having! Wasn't she?

"Yes—that's what you said, I remember. And you did—and it trapped me, Fran, don't you see? I'm trapped here because I can never grow up, even though I've grown so—so old. So ugly." She whispered this last. "It's all your fault, Fran."

"Mary, those were movies. Just movies."

"No! They weren't just movies, you know that better than

anyone—*you* saw how the public worshipped their Little Mary! You were right there! And they were never only movies to me—they were my *life*. And so I haven't any other, I never have. But you—you had a life! With Fred, your boys, your career. Mine crashed but Frances Marion was the writer everyone wanted—you made sure of that, didn't you?" Mary smiled a crooked, resigned smile. "No one wanted me. I was trapped. So you can't rescue me, you see—that's not your role. Because you're the one who trapped me in the first place."

I couldn't move; I couldn't speak. I was cold and shivering, just as I'd been on the road from Verdun, and I felt just as desolate, lost. She couldn't mean what she said. She couldn't. It wasn't true! It—

"You've got it all wrong, Mary," I stammered weakly. "You're—"

But for the first time, it struck me that none of the movies I'd written for an adult Mary had been a success.

"Oh, but, Fran, darling, don't you see? I'm *right*." And the way she said it, so sweetly, so sadly—not accusingly, not at all—made me slide off the bed, desperate to get as far away from her as possible. I nearly tripped over a robe on the floor in my hurry to flee this place, this house of horrors.

Forget Mary—it was too late for Mary. I could see that now; too late to turn back the hands of time, to go back to how it used to be, no recriminations, no regrets. Had I really believed that was possible? It was folly, pure and simple; she was too far gone. But I wasn't—blindly, I pushed my way out the door and hurried down the stairs, hanging on to the bannister for dear life. For the first time, I slipped on the marble foyer of Pickfair, but somehow I righted myself; I had to, I had to get out of this place, this mausoleum that according to the madwoman upstairs I was just as responsible for building as she was. I had to flee before it entombed me, too.

The door slammed shut behind me as I tumbled out of the house; the startled doorman didn't even have time to give me his headshot. As desperate as I was to escape, my car had been whisked around to the garage, so I had no choice but to wait for one of the chauffeurs to fetch it. It was just as well; I needed to catch my breath. I was clammy, wrung out, and after the stifling, cloying atmosphere of Mary's bedroom, I was shivering. Lifting my face to the sun, I vowed that for whatever time was left to me, I would seek its embrace, its benediction. I deserved that, no matter what Mary said.

I ached for a cigarette but I hadn't smoked in years; the doctors made me quit after a bout of pneumonia. I needed something in my hands—those hands that were always so restless. *Restless hands to go with a restless mind*—wasn't that what Mother always told me?

But then I realized there *was* something in my hand; to my astonishment, I was still clutching that photograph.

Damn.

Turning, I looked back up at the house; her bedroom wasn't visible from this angle, but I knew she was there anyway, still smiling so sadly, lost in her false memories. I'd have to go back inside. But no, I couldn't. I couldn't imagine being able to look her in the eyes again. Spying a trash container beneath a potted palm, I tottered unsteadily over to it, ready to toss the photograph inside; surely someone would find it and return it to her. Or not—I really didn't care.

But something stopped me before I could drop the heavy silver frame into the container; something beckoned at me from behind the glass.

Mary. The expression in her eyes—so different from what I'd just witnessed! Instead of resignation and bitterness, I saw confidence and joy in her eyes. And in mine. In this photo, both of us looked successful and happy. Well, Fran—of course you were happy. You were in love with Fred and Mary was in love with Doug. Still, we were so attuned to each other, you could see it—it was as if there was an invisible thread between us, even though we were both looking at the camera. Both smiling confidently. Joyously.

The only girls in the picture.

It occurred to me then that we were *always* the only girls in the picture—or even in the room. The two of us huddled together in that dark, forbidding screening room, surrounded by disapproving men, as *The Poor Little Rich Girl* was previewed. Me during the war, unwanted, bullied, propositioned, everywhere I turned another man scowling at me in disapproval, asking me why I was there, in a man's world. Mary at United Artists, sitting in a boardroom surrounded by Chaplin and Doug and Griffith. A flower in her elegant dress, bordered on all sides by men in dark suits. Even when it was only one of us, it was always as if the other was there in spirit, too. We might have been alone, but we were never lonely. Because we always were there for each other.

When I thought back to those years, *those golden years,* that was how I remembered it. At least—that's how I chose to re-member it; I knew now that Mary remembered something dif-ferent. Something darker.

Something closer to the truth?

No. Just a different truth; like in a movie shot from different points of view—like *Rashomon,* which I'd admired so when it came out—our experience was the same. We remembered these identical experiences differently—but that didn't make them any less truthful. Two people could look at something— like this photograph—and see two different stories. I knew, now, what Mary's story was.

I could accept it—not willingly, but still—as her truth. I could see my role in her imprisonment, just as I could see—had always seen, try as I might to deny it—my role in Fred's career and, ultimately, his death. For if he hadn't been successful, if we hadn't built our own monument to Hollywood in The Enchanted Hill, he wouldn't have stepped on that nail. He might still be with me, the two of us rocking comfortably together in the evenings, holding hands and chuckling over the antics of our grandchildren. But he was gone, truly gone.

Mary, however, wasn't.

As I continued to look at the photograph, I saw another story—*my* story. And it was just as true, just as valid, as Mary's.

A story that began with two women—once girls. One golden-haired, one with raven locks. Standing next to each other on a porch, gazing up at a night full of stars. Laughing together on a set crowded with lights and cameras and cables, Mickey high on a ladder teasing them as they played jacks, getting their hands and knees dirty. Rejoicing in each other's true love. Falling in love, growing old—growing bitter.

Feeling alone.

But ultimately, forgiving each other—*saving* each other. For if we didn't, wasn't everything we'd sacrificed, every inch of accomplishment for which we'd struggled—movies, studios, Academy Awards, millions of people made happy because of two hours in a dark theater—all in vain?

Mary and I *were* these women; we were the girls in the picture, still. The girls whose brave and tender hearts were still beating beneath the wrinkled breasts, the old-fashioned night-gowns and sensible grandmother blouses. The girls we'd become the moment we'd said hello in that other dark room, so many years ago.

The girls we'd believed to have been lost in the haze of regret and recrimination that comes with *surviving* in this unscrupulous business; this unjust world. But it turned out they'd been here all along, these two; caught forever in a shared moment, preserved together in a silver frame.

Lovingly, I touched the faces of the girls in the picture, faded a little with time but heartbreakingly perfect. I couldn't throw the photo away. I couldn't throw *her* away; I couldn't leave her alone in that room. If she didn't want to come out, then I could stay there with her. I could be her comfort in the darkness. No—not her comfort. And not her savior, either.

Her *friend.*

I took a shaky breath; rescuing was easy. Accepting was much more difficult—and terrifying.

But I opened the door and walked back inside. Back to who I used to be, before Louis B. Mayer and MGM and bad reviews and rusty nails and heartbreak and phone calls that were never returned, queries of "Frances who?" and "Didn't you used to be—?"

Back to my truest, my very best self—

Back to my friend Mary.

ACKNOWLEDGMENTS

As always, I am not alone in my journey; there are many people who have earned my gratitude for their roles in the publication of this book:

Kate Miciak, my indefatigable editor who always pushes me to be better.

Laura Langlie, my agent, who is always on my side.

Gina Centrello and my invincible team at Penguin Random House, who never fail to touch me with their support and enthusiasm: Kara Welsh, Kim Hovey, Gina Wachtel, Sharon Propson, Susan Corcoran, Quinne Rogers, Leigh Marchant, Allyson Pearl, Robbin Schiff, Benjamin Dreyer, Loren Noveck, and Julia Maguire. And my team at the Penguin Random House Speakers Bureau, who are always looking out for me: Anastasia Whalen and Caitlin McCaskey.

Bill Contardi, who leaves no stone unturned.

The kind professionals at the Margaret Herrick Library at the Academy of Motion Picture Arts and Sciences.

The enthusiastic sales reps at Penguin Random House, so many of whom I'm proud to call friends.

All the booksellers.

And finally, Norman Miller, Mark Miller, and Stephanie Miller. And most of all, my sons, Alec and Ben, and my rock, my husband, Dennis Hauser.

AUTHOR'S NOTE

I'M ASKED WHAT I'VE MADE UP, AND WHAT HAPPENED in real life, when I write my novels. The dialogue, the emotions, the reasons why people do what we know they did—those are imagined. Imagined based on research, of course. But still, imagined. Did Mary and Frances have a fight on the set of *Secrets*? We don't know. But we do know they didn't work together again. Was Mary bitter about the fact that Frances imprisoned her as a little girl on-screen? Again, we don't know. But every time she tried to grow up in a movie, her public demanded that she return to playing children. Mary Pickford was the first—but not the last—actress to become a casualty of her own image. An image first created by Frances.

When writing a novel, as compared to a biography, storytelling is the primary intent, and in order to do that, I naturally have to condense parts of the characters' lives and leave other parts out. Things I omitted include many of the movies Mary and Frances made with other people, and some of the studios at which they worked. Frances's first two marriages are glossed over, as is her fourth. That marriage, to George Hill, had more of an impact on her life than I depict; George was an alcoholic, and he committed suicide after they divorced. I also don't explore the depth of Frances's friendships with other women, particularly Marie Dressler and Hedda Hopper. And again, I don't fully write about Frances's post-silent career, when she made the movies she's actually best known for today, including *Dinner at Eight, Anna Christie,* and *The Champ.* Her involvement in forming the Screen Writers Guild, too, isn't really explored here. Frances stopped writing for the movies in 1946, and then wrote some novels and plays—again, not mentioned here.

Mary's marriage to Buddy Rogers is only touched on, and I had to (reluctantly) omit one major aspect of Mary's life—her adoption, in the 1940s, of two children. That could be a novel in itself! There are many rumors as to why Mary never had biological children, but when she and Buddy decided to adopt, it had terrible consequences. Simply put, Mary was not cut out to nurture children. She fussed over them as babies and then when they grew, she couldn't handle them. The two children were never fully part of her life; at early ages they were sent off to boarding schools. And at the first opportunity, they each struck out on their own.

Mary didn't retire from Hollywood as abruptly as I depict here. She never performed in another movie after *Secrets,* but she toyed with ideas, one of which was to star in a live action/cartoon version of *Alice in Wonderland* for Walt Disney, although the project never was made. She produced movies through United Artists, and at one point hoped to have Shirley Temple star in a biopic of her life. She remained active on the board of United Artists—continually clashing with Charlie Chaplin, the other remaining founding partner—until 1956, when she finally sold her shares.

In her golden years, Frances traveled widely but maintained

a small apartment in Hollywood. Near the end of their lives, Mary and Frances did write each other often, sending flowers for birthdays or holidays. I don't know that Frances had one final visit with Mary, as I've written. I do know that their last letters were full of emotion; they both wrote that they were at their best with each other, back in the early days. They seemed to come to peace with their legacies, and with each other.

Both women wrote memoirs, and both are frustrating. In her autobiography, *Off with Their Heads!,* Frances does not write with depth about her own life; even Fred's death garners only a couple sentences. She seems always to cover her true feelings with a joke or a quip. Mary's autobiography, *Sunshine and Shadow,* is similarly unfulfilling. Always conscious of her image, she glosses over every setback, and omits quite a lot, especially about her first marriage and her siblings' tragic lives. And her own drinking, of course.

But for further information, these two books, as well as Cari Beauchamp's *Without Lying Down,* are worth your time, as are these others: *Pickford: The Woman Who Made Hollywood* by Eileen Whitfield; *The First King of Hollywood: The Life of Douglas Fairbanks* by Tracey Goessel, and *Mary Pickford and Douglas Fairbanks* by Booton Herndon. For further information about United Artists, I recommend the book *United Artists: The Company Built by the Stars,* vol. 1 by Tino Balio.

For more reading about early Hollywood, I highly recommend *The Parade's Gone By* by Kevin Brownlow; *American Silent Film* by William K. Everson; *My First Time in Hollywood* by Cari Beauchamp; *Silent Lives* by Lon Davis and Kevin Brownlow; *Silent Stars* by Jeanine Basinger; *The Speed of Sound: Hollywood and the Talkie Revolution 1926-1930, Lion of Hollywood: The Life and Legend of Louis B. Mayer,* and *Empire of Dreams: The*

Epic Life of Cecil B. DeMille, all by Scott Eyman; and Adela Rogers St. Johns's autobiography *Love, Laughter, and Tears*.

All my novels ask the reader to step back into another era and accept that era's limitations and conventions, no matter how unacceptable they may seem to us today. *The Girls in the Picture* is no different; we must remember the different expectations imposed upon women more than a century ago, for example. We must also recognize that one of the films I mention, *The Birth of a Nation,* was very important to early Hollywood and to filmmakers like Mary and Frances, even as we shudder at the despicable racial stereotypes and glorification of the KKK depicted in it. But to ignore its impact on these two women, and to Hollywood in particular and the movie-going public in general, would be wrong; the film represented such an enormous leap forward, technically speaking. And for this, it deserves to be included in a novel about early Hollywood.

Too often we think of silent films as ridiculous, jerky images on a screen; silly relics, dull as dust. I hope, after reading my novel, you see this era for what it was: a breathtakingly innovative time in which literally anyone with a new idea could suddenly become the head of a department, and women were just as important as men.

I also hope you remember Mary Pickford and Frances Marion as not just long-forgotten names in a book or screen credits from an old movie, but as innovators, artists. As loving friends who helped each other grow and flourish; as passionate people who fell in love with an idea, and made it into an art form.

As courageous women who were just as responsible for creating Hollywood as Louis B. Mayer or Sam Goldwyn, and who paved the way for the women working in film today. Hopefully, one day soon, there will be more of them.

THE GIRLS IN THE PICTURE

A NOVEL

MELANIE
BENJAMIN

RANDOM HOUSE
READER'S CIRCLE

QUESTIONS AND TOPICS FOR DISCUSSION

1. Frances and Mary, especially in their younger years, feel they have to choose between pursuing careers and fulfilling traditional expectations of marriage. Did these conversations surprise you? Do you think these pressures still exist for women today?

2. How did you react to the sexism Frances and Mary face in the movie industry? How do the women confront their male superiors, and do they ever prove the men who doubted them wrong?

3. Mary's role as an actress places her in the spotlight, while Frances works behind the scenes as her "scenarist." Does Mary's fame work for or against her? What about Frances's relative anonymity?

4. Did you identify more with Frances or with Mary? Why? Whose chapters were more intriguing to you?

5. Benjamin references many movies produced in the early days of Hollywood, such as *The Birth of a Nation, The Poor Little Rich Girl,* and *The Big House.* Have you seen or heard of any of these movies? If not, did the novel make you want to seek them out?

6. Have you ever had a friendship as supportive, productive, and collaborative as Frances and Mary's? Do you think that kind of friendship can only thrive between the young and ambitious, or can you find it at any age?

7. Are Frances and Mary truly equal creative partners or does one woman hold power over the other? How do the power dynamics of their partnership change over the course of their lives?

8. Consider the opening line of Mary's first chapter: "Mama, I made a friend!" How does Mary's relationship with her mother affect her throughout her career? Does Mary feel as though she needs to prove something to her—and if so, what?

9. Seeing the frontlines of the war—and the war's brutal ramifications for women—is a turning point for Frances. Why do you think Frances makes the decision to leave her flourishing career and go to war? How did Mary's decision to stay in Hollywood and work on her movies affect her relationship with Frances?

10. Mary Pickford and Douglas Fairbanks were the most celebrated couple of their age. Can you think of a similarly iconic couple alive today?

11. Despite their remarkable success, Frances and Mary experience anxiety in their personal and professional lives. What is Frances most insecure about? What makes Mary feel imprisoned?

12. What do you think causes Frances and Mary's friendship to fracture? Do you think it was one incident or many over time? Was it inevitable?

13. Throughout the novel, Benjamin sprinkles appearances from celebrities and illuminating details about the time and place of the story. What did you learn about early Hollywood and the naissance of the movie industry?

14. What female screenwriters or directors do you know of? How do sexism, gender bias, and inequality manifest in the film industry today?

IF YOU

ENJOYED

THE GIRLS IN THE PICTURE

read on for a preview of
Melanie Benjamin's next enthralling
work of historical fiction

...

MISTRESS OF
THE RITZ

...

LILY

Blanche is dead.

Sometimes death is a mercy, and I believe this is true for her. Because she was once so vibrant and spirited, and that's how I'll remember her. I have so many memories of Blanche—Blanche singing a sailor's sea chantey with a glass of champagne balanced on the back of her hand, Blanche showing a streetwalker how to dance the Charleston, Blanche being gently compassionate to someone who didn't deserve it, Blanche stubbornly turning her back and stomping her foot like a child.

Blanche blazing with courage, defying—foolishly—those she should not.

But the memory of Blanche that remains the most vivid is the memory of seeing her for the first time, in the setting that suited her best: At the Ritz. Her beloved Ritz.

Blanche wasn't there the day the Nazis first arrived in 1940; she was still making her way back home from the South of France. But she told me how it happened that day.

How at first, the Ritz employees and guests only heard them; the tanks and jeeps roaring into the vast square, positioning themselves around the tall obelisk as Napoleon himself stared down in horror from his lofty perch. Then the metal heels of their boots ringing out on the cobblestones and pavement, faint at first but increasing in volume as the Germans came close, closer, closest. They wrung their hands; they *looked at one another, and some of them bolted for the service entrance downstairs. But they didn't get far.*

Madame Ritz herself, small, gallant, dressed in her best black dress, still in the old Edwardian style, waited inside the entrance to her home that was the grandest hotel in all of Paris. Her bejeweled hands trembled as she clasped them in front of her; more than once she glanced up at the enormous portrait of her late husband, as if his painted likeness could tell her what to do.

Some of these employees had been with her, with him, in the beginning, in 1898. They remembered the first time these same doors flew open; the glittering, gay guests venturing into the richly appointed hall—no lobby for Monsieur Ritz's new hotel; he did not wish for mere citizens to darken its gilded portals—eyes shining with awe. Princes and duchesses and the wealthiest of the wealthy: Marcel Proust, Sarah Bernhardt. Then, as musicians played, as chandeliers gleamed, as the kitchen sent up trays and trays of Auguste Escoffier's finest creations—meringues of vanilla cream decorated with sugared petals of lavender and violet; tournedos Rossini, rich pâtés, even peach melba, in honor of Dame Nellie Melba, who had agreed to serenade the guests later—they gave one last touch to their new uniforms and smiled, eager to do their jobs. To fetch, lift, provide, polish, dust, mop, chop, fold, soothe, fix. To pamper; to cosset. They were thrilled to be part of this—the opening of a grand new hotel, the only one in the world with bathrooms en suite, telephones in every room, completely wired with the new electricity instead of gas light.

The Hotel Ritz, on the Place Vendôme.

This day, they did not smile. Some wept openly as the Germans stormed through the front doors, their dusty black boots sullying the carpets, their guns slung across their shoulders or holstered. They did not remove their caps, those imperious caps with the eagle insignia. Their uniforms—gray-green, the color of haricots verts—were ugly and of-

fensive against the brilliant gold and marble and crystal of the hallway, the ornate tapestries on the walls, the regal blue of the carpeted grand staircase.

The blood-red band on their arms—the ugly black spider of the swastika—made everyone shiver.

The Germans were here. Just as everyone was told they would be, after the French army crumbled like one of Monsieur Escoffier's fine flaky pastries, after the Maginot Line proved to be a child's illusion, after the British allies abandoned France, fleeing across the Channel at Dunkirk. The Germans were here. In France; in Paris.

At the Hotel Ritz, on the Place Vendôme.

CHAPTER I

BLANCHE,

JUNE 1940

H ER SHOES.

It's her shoes that worry her, if that can be believed. Of all the things this woman should be concerned about on this horrific day, it's her shoes.

But in her defense, given who she is and where she is headed, her shoes *are* a problem. They're filthy, caked with dried mud, the heels worn down. And all she can think about, as her husband helps her off the train, is how Coco Chanel, that bitch, will react when she sees her. How they'll all react when she shows up at the Ritz with filthy, worn-down shoes, her ripped stockings practically disintegrating on her shapely calves. While she can't do anything about her stockings—even Blanche Auzello would never dream of changing her stockings in public—she is desperate to find a bench so that she can rummage through her suitcases and find another pair of shoes. But before she can speak this wish, she and her husband are swept up in the wave of bewildered—well, what the hell are they now? French? German? Refugees?—who are flooding out of the Gare du Nord, eager, terrified, to see what has become of Paris in their absence.

Blanche and her husband are part of the great unwashed;

dirt and cinders have coagulated in pockets of perspiration beneath their chins, behind their ears, their knees, in the crevasses
of their elbows. Greasy faces streaked with soot. They haven't
changed clothes in days; Claude packed away his captain's uniform before they left his garrison. "To be worn again," he assured Blanche—or more likely, she suspected, himself. "When
we fight back. As we most certainly will."

But no one knows when, or if, that time will come. Now
that the Germans have taken France.

Outside, the pair finally push their way out of the crowd, so
that they can catch their breath, try to corral all the luggage
that is slipping out of their hands; when they packed, nine
months ago, they had no idea how long they'd be away. Automatically, they look for a taxi in the usual line outside the station entrance, but there are none; there are no cars at all, not
even horse carts.

The Auzellos are still a long way from the Ritz.

"I would have telegrammed to have someone meet us,"
Claude says, mopping his forehead with his filthy handkerchief; he looks at it and winces. Blanche's husband craves a
clean handkerchief as much as she craves clean shoes. "But . . ."

Blanche nods. All the telegraph and telephone poles linking
Paris to the outside world had been cut during the invasion.

"Monsieur! Madame!" Two enterprising young boys appear, offering to carry the Auzellos' bags for three francs;
Claude agrees, and they start to follow the urchins through the
streets of Paris, normally so chaotic. Blanche can't help remembering the first time she tried to navigate the circle around the
Arc de Triomphe, so many lanes full of honking vehicles going
every which way. But today she's stunned by the complete absence of traffic.

"The Germans are confiscating every car," one boy, a tall, pale lad with blond hair and a broken front tooth, says with the cockiness of a youth in the unusual position of knowing more than his elders. "For their army."

"I would blow it up first, rather than give my car to the *Boche*," Claude mutters, and it's on the tip of Blanche's tongue to remind him that they don't own a car. But she doesn't; even Blanche knows that now is not the time to make that particular point.

While the ragtag little group straggles along, she becomes aware of something else: silence. Not just from the crowd of stunned citizens stumbling out of the station, spreading out through the city like a muddy puddle of rain, but *everywhere*. If there is one constant in Paris, it is *talk;* café tables crammed with volatile patrons arguing about the color of the sun; sidewalks, too, crowded with Parisians stopping to make a point, jabbing a finger in a companion's chest as they debate politics, the cut of one's suit, the best cheese shop—it doesn't matter, it never matters. Parisians, Blanche knows too well, love to gab.

Today, the cafés are empty. The sidewalks are bare. There are no noisy schoolchildren in uniforms playing in the vacant gardens. No vendors singing while they push their carts; no shopkeepers haggling with suppliers.

But she feels eyes upon her, she's sure of it. Despite the warmth of the cruelly sunny day, she shivers and tucks her hand beneath her husband's arm.

"Look," he whispers, nodding his head skyward. Blanche obeys; the windows beneath the mansard roofs are full of people peering out furtively from behind lace curtains. Her gaze is pulled toward the sky, caught by something shining, reflecting the light, up on the very rooftops.

Nazi soldiers, carrying polished rifles, looking down at them.

She starts to tremble. They haven't encountered any soldiers until this moment. The Germans had not reached Nîmes, where Claude had been garrisoned at the start of the Phony War. Even on the train to Paris, where everyone was terrified that they would be strafed by bombers as so many people who fled had been; even though every scheduled—and unscheduled—stop caused all conversation to cease as they held their breath, afraid of hearing German words, German boots, German gunshots—the Auzellos hadn't encountered a single Nazi.

But now that they are here, home, they do. It's really happened, goddammit. The Nazis have really conquered Paris.

Blanche takes a breath—her ribs ache, her stomach churns, and she can't remember when they last ate—and walks on in her destroyed shoes. Finally, they come to the enormous paved square of the Place Vendôme; it, too, is empty of citizens. But not of soldiers.

Blanche gasps; so does Claude. For there are Nazi tanks in the square, surrounding the statue of Napoleon. An enormous Nazi flag, with its twisted black swastika, hangs above several doorways—including that of the Ritz. Her husband's beloved Ritz. Hers, too. *Their* Ritz.

And at the top of the stairs leading to the front doors stand two Nazi soldiers. With guns.

There's a clatter; the boys have dropped the bags and are sprinting off like hares. Claude looks after them.

"Perhaps we should go to the flat instead," he says, taking out his dirty handkerchief again. For the first time today—for the very first time since Blanche has known him—her husband looks uncertain. And that's the moment when she understands, for certain, that everything has changed.

"Nonsense," Blanche replies, feeling hot blood surge through her—strange blood, not her own, but the blood of a courageous woman with nothing to hide from the Nazis. To her own surprise, not to mention Claude's, she gathers up the suitcases and marches straight toward those two soldiers. "We are going in the front door, Claude Auzello. Because *you* are the director of the Ritz."

Claude begins to protest but for once does not argue with her; he lapses into silence as they approach the two sentries, who each take two steps toward them, but don't, thank Christ, raise their weapons.

"This is Herr Claude Auzello, director of the Ritz," Blanche announces in her best German, a German that surprises her with its smooth confidence, as it obviously surprises her husband. After all, according to him, his American-born wife speaks French with the most atrocious accent he's ever heard, so it's more than a bit stunning to hear this flawless German.

But then, the Auzellos have been surprising each other since the moment they first met.

"I am Frau Auzello. We want to speak to an officer at once. *Mach schnell!*"

The soldiers look startled; one runs into the hotel. Claude whispers, "*Mon Dieu,* Blanche," and she can see, by the way he tightens his grip on his bags, he's doing his earthly best not to cross himself in that infuriatingly French Catholic way.

Blanche—despite trembling limbs—remains upright, even imperiously so, and by the time the officer, a short man with a red face, emerges, she knows exactly what she is going to say.

For she is Blanche Ross Auzello, American. Parisian. Among

other things, many other things, past, present, future, that she will have to conceal from now on, but then again, hasn't she been concealing most of them these past twenty years anyway? So she is very good at this, deception. As, she must acknowledge, is her husband.

It is, perhaps, the thing that binds these two even more closely than it tears them apart.

"Herr Auzello! Frau Auzello!" The commanding officer tumbling out the door to greet them has a voice that is both slippery and guttural in the German way, but his French is flawless. He bows to Claude and reaches to kiss Blanche's hand, which she hides behind her back just in time.

For it, too, is suddenly trembling.

"Welcome back to the Ritz. We have heard so much about you. I am here to explain that management has been relocated to the other side." The Nazi bobs his head to indicate the rue Cambon, which runs behind the building. "We—we Germans—have made ourselves at home, thanks to your staff's hospitality, here on the Place Vendôme side. Your other guests are all over on the rue Cambon. And we have taken the liberty of removing your personal items from your office and installing them in another, in the gallery above that side's lobby. You will find much of your staff intact and awaiting your instructions."

"Fine, fine," Blanche hears herself replying—as if she encountered a Nazi officer every day, and she can't help but marvel at her own performance. Damned if it didn't take a German invasion to mold her into the kind of actress she'd always wanted to be. "I expected nothing less. Now, will you have your men take our bags around for us?"

She turns to smile reassuringly at Claude, whose face, she's startled to see, has paled beneath the ruddy tan acquired in the South of France. As the two soldiers begin to gather up the luggage, she can't help but notice that Claude grips his attaché case tightly when they motion for it, the knuckles on his hand white with effort, the ropy muscles in his neck twitching. She shoots him a questioning look, but his face, anyway, remains smooth and unworried.

They follow the two soldiers through the square, taking a left to the narrow, yet impossibly chic, rue Cambon. Once again, she's aware of eyes watching. She reaches out to grasp Claude's other hand; he keeps her tightly within his grip. The two of them, linked this way, won't falter. Of this, she is sure; it's the only thing of which she's sure, at this incredible Wonderland moment, when nothing is as it should be.

When Nazi soldiers are escorting the Auzellos to the rear entrance of the Ritz.

They follow the soldiers through the smaller entrance, and at once the pocket-sized lobby is filled with familiar faces, stricken and pale but breaking into smiles of relief at seeing the Auzellos return. Blanche, too, smiles and nods to one and all, but they don't stop to chat. Blanche senses that her husband is not up to the emotion of homecoming, of being greeted by the staff he left almost a year ago, his family, his children in the truest sense. Normally her husband would have deserted her while he caught up with staff, broke open a bottle of port in his office, listened to all the stories that have waited until his return to be told—the young florist is gone, married to her lover; there is a new provider of butter, because the old one died and his children sold the dairy.

But today, Blanche suspects that he knows the stories he will be told are not pleasant, trivial ones. Stories of staff disappearing in the chaos of the invasion, of young bellhops dying in battle, of that pretty young florist—last name of Chabat—not marrying after all but trying desperately to get a visa to England. Stories of how the Nazis want things to run here in his hotel—yes, her husband thinks of the Ritz as his own, despite the fact that the family of César Ritz are the true owners. He is arrogant in that way, her Claude; if Blanche were honest—something she allows herself to be at least once a day—it's one of the things she most admires about him.

Claude is in an awful hurry to get to their rooms; Blanche breaks into a jog to keep up with him and the soldiers in their black boots with the steel toes striking hard against the plush carpets. And she finds herself worrying—always the wife of the director of the Ritz!—that the carpets will not be able to stand up to this kind of treatment. Not carpets more accustomed to slinky heels of leather. Again, she remembers her own shoes, grinding dirt into the carpets as well, and for the first time in a very long time, she feels less than her surroundings.

Blanche has grown accustomed, over the years, to dressing up to the Ritz; there's just something about the place that inspires you to wear your best, to sit up straighter, talk more quietly, drape your best jewels about your neck, check your reflection one last time before venturing out into its marble halls, every surface always shining and polished, those whose job it is to shine and polish retreating into hidden cupboards and corners the moment they see a guest, so that the overall effect is that of a magic castle lovingly tended to by sprites who only come out at night.

But now she notices the Nazi flag on display in the enormous urns that hold palm trees. The utter silence in the opulent

halls and sitting areas; the sense that lurking behind every polished door is an ear, pressed, listening. And she forgets about
her shoes again.

The Auzellos are shown to their old suite, conveniently already located on the rue Cambon side of the hotel; the bags
are stacked neatly for them but damned if Blanche is going to
tip a Nazi; she merely nods as the soldiers leave. Claude and
Blanche both turn away from each other, as if the moment of
homecoming—nightmarish as it is—after so long away is simply too much to acknowledge. So the two of them, like tour-
ists, begin to walk about the rooms, surveying. Blanche is
startled to see that there's a layer of dust on every surface—
impossible to imagine, before. There are some small fault lines
in the gilded wallpaper—were there bombs dropped nearby,
prior to the occupation? There's a staleness to the air, as if the
small suite—by Ritz standards, anyway—has been holding its
breath until their return. She opens a window; below her is a
cluster of Nazi soldiers talking, laughing, as gleeful as school-
boys on holiday.

"Why were you behaving like a guilty kid out there?" She
draws away from the window with a shudder and finally turns
to Claude, who is still gripping his case.

"I have . . ." he begins to laugh, shakily; his neat little mustache quivers, and his slightly-protruding eyes blink repeat-
edly. "Oh, Blanchette, you foolish woman. I have papers with
me." He thumps the case. "*Illegal* papers. Blank travel passes
and demobilization papers. I stole them from the garrison, so I
could use them here in Paris for—for whomever might need
them. I could have been thrown in prison if the Nazis had discovered them."

"Jesus Christ, Claude!" Now it is Blanche's turn to pale; she collapses into a chair, imagining the scenario playing out. "Oh, Claude. You should have told me when we left Nîmes."

"No." Claude shakes his head, fingers the collar of his shirt, loosening it a bit. "No, Blanche. There are things you shouldn't know. For your own good." And he's back to normal, Blanche's husband; her infuriatingly *French* husband with his rules and pronouncements and lectures. They've been married seventeen years, and still he's trying to make a docile French wife out of a rebellious American flapper.

"Oh, Claude, we're not back to this old song and dance again, are we? After all we've been through this past year? After *today*?"

"I have no idea what you mean, Blanche," her husband says in his priggish way—and normally, this would be the red cape that would incite her to fury. She remembers, with a guilty start, that some of those rips in the wallpaper were there even before they left. Courtesy of flying vases and candlesticks; courtesy of one of their innumerable arguments concerning the very nature of marriage. Specifically, theirs.

But today, Blanche is too exhausted and bewildered to fight. And suddenly, too thirsty. When was the last time she had a drink? Days. She laughs, although it sounds tinny to her ringing ears. A German invasion is a hell of a way to dry out.

"Well, that's that," she says, and finds, to her astonishment, that she has to wipe an unexpected tear from her eye. "It was good while it lasted, I guess."

"What do you mean?" Claude, who is searching the rooms for a place to hide his contraband papers, frowns.

"I mean that nothing's changed, after all. After that time at Nîmes, when we—when we almost had a marriage. Paris might be under German rule, but you're still lying to me."

"No, no, it's not like that at all," Claude says—sadly, to Blanche's surprise. He drops his case on a table, as if he no longer has the strength to carry this burden; his face softens, and it looks almost as young and pliant, able to smile and laugh, as it did when they first met. For a moment, he looks repentant, and Blanche leans toward him, her hands clasped over her heart like a young girl. A foolish, but hopeful, young girl.

But then Claude doesn't bother to explain exactly what it is like and so Blanche shrugs—the one thing, according to her husband, that she does as well as, if not better than, any French woman—and begins to unpack.

"Now." Claude stretches, arching his back which creaks alarmingly, his usually composed face so weary that, despite her disappointment, she has a momentary longing to draw him a bath and tuck him into bed. "I must go to Madame Ritz and see what is going on over on the other side, where the Germans apparently are residing. Nazis in César Ritz's palace—*mon Dieu!* He will be turning in his grave."

"Go, go. You'll be useless until you've walked over every inch of your beloved Ritz, I know you, Claude Auzello. But—should we go back to the apartment later, though? To check on it?" For the first time Blanche remembers their roomy flat on the Avenue Montaigne in the shadow of the Tour Eiffel. The Auzellos' destination, always, from the moment they left Nîmes in the chaos of retreat, had been the Ritz. It is their true north. But they do have another place to stay—a place that is not inhabited by Nazis and thinking about them lurking around every corner here at the Ritz makes Blanche's skin thrum with the desire to flee, to hide. The fearless imposter who stood outside and ordered Nazis around like peasants is gone; in her place is—a woman.

A frightened woman with no real home—an alien in a country occupied by a terrifying enemy—making her infuriatingly dependent on a husband who disappoints her more often than not.

Almost as much as she disappoints him.

"I think not," Claude says with more than a trace of his usual infuriating superiority, and Blanche, in her current state, is relieved to see it. "If there is rationing or shortages, it's best we're here at the Ritz. I'm sure the Germans will see to it that they have the best of everything, and perhaps we can live on the scraps." Claude, after a moment's hesitation, goes to his wife; he folds her in his arms and whispers into her ear.

"You were brave today, my Blanchette," he croons, and Blanche can't help but shiver a little, and nestle closer into his chest. "Very brave. But perhaps it is best for you to try a little cowardice, instead? Until we see—? Until we see."

She nods; he makes sense. Oh, he always makes sense, her Claude—except in one area. One very important area. Still, she allows herself to slump a little against him; he is not tall, he is not broad or muscular, her husband. But he manages to make her feel protected anyway, as he has from the very beginning; a man who is as certain as he is, as infuriatingly upright and proper, can do that. Even when his hands are small, and his throat as slender and fine as a dancer's. So she clings to him; he is, after all, the only thing she has left. She could have gone back to America when the world started to go to hell; she could have joined an old lover in a different country, one that most likely would remain safely on the sidelines of this grotesque circus. But no, she'd stayed here in France, with this man, this husband.

Someday, she really should get around to asking herself the

question of why. But not today; she's already been through too much. And she needs a goddamned drink.

As soon as Claude leaves, with a promise not to be long— a promise they both know he won't keep—Blanche decides to take a good look at herself in the mirror; she hasn't seen her reflection in days. The blond hair—not natural; the ruby ring on her right hand—not authentic; she hocked the jewel years ago and had it replaced with a fake, and never did tell Claude, who would not have approved of her reason. The delicate gold cross at her throat, a wedding gift from her husband—a joke, she had thought at the time, but soon realized it was anything but; the passport in her handbag, creased and soft from carrying it with her, day in and day out—well, they're all a joke, really, when you come right down to it, she thought bitterly.

Everything's a joke now. A farce. A sham.

This new reality, this new nightmare that she finds herself in; it's so far removed—lightyears, *Biblical* years—from the Paris, the Ritz, the man she met when she first sailed from America. Seventeen years ago, it was. A lifetime ago.

A dream ago. Several of them, actually—dreams. Mostly unfulfilled.

As dreams, Blanche Auzello knows all too well, tend to be.

PHOTO: © DEBORAH FEINGOLD

MELANIE BENJAMIN has written the *New York Times* bestselling historical novels *The Aviator's Wife* and *The Swans of Fifth Avenue,* the nationally best-selling *Alice I Have Been,* and *The Autobiography of Mrs. Tom Thumb.* She lives in Chicago with her husband, and far enough from her two adult sons not to be a nuisance (she hopes). When she isn't writing, she's reading.

Melaniebenjamin.com

Twitter: @MelanieBen

Look for Melanie Benjamin on Facebook.

ABOUT THE TYPE

This book was set in Bembo, a typeface based on an old-style Roman face that was used for Cardinal Pietro Bembo's tract *De Aetna* in 1495. Bembo was cut by Francesco Griffo (1450–1518) in the early sixteenth century for Italian Renaissance printer and publisher Aldus Manutius (1449–1515). The Lanston Monotype Company of Philadelphia brought the well-proportioned letterforms of Bembo to the United States in the 1930s.

Chat.
Comment.
Connect.

Visit our online book club community at
Facebook.com/RHReadersCircle

Chat
Meet fellow book lovers and discuss what you're reading.

Comment
Post reviews of books, ask—and answer—thought-provoking
questions, or give and receive book club ideas.

Connect
Find an author on tour, visit our author blog, or invite one of
our 150 available authors to chat with your group on the phone.

Explore
Also visit our site for discussion questions, excerpts, author
interviews, videos, free books, news on the latest releases,
and more.

Books are better with buddies.
Facebook.com/RHReadersCircle

RANDOM HOUSE